The Queen in Winter

THE
Queen
IN Winter

✳ ✳ ✳

CLAIRE DELACROIX
LYNN KURLAND
SHARON SHINN
SARAH MONETTE

BERKLEY BOOKS, NEW YORK

THE BERKLEY PUBLISHING GROUP
Published by the Penguin Group
Penguin Group (USA) Inc.
375 Hudson Street, New York, New York 10014, USA
Penguin Group (Canada), 90 Eglinton Avenue East, Suite 700, Toronto, Ontario M4P 2Y3, Canada
(a division of Pearson Penguin Canada Inc.)
Penguin Books Ltd., 80 Strand, London WC2R 0RL, England
Penguin Group Ireland, 25 St. Stephen's Green, Dublin 2, Ireland (a division of Penguin Books Ltd.)
Penguin Group (Australia), 250 Camberwell Road, Camberwell, Victoria 3124, Australia
(a division of Pearson Australia Group Pty. Ltd.)
Penguin Books India Pvt. Ltd., 11 Commuity Centre, Panchsheel Park, New Delhi—110 017, India
Penguin Books (NZ), Cnr. Airborne and Rosedale Roads, Albany, Auckland 1310, New Zealand
(a division of Pearson New Zealand Ltd.)
Penguin Books (South Africa) (Pty.) Ltd., 24 Sturdee Avenue, Rosebank, Johannesburg 2196,
South Africa

Penguin Books Ltd., Registered Offices: 80 Strand, London WC2R 0RL, England

These are works of fiction. Names, characters, places, and incidents either are the product of the authors' imaginations or are used fictitiously, and any resemblance to actual persons, living or dead, business establishments, events, or locales is entirely coincidental.

THE QUEEN IN WINTER

"A Whisper of Spring" copyright © 2006 by Lynn Curland
"When Winter Comes" copyright © 2006 by Sharon Shinn
"The Kiss of the Snow Queen" copyright © 2006 by Claire Delacroix, Inc.
"A Gift of Wings" copyright © 2006 by Sarah Monette
Collection copyright © 2006 by Penguin Group (USA) Inc.
Cover design by Lesley Worrell
Book design by Kristin del Rosario

First Edition: February 2006

ISBN: 0-425-20772-2

This book has been catalogued with the Library of Congress.

PRINTED IN THE UNITED STATES OF AMERICA

10   9   8   7   6   5   4   3   2   1

CONTENTS

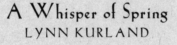

A
Whisper
of Spring

LYNN KURLAND

Prologue

She woke to blackness.

It took her several moments to decide if her eyes were open or not. Once she was quite certain she was awake, realization dawned—the realization that she was lying on a cold floor, without benefit of bed, fire, or even the meanest of quilts to shield her from the chill.

She paused, disoriented and confused. Was she dreaming? She supposed she might be, but this was a dream she had little liking for.

She very carefully closed her eyes and sank back into the darkness. She struggled to make herself smell air that was cool and fragrant. She listened for the crackle of the fire in her hearth and the faint sound of wind moving through bare winter branches.

She waited.

In time, she had to admit that the only sound she could hear was her own harsh, uneven breathing. The air smelled not of roses, but of something foul, and the darkness did not abate, not even when she could no longer pretend to sleep.

She shivered.

At length, the room lightened, though not overmuch. She could see but a sliver of gray sky from the slit of a window set deep into a casement across the chamber from her. She sat up and pulled her sleeping gown over her knees, then hugged her knees to her chest in a futile attempt to warm herself, and stared in disbelief at her surroundings.

Gone was the riot of color that surrounded her in her own chamber, color that spread outside her window as far as the eye could see. Gone was the large bed with piles of beautiful quilts and fine blankets knitted of the softest cashmere. Gone was the magnificently carved furniture, the finely wrought tapestries, the plush rugs of muted hues and exquisite softness beneath her feet. Gone was the smell of rich earth, clean rain, and perfumed blossoms.

In its place was the smell of evil.

What, by all that was wondrous, had befallen her?

When she had the courage, she looked about herself. She was in a stone chamber. It was small, and without any furnishings at all, not even a worn cushion for her head or a scrap of quilt with which to make a poor bed. The stone was gray, a dark, unrelenting gray that was not relieved by even the stingy bit of daylight that struggled in through the window slit.

After a time, she noticed a doorway across from her. She scrambled to her feet and ran across to it, jerking it open.

It was a privy.

A pity the hole there was so small. Had it been larger, she would have crawled through it, no matter where it led. She shut the door slowly, then leaned her forehead against it, wondering what she would do now. The chill of the floor bit into her feet, forcing her away from the door and back into her corner. At least there, her own warmth had made some minute change in temperature. She resumed her crouch and did her best to still the fear that threatened to choke her.

Apparently, she succeeded, and so thoroughly that it took her several minutes to realize she was no longer alone in her prison. A man was leaning against the wall to her right, watching her.

She forced herself to her feet and wrapped her arms around herself, more for the comfort of that embrace than any protection it might have offered.

The man pushed away from the wall and made her a low bow.

She recoiled. She couldn't help herself. There was something quite fraudulent about that appearance of deference. The back of her head touched the wall as she flinched; she reached up to find a lump there.

Memory flooded back. She'd been tending her fire for the final time before bed when a shadow had fallen across her. She remembered a sharp pain, then nothing more. Had this been the man who had dared enter her chambers? Obviously so, else she wouldn't find herself captive in his hall. Perhaps he had also dared attack her. Clearly he knew nothing about her or he never would have.

"You struck me," she said disapprovingly.

"Aye," he replied simply, without remorse.

She frowned. "No one has dared strike me before."

"I daresay they haven't."

She looked at him, quite unable to believe he was so bold. "Have you no idea who I am?"

"Aye," he said. "You are Iolaire, daughter of the High King of Ainneamh."

"You know, yet you dared steal me?" she said, incredulous.

He only shrugged, apparently unrepentant.

"Have you no idea what my father will do to you?"

He smiled, but somehow that smile did not reach his eyes. "Elves do not come after those who dare leave elven lands, do they? So, given that your father will remain comfortably and safely ensconced upon his throne, I daresay I know exactly what he will do to me."

She suppressed the urge to rub her arms. "Who are you?"

"Lothar of Wychweald."

Wychweald? She knew Yngerame, the mage king of Wychweald,

but there was only good attached to his name. Did this man seek to borrow some of that reputation to burnish his own? Surely the two men were not related . . .

A pity she had not bothered to learn more about the kingdoms of men. She knew enough to be pleasant at supper to those rare mortals who were allowed into her land to curry her father's favor. She had been destined to wed another of her kind, so what need had she had to learn of the outside world?

She wished now that she had made the effort.

Well, whoever this man was, he was surely not her equal, either in power or station. She put her shoulders back. "What do you want?" she demanded.

"You."

She blinked. "Me? Why?"

"I need a bride."

She looked at him, dumbfounded. "A bride?"

"I tried your cousin Ceana." He shrugged. "She said nay."

Iolaire swallowed past her parched throat. So that was where Ceana had gone. She'd thought her cousin had gone mad and left home for the love of a mortal. "Where is she now?"

"Dead."

She smothered a cry of horror with her hand. What kind of man . . .

"Think on it," he said simply. "I'll return." A doorway appeared in the rock, he left through it, then the doorway disappeared.

Iolaire rushed to it, ran her hands over it, but found nothing.

No opening.

Nothing but rock.

Nothing but her doom.

She walked back to her corner, sank down to the cold floor, and wept. Whoever he was, Lothar of Wychweald knew of what he spoke. Her people would not come for her; they would assume she had gone because she had chosen to. A part of her suspected that even if her father had known she had been abducted, he wouldn't have come to search for her. The intrigues of men held no interest for him. He would, no matter the truth of it, consider her to have dabbled in those affairs at her own peril.

She was alone and without aid.

She closed her eyes and squeezed herself back into the corner as tightly as possible. Perhaps if she tried hard enough, she would wake and find it had all been a very foul dream.

But she suspected she wouldn't.

Her heart broke, and the sound of it echoed in the stillness of the chamber.

One

THE FIRE BURNED BRIGHTLY IN THE HEARTH,
warming not only the rugs before it, but also the dogs
lying upon those rugs and the man sitting in the least
uncomfortable chair in what was almost a snug gathering chamber. Tapestries depicting glorious scenes of the
hunt lined the stone walls and drove away yet more of
the chill. The dogs dozed, their hind legs twitching now
and again as they dreamed of the chase. Winter raged
outside, but inside all were safe and secure, if not quite
cozy, before that cheery blaze.

But as Symon of Neroche sat before the fire with a
cup of ale in one hand and his other hand pressed over
his eyes, he found that even a pleasant fire could not
drive away the chill of the tidings he was receiving. He
rubbed his eyes, sighed, then looked at his oldest friend
who was, as fate would have it, also his chief advisor and
captain of his guard.

"Say that again," Symon instructed. "But slowly. I
didn't sleep well last night."

"Bad beds," Hamil said promptly. "This is, as you may or may not remember, your father's hunting lodge. There is a decided lack of creature comforts here."

"We have a roof, a fire and food," Symon replied. "It will have to suffice us at present. Now, please give me the tidings again."

Hamil blew out a gusty breath of impatience. "Again, there are still reports of attacks from the north, rumors of things coming across the border at night—"

"What sorts of things?" Symon interrupted, but he didn't need to ask the question; he already knew the answer. He listened to Hamil recount the tidings, but he'd already heard the scouting reports filled with tales of creatures that had once been men but now were not, rumors of abductions of innocent crofters, tales of narrow escapes from horrors normally confined to nightmares, glimpses of a castle near the sea that bled darkness across the land it controlled, darkness that had begun to seep southward across Neroche's northern border.

Nay, Symon was not sleeping well at all.

"Will you hear more?" Hamil asked.

Symon shook his head. "I've heard enough, thank you." He spared an unkind thought for his father. It was that old fox's fault that Symon was freezing in a drafty hunting lodge, unable to wear the crown of Neroche (which fit so poorly that Symon's cook was using it for a pastry mold), and facing an unrelenting onslaught from the north, an onslaught that his father had suddenly tired of a year ago.

Damn him anyway.

Symon sighed heavily. "Is there anything else? Something I can solve easily?"

"Your father sent word," Hamil offered. "He wishes to know how your search for a bride proceeds."

Symon rubbed his forehead with a bit more vigor. "I imagine he does."

"He has given up on sending you suggestions. Instead, your mother sent along a list. I have it here"—he patted his breast protectively—"should you care to have a look at it."

"I wouldn't."

"She claims it will inspire you," Hamil said, as if he hadn't heard Symon's answer. "And if you don't mind me pointing this out to you, my unwed but quite eligible friend, you have no roster of potential brides loitering upon your person."

Symon now used two hands to rub his face.

"Of course," Hamil continued, "I can make you a copy of your mother's suggestions for your own study, if you like, whilst I retain the original in case you strike through a name or two, then regret your haste later—"

The door burst open. Guards who had been standing silently in the shadows leapt forward, then stopped still. Hamil was up with his sword drawn, then he froze as well. Symon found himself on his feet along with the rest, without really knowing how he'd gotten there. He stared at the intruder, supposing idly that he might be allowed a bit of surprise. It wasn't every day that an elf deigned to visit a mortal's dwelling. But the elf in question seemed unfazed by his break with tradition. He merely walked across the small hall calmly, as if it were no great thing to be who he was, where he was.

Symon cleared his throat. "Ehrne of Ainneamh, son of Proìseil the Proud," he managed, scrambling to dredge up a few polite phrases in his somewhat unused elvish. "You grace my hall with your presence."

"I congratulate you on that honor," Ehrne replied easily in his own tongue.

"Foolish is the man who does not realize when such an honor is bestowed upon him."

"And wise is the king who recognizes when he is being so honored. Wise in spite of his youth and inexperience with his crown," he added.

Symon suppressed a sigh. He was five and thirty, old enough to manage the affairs of one small kingdom. Never mind that Neroche was a vast land surrounding several smaller of the Nine Kingdoms. Never mind that he'd spent so much of his time over the past year trying to keep the evil from the north at bay that he hadn't seen a fraction of that kingdom. Never mind that instead of giving him decent warning, his father had, a year earlier, plopped that ill-fitting crown on his head one night at supper and bid him pack his bags the next morning and be about his next adventure. He would rule well enough, if he could just have the peace to do it in.

Symon gestured with his most regal gesture towards Hamil's chair. "Will you take your ease?"

Hamil, mercifully, vacated his chair without comment. He fetched a stool from the hearth and sat down upon it, still silent and slack-jawed.

Symon waited until Ehrne had seated himself with a grace that belied the great distance he'd come and, by the telling condition of his clothes, the haste in which he'd traveled it, before he slowly took his own seat. Why in the world a prince of Ainneamh would find himself in a snow-bound hunting lodge leagues from his own comfortable home—

"I came to seek your aid."

Symon stared at him, dumbfounded. "I beg your pardon?"

"You have magic, I assume, being the son of a mage king."

"Aye, well, I suppose I do."

Ehrne looked at him appraisingly. "Let us be about discussing the depth and breadth of it before I decide if I've chosen amiss—"

"Use the common tongue!" Hamil said suddenly. He looked at Symon crossly. "You know I cannot decipher that elvish babbling."

Symon supposed Hamil deserved the long look Ehrne gave him, but then again, Hamil had a point, even if he could speak the language of Ainneamh as well as Symon himself could. There was safety in having a relative stranger think Hamil incapable of understanding his tongue; it might prove useful in the future.

"Your magic," Ehrne repeated, turning his attention back to Symon. "I would know—"

"And I would know what your business is first," Symon said as politely as he could. "Lest there be no need for a discussion of whatever paltry skills I might possess."

Ehrne paused only for a moment before he shrugged. "'That is fair enough, I suppose. I am here because I was banished."

Symon blinked in surprise. "You were what?"

"I was banished. By my father, in case you were wondering."

That answered one question, but raised several more. "Why?"

"I was accused of trying to kill the queen."

"The queen," Symon said slowly. "Morag."

"Aye."

"Morag, your mother."

"Aye there, too." Ehrne looked about him purposefully, but apparently fruitlessly.

Symon handed him the half-full cup of ale he held in his own hands. Ehrne drained it, then dragged his sleeve across his mouth.

"Drinkable. Barely."

"We do our best," Hamil said stiffly from his corner.

Ehrne looked at him, or through him rather, then turned back to Symon. Symon motioned for his page to refill the prince's cup, then accepted another for himself.

He sipped slowly while his guest quenched his thirst with barely drinkable ale and while he waited, he considered. This was a remarkable visit, no matter the true reason. It wasn't every day a man entertained an elf of Prince Ehrne's pedigree and station.

Though, it wasn't that Symon hadn't treated with elves before. He had. He'd become acquainted with their fine tastes, their diplomatic speech, their painful beauty—on those rare occasions when they had come to make visits of state to his father. He had also been to Ainneamh—and for longer than most men could claim.

Long enough to look on things he never should have seen, to be burned by a beauty so painful, even the memory of it made him want to draw his hand over his eyes.

A beauty whose brother had apparently finally drunk enough to find his voice.

Ehrne looked about him as if he sought a distraction. "We heard that your father had divided his lands and made you king over the greater part of them. Passing foul of him to leave you this hovel as your palace."

"He thought it would do me good to begin my reign humbly."

Ehrne snorted. "It would do you good to build something more suitable, lest important guests such as myself find themselves slighted."

"I'll see to it—right after we've discussed your business," Symon said. "Give me all the particulars, if you will. You say your father banished you, but I don't understand why there was no one there to protest your innocence."

"That was a bit hard to find, given that I'm quite guilty."

Symon was actually grateful for the magnitude of Hamil's gasp, for it quite handily covered his own. He tried to look as diplomatically unsurprised as possible. "Well," he said, finally. "I assume you had good reason for it." He paused. "Did you?"

Ehrne shrugged. "I suppose it depends on your perspective. I thought I had reason. You see, my mother betrayed an elf to a black mage."

Well, that would do it. "Not many of those about," Symon said, holding out his cup to his page for another filling. "Black mages, that is, not elves."

"Very few indeed," Ehrne agreed.

So few that Symon could bring all three of them to mind without effort. "So why come to me? Especially considering—"

"The fact that we hold wizards, their get, and mage kings in the same high regard we hold rats, dwarves, and ill-dressed brigands?"

Symon smiled. "Something like that."

"The elf was kidnapped by Lothar of Wychweald."

"Ah," Symon said, somehow quite unsurprised. Aye, there was one of the three.

"And given that Lothar of Wychweald is your brother, I thought perhaps you might have an idea how to kill him."

Symon pursed his lips, even less surprised, if possible, than before. Why had he not seen this coming? "You attempted matricide and look where it got you. Is fratricide any less grievous?"

"You're the king. You'll pardon yourself."

"And you're Proìseil's heir; that didn't serve you any." Symon expected no reply and he didn't get one. "Well, who did Lothar steal?"

"My sister Iolaire."

Symon heard a cup hit the stone floor. There was also a splat, as if a goodly amount of ale had abruptly left that cup. He looked down and realized that it had been his cup to deposit its contents on his boots and the floor both.

"Do you know her?" Ehrne asked mildly.

Symon looked up. Ehrne was watching him with clear, untroubled eyes, waiting. Symon took a deep breath. "You know damned well I do."

Well, if one could call gazing at the radiant beauty of the moon whilst knowing you would never touch it, knowing. Hadn't Ehrne watched Symon watch Iolaire from across Proìseil's glittering hall? Symon had been one of the few of those perennially unpopular wizard's get to be allowed, however reluctantly it might have been, inside Proìseil's hallowed halls. Obviously being Yngerame of Wychweald's son had its advantages.

Of course, not advantage enough to do aught but look on Proìseil's fairest daughter and wish he might manage to exchange the odd courtly pleasantry—not that the princess would have wanted to exchange anything else, especially rings of betrothal or passionate kisses in her father's ever-blooming gardens.

Elves and mages did not wed. It was just one of those things that was as accepted as the sun rising in the east or the seasons changing from year to year. Then again, in that blessed land of Ainneamh seasons didn't change all that much, so perhaps there were other things that might not be as true as he'd been led to believe.

He closed his eyes briefly and brought to mind the vision of a slender young woman dressed in a gown of hues that seemed to shift as she did. But what didn't change was the sheet of darkness of her hair falling down her back and the vivid blue of her eyes. Aye, he'd been close enough to see that much, and to smell the sweet scent of her perfume as she passed by him, and to take note of the flawless perfection of her skin. If there was grace, beauty, or goodness to be found anywhere in any of the Nine Kingdoms, it was in Ainneamh, where Iolaire the Fair walked over green grass that never faded to brown—

Aye, he knew her.

He also knew that he could never have her.

"Will you help me?"

Symon came back to himself in time to hear the question. "Aye," he said, without hesitation.

"What?" Hamil bellowed. "Have you gone mad?"

Quite likely, Symon thought to himself. He listened to Hamil make increasingly loud and quite reasonable arguments as to why the entire adventure was doomed from the start, not the least of which was that even should they manage to free Iolaire from Lothar's hall, Symon could expect no more than a nod in thanks—if that. Was that worth putting his own life and kingdom at risk? He was unwed; he had no heir. Should he die, who would inherit his lands? His elder brother, the black mage in question, would have gladly and quite legally taken the title of Neroche, but what would have been left of his lands after a single season?

Darkness, death, destruction.

"Dangerous," Hamil was saying. "Dangerous and pointless. What you need to be doing, my liege, is following your father's advice and seeking a bride. You cannot wed with elven get and even if you did, what would it serve you? She is as banished as he is."

"My sister will wed in time," Ehrne said confidently. "Perhaps to a wizard from the east with immense wealth and power to match." He swept Symon's hall with a glance that spoke much of his opinion on the place and the depths of Symon's purse.

"Do you *want* him to help you or not?" Hamil demanded. "Why don't you go instead and pester one of those other wizards with gold enough to raise an army to contend with Lothar?"

"He is Yngerame of Wychweald's son. One would hope that some of the father's power became the son's upon taking his crown." Ehrne smiled grimly at Symon. "Though Wychweald is still a powerful kingdom and Yngerame a powerful king, Neroche is larger and you are younger."

"And I am Lothar's brother," Symon added wearily.

"Slaying your brother is easier than slaying your son. Another reason for my appearance here and not at your father's hall."

Hamil only grunted. Perhaps he could decide on no decent retort for that.

Symon sighed. "I'll go, and expect nothing in return."

"Which is what you will have," Ehrne agreed. "That is assuming you can be of any use to me. Your father is powerful, but of you I know little—"

"I daresay you know nothing at all!" Hamil exclaimed. "My liege not only earned the rings of mastery from all six schools of wizardry at Beinn O'rain by the time he was a score, he earned the last and final ring as well."

"I didn't know there was a seventh ring," Ehrne said, looking at Hamil skeptically.

"There is a seventh ring, though only five of them have been fashioned given that only five have been achieved," Hamil said importantly.

"Hamil," Symon warned, trying to stave off what would no doubt prove to be a very long retelling of a tale better left for a night when everyone had slipped well into their cups.

Ehrne looked at Symon's hand. "I don't see any ring there."

"I think that we—" Symon began.

"It's hidden in the rye bin," Hamil supplied helpfully. "My liege tends to lose bits of his gear if they're small."

Symon rubbed his hands together purposefully. "Let us be about this—"

"Still, how will you do what needs to be done, I wonder?" Ehrne asked, doubtfully. "I've seen no performance of your skill—"

"Don't waste your strength fretting over it," Hamil said briskly. "We'll tell you of it all when we return."

"But I'm coming along," Ehrne said blankly.

"You are not," Hamil said, sounding horrified.

"But of course I am. I have my own magic."

"Aye, causing flowers to bloom and clouds to drop only as much rain as you need to keep those flowers blooming." Hamil snorted. "Look at you. You even look like a weak-stomached, flower-picking—"

Symon watched with only faint alarm as Ehrne rose and drew a sword from a previously nonexistent scabbard and made a ferocious swipe at Hamil. Hamil rose to his feet with a yawn, which would have made Symon laugh, but this was no time for levity. It was also no time to have all the decent furniture he owned carved up unnecessarily— and elf though he might have been, Ehrne was in every respect Hamil's equal. Too much longer and those two would reduce everything usable to rubble.

Symon sighed, then lifted a finger and murmured a word of command. Ehrne's and Hamil's swords both went flying across the hall.

Hamil cursed and sat down.

Ehrne turned and looked at Symon with what Symon was sure had to be one of the first times in his life he'd been surprised. But the look of surprise quickly faded to satisfaction.

"I chose well, I see," he said.

"You still look like an elf," Hamil muttered.

Ehrne's stained but obviously finely made clothes disappeared and were replaced by what Symon was certain Ehrne considered ill-dressed brigand's gear.

Hamil threw up his hands and heaved himself back to his feet. "Very well, I give in. I'll go see to supplies." He looked at Symon. "When do we leave?"

"Now," Ehrne said.

Symon smiled at his captain. "Within the hour, if you please. Even elves must eat now and then."

Ehrne followed Hamil from the chamber. "I'll go with you and see to the supplies. I am no doubt the only one with the ability to see us fed well."

"I daresay that if you don't stay out of my way, the only ability you'll have will be to lie on the floor and let me use you to wipe my feet on."

Symon sighed. It was going to be a very long journey.

He wondered about the end of it. First was the question of even freeing Iolaire from his brother's castle. Perhaps it was possible. But then he thought again of those first-hand accounts of what crept over Neroche's most northern borders. To think on what Lothar had done to his own people was horrifying.

But to think on what Lothar would do to an elf of Iolaire's beauty and grace?

He rose to his feet. An hour was too long to sit and wait for preparations to be made. Indeed, he rued the time he'd spent in conversation with Ehrne.

Nay, he would have nothing more than thanks from her, if that, but it would be enough.

Two

✳

IOLAIRE DREAMED OF AINNEAMH.

The dream was so pleasant and so real that she smiled and stretched in her sleep. Water trickled over and down chiseled bits of polished granite from the mines of Dèan An, unearthed from deep in the elven mountains of Tòrr Dòrainn. The sounds of water softly filling the air were accompanied by heady smells from the twisting vines of jasmine and curling branches of climbing roses that framed her window. Her room was drenched in the scents of the flowers that bloomed all year round save that pair of months in the chill of winter when the earth rested and regained her strength.

The scene changed. She walked through her father's hall with the enormous hearths at each end, where a fire was lit each night to stave off the cool of the evenings. Her father was there, her brothers, her cousins, her friends, all in their finery, all eating the most delicious things her father's cooks could produce and sipping sweet wine that tasted of dew. Everything glittered, from the whisper-thin goblets hand blown by her father's most skilled glasswrights to the gowns that seem to have been spun from the gossamer wings of Ainneamh's most beautiful butterflies.

She looked about her. Her mother was gone, but that was not unusual these days. Her mother had withdrawn from them more and more often of late, as if she found their company painful. Perhaps she was grieved for the loss of her niece, Creana. Perhaps she merely wearied of their company. Iolaire did not know and it troubled her.

But despite that niggling doubt over her mother's absence, Iolaire relished the feeling of being comfortable, safe, and surrounded by those who loved her and whom she loved. Was there a more beautiful place than Ainneamh? Was there a more luxurious and appealing hall than her father's, where the colors, sounds, and smells all blended in a perfection that was only to be found here? She drew a shawl of the finest cashmere about her shoulders and closed her eyes briefly to better savor the pleasure of it. She was certain that the bliss of her life could be no richer.

And then she saw him.

Even in her dream, she felt a tingle of something that was not dread and certainly not fear run through her. The man was not altogether mortal, but not elvenkind either. Who he was might prove to be as much a mystery as what he was. A guest of her father's surely, else he would not have dared enter the king's innermost hall. No crown sat upon his dark hair, but he carried himself in a straight, confident way that bespoke noble breeding. He was deferential to her kin, speaking in their tongue, which was a most unusual thing for one who was not of Ainneamh, but even so, he did not abase himself . . .

She watched him look about the chamber as politely as good manners would allow, but with an awe she supposed she could understand well enough.

But then he turned that looking upon her.

And she watched him go still.

That same stillness came over her, leaving her feeling as if it were just they two who stood there, connected, silent and unmoving in a sea of strangers. That same feeling came over her, only this time she recognized it for what it was: a remembering. It was as if she had always known him, but only forgotten until this moment that she did.

Even eternity held its breath.

She wanted to go to him, to take his hand, to go into his arms and find herself whole. But before she could move, her brother had taken her by the arm and pulled her away. She wasted time convincing him that she was well and not consorting with mortals beneath her station, but by the time she turned back to look for the man, he was gone, lost in a sea of elves who suddenly looked all the same.

She almost wept. She looked amongst her family, but could not find him for the press of her kinfolk. After a time, she gave up and left the hall. As she walked past the mingling crowd, she thought she heard her name. She looked up quickly and saw the man again, briefly, only to have the crowd draw together before her and hide him from her view.

She didn't dare ask who he was. Her father would have wanted to know why she desired the name of a man who could not possibly interest her. Ehrne would have come undone at the thought of her looking twice at a man whose clothing was likely quite serviceable in a mortal kingdom, but made him look a rough peasant in her father's grand hall. She half wondered, now, if she would recognize him at all, or if she would pass him on a deserted road and not know it was he.

The sorrow of that was so great that she woke with tears streaming down her cheeks. And once she was awake and again facing the hard, unyielding stone of her prison, she wept for other reasons.

She would never see her home again. Even if she could free herself, she would be forever barred from it. The law was such and her father was bound to uphold it. She could break herself and her shattered heart against that law, but it would not yield.

She was alone now, without home or lover.

How she longed for both.

She leaned her bruised head gently against the wall and gave herself over to daylight dreaming. Of her home she could think no more. Her grief would be endless and thinking on it only deepened that grief.

But that man, aye, that was something she could think on idly and not have it pain her so much. Was he mage, prince, or stableboy? It had been impossible to tell, though she supposed no stableboy could have spoken her tongue, and she had watched him converse with her kin. And no stableboy she'd ever encountered had ever possessed such a handsome face and such piercing, pale eyes. Blue or green? She could not say, and she found that it became increasingly difficult to imagine up the contours of his face. She struggled, trying to make out his features in the semi-dark of her prison.

And then the face began to speak.

She came to herself to find Lothar of Wychweald standing on the other side of the stone chamber, speaking to her. It took her a moment or two to drag herself from the comfort of her dreaming and understand him. She frowned.

"I beg your pardon?" she said.

His look was mild, but she was no fool. And only a fool would have missed the malice behind that pleasant expression.

"I asked you if you had decided upon an answer."

Somehow, sitting there hugging her knees and pressing herself back into a corner was far too powerless a position to be in. She scrambled to her feet. "I am unsure of the question."

His snort of laughter was humorless. "I asked you if you were ready to leave the chamber."

She studied him, wondering what it would mean if she said aye. "If I say I am, to what have I agreed?"

"I think you might know," he said.

She wrapped her arms around herself, somewhat alarmed by how chilled her flesh was. "You cannot keep me locked in here forever."

He only looked at her placidly, without comment.

"Is that how you must convince me?" she demanded, her teeth beginning to chatter. "By starving me? By denying me even the most paltry of comforts?"

He shrugged. "I hope to inspire you to come willingly." He looked at her without the slightest bit of interest or affection. "I can force you, but I imagine you wouldn't care for that."

She would have answered, but found that her mouth was suddenly too dry with panic for sound.

And she feared greatly the sound she would make if she began to give voice to her fear.

Lothar pushed away from the wall, much as he had done the first time. He spoke no word, but suddenly a doorway appeared and a door swung open.

He left, silently.

Once he was gone, Iolaire stumbled across the chamber. She ran her hands fruitlessly over the place where the doorway had been. The magic there was strong, stronger than she was accustomed to. Then again, her magic was given to more noble purposes than locking unwilling prisoners in cold, comfortless cells of stone.

She sighed deeply, then turned and went to the window. It was far too small for her to crawl through; indeed, she could scarce shove her hand through the narrow, vertical shaft that afforded her all the light her chamber possessed. She tore off the hem of her nightgown and held it bunched in her hand. Rain fell softly, slowly, but eventually long enough that the cloth was wet and she managed to draw off a small bit of moisture.

It tasted far better than anything she had ever savored at her father's table.

She spent the better part of that day trying with only scant success to ease her thirst. When evening fell and the misting rain ceased, she retreated to her corner where the draft was less, drew into the smallest folding possible of herself, and gave thought to her future.

She could wed with Lothar, she supposed. It might at least gain her an exit from her prison. She might be able to flee at some point in the future, when she had the means of escape and hope of a refuge.

But if she wed with him, she would no doubt bear him children. Unbidden, came the vision of a small, fair-skinned maid child with curling hair and soft blue eyes. Iolaire fancied that if she'd had the light for seeing, she could have looked down in her arms and seen that wee girl snuggled there, sleeping peacefully with her hands clasped together and her face turned upward, untroubled by unpleasant dreams.

Iolaire shuddered. How could she doom that child—and the rest of the world—to the specter of Lothar's manifest evil coupled with her magic?

If she had any magic left.

She gave thought to that. She had been born with magic in her blood; all elves were so blessed. At least they were as long as they remained within the borders of their land. There, spells fell over everyone and everything as effortlessly as sunlight sparkling and glistening through dew-laden trees. Elves walked through those spells, over them, under them, making the magic a part of themselves as they passed. And Ainneamh was the source of it all.

Or so she had been led to believe.

Now, though, she wondered. Losing that magic was part of what made the specter of banishment so awful. But what if the magic was in her and of her, in spite of where she dwelt?

She tried to draw magic from the stones beneath her feet, from the air, from the gray light that came in the window. In Ainneamh the magic so drawn would have shimmered in her hands and effortlessly become what she required. Here she only drew evil to her. She gasped and ceased immediately. She would have no part of this place or its power.

Though that she had even managed to gather some of it to her was something to think on.

She allowed herself another moment or two to envision again that sweet, pure child who had not yet rested in her arms, then forced herself to give somber thought to just what she might do.

She crossed the chamber to where she knew the door to be and ran her hands over the stone. She tried *door* and *open* in all the languages she knew, but to no avail. She cursed it with all the vile things her younger brother Artair had taught her when their tutor had been snoozing in the afternoon sunlight. That brought no better result.

But as she stood there with her hands pressed against the wall, her head bowed, tears she could not spare falling down her cheeks, she realized Lothar's spell lay over where she knew the doorway to be like a piece of cloth. She pulled back with her palms still flat against that invisible bit of magic and stared at it in surprise.

Could she unravel it?

And what would Lothar do to her if she managed it?

She decided immediately that it was best not to think on that. She would seek to undo his evil quietly and perhaps she would manage to free herself from her prison, escape out the front door, and be on her way before he was the wiser.

It did not serve her to think on what would happen to her otherwise.

Three

✳

SYMON SURVEYED HIS BROTHER'S DOMAIN and could scarce believe his eyes. Gone was the lovely castle on the edge of the sea, surrounded by fair meadows full of wildflowers. Gone too were the beautiful stretches of beach before the castle, the clutches of rocks with wild birds perching thereon, the lovely white cliffs that provided a bastion of safety from the crashing waves.

In their places were ruin and decay.

"By Crea of Meith's knobby knees, will you look at that!" Hamil exclaimed. "He's ruined the place!"

Ruin had been Symon's own word, but he saw now that 'twas too mild a term. But hadn't he suspected as much when he thought of Lothar overrunning Neroche?

Darkness, death, destruction.

He'd wondered, over the past year since he'd been king, and for several years before that, if he was imagining Lothar's potential for evil. He'd wondered it as he had watched his elder brother whilst they grew to manhood together. Lothar's power was perhaps unmeasured, but his capacity for cruelty had been amply demonstrated over the years. Symon had also wondered, when their father had given Lothar his most beautiful bit of land but no crown as an inheritance, what would become of the magnificent castle on the sea. When he'd asked as much, his father had only looked at him in that way he had, placid and patient, and said that 'twas no longer his affair and that Lothar would have to find his own way.

Did a father know, then, when a son was a babe, that the son would go so astray?

And if so, what could he possibly do to stop it?

Ah, but such a departure from good sense and goodness. Symon shook his head. Slabs of rock from ill-conceived and poorly executed mining ventures littered the land, blackness from fire, debris and refuse covered the strand—and not a green thing in sight. It was as if anything within Lothar's reach that had possessed any life at all had given up.

"What does he eat?" Ehrne inquired politely.

"I wouldn't want to know," Hamil said with a grimace. "Well, my liege, what now?"

Symon looked at Ehrne. "Can you sense her?"

Ehrne stood there with a look of distaste on his visage. "The stench of evil that lingered behind in Iolaire's chamber is the same as what comes from this place." He sighed and turned to Symon. "But I have no sense of her." He paused. "In truth, I have no sense of anything living."

Hamil shifted. "I do not know about that. I have little magic of my own, but I'm well acquainted with Lothar's use of his. Are there invisible companies of his monsters lying in wait to attack upon his command?"

Symon looked, but could see nothing but what appeared before him. If the castle was covered by some sort of spell, Symon could not tell.

And he was not the lesser of his father's sons.

"I daresay he has used no magic to augment the destruction," Symon said slowly, "and I can see no souls lying in wait for us."

"How does he convince people to serve him?" Ehrne asked idly.

"He steals them," Symon said. "Or perhaps I am wrong and he draws to him those who love his particular sort of magic." He shrugged. "I do not know and I wish to know no more of it than I must to rescue your sister. So, let us be about this business and quickly, before she must spend another night in this accursed place."

"Aye," Ehrne agreed. "But let us approach as if we were lords come for a parley." He paused and looked at Symon. "Well, I will go as a lord; you may come along as my lowly squire."

"And what of me?" Hamil demanded.

"Can you shape change?" Ehrne asked Symon.

"Aye," Symon answered.

"Can you change that one there," Ehrne asked, pointing to Hamil, "into a jackass?"

Symon laughed in spite of himself. "I have no idea why there is such enmity between the two of you, and nay, I will not change him into the like."

"Is it that you cannot, or that you will not?" Ehrne pressed. "Does your magic extend to those kinds of things, or can you only manage the simple spells a village witch could cast?"

Hamil rolled his eyes. "Know you nothing of the rings of mastery? Any fool might win the first, or even the second, but the rest are only taken by those with an affinity for the business or strong power found running through their veins. But the last ring—"

"I can manage what needs to be done," Symon interrupted with a warning look shot Hamil's way. It wasn't as though he cared what Ehrne knew of him, but there was no sense in boasting of any skill so near to Lothar's front stoop. He looked at his men and considered. "Perhaps you lads would be safer if you went about disguised as something of the equine persuasion."

The small company of his most elite guardsmen who had accompanied him north sighed almost as one. Symon supposed they could expect no less, being his men. He looked at Hamil. "And you? Shall you be the wind?"

"Make it an ill-wind and I'll say no more."

Symon nodded. As quietly as possible, in a magical sense, he made the necessary changes to his company, then changed his own appearance. Whether or not it would fool his brother remained to be seen.

Lothar had magic, 'twas true, but he had learned it not from those who taught restraint and honor in its use, but rather from rogue wizards who had learned enough to be dangerous but hadn't managed to earn any of the rings of mastery. Nay, Lothar would wear only the first of mastery, if he wore one at all. Even so, that did not mean he had no power.

Ehrne led them down the path to the hall door in a lordly fashion. Symon followed, too busy watching the surrounding desolation for the potential of attack to worry overmuch about what Ehrne would do. If they gained the great hall, hell would be unleashed upon them no matter how pretty Ehrne's introductions were.

All, however, was quiet.

Too quiet.

Ehrne banged on the door. It was opened eventually by a stooped, misshapen old man.

"I'm here to see the lord of Rathlin. Let me pass."

He did not wait for a reply, but pushed past the old man. Symon slipped in behind him. He used Ehrne's blustering calls for service as a shield so he could be about his own business. He could not hear Iolaire, nor could he sense her. He followed Ehrne into the middle of the hall near the fire pit, mentally searching frantically through passageways that were cobwebbed by rotting, though dishearteningly strong magic.

And still no trace of her.

Ehrne's calls for ale grew stronger.

"Looking for someone?" cackled the old man near Symon's ear.

"I'm but the servant," Symon muttered, brushing him away.

"The hell you are."

Symon turned, realizing too late that his brother was lord and doorman both—and perilously good at hiding his identity. Before Symon could lift a finger or spew out a spell of his own, Lothar had cast a net of his own magic.

Symon watched it fall.

IOLAIRE SELECTED A THREAD OF MAGIC THAT LOOKED as if it might be weak enough for her to break. It had taken her most of the night to manage to find even that. Of course, she had been clumsy with fear, certain that Lothar would surprise her with another visit as she was about her work.

But now, as the chamber had lightened enough to signal full daylight, she had found what she sought. She unraveled a bit more on either side of that weakened thread, and then with a great rending sound that she feared would shake the castle to its foundations, she tore the spell asunder.

The door was revealed.

SYMON COULD HAVE SWORN THE CASTLE ROCKED on its foundations. The sound of rending was nothing short of deafening. Lothar, startled, turned.

And by the time he turned back, it was too late. Perhaps he was powerful. Perhaps he was determined. But Symon fought for a more noble purpose. It was the smallest of advantages, but perhaps it would be enough.

He countered Lothar's spells one by one. They were unpleasant spells, ones full of evil portents Symon had never before considered. It took all his wits to fight them off while doing his best to lay his own snares about his brother.

"Do you need aid?" Ehrne asked from beside him. "Shall I put the kettle on? Toss herbs onto the fire? Brew up a potion or two?"

"Shut up," Symon said, through gritted teeth. "Be about our other business."

"And what is that?" Lothar said, sounding equally as taxed. "The rescuing of an elven princess? You needn't bother. She's dead already."

Symon gasped in surprise, then staggered under the renewed on-slaught of Lothar's spells. He would have bid Ehrne make a search, but he didn't have the breath for any speaking.

And then Lothar smiled and began the words of essence changing. Symon was torn between a desire to point out to his brother where he was doing it wrong and the horror of realizing that his brother was trying to weave such a spell around him. It took all his strength to counter the spell, to fight it off with his own magic.

He felt himself, after what seemed like hours, begin to weaken.

The ground beneath him began to slip.

And slip a bit more.

As eternity passed, he began to wonder if he would manage to best his brother after all.

Out of the corner of his eye, he saw another old man enter the hall. Damnation, was he to be plagued by these geriatric pretenders until the end?

He realized perhaps the instant before his brother did, that this old fool was not quite what he seemed either. If Symon had had the strength, he would have sighed in relief, no matter how unkingly it might have made him look.

Yngerame of Wychweald had arrived and he did not look pleased.

Four

✹

Iolaire crept toward the stairs, her bare feet crunching things she didn't stop to identify. She was free of her prison and on her way to being free of the castle. There was noise coming from the stairwell before her, as if there were a great ruckus happening below in the great hall. That cheered her slightly; perhaps no one would notice her in the confusion. Her feet hurt with every step, but that could be remedied later. For now, she would do what she had to.

She hobbled as quickly as she dared down the circular stairs to the great hall. Then she came to a teetering halt. Before her was a scene she was sure she would never forget.

Her brother stood there, along with Lothar and two strangers who stood with their backs to her. And around them all swirled a whirlwind that seemed to delight in blowing ashes from the fire into Lothar's face.

Lothar's servants stood all in a huddle at the back of the hall next to her. They made no sign of intending to stop her flight, but she supposed she should have expected nothing else. They might have been human at one time, those souls there, but they were that no longer. It was a terrified mass of creatures who shrank back against the wall when she looked at them, so she turned away, unwilling to torment them more.

Ehrne watched silently, his mouth agape, as Lothar and the older of the two strangers screamed at each other. Actually, Lothar was screaming. The older man stood there calmly, speaking every time Lothar would take a breath. This seemed to anger Lothar more each time, but somehow, with each firm word or two spoken by the older man, Lothar seemed to have less breath and vigor for shouting until all he was able to do was stand there with his mouth in an open scream and glare at the older man with hate in his eyes.

The other man, a younger one, stood with his hand upon the old man's arm, as if he leaned on him for strength, though she could not understand how that would be. She could not see his face, but he was possessed of a powerful form and stood straight and tall, as if he were someone to be reckoned with. The power that emanated from them both was like waves of heat from a fire; she could distinguish that even in her current state. Who were these two, then, to be dressed so humbly yet possess such power? Enemies Lothar had made long ago? Powerful noblemen fetched by Ehrne to come battle the foul mage and rescue her?

"Iolaire!"

She heard Ehrne's glad cry the moment before he ran across the hall to where she stood. He took hold of her and pulled her back with him toward the front door. She was almost all the way there before she managed to stop him with complaints over the condition of her feet. He swept her up into his arms and ran.

"But those men—" she protested

"Will survive," he said curtly, "or they won't." He elbowed his way out the door and ran down the handful of steps to the ruined courtyard. He put her up onto a horse standing there unhappily. "Take my horse," Ehrne said. "I'll find something else to ride." He hesitated, then looked at another horse shifting restively nearby. "Are you man or beast?" he asked.

Iolaire stared at her brother, wondering if the journey from Ainneamh had damaged his wits.

"Do you mind if I ride you?" Ehrne asked uneasily.

The horse didn't answer. It looked at Ehrne as if it thought him daft as well.

Ehrne cursed, vaulted onto the horse's back and yelled at Iolaire to ride, and quickly, too. She did, regretting deeply not having thanked the men inside for making her escape fully possible.

She hoped they would know just the same.

IT WAS VERY LATE IN THE DAY WHEN EHRNE FINALLY allowed them to stop. Iolaire sat by the poor fire he'd built, shoving her numb, bare feet as close to the blaze as she dared. Ehrne dropped his cloak around her shoulders and sat down next to her. She looked at him.

"Ehrne—"

"Please, sister, not yet." He held his hands to the fire with his head bowed. It was quite some time that he sat there, silent and unmoving.

She understood. Any time spent in Lothar's hall was enough to render a body sick at heart. And if Ehrne were sitting next to her, not on his comfortable chair in their father's throne room, then that meant he had been banished as well. She reached out and put her hand on his arm.

"I'm sorry."

He looked at her quickly, then gave her a wan smile. "You have endured far worse than I, yet I begrudge you the ridding yourself of its burden. You must have things you wish to say, or questions to ask."

She nodded. "I do, actually. Why are you here? To rescue me?"

"That is part of it," he agreed. "The rest is complicated."

"I think I can wrap my mind around it," she said dryly, "if you say it slowly and simply."

He took a deep breath, looking uncharacteristically hesitant. "I was banished."

"Aye, I gathered as much."

"This is the complicated part." He paused. "You see, I tried to kill Morag."

"Mother?" she gasped. "But why?"

"Because, sister dear, she sold you to that black mage back there for money and the promise of power. I listened to her fix just such a bargain with him, but didn't realize whom she intended to betray until you went missing and I confronted her with my knowledge."

"And what did she say?"

"She admitted to it all with a callousness that still shocks me when I think about it."

"What did you do to her?" Iolaire asked faintly.

"I tried to stab her."

"Ehrne!"

He shrugged. "She's slipperier than you might expect. Father came upon me attempting the deed and cast me from our land. He was rather unwilling to listen to my tale."

She shivered. "What will happen to Sìne and Artair? If you are not there to see to them and Father does not believe what you've told me, then where does that leave them? If mother is capable of this offense to me, why not something similar to our younger siblings?" She looked off past the fire. "I can hardly believe it of her. How will we save them?"

"I do not know, given that the borders are closed to us," he said grimly.

Iolaire stretched forth her mind in an effort to take hold of the sense of her land. Before, before her time in Lothar's hall, it had been a continual stream of beauty and peace that ran through and under her thoughts. That connection with her land had been a part of her for as long as she could remember, coloring all her thoughts, her emotions, her desires.

It was gone.

'Twas no wonder her life seemed as bleak as Lothar's land had been.

"We should sleep," Ehrne said.

She looked at him wearily. "Are we safe?"

"If Lothar is vanquished, aye. If not, it matters not what we do, for we are all lost."

She nodded.

She understood completely.

S YMON SPOKE THE LAST WORD OF HIS OWN SPELL of binding, then hunched over with his hands on his thighs as he tried to catch his breath. The fact that his father was in much the same position made him feel slightly better.

"That will have to do," Yngerame gasped.

A stiff breeze blew Symon's hair into his eyes. With a curse, he grunted out another spell that left Hamil standing suddenly there, bouncing on his heels and looking far too lively for his own good.

"Well done," Hamil said, rubbing his hands together. "Very well done. Look at the fool, standing there with his mouth gaping open."

Symon managed to straighten and survey their handiwork. Lothar was trapped, mid-scream, and bound by so many unbreakable spells that he would have looked like a large, very plump chrysalis if the spells had been visible to any but those who had woven them about him.

"Well," he said, "all we can do is hope they hold."

"Even if he lives long enough to understand how the spells are fashioned," Yngerame said, straightening with an effort, "it will still take him years to unravel them all." He put his hand on Symon's shoulder. "Come, my son, and let us leave this awful place. It will be up to your children, I daresay, to see that his evil stays within its bounds. I am sorry for that, for I could not—"

Symon shook his head. "I could not kill him either, Father, much as he deserves it. We will just be vigilant."

"Aye, we will. Now, perhaps you would care to come to Wychweald and rest after all this."

Symon considered. He would have something decent to eat for a change, if he went to Wychweald. He also might have a good look or two at that elven princess he'd had the pleasure to mostly rescue.

Aye, that was what he wanted—to sit at his mother's table and stare at a woman who had haunted his dreams for years and be no closer than he had ever been to having her, given the fact that he would still be unable to spew out two coherent words in her presence.

"I'd best return to Tor Neroche," Symon said with a sigh. "I do have a kingdom to see to."

"A decent meal, son," his father tempted.

Symon grunted. "You know, you could have gifted me a decent cook along with my crown."

"I thought to, but your mother feared you would find the combination of that lovely cabin and good food so pleasing that you would never return home."

Symon found it in him to laugh. "She knows I would have returned often."

"Then come now. Besides, I'll no doubt need help protecting that elf maiden young Ehrne of Ainneamh whisked away so quickly. It is a long road to Wychweald. I am quite sure you are just the lad to render such aid."

"You are a meddlesome old man."

Yngerame laughed. "I want grandchildren. Come with me at least for a few days. You can turn off the road at the great crossing easily enough if you decide otherwise."

"As you will," Symon agreed. "I've no stomach to argue with you."

"Ah," Yngerame said, slinging his arm companionably around Symon's shoulders, "I daresay even if you did, you wouldn't."

Symon started to follow his sire from the great hall when he caught sight of Lothar's servants standing in a terrified mass near the back of the hall. He paused. "Should we undo that?"

Yngerame frowned. "I don't know if it will serve them. The damage may be too great."

"Or it might not."

Yngerame looked at him. "Then let us try. Can you not do this?"

"You know I can, as you were the one to teach me how."

His father smiled. "My best pupil."

Symon chose a misshapen man and led him across the floor to the fire, under the watchful and blazing eyes of an immobile Lothar. He began to undo his brother's foul work—and that with great effort—but as he did so, he realized the changes were wrought so deeply and so poorly, that they could not be undone.

He kept at it, though it cost him dearly in energy and hope. When he was finished, the man was again a man but still quite damaged in mind and spirit.

Symon looked at his father. "You were right."

Yngerame shook his head slowly. "There was little hope from the start. I daresay there is no evil in them. When I return to Wychweald, I will find a steward for them. Then at least they will finish out their lives in some peace." He put his hand again on Symon's shoulder and led him toward the hall door. "Let us be away. I cannot bear to stand in this place of evil a moment longer."

Symon followed his father out into the winter sunshine and took a deep, cleansing breath. He used one last bit of precious energy to change his guards back from horses to men before he dragged himself over to his own horse. He found himself with no strength to mount.

"Symon."

He turned at his father's voice. The older man was smiling faintly, but his color was poor. Symon understood fully. "Aye?"

"Send the lads on ahead to look after Proìseil's children. I am not ashamed to desire a slower pace for a bit."

Symon did as his father requested, then heaved himself onto his own horse. He took a final look at his brother's ruined hall before he turned away and rode with his father away from the sea and into the peaceful, welcoming dusk.

IOLAIRE RODE NEXT TO HER BROTHER THE FOLLOWING morning, cold, but grateful nonetheless for the pale winter sunshine. It was sublime to have not only liberty from Lothar's hall, but limitless freedom to do what she wished with the rest of her life.

At least she told herself it was so.

Something fell on her hands. She looked up, expecting to see rain clouds, but the sky was cloudless. She realized then that she was weeping. She looked down at her hands and watched them grow increasingly wet.

She took a deep breath. This would not do. There were many advantages to being banished. She would no longer have to endure those endless suppers where she was watched as covetously as a lone bottle of her father's rarest wine that was to be shared amongst the entire company. No longer would powerful elves from other families come to see if they could bluster their way into her father's good graces. Never again would she be forced to learn the languages of foreign kings so she could reject their suits in their own tongues. She was free to do what she liked, to converse with whom she cared to, to make a life where it suited her.

More tears fell.

The thought of never being allowed to return to Ainneamh was more devastating than she could bring herself to admit. How was she to go on? Where was she to go on *to*? Her life, her family, even her home was now forbidden her.

She dragged her sleeve across her eyes and cast about desperately for a distraction. She found one immediately in trying to divine the true identities of the half dozen men who rode in front of and behind her. Most of them had caught up with them the evening before, giving her a terrible fright. Ehrne had identified them as men-at-arms, though he had declined to name whom they served—as if that somehow was going to ease her mind more than knowing who commanded them.

Two other men had joined them as they broke camp that morning. She hadn't had a chance to converse with them—as they had kept firmly to themselves—but she had recognized them from the day before. She supposed she couldn't blame them for their silence, given that they had been the ones to deal whatever blow had been dealt to Lothar.

"Were they victorious, do you suppose?" she asked Ehrne quietly. "Those two who fought with Lothar?"

"Aye, else they wouldn't be here."

Iolaire looked at the back of the older man who rode a fair distance in front of her. "Who is he anyway? A renegade mage from the eastern lands you hired to help you?"

Ehrne looked at her with faint amusement. "Hardly. Don't you recognize him?"

"I doubt I would recognize Father in my current state," she said defensively.

"Well, that renegade mage, as you name him, is none other than Yngerame of Wychweald."

Iolaire caught her breath. "The wizard king of Wychweald," she breathed. "I never would have thought it. He does not look so powerful."

"Nor do I," Ehrne said loftily, "yet mortals quiver in fear before me."

She let that pass as she studied King Yngerame's back. "I've met him before. He looked younger then."

"He just battled his eldest son. Perhaps he's weary."

"I daresay."

"He's invited us to his palace," Ehrne continued. "I understand a body may enjoy uncommonly fine victuals there."

"Well, you'll be happy at least," she murmured, but she ceased quickly to listen to Ehrne recounting the rumors he had heard about the lady of Wychweald's supper table. She had other things to think on.

And to look at. She rode on for a very long time before she dared hazard a peek behind her. Closest on her heels, in front of the other half of the men-at-arms, rode the other man she'd seen with King Yngerame. He was weary as well; that she could tell from the set of his shoulders. She couldn't examine his features, though, thanks to the hood he had pulled close round his face.

"And what of that man back there?" she asked her brother casually. "Is he one of King Yngerame's retainers?"

Ehrne looked at her with his mouth open, then threw back his head and roared out a laugh that made her horse rear. She managed to bring the beast back under control, then she glared at her brother. "Why is that amusing?"

Ehrne laughed again. "I must tell him. It will devastate him."

"Who is he, damn you for an empty-headed fool—"

"He is Symon, Yngerame's son," Ehrne said, grinning with a most inappropriate bit of humor. "Symon, king of Neroche." He laughed again. "At least you didn't reduce him to pig keeper. But I must tell him—"

"Do, and I will turn you into a toad."

His grin faded only the smallest bit. "You couldn't."

"I can and I will."

"I don't believe you."

She glared at him. "If you humiliate me by repeating my words, I will not only turn you into a toad, I will weave the spell so only I can undo it, I will carry you to a pond full of large, poisonous snakes, and I will make it so you cannot hop away. You will die a terrible death and I will not mourn your passing. And if you think I cannot do it, then think on all the times you snuck out of your lessons whilst I applied myself to them."

"You have spells to grow better smelling roses," he bluffed, "and nothing else."

"Blather on to him and see," she said.

He looked at her seriously, then pursed his lips. "I will think on silence."

"That might be wise." She looked at him once more to make certain he held her in the appropriate amount of awe, then turned her mind to what she'd just learned.

Symon of Wychweald, lately the king of Neroche, had come to rescue her.

"I went to him for aid," Ehrne supplied. "In case you wondered."

She tried to look uninterested. "Why to him?"

"Several reasons. One, he is Lothar's brother and has no love for him. Two, I assumed he had inherited some of his father's power and might be willing to use that power to aid me. And, lastly," he added, "he was the one monarch of the realm who had not fallen at your feet and begged for your hand upon seeing you. I thought that might be a boon."

"How so?" So, he had not wanted to have anything to do with her? She wondered if she should find that offensive or not.

"I determined that having my companion on a rescue ruining the rescue by pledging you undying love whilst he should have been about the business of freeing you might have been not only annoying but unproductive. I wanted him for his sword and his spells, not his spouting of wooing poetry at inopportune moments—"

"Ehrne?"

"Aye?"

"Shut up."

He closed his mouth, then huffed as he urged his mount forward where he commenced a spirited discussion with King Yngerame on the politics and corruptions of the schools of wizardry. Iolaire rode for quite some time in silence, giving thought to what she'd learned.

So, the king of Neroche had come to rescue her, quite possibly because he was the one man in the Nine Kingdoms who had no desire at all to seek her hand.

She wasn't certain how she should feel about that.

Well, no matter. She hadn't any more use for him than he apparently had for her. She had someone else in mind. And since she was no longer destined to wed with an elven prince, perhaps she would set herself the task of looking for that dark-haired, light-eyed man who had come to her father's hall. Finding him might take a goodly amount of time. And given that she had nothing but an excess of that on her hands, it seemed a task worthy of pursuit.

Still, it would be impolite not to at least thank the man behind her for his efforts, misguided though they might have been. She slowed her mount just a hair. In time, and over several miles, she managed to find herself riding next to the king of Neroche. She stole a look or two at him from under her hair—which was in sad need of a good brushing, but there you had it. It was difficult to look tidy after having been held captive without any of the appropriate creature comforts.

Symon's hands were strong, but graceful. She supposed he was equally proficient at wielding a sword or weaving a spell. A pity she knew next to nothing of him.

She knew a good deal about his father. Yngerame was as famous for his skill with magic as he was for his gilded tongue. He had not founded the schools of wizardry at Beinn O'Rain, but while still a student he had forged bonds between them that courses of study might be shared between the apprentices. He had mastered all the lessons available there, bested each of his masters in turn, and roamed far afield in exotic lands searching for strange and mysterious spells not known in the Nine Kingdoms. He had returned in time, wed himself the daughter of Murdach of Meith, built her a marvelous palace at Wychweald, then settled down to keep bees and dig in the dirt, shocking everyone who'd thought they'd known him. Iolaire had suspected, once she had learned his history, that his purposes were far deeper and more serious than weeding out the pea patch—though she had to admit she had always liked that about him, being something of a gardener herself.

But what of his son? She stole another look at Symon and wondered how much like his father he was. Was he equally as skilled? Was he kind or cruel? Was he like his brother, or not like him at all? These were questions worthy of an answer and since she had nothing to do until she was about her self-appointed quest to find that missing stranger, she would go ahead and ask him. But first a bit of small talk. She was certainly adept at that. She cleared her throat purposefully.

"Thank you," she said politely.

He didn't answer for quite a while. Then he slowly pushed his hood back from off his face and looked at her. "You are most welcome, Your Highness."

If she hadn't been such a good rider, she would have fallen off her horse.

It was him.

The man she had dreamed about since the night she'd first seen him.

Symon of Neroche. He had been near her all along, first at Wychweald, then as king of his own lands. And she hadn't known.

Symon of Neroche.

And he had come for her.

In a roundabout way.

She could only stare at him, speechless and unable to force herself to look away. He was as beautiful as she had remembered him being, gray with weariness though he might have been. His brow was just as noble, his face just as chiseled, his bearing just as regal.

And his eyes were blue.

A pale blue that was mirrored in the late afternoon winter's sky above them.

He was not smiling, but his look was pleasant, if not just the slightest bit inquiring, as if he wondered why it was she had not a useful thought in that empty head of hers. Iolaire wondered as well. There she was, the well-seasoned daughter of a powerful king who was used to smoothing over all sorts of diplomatic disasters and unacceptable proposals of marriage, yet she could not bring herself to spew forth two decent words that might make her sound something more than a fool.

"Ah," she managed, "ah, is this horse yours?"

Symon tilted his head to study her. "It is."

Well, he was economical in his speech, she would give him that. Perhaps she looked worse than she knew and he feared to overwhelm her in her current state of disarray. She smiled weakly. "I rode my brother's yesterday."

"Aye," Symon agreed with a solemn nod.

Iolaire had a thousand things to tell him, but every one of those things was completely daft. How could she say that though she had never spoken to him, she felt as if she had known him all her life? That he had haunted her dreams for years? That she had rejected suitor after suitor because they were not him?

He would think her mad.

But now he was here and she was free. She had to say something. There had to be a way to start the beginning of something she desperately wanted to grow and blossom like the beautiful, rare meadowqueen flowers in her father's most private garden. But she could not speak; she could not look away.

Disastrous.

"Do you breed horses?" she blurted out in desperation.

"Among other things."

Well, of course. He was the king of Neroche, after all. He likely had all sorts of kingly activities he went about each day. After all, Neroche was an enormous country. She'd paid attention long enough in her lessons to know that, at least.

He did not look away. Perhaps he had never seen a woman come undone in his presence as she was presently doing. She took a deep breath. She would have given herself a brisk slap, but who knew what that would lead him to believe. "I understand Yngerame of Wychweald is your sire."

He shifted in his saddle. "Aye, that he is."

Was he uncomfortable talking about his family, or had he decided she was too odd to tolerate? She sighed. "Well," she said finally, "at least you are nothing like your brother."

He looked at her with the faintest of smiles.

She could have sworn her mouth went dry. Aye, he was nothing like Lothar and somehow it had nothing and everything to do with his beauty. There was something else about him that bespoke steadiness in crisis, sureness in deed, unwavering loyalty in the face of criticism and libel. She could scarce believe he was not wed; Yngerame's list of potential brides for his son was almost as long as his list of what to plant in his garden and equally as famous.

"How so?" he asked.

"How so, what?" she asked.

"How so am I different from Lothar?"

"Oh," she said. "Well, he could not seem to stop talking."

And then she realized what she had said and how offensive it was. She shut her mouth with a snap.

But he laughed. It was a small laugh, but the sound of it fell around her like soft sunlight, warming and cheering her both.

"I must admit, Your Highness, that in your presence, words fail me."

Well, words might have failed him, but they certainly hadn't her. A pity the only words she could find to say reflected so poorly on all her years of princess training.

"Why? I am a woman just like any other."

He smiled again and shot her a look from under his eyebrows. The sight of it was so delightful and so unexpectedly charming, she felt a little unsteady and quite a bit more flushed than conditions outside warranted.

"You are not like any other," he said seriously.

She swallowed. "You would be surprised."

He only smiled and shook his head, but he seemed to settle more comfortably in his saddle and that small smile did not leave his face.

Iolaire felt the breath of beginnings wash over her. It was just a hint of the kind of spring she'd felt at home, but it was enough for now.

"May I continue to ride with you?" she ventured.

He looked at her for a moment or two in silence, then smiled again. "It would be my honor and pleasure, Your Highness, and surely more than I could dare hope for."

"See," she said, "you have words enough there."

He smiled again, but didn't reply.

Iolaire turned her face forward as well, though it fair killed her to do so. She told herself it did not matter, for she would possibly have days to look on him and marvel at the coincidence that had brought them together.

It could not replace what she had lost, but somehow, the sweetness of it began to ease the ache in her heart.

And for now, that was enough.

Five

SYMON BRUSHED HIS HORSE THOUGHT-fully. It was a very unnecessary task—any of his men could have seen to it for him—but it gave him time to think. Perhaps that was an unhealthy and useless pursuit as well, but he couldn't seem to help himself.

Iolaire had thanked him.

She hadn't needed to, of course. Whatever else he might have been, he was Màire of Meith's son and as such knew his chivalric duty when it came to maidens in distress.

Though he suspected that fighting his brother for the treasure of Ainneamh hadn't been what his mother had had in mind all those years ago when she had ceaselessly drummed into his young heart the need to protect women and children from evil and hurt.

He would have to thank her, when next he saw her.

He stopped his grooming and peered over his horse's back to see what went on in their small camp. Iolaire was there, clodding about in boots that were several sizes too large. His boots, if anyone was curious. He'd brought them for no good reason he'd been able to divine at the time, but he was grateful for it now. At least Iolaire had something keeping her feet warm.

And given that he could hear her tromping from where he stood, at least he had a way to know where she was at all times. Not that he needed boots for that. Her very presence was a whisper of spring that seemed to brush over him whenever he was within a hundred paces of her. But since he now knew where she was and could gape at her as often as he liked without having to explain himself or make excuses for it, he did. Freely.

She was grace embodied, so drenched in beauty that he had a hard time looking at her, and he was not unacquainted with beautiful queens and princesses. Her hair was not much more tamed than it had been when he'd glanced at her in his brother's hall, but she had found some way to at least pin some of it back away from her face. He wasn't sure if that was a good thing or not. Staring into those fathomless blue eyes made him feel as if he were falling off a cliff, never to land, never to find his feet again.

Worse yet, he wasn't sure he wanted to.

She paced aimlessly, as if she suffered pain that could only be relieved by mindless movement. His heart ached for her. If he'd dared, he would have gone and offered her his companionship if for nothing more than what comfort it might provide.

And for the short time he could provide it. They were traveling slowly, but still the crossroads would be reached in a matter of days. He sighed. It was as he had told his father: He had no pressing reason to go to Wychweald and a handful of quite pressing reasons to return home. Therefore, three days alone remained before he had to either be about his duties as king or conjure up a decent reason to visit his father's hall.

Three days to drink in the sight of the eldest princess of Ainneamh.

Three days to wish he could look on her forever.

"A bit of swordplay, my liege?"

Symon jumped, then scowled at the suspiciously solemn captain of his guard who had appeared quite suddenly beside him.

"Not today, I don't think."

Hamil rolled his shoulders. "It would do you good. I always find that a bit of hard labor after serious magic is quite restorative."

"So says my father," Symon agreed sourly.

"A wise man, your father. A wise woman is your mother, as well." Hamil patted his chest meaningfully. "I have her bridal suggestions here still."

"Not interested," Symon said. He looked back toward the princess stomping about in his too large boots. She said something to her brother, then walked away from the pile of wood Ehrne was having a hard time making burn. "I think I'm needed elsewhere."

Hamil looked at him pityingly. "Poor fool."

"I am your sovereign lord," Symon said. "Show some respect."

Hamil grunted. "Count yourself lucky I'm better with a sword than with spells, else you wouldn't have me at all." He patted his chest again and nodded knowingly. "When you're curious . . ."

Simon grunted, handed Hamil the curry comb, and walked back to camp. He paused next to Ehrne who was cursing quite inventively at green wood that simply would not light.

"Might I offer aid?" Symon asked.

Ehrne swore again. "What I need is dry wood. What my sister needs are boots that don't make a bloody ruckus every time she stomps next to me in them. Have you a solution to either?"

Symon watched Iolaire walking toward the woods. The boots were unwieldy, that he would admit, but he had no doubts that 'twas more than simply her gear that troubled her. She had passed an as-yet-undetermined number of nights in his brother's hall, and who knew what torments she had there suffered?

"She claims he did not touch her," Ehrne said quietly, rising to stand next to him, "yet still I see her much changed. She has lost her beauty, her fire, her passion for life."

"I pity us all if she finds any of the three," Symon muttered to himself, then reached down to toss a handful of dry grass on Ehrne's attempt at a fire. He called a flame from elements in the air and wrapped it firmly around the green wood.

The blaze began to burn quite cheerily.

Ehrne grunted. "A pity you cannot so easily do something about those boots."

"Who says I cannot?" Symon considered for a moment or two, then walked off into the forest. It took him a bit, but in time he found a patch of weeds plucky enough to survive the layer of snow. He chose what he needed, returned to sit down next to his fire, then began to weave.

"What are you doing?" Ehrne asked suspiciously.

"What does it look like I'm doing?"

"It looks, and I can hardly form the words due to my astonishment, as if you are weaving."

Symon did not look up. "And so I am."

"We are fugitives, out without proper escort, homeless, helpless, and hungry," Ehrne said, sounding increasingly incredulous, "and you choose to weave grass?"

Symon did look up then. "You aren't without proper escort," he pointed out mildly. "You have my men to guard you. My father has offered you refuge in his hall for as long as you'll have it, so you won't starve. Failing that, you have magic of your own." He looked back down at what he was doing. "Since you have complained so much about my boots, I am now making your sister a pair of shoes that fit."

"Out of grass?" Ehrne said in disbelief.

"Apparently," Symon answered. He wove a simple pattern that his mother had taught him one afternoon when he'd been ten, on an endless summer day before he'd left for the schools of wizardry at Beinn O'Rain. And as he wove, he considered the possibilities of Ehrne and Iolaire living at his father's hall.

They would be protected, that was true. They would be well fed and suitably entertained. Indeed, he suspected that it wouldn't be long at all before there was a line of mortals for each of them, mortals come to offer themselves as spouses to two such beautiful and desirable members of the elvish kingdom. Symon worked the final strands of grass into the slipper. Who was to say that Yngerame wouldn't offer to adopt the pair, so as to better see to matches for them?

Symon felt slightly queasy.

Of all the things he thought he might want of Iolaire of Ainneamh, becoming her brother was *not* one.

He set one bit of weaving aside and began a second before he could think any more.

Iolaire came to watch.

He knew this because the very air itself tingled when she walked through it. Symon kept on with his head bowed over his work, ignoring Ehrne's comments about his choice of pastimes and how his lack of skill would make itself apparent at any moment.

Iolaire, quite pointedly, bid him be silent.

At one point, Symon got up and went to roam in the meadow across the road from their camp. He had to search, but finally found a small handful of mountain flowers brave enough to poke through the snow. He returned, then stuck them into the shoes with as much artistry as he possessed, which wasn't much. He set the slippers down, then silently wove a spell of essence-changing over them.

Iolaire's breath caught. "Oh, how lovely."

Symon waited until the weariness passed before he picked up the shoes. Such spells, even for something so trivial, were not wrought without cost. He took a deep breath, waited until he thought his legs were up to the task of holding him, then rose. Even so, his hand shook a little as he handed the slippers to Iolaire. He was no artist, to be sure, but his magic and the beauty of the flowers compensated for it. He made Iolaire a low bow.

"I hope they please you, Your Highness."

"Illusion," Ehrne scoffed.

Iolaire shook her head. "I think not."

"They'll disintegrate into a pile of dead grass at an inopportune moment," Ehrne warned.

"Fool," Hamil said clearly from behind them, "can't you recognize a true change when you see one? And you with all your magic."

"'Tis but illusion," Ehrne insisted.

"Nay, it is not," Hamil said. "I've been around magic all my life and I know the difference."

Ehrne stared at Symon in shock. "But to learn to change the essence of a thing requires years of study, and . . . " He paused.

"And that coveted seventh ring of mastery," Hamil said smugly. "Now do you believe me?"

Ehrne looked a little pale. "Only a handful of men in this world have been so entrusted. Your father is one."

Symon looked at him as blandly as he could. "Aye, that is so."

"But you . . . you . . . you," he spluttered.

"He, he, he," Yngerame said, sounding quite amused as he walked into the clearing. "Symon is a legend in Beinn O'Rain, only surpassed by one other lad of equal skill who, I might add, managed to win all his rings of mastery in like manner, but at tender ten-and-six and not a score. Four years earlier, if anyone cares to count."

"And who is that other lad?" Ehrne asked in admiration.

"It was he himself, the immodest old fox," Symon said dryly. "Where have you been all these years, Ehrne?"

"Ducking out of his lessons," Iolaire supplied cheerfully.

Ehrne scowled, then looked at Symon. "Lothar's men were altered. How do you explain that? Did he learn the spells along with you?"

Symon shook his head. "He lost interest in the discipline of magic before he earned his first ring. Lothar knows the spells of essence changing, but he was not given them freely. 'Tis my theory that he poached the spell from our good King of Wychweald's top desk drawer, the one with the lock that can only be opened by the three-headed key."

"Or by a sharp knife wielded with fiendish determination," Hamil put in.

Yngerame smiled faintly. "It is not a spell that one dares write down, as you both know, so I daresay we can credit him with a goodly bit of eavesdropping." He sighed. "At least we may count him well contained for the next few decades—or perhaps a pair of centuries if we did our work well. Then I'll trot out my old tired self to see to him again. Until then, I'm off to hunt for supper. Anyone care to come along?"

"I'll come," Hamil sad. "You set a fine table, sire, but I never quite trust your greens."

Yngerame put his hand on Hamil's shoulder and proceeded to give him a lecture on the virtues of all things bitter. Symon watched them walk off and thought again that his father looked more at ease than he had in years. A pity it had to come at the cost of his elder son. Symon would have pondered the irony of that, but Ehrne seemed disinclined to allow him the peace for it.

"Why didn't *you* kill Lothar when you had the chance?" Ehrne asked.

Symon sighed. "My father could not and I could not do it in front of him. Perhaps later. For now, he is well bound."

"What does your sire mean when he says centuries?"

Symon smiled faintly. "Think you that only elves live a thousand years?"

"You do not," Ehrne scoffed.

"We'll see, won't we?"

Ehrne merely looked at him, silent, as if he simply could not take another shocking revelation.

Symon looked at Iolaire who was holding up the hem of her gown to look at her shoes. "Do they please you, lady?"

"Greatly," she said, looking at him with a smile. "Thank you."

He felt, quite suddenly, much like a deer frozen in a meadow in the face of a hunter. He searched for something to say, something charming, something amusing, something coherent even, but found that, as usual, just the sight of her was too much for him. Maybe 'twas best he would never have her. It would have been a very silent marriage.

"Shall we hunt for berries?" she asked. "For a sweet after the meal.

I fear that after last night, I too have grave doubts about your father's greens." She shivered delicately. "Passing bitter."

Symon struggled briefly, then gave up on speech and contented himself with a nod.

"Ehrne, tend the fire," Iolaire instructed, taking Symon by the hand. "The king of Neroche and I will return later."

"Do not become over friendly with him," Ehrne warned. "He is not—ow, damn you!"

Symon saw the rock stick for the briefest of moments between Ehrne's eyes before it dropped down into his lap. He looked at Iolaire and had to laugh.

"You are dangerous."

"You've no idea. Best come along then, lest I turn my wrath upon you."

He laughed a little more, mostly to himself, and mostly because it kept him from being completely undone by the feeling of Iolaire of Ainneamh's fingers entwined with his. To be sure, he was a man full grown, and he was not unacquainted with the ways of men and women. He had managed bouts of half-hearted wooing at his father's command, to useful and well-bred princesses and wizardesses of good repute.

All of that meant nothing now. He was walking through a forest still sleeping under winter's spell, falling under the spell of an elven princess who seemed not to notice that he was as tongue-tied as a bastard village lad come to his lord's castle for the first time.

"I'm sorry," he said, when he thought he could spew out two words in succession and succeed.

"About what?" she asked.

"That you were there," he said slowly. "And that you cannot return home."

She smiled gravely. "I thank you for your words, but do not pity me overmuch. Freedom is more greatly prized after it is lost for a time." She looked off into the distance, but seemed not to see what was before her. "It is some small comfort, that freedom."

He couldn't imagine. He had never been barred from his home, never not found a way to be welcomed wherever he went. And though he loved his father's hall, he had spent a goodly part of his life in other places and did not find traveling unpleasant.

He very much suspected Iolaire had never been outside Ain- neamh. She had lost not only her home, but also the pleasure in her memories of her past and her dreams for the future.

"Poor girl," he murmured, then realized what he'd said. He was digging for words of apology when she smiled at him and squeezed his hand.

"No matter," she said. "I am free, with my life before me, and all things possible."

He could say nothing. His heart, overused thing that it was, was too full of her loss.

"I begin to wonder," she said, tilting her head to look at him side- ways, "if it is because you do not like me that you find nothing to say."

"Nay," he managed. "Nay, that is not the reason."

"Good," she said, then she turned her attentions to what was before them. "Ah, look over there. Wintergreen. Just what your father's salad needs."

And she was just what he needed. He still was not convinced he would have her, but he had also never expected to be hunting berries with Proìseil the Proud's most beloved daughter.

As she had said, life was before her and all things were possible.

He wondered if he dared believe that for himself as well.

Six

"WHAT, BY UISDEAN OF TAIGH'S GLITTER-ing crown, do you think you are doing?"

Iolaire didn't move from where she sat on a log, resting her chin on her fists, which rested on her knees so she might more easily observe the two men exercising in the open field before her. But she did condescend to glance her brother's way. "What does it look like I'm doing?"

"It looks as if you're contemplating having some sort of, oh, I don't know, *liaison* with that man."

"Which man? The one who risked his life to rescue me? The one who wove me slippers from grass and made them beautiful with his own generosity? The one who has endured your vile complaints for longer than he was obligated to and should likely turn you into a burr under his saddle except that it would irritate his good horse?" She looked up at him mildly. "That man over there?"

Her brother folded his arms over his chest and pursed his lips. "Swordplay is so pedestrian."

"You engage in it."

"It becomes a thing of magnificence when I apply myself to it."

She laughed. "Ehrne, you pompous ass, get you gone and cease distracting me. I've business here."

He squatted down next to her. "Iolaire, do not give your heart," he said seriously. "There might be a chance to return home. I daresay you will not endear yourself to Father if you try to do so with a mortal scampering at your heels."

A dreadful hope bloomed and died almost before she could breathe in and out. "Ehrne, we will not be allowed in, no matter if I bring Symon or not. And in case you've overlooked it, I suspect our good king of Neroche isn't quite all as mortal as he seems. I daresay even you didn't manage to sleep through *all* Master Cruinn's lectures on the genealogies of the Nine Kingdoms."

Ehrne grunted. "I'm uninterested and I still say you should leave him be."

"I'm not doing anything with him," she said easily. "Just talking."

He pursed his lips, rose, and walked away. Iolaire watched him go, then turned back to the exercising going on in the well-trampled meadow in front of her. It didn't continue much longer, which did not displease her. It was a pleasure to watch Symon hoist a sword like any other man of substance; it was even more pleasant to have him pay her heed like any other man of good breeding.

Never mind that sometimes he looked at her, when he thought she wasn't looking, in a way that made her want to sit down.

It made her, against all odds, forget even for the briefest of times, the pain of her banishment. And given that such was a gaping wound in her heart that she feared would never heal, the distraction of Symon was something to be prized indeed.

The king in question resheathed his sword, then exchanged a few pleasantries with his captain before he tromped across the field and stopped in front of her.

"You look well."

"Winter's chill suits me somehow," she said with a smile. "It helps that my slippers seem to carry a hidden warmth. I wonder if that is a happy accident?"

"I should think not," he admitted. "But who's to say? If they please you, then I am pleased." He hesitated. "Perhaps you would care to walk a bit before we break camp? These long rides can be wearying."

She nodded and rose with a smile. Soon, she was crunching along a snowy road with him, looking down at the beautiful, flowered slippers that seemed to dissolve the snow whenever they touched it so she walked upon dry ground. She looked up at Symon walking next to her and couldn't help a smile. He was handsome, aye, but more than that he was just genuinely himself, unlike so many men who had courted her. He gave her gifts apparently without expecting anything in return, and merely because it pleased him to do so. He would have baffled her sire. She knew he confused Ehrne quite thoroughly.

She liked that about him.

"So," she said, stepping over a particularly slushy patch of road, "what is it you do each day?"

"Tend horses. Muck out stalls. Stoke fires."

"In between entertaining envoys from other powerful kingdoms?" she asked politely.

"Aye, well," he said depreciatingly, "I generally invite them to pick up a pitchfork and dig right in with me."

She laughed. "Much like your sire, I see. He is notorious for forcing the mighty ones to putter with him in his pea patch."

"I admire my father very much," Symon admitted. "And his techniques seemed to have worked for him."

"He is a powerful mage," Iolaire ventured. "Perhaps they feared to incur his wrath so they humor him."

She waited, but he neither agreed nor disagreed with her. He also didn't offer any comparisons of his own power to his father's. She studied him surreptitiously. She had seen him in Lothar's hall, but it had been his father weaving the spell to bind Lothar—or so she had assumed. If Symon knew spells that would change the essence of things, then he must be powerful indeed.

But somehow, despite that, he did not look it. He looked like a man who might happily muck out his stables then return inside and desire nothing more than a hot supper and a blazing fire. Did men fear him or did he have trouble with the ambassadors who came his way?

"You're staring at me with a frown," he remarked.

"I should know more of the outside world," she admitted, "and more about the souls who people it. It is a very easy thing to be comfortable in my land and never wonder what goes on outside it."

"Were you not required to learn anything of mortal kings?" he asked.

"Aye, I was. I learned much of your father."

"I take it you were off on holiday the day they discussed me?" But he laughed as he said it. "It is unimportant. I am but a small cog in a very large wheel."

"Are you?" she mused. She looked down at her slippers again. It occurred to her that if this man could take notice of a banished elf maid's cold feet and use his gifts to ease her discomfort, then his land and the people dwelling thereon were fortunate to have him. She looked up at him. "I daresay not."

"Thank you."

She laughed a bit shakily. "I cannot imagine my opinion matters much."

"You would be surprised," he said dryly. He smiled down at her as he walked with his hands clasped behind his back. "Nay, Neroche is vast and it requires much effort to tend it properly; I feel hard-pressed to see to it all."

"Your land is beautiful, even under winter's chill," she offered.

He smiled a little ruefully. "Winter is hard here, but Neroche is beautiful even then. It is not Ainneamh, of course, but there is much about it that is lovely and grand. We've a long, beautiful coastline to the west, mountains to the north and south, and beautiful valleys scattered throughout. I daresay I haven't traveled over as much of it as I would like. A king should know the vales and hamlets that are in his care, don't you think?"

She nodded. How would it be to wander that land with him, binding the little boroughs and villages together, coming to know the people who would depend on him for their safety and security? Would he make shoes of grass for small children or bind up cracks in kettles for women who had no men to see to it for them?

All of a sudden, a vision of a freshly plowed field came to her, replete with the smells of spring and possibility. Symon's land waited for the seeds of a new reign to be planted and the touch of the king's hand to do it. How much better would it be if there were a queen to set things to growing as well? That feeling of possibility, of laboring with her hands for something she had cultivated herself—it was almost enough to take her breath away.

"Iolaire?"

She closed her eyes briefly. Ah, the way he said her name, as if he found it beautiful. She looked at him and smiled.

"Aye, my king?"

He smiled. "You were very far away."

She shook her head. "I think I begin to understand why your father spends so much time in his vegetable garden."

"I should think you do. Your land is lush and verdant as well."

She smiled, even though she thought she might have preferred, quite suddenly, to weep. Symon took her hand and held it in his.

"Forgive me, Iolaire," he said. "I did not mean to grieve you."

"You did not grieve me," she said with a wan smile. "I cannot forever avoid speaking about it. The truth of it is, I will have to make a new home—"

A voice called from behind them. Iolaire looked over her shoulder to see her brother shouting at them and waving for them to return.

Symon sighed. "They are ready, it seems."

She nodded and turned with him back to where their company was waiting. "How much longer until we reach Wychweald, do you think?"

"Three days," he said.

"You sound quite sure of that," she said, faintly amused. "Are you so eager to reach your mother's cooking pot?"

He paused for such a long time that she began to wonder if she'd said something amiss.

"Symon?"

"I'm not going to Wychweald," he said finally.

"You aren't?"

"We'll reach the crossroads tomorrow. I must turn aside from this road then."

She felt foolish for being caught so by surprise. Of course he wouldn't go to his father's hall. He had his own kingdom, his own hall, his own affairs to see to. Perhaps he had a woman to woo and had been interrupted in his plans by Ehrne's insistent demands for aid.

She slipped her hand from his. "Of course," she said with a brightness she most certainly did not feel. "You must miss your hall."

"There isn't much to miss," he admitted. "'Tis my father's hunting lodge. It is, as your brother might say, a hovel."

"Ignore him. He has no imagination."

Symon stopped suddenly. "'Tis no place for a queen, to be sure."

She looked at him blankly. Why should she care whether or not his hall was sufficient for him to take a bride there? Indeed, she began to hope the bloody roof leaked—

"I will build you a palace," he said, taking her hands. "In the valley of Chagailt, where 'tis warmer." He paused. "It rains a great deal there, so I understand."

Iolaire blinked. "A palace?"

"Aye, a palace. A beautiful palace made of granite from the hills of Iarmil, fine furnishings carved by the dwarves of Sgùrr, tapestries woven by the Wizardess Nimheil, who dyes her yarn with her own tears—"

She found words had failed her entirely. Was he proposing to her? Where were the other women she'd been certain he was planning to woo?

"Are you a gardener?" She heard words and realized belatedly that she was the one to speak them. He was going on about priceless wonders, and she was wondering if he needed someone to scratch in the dirt for him?

"A gardener?" he asked blankly.

Well, there was no sense in not continuing down that path to true madness. He was already looking at her as if she'd lost what few wits remained her; she might as well give him more reason to believe it.

"Do you need a gardener?" she asked.

He frowned, as if he actually spared the effort to try to understand just what she was getting at.

"You didn't mention gardens," she finished lamely.

A corner of his mouth twitched.

"I amuse you," she stated.

"Nay," he said slowly, "nay, 'tis a fair question. But actually, I was more concerned with putting some kind of roof over your head than I was with shrubberies and such, but gardens would be lovely as well."

"A roof over my head?"

"That is usually what a husband sees to, is it not?"

"A husband?"

"Aye."

"Is this a proposal of marriage?"

"Am I doing it so poorly?"

In all honesty, she'd had so many proposals over the course of her majority that she'd long since ceased to give them more thought than was required in order to reject them.

"It was lovely," she said honestly. "Truly."

"It was spur-of-the-moment," he admitted.

Iolaire would have listened more closely but her brother was beginning to shout at her quite frantically. She motioned impatiently for him to be quiet.

"A proposal," she said to Symon. "Well—"

"I never thought to ever blurt out the words," he said, "given that I thought I would never stand this close to you—"

Ehrne was almost beside himself now. Iolaire swore at him loudly, then turned to Symon. "What did you say?"

"I said I never thought to even stand so close to you without your father taking a sword to me for my cheek—"

"Which I will do, mage king," said a voice from her right, "if you do not stand aside."

"Father!" Iolaire said, turning around with a gasp. She could scarce believe her eyes. Now she understood why Ehrne had been so distraught. "Father, what are you doing here?"

"Saving you from a life of misery," Proìseil said promptly. "Neroche, release her."

Iolaire didn't give Symon the chance to do it on his own. She let go of his hands and stood between him and her father, lest her sire use that sword hanging at his side for unwholesome and untoward purposes.

"He came for me when you would not," she said, pointedly. "And for that I am grateful."

"Your gratitude does not need to extend to binding yourself to him," Proìseil said sternly. "Besides, I've come to fetch you home. I have convinced all necessary that the banishment was unjust. It is lifted."

She swayed. Indeed, she suspected she might have landed quite untidily upon her backside had she not swayed back into Symon. He steadied her with his hands on her shoulders. When he would have released her, she reached up and put her hands over his.

"He is building me a palace," she said weakly. "With fine stonework and carvings. Tapestries by Nimheil. I plan to make the gardens the envy of the Nine Kingdoms."

Proìseil snorted. "How can that possibly compare to Ainneamh, where there is beauty as far as the eye can see, music that touches the soul, those of your family about with whom you have had association all your days! Will you give all that up for that mortal there?"

Iolaire looked over her shoulder at Symon, but he was steadily regarding her father, his expression inscrutable. Iolaire turned back to her sire.

"And if I choose him?"

Her father's expression told of his determination. "We do not wed with mage's get."

"But what of Sgath—"

"Do not speak to me of others," Proìseil said curtly. "Here is a horse, Iolaire—"

"What of me?" Ehrne said suddenly from behind her. "Do you have a horse for me as well?"

Proìseil glared at his eldest son. "You tried to murder your mother."

"She deserved worse."

"Well, she'll have it," Proìseil said grimly, "but not from you. As for your fate, I've not decided yet. Grace Wychweald with your delightful presence until I come to a decision." Proìseil then looked at Iolaire. "Well?"

She looked down. She saw her slippers and thought of Symon. Granted, she had only known him a few days; she had dreamed of him for far longer than that.

But to return to Ainneamh . . .

Without him.

She took a deep breath, put her shoulders back and lifted her chin. She did not dare look at either her father or her love.

"I will go—"

"Home," Symon interrupted.

Iolaire whirled around to look at him. "What?"

"You will go home," he said.

"But I thought—"

He pulled her into his arms and held her tightly. She could have sworn he trembled, just once. He buried his face in her hair, then he spoke against her ear.

"Go with your father."

"You do not want me," she managed.

"I want you more than I desire my own life, and for far longer than it will be granted me, but I cannot keep you from Ainneamh."

She could say nothing. *Home.* All that she held dear, all that she knew, the only place she had loved . . .

"Take him at his word, Iolaire," Symon said quietly, "and return with him."

"Well spoken," Proìseil said. "I will credit the king of Neroche with sense in this matter. Now, Neroche, get you back to your father's cabin of wattle and daub and allow me to take my daughter back to the magnificence she's accustomed to."

Iolaire turned to her father. "He rescued me. You owe him at least a supper in thanks."

"I'll think on it."

She turned and threw her arms around Symon's neck, hugging him tightly. "I will miss you," she said, her voice cracking.

"I will come for supper," he whispered into her hair, "and then we will discuss plans for your gardens."

She nodded, then sank back down on her heels. She looked into his pale eyes and saw her own torment mirrored there. She wanted home; she wanted him. He wanted her; he could not keep her from the place that would heal her heart.

Symon released her finally and took a step or two backward. "My heart is glad for your chance to return to the land you love," he said with a grave smile.

"You will come soon," she said, not making it a question.

"He will come at my invitation," Proìseil put in immediately, "and I suggest he not waste his time watching for my messenger."

Iolaire turned and with a deep sigh walked to her father's company.

She watched her shoes as she did so.

Flowers bloomed on her slippers, but she wondered how they would ever bloom again in her heart.

Seven

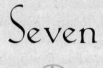

Symon stared off after Iolaire as she rode with her father's company southward. He wanted to believe he'd done the noble thing. Indeed, how could he have done otherwise?

"Well, are you going to just stand there, or are you going to go after her?"

Symon smiled at his father. "I'm thinking."

Yngerame laid his hand briefly on Symon's shoulder. "The reason you matriculated through all the schools of wizardry so quickly is because you are quick of hand and of thought. But, my son, in this, I tell you that you think too much."

"I haven't yet begun to truly contemplate this."

"The world will tremble when you do," Ehrne said. He shook his head with a sigh. "I cannot believe you let her go."

Symon looked at him archly. "You wanted me to."

"That was before I resigned myself to the fact that she loves you," Ehrne said with pursed lips. "Not even the incomparable wonders of Ainneamh can root that out of her poor breast."

"Well, apparently your father left me you in trade."

Ehrne snorted, but declined to reply.

"And fortunately so," Symon continued, "as I've a question or two to put to you."

"Then unpack the luncheon gear," Ehrne said, flexing his fingers purposefully. "I have the feeling I'll need a little something to tuck into as you pepper me with questions I will likely find unpalatable."

Symon smiled briefly. "Later. Answer me this first: What exactly are the laws of banishment?"

"I've had more experience with them of late than I ever thought to," Ehrne grumbled, "but as I understand it, once an elf leaves Ainneamh that elf may not return. Unless they go for diplomatic reasons, of course," he added. "But we have as little traffic as possible with you lowly mortals. Dulls the blood, you know."

Symon ignored Hamil's very loud snort. "It seems harsh," he said thoughtfully, "to forbid your family entry back into their home for such simple things."

"Aye, but it has been done, and more than once, without any remorse. Witness Sgath, who wed with Ealusaid of Camanaë. I daresay he longed for home, but his banishment was never lifted." Ehrne paused. "Do you know their tale?"

"Only that they wed and Ainneamh mourned," Symon said. "Sgath was your grandfather's brother, was he not?"

"He was. He was out riding one day when he found Eulasaid fleeing from ruffians chasing her along the border of Ainneamh. He took her back to the palace, gave her refuge, and fell in love with her."

"And how could he not?" Yngerame asked. "She was, and still is, a remarkable woman. As you may or may not know, Eulasaid is the one who expelled Lothar from Beinn O'Rain when he overstepped his bounds." Yngerame shook his head in admiration. "Her power is luminous. I daresay Sgath loves her more today than he did when he wed her, and he loved her greatly then to give up his home."

"I daresay you have it aright," Ehrne agreed, "though the giving up of his home wasn't exactly his choice."

"Then he was banished as well?" Symon asked.

"It was a failed attempt at trying to remain in both worlds, the mortal and the immortal. Sgath convinced his brother the king to come riding with him. When they reached the border, Sgath stood half in Ainneamh, half out, and Eulasaid claimed him for her own."

"Romantic," Symon noted.

"And off by about ten paces," Ehrne said dryly. "They misjudged the border that badly, you see. I smile now, but 'twas a tragedy that provided fodder for Ainneamh's bards for years. My grandfather banished Sgath on the spot. The banishment has remained in force, even through the succession of kings."

"Interesting," Symon said, calculating furiously. It wasn't as if Eulasaid had possessed a good map to determine where the border was. Sgath should have known, of course, but perhaps he had been distracted—

"'Tis likely for that reason that my father is so unwilling to see Iolaire go with you," Ehrne said with a sigh. "He has not spoken to Sgath since that day. Perhaps there is a place in that hard heart of his that grieves at the thought of never having speech with my sister again—even if that would be his choice and not hers."

Symon rubbed a hand over his face. "If I manage to claim Iolaire on the border, then she will be allowed to come and go as she pleases?"

"It has never been successfully done, but aye, in theory that is the case."

Symon frowned at Ehrne. "Does your father not consider the fact that perhaps Iolaire might *want* to wed me?"

"He no doubt thinks time away from her land has dimmed her wits," Ehrne said. "Besides, you are mage's get." He shot Yngerame a faintly apologetic look.

Yngerame only smiled easily. "What your father refuses to see is that Symon is his equal in every respect."

"Ha!" Ehrne exclaimed, then fell silent.

"Am I?" Symon said with a smile. "I daresay not, Father, though the comparison flatters me."

"You forget your genealogy, my son."

"Perhaps our good elven lordling might like to hear a recounting of it," Hamil said.

"Perhaps you should attend to that light afternoon tea first," Ehrne suggested.

"I'll be brief," Hamil said. He made himself comfortable on a fallen log. "There was once a lad from a small, obscure village called Wychweald. He was deft-handed and quick-tongued and when he talked the lowest master of the school of Wexham into letting him attend on a trial basis, he began on his path to greatness."

Ehrne sighed deeply and sought a seat on a rock.

"As you might or might not know, being from Ainneamh and all, and as I may or may not have told you already," Hamil continued, "our good King Yngerame won all seven rings of mastery from the schools of wizardry by the time he was ten-and-six. Having nothing more to learn there, he went in search of other knowledge in strange and diverse places. And when that search yielded nothing of interest, he began to create his own magic. And it was whilst he was about his labors that he wandered into the kingdom of Meith and saw Màire of Meith walking along the shore near her father's palace."

"Màire of Meith," Ehrne repeated faintly. "Granddaughter of Sìle of Tòrr Dòrainn."

"Tòrr Dòrainn being that little mountainous village well within Ainneamh's eastern borders, if memory serves," Hamil said blandly. "Do I have that aright?"

Ehrne nodded weakly. "Iolaire hinted Symon bore elven blood, but I feared that blow to her head had done more damage than I feared."

"You were wrong," Hamil said bluntly. "But now back to our tale. Yngerame asked King Murdach of Meith if he could have his daughter to wife. I believe his reply was something akin to 'Come home, daughter, without this worthless mortal here.' Or it could have been merely 'ha!' bellowed with great disdain."

Ehrne snorted out a laugh. "Indeed."

"Meith also added that he would be damned if he would give his beloved daughter to a landless, less-than-well-scrubbed wizard of no repute. Of course our good king who was not king yet had reputation enough, but Meith had arrogance to match, so they were at an impasse. Yngerame promised Màire that he would return for her when he had satisfied her father's demands, then set off to see to that satisfying. He happened a few weeks later upon Petier of Neroche and challenged him to a game of draughts, with Neroche as the prize. Actually, King Petier would have preferred to have had the changing of his mother-in-law into a set of fire irons as his prize, but Yngerame did place certain limits upon the use of his powers."

Symon smiled to himself as Hamil warmed to his tale.

"Now, as you might guess," Hamil continued, his eyes alight with pleasure, "Yngerame won that game of draughts fairly. Neroche surrendered his vast territory, which included that little village of Wychweald, and went to stay with his quite lively and unquiet mother-in-law in her manor house, miserable to his dying day. Yngerame, quite content with his victory, returned to Meith and asked if it were enough."

"I take it King Murdach said aye, when the alternative was no doubt gracing Wychweald's most elaborate hearth as fire tools himself?" Ehrne asked with half a smile.

"He did," Hamil agreed, "though he complains about it to this day."

Symon yawned. "I thank you for the tale, Hamil. It was quite instructive. I, for one, am grateful for my mother's choice."

"Speaking of your mother, I still have her list here if you're interested," Hamil said. "To take your mind off Princess Iolaire."

Symon ignored him and turned to Ehrne. "So if I am to succeed, she must be in both kingdoms."

"So I would expect."

"And I wonder how I'll possibly ask her to do that without your father rushing off with her before I can claim her."

"I've no idea, but I don't suppose you could turn me into a little bird to sit on her shoulder while you try, could you?"

Symon smiled. "I'm going for a walk. I'll need peace to think on this."

"I cannot believe you're not the least bit curious about your mother's suggestions," Hamil said.

Symon sighed. "Very well, to silence you once and for all upon the matter." He took the list Hamil produced, read it, then handed it back with a smile. "One name," he said. "Read it yourself."

Hamil did so. He looked at Symon and laughed. "Iolaire of Ainneamh."

"A wise woman your mother," Yngerame said with a nod. "Very wise indeed."

"And to think I carried this for this long for no reason," Hamil said. "I'm surprised it didn't blow off me whilst I was that ill wind about its foul business."

"If it eases you any," Symon said with a smile, "hers would have been the only name on my list, if I had possessed the courage to make one." He started to walk away, then stopped and looked at his captain. "An ill wind," he said. "Well, that is something to think on."

"Turn me into a leaf and carry me along," Ehrne begged. "I must see this. Perhaps you can claim me as well and save me from a life in this dreary bit of world."

"Claim you as what?" Hamil snorted. "His squire?"

"I'm desperate enough to consider it," Ehrne said.

Symon exchanged a smile with his father, then walked away, leaving Hamil and Ehrne arguing over what form would suit him best.

The wind stirred in the trees.

Symon smiled.

Eight

IOLAIRE RODE BESIDE HER FATHER, FEEL-
ing with every beat of her horse's hooves that she was
going in the wrong direction. She wanted to see Ainneamh again, truly she did. But she didn't want to be
put again to market, no matter her father's great sacrifice in coming to fetch her. She didn't want an elf, no
matter his beauty; she didn't want a wizard, no matter
his power; she didn't want a king from the east beyond
the Nine Kingdoms, no matter his exotic strangeness
nor the fathomless depths of his purse.

She wanted a man whose boots were worn, whose
clothes were serviceable, whose fingernails showed telltale signs of being familiar with the dirt of his realm.

A gentle breeze whispered over her suddenly.

She caught her breath, then lifted her face to the
sun. She smiled for the first time in days. The breeze
encircled her, enveloped her with a joyousness that stole
her breath, then made her laugh from the delight of it.

He had come for her.

And if this was what it felt like to be loved by Symon of Neroche, then she had chosen well indeed.

You will soon come to the border of your land, the wind whispered to her. *You must have one foot in Ainneamh, one in Neroche.*

And just how was she to see that, she wondered. She allowed herself the consummate pleasure of being enveloped by that sweet breeze and supposed she would know when the time came.

If you're willing...

Iolaire smiled to herself.

The wind swirled around her, ruffled her hair gently, then flung itself before her.

Iolaire waited a few moments before she reigned her horse in. "Father, I must walk for a bit."

Proìseil looked at her kindly. "As you will daughter. I daresay it has been a trying few days."

She had a twinge of regret at her subterfuge, but she squelched it. She loved her father and when he wasn't about his business of being king, he was the kindest of men. But her heart had been given and that to a man who was never just king and never just a man, but always Symon. Whatever she had to do to be his, she would do.

She dismounted and walked a little ways until she saw in front of her a very thin silver line that shimmered upon the snow. She stopped and very carefully put one foot in her old home and kept one in her new.

The breeze blew about her father, stirring leaves and his cloak, then stopped to swirl fiercely in a space ten paces before him. The whirlwind became Symon. He stood there with his hair wind-blown and a wildness in his eyes that should have given her father pause. True to himself, Proìseil merely drew up and scowled.

"You are in my way, mage king."

"And you're leaving Neroche with something that's mine," Symon answered.

Proìseil sniffed. "I will not wed my daughter to a lowly wizard—"

Symon strode forward, took Iolaire by the hand, and looked up at her father unflinchingly. "I now claim Iolaire of Ainneamh for my own while she stands in my land and yours. I do it in accordance with your law which was before you took the throne and will remain after you have given that throne to another. And thus it is done."

Iolaire looked at her father to find him gaping at Symon in astonishment. Then his expression darkened. He shut his mouth with a snap.

"Damn you."

"Father!"

Proìseil glared at Symon. "You may *not* have her."

Symon merely lifted one eyebrow, but said nothing.

Iolaire watched her father with fascination, wondering what he would do now. He continued to glare at Symon, as if by his very look he could force him to give up. It took several minutes of quite uncomfortable and very charged silence before Proìseil actually sat back in his saddle, cursed quite inventively, and heaved a gusty sigh. He scowled at Iolaire.

"I suppose if he is that clever, he deserves his heart's desire." He fixed Symon with a steely look. "I assume she is your heart's desire. If not, you will find yourself quite unable to wed her, whether or not you've claimed her."

"Father!" Iolaire exclaimed again. She looked at Symon and felt that same joyous breathlessness wash over her. "You came for me."

"I apologize it was not sooner," Symon said. "I had to wait until you reached the border."

She shook her head. "It does not matter. Now, my liege, shall you wed me in Ainneamh, or in your father's lodge in the mountains?"

Her father began to splutter.

"I would wed you in the vale of Chagailt, but I would begrudge myself the time it took to build a palace there," Symon said. "I will wed you where you choose—"

"It is *not* her choice," Proìseil cut in loudly.

Iolaire looked at him. And for once, he paused, considered, then relented.

"Mount up," her father said wearily. "Neroche, meet us in my hall in a month's time. All will be ready."

Symon inclined his head. "I thank you for the honor you do me, not only in the gift of your daughter, but by allowing me inside your hall."

"How else am I to see my grandchildren in times to come, damn you? Iolaire, come. We'll go home."

Symon kept hold of her hand. "I will see her there."

Proìseil scowled. "'Tis a very long ride and you have no horse."

"We won't be riding."

Iolaire looked at him. "We won't?"

"Have you ever shape changed?"

Proìseil's eyes bulged and his face turned an alarming shade of red. "Elves do not . . ." he spluttered. "They most certainly would never . . . ever . . ."

Iolaire caught her breath. "I've never tried. Do you think I can?"

"You are Proìseil of Ainneamh's daughter," Symon said with a smile. "I daresay there is little you cannot do." He pulled her farther down the path away from her still protesting father. "Here is the spell . . ."

Iolaire looked back over her shoulder to find her father looking as if he might explode at any moment. She whispered Symon's spell along with him, then suddenly found herself blowing through the leaves of the trees, intertwining with the wind that was the king of Neroche.

And then she somehow lost her grasp of who she was. She became the breeze rustling through the trees of the forest, transparent as the sun filtering through her, carrying with her the scents of flowers and pines and the calls of eagles that soared above her. And all the while, Symon was there, around her, woven through her, bearing her aloft.

She thought she might perish from the joy of it.

Nine

✹

SYMON STOOD IN THE KING OF AIN-
neamh's hall with a breath-stealingly beautiful elven princess by his side and wondered several things.

One, was it possible for him to have imagined as he
visited this selfsame hall years earlier that he might at
some future time again walk over that floor of polished
midnight-colored marble only this time as the groom of
an elven maid?

Two, would he survive a lifetime spent looking at
the lovely, remarkable woman standing at his side?

Three, would Proìseil survive the ceremony, or would
his heart fail him before it was finished?

Symon felt Iolaire take his hand and he smiled
down at her. The past month had been beyond what
he'd expected. They had laid out the palace of Neroche
at Chagailt. They had roamed over his land in whatever
shape Iolaire, who had proved to have a magic easily as
strong as his, had fancied.

They had already begun to visit his people, going

wherever they had felt needed. Symon had watched with awe and a full heart as Iolaire had bestowed her radiant smiles on noblemen and poor farmers alike. She had welcomed children of all classes and states of cleanliness into her arms and onto her lap, drawing them close and showing them the beauty of their lives and their land in the way only she could see it, she who had grown to love it as much as he, Symon, did.

And then they had retreated to Ainneamh to await the arrival of their guests. Symon had had a crowd of four—including himself. But his parents and Hamil made up only a small fraction of all the souls, powerful or not, who had come to witness Proìseil willingly, or almost willingly, giving his daughter to a mage king.

He had chosen well indeed.

She whom he had chosen turned her lovely face up and smiled at him. "Are you ready?"

"From the moment I saw you."

She laughed. "For me, as well."

"Will your sire survive the day, do you suppose?"

"He has softened toward you," she said. "He has, after all, prepared the wedding feast."

"I'll bid him taste my portion before I eat it," Symon said dryly, but his heart was light as he said it. Perhaps 'twas a small thing, but his marriage to Iolaire had opened up some bit of exchange between Neroche and Ainneamh. He supposed that at some point in the future that might be a boon in dealing with Lothar, should he find himself free.

But that was far in the future and today was the day for other beginnings. He took Iolaire's hand in his and walked with her through that glittering hall to stand before the king of Ainneamh and there claim her as his wife and queen.

They passed the evening most pleasantly in dancing and feasting. Symon glanced about him at one point to find Ehrne engaged in conversation with Sgath and his wife Eulasaid, the wizardess of

Camanaë. Symon shook his head in silent wonder. First it was Proìseil lowering himself to wed his daughter to a mage, then it was allowing his banished and subsequently quite teary-eyed great uncle to see his home again. Where would it end? The world no doubt held its breath . . .

Symon looked for his bride. Iolaire stood near her father, laughing with her younger brother and sister. Symon looked at her and marveled. She looked much as she had when he'd first looked upon her. She was dressed in a gown of hues that seemed to shift as she did; she still had that cascade of dark hair falling most of the way down her back, and her eyes were the same vivid blue. If there was grace, beauty, or goodness to be found anywhere in any of the Nine Kingdoms, it was in Ainneamh where Iolaire the Fair walked over green grass that never faded to brown—

Only now she was his and she was walking to him with a smile that was for him alone.

For a moment, he felt as if he were still in his father's winter retreat, making his own very short list of women he might want to wed and having but one name on it. He wondered if he would ever catch his breath from the wonder of being able to call that one name and have her answer as his.

"You are far away, my liege."

He shook his head. "I was thinking that you are like a whisper of spring in the middle of winter." He laughed, a little unsteadily. "I admit there are times I wonder if I will survive you."

She shook her head with a smile. "Nay, I will be winter's queen and happily so, for even in the quiet of the snow, we will have hope for the spring."

"Aye, there is that as well," he mused, feeling a deep peace sink into his heart.

And with that peace came a great joy in knowing that Iolaire would be his forever, her eternal springtime intertwining with the stillness of his winter kingdom.

"Come, my king," she said with a smile, "and let us celebrate while the evening lasts."

And so Symon, king of Neroche, took the hand of Iolaire, princess of Ainneamh, and walked into his future, clear-eyed and content.

When Winter Comes

SHARON SHINN

One

PEOPLE ALWAYS SAY THEY'RE WILLING to die for the ones they love, as if nothing else they could do would be so hard. But it is harder to keep living for someone else, doing everything in your power to keep that person safe and breathing. I know. All these past weeks I have been living for my sister and her son, battling everyone else in the world, or so it seems, to keep Annie and Kinnon alive. I have defied my father, broken my mother's heart, traveled in secret, gone without sleep, gone without food, and hidden from violent strangers trying to kill all of us because of the magic in Kinnon's veins.

Most days it would be easier to be dead.

We left our parents' house when Kinnon was only three weeks old. Too soon by any measure. Annie had nearly died giving birth to him, and only survived because of two mystics who happened to be passing through our tiny village the very hour we needed them most. Until the night Kinnon was born, I'd never had any dealings with mystics—I'd been as afraid of their sorcerous abilities as my father was, or most of the other people I knew. But it had been clear all during the pregnancy that the baby in my sister's womb possessed a strange power, for there was a heat and a glow to her skin that ordinary women never had. She confessed that her lover had been a mystic and that she feared her baby would be as well. The night she went into labor, my father attempted to cast her out of the house. I ran to the tavern for help.

And help was there. Two women I had never seen before and never expect to see again. Both of them were healers and one of them—the strange one, the pale-haired one called Senneth—had the power of fire in her hands. They saved Annie, they saved Kinnon, they warded the bedroom door so that my father could not come in and hurt us. Senneth even enchanted two ordinary stones for my sister and me, embuing them with a magical power that would give us strength when our own strength was at its lowest. And then they left.

Three weeks later, we left as well. It was not safe to stay. Not just my father, not just my brothers, but all the neighbors from our little town hated us and wanted us gone. I knew this, because I was Annie's only link to the world outside. I brought food and milk to my sister and my nephew, I carried their soiled clothes out through the warded door and brought clean linens back inside. I suffered my father's blows when I could not avoid them and was chased out of the tavern more than once by neighbors who jeered and threatened. Until this time, I had always been well-liked. The blacksmith had been pleased when I flirted with his son, and the tavern-master had hired me to wait tables on busy days. Now the tavern-master shouted at me to get out, and the blacksmith's son flung a molten horseshoe at me, barely missing.

Everyone felt revulsion for the mystic and his mother and his aunt. Better off gone.

We left one bright winter morning that was so cold I could feel frost forming on my ribs inside my body. Annie swore she was strong enough to walk, though she'd had no exercise for three weeks except for moving between the bed and the crib. I had sewn a carrier for Kinnon, a soft cloth pouch that held him close to the chest while its straps buckled over his mother's back. Annie wrapped him to his eyebrows and then buttoned her coat over both of them. She was not strong enough to carry anything else except a basket of bread and cheese. I had appropriated a two-wheeled cart from my father's toolshed and filled it with as much as I thought I could manage—clothes, blankets, more food, a knife, a piece of flint, the barest essentials for surviving on the road—and even so, I knew it was not enough. No one tried to stop us as we left, though our father and our brothers glared at us and our mother lay on her bed and sobbed. Through the main room we went, through the front door, out into the brilliant and bitter day.

And we walked. We walked away from everything we had ever known, a place we had lived since both of us had been born. I had never felt so afraid and so helpless in all my life.

SENNETH HAD TOLD US TO HEAD FOR RAPPENGRASS, where we could take shelter with another mystic. But she had warned us there would be no safety on the road, and perhaps no safety even once we arrived at our destination. For mystics, there was no safety anywhere.

For some reason, we had not realized how much trouble Kinnon could bring us in our travels, small as he was. Oh, from the minute he was born, it was clear he was rife with a power even his mother did not know how to control. His rage could cause shoes to fly across the room, plates to hurl themselves from the table to the floor. Senneth had taught us to wrap a moonstone in a scrap of cloth and tuck it beside him in his blankets. A bare moonstone could burn a mystic's skin, which was why it must be covered, but it could also dampen a mystic's power, which was why it worked. Most of the time.

The first day we traveled, we only covered twelve or fifteen miles, and even that was a hard-won distance. Annie had moved slowly, so slowly, her face pinched with pain and weariness and determination. She had no breath to speak, though now and then she murmured into Kinnon's hair, so either I did all the talking or we walked in silence. We did not encounter many other travelers, and when we did, we crowded to the side of the road so they could pass. There is always some risk for two young women out in open country with no protectors, but no one harassed us. I had a knife up my sleeve and was prepared to use it, but the need did not arise.

No, trouble did not come until that night. We had made an uncomfortable camp a little way off the road. It was so cold that we had to build a fire or risk freezing to death. We traveled through lightly wooded countryside, so fuel was plentiful, but there was so much to do and no help to be expected from Annie. She sat numbly beside the cart where I had left her, nursing the baby and looking tired enough to sleep sitting up. I gathered food, started the fire, laid out a meal, cleaned up after we'd eaten, changed the baby, pulled out the blankets, and gently pushed Annie to the ground.

"Lie down," I said. "Get some sleep. We have to go on tomorrow."

Obediently, she stretched out on the hard ground. "How far?"

"As far as we can make it."

"For how many days?"

As many as it takes us, I wanted to say. "I don't know. I have a map that Senneth drew. We're going to the house of another mystic. We'll walk till we get there."

She sighed and closed her eyes. I expected her to say "I'm so tired" or "I don't know if I can make it." Instead she said, "I don't deserve a sister like you, Sosie."

"Why would you say that?" I demanded in a rough voice.

She opened her eyes. They were dark green on a normal day, or at least before she'd had Kinnon. Now they were paler, grayer, as though Kinnon's small greedy life had sucked even this small bit of color out of her. "You have been so good to me," she said. "You have given up everything for me. Everything."

"I've given up nothing," I said, still brusque. "I wouldn't have stayed at our father's house. Even if you and Kinnon had both died that night. I couldn't have stayed any longer."

I could tell she was struggling to keep her eyes open, but the lids dropped. "What will happen to you now?" she whispered.

"What will happen to any of us?" I whispered back. I was certain she was already asleep.

Kinnon, who slept beside her, waited about four hours before he decided to make things interesting.

I was deeply dreaming when the bird's nest dropped on my face from an overhanging branch. Choking and disoriented, I scrambled to my feet, trying to understand where I was, what was happening. Twigs and hard bits of icy snow and loose acorns were raining down on us from the tree above. It was as if a giant had grabbed the trunk and was shaking it with all his might, as if a strong wind blew through, hard enough to bend the tree over double. But the tree was not shaking. The wind was not blowing. Seeds and kindling and nests came tumbling down as if the tree had simply opened its sticky fingers and let go of everything it had ever possessed.

I put my hand up to fend off debris and glanced over at my sister. She was still sound asleep, but Kinnon was awake, the shine of his eyes barely visible in the fading flicker of firelight. Somehow he had twisted free of the blanket he shared with his mother. His tiny, fisted hands waved uncertainly at his sides as if he was not sure how to move them or what would happen when he did. The wrapped moonstone, the charm designed to keep his power in check, lay uncovered on the ground a few inches away. He waved his arms again, and a piece of dried wood fell with a thump right at Annie's feet. She did not stir.

"You dreadful child," I exclaimed in an undervoice, retrieving the moonstone, tying the cloth around it again, and tucking it under his collar. Twigs and acorns immediately stopped falling from the tree. "If there was any malice in you, I'd have to leave you for the wolves to find, but I suppose you don't even know you're the bane of my existence. Go to sleep, Kinnon, please do."

Of course he didn't. Having napped most of the day, he was wide awake now. Thank goodness he didn't seem hungry, too, because I wouldn't even dream of waking Annie at this hour. I played with him and rocked him and whispered lullabies in his ear. It was still another hour before he slept.

I knew that dawn would come too soon, and it did. Both Annie and I were cold, exhausted, sore, and hungry when we woke in the morning. And afraid. Was this to be the pattern for the rest of our lives? A slow journey, an insufficient meal, an unsatisfying sleep, and nothing ahead but a repeat of the dreary day just passed?

"This will be a hard way to live," Annie said, attempting to smile as she said it. She was nursing the baby. I had built up the fire again, just so we could be warm for as long as it took to eat breakfast.

I gave her a very serious look. "But at least we'll live."

"And it will be better when we're at the mystic's house," she said.

If we make it that far, I wanted to say. I didn't. "It will be better once we're up and moving," I said. "Once the sun rises. We'll get warm. By sundown we'll be one day farther from our father's place, one day closer to our destination."

Annie hauled herself to her feet, Kinnon in her arms. "Then let's start walking."

THIS DAY WAS JUST AS COLD AS THE ONE BEFORE and just as sunny. Annie seemed stronger, somehow, though I myself was wearier than I'd been the previous day. Kinnon was awake most of the day, and Annie kept smiling down at him, bouncing him in her arms and cooing his name. It was as if his presence gave her strength or as if, awake, he could transfer some of his magic from his body to hers. I had no such source of renewal, though from time to time I clutched the rose quartz stone Senneth had bespelled for me. I couldn't say that it actually made me feel stronger, but I honestly thought I could feel fire in its depths. Every time I unclasped my fingers, my hand was no longer cold.

The next day was much the same, but cloudy. The next day, the same, but warmer. Then a day of drizzle, which was miserable, though it stopped by nightfall. We took shelter under the branches of a huge, spreading oak, where the ground had stayed mostly dry, and huddled together all night for warmth.

We got lucky the following night. An hour before sundown we came across a little village, much like our own, straddling the main road. A tavern with a stable out back, a blacksmith's shed, a few houses, then road again.

"We don't have money," Annie said, wistfully staring at the sign in the tavern window that advertised rooms to rent.

"Someone might let us sleep with the horses," I said, resting my wrists on the handle of the cart. "I'll ask."

I stepped around to the back of the tavern and peered in the door. I saw a harried middle-aged woman stirring something on a stove and snapping orders to a sullen girl seated at a small table. "What?" the older woman demanded when I appeared.

"I'm sorry to disturb you. My sister and her baby and I have been traveling and we can't pay for a room," I said. "If you're willing to let us bed down in the stable, I'd take it as a kindness. I'd help with some chores if you wanted payment."

She gave me a sharp look, then frowned at her assistant again. "No! Girl, can't you even roll out a pie crust? Look, and now you've spilled the flour."

"I'm telling my father," the surly young woman said, and slouched out of the room.

The cook returned her attention to me. "I simply hate her," she said in a calm voice. Then, as if this interlude had never happened, she answered my first comment. "Doesn't seem like you should have to do chores just for the privilege of sleeping with my cows," she said. "But if you're willing to work beside me this evening, you and your sister can have your meal for free and bed down in the barn. Or take a room upstairs and pay for your meal. One or the other."

I had already been worried about how quickly we were running out of food. "We'll take the meal," I said.

The woman nodded across the room. "Fresh milk and bread over there. Take some out to your sister and get her settled. Then come back in and help me. There's plenty to do here and my husband's daughter won't be much help. That's for certain."

"I'm good in the kitchen," I told her. "I'll be right back."

WE ACTUALLY STAYED TWO NIGHTS IN THAT LITTLE town, waiting out another stretch of bad weather and catching up on our sleep. The cook slipped me a couple of coins in addition to letting us eat as much as we wanted; despite her gruff ways, she had the kindest heart. Maybe the world was not so bad as it had seemed in the view from my father's house, I thought when we left that second morning. Maybe most people really were compassionate and caring. Or maybe, as I had thought at first, we had just been lucky.

Two days later we had an entirely different kind of luck. The worst kind.

It was another cold, clear day, and we had been walking for hours. The ruts in the road were frozen in odd shapes that would make you stumble if you weren't careful; both Annie and I had almost fallen half a dozen times. Sunset was starting to paint the western horizon in peach and crimson, and night crouched low in the sky just over our backs. Kinnon, who had drowsed all day in Annie's arms, woke and set up a fretful, mewling cry, and nothing Annie did could comfort him.

"Sosie, let's stop a minute, maybe he's hungry again."

"We only have about a half hour of daylight left. If we stop now, we won't be going any farther."

"Then maybe let's just step off the road and make camp."

I looked around somewhat hopelessly. We were in the middle of a long, dispirited sweep of road, lined on either side with low, straggling bushes, patches of hard, bare ground, and the occasional surprise boulder, rolled here by no recognizable force. "Here? There's no place to set up." I liked to camp near trees or by a stream, so we had either fuel or water close by, and I preferred it when we had even the sorriest excuse for shelter.

"We'll just pull off the road a ways so no one tramples us in the dark." Kinnon's cries intensified and she rocked the baby in her arms. "Sosie, I have to stop. I have to see what's wrong with him."

Reluctantly I followed her a little distance off the road. She dropped to the ground on a dried slick of mud and unbuttoned her shirt for Kinnon. I left the cart beside her and began foraging. A few thin and dried-up scrubby brushes—we might get a fire out of those for twenty minutes or so, enough to heat up some water and warm our hands. But it would be a cold night for certain. We would have to lie wrapped in the same blankets, the baby between us, or else die from cold.

The sudden dark of winter had fallen on our sketchy camp by the time I knelt beside Annie and fumbled through my belongings for my flint. Kinnon was still fussing, twisting in Annie's arms and refusing to nurse, his little fists clenched and pressed against his eyes.

"What's wrong with him?" I asked, pausing in my search to look over at Annie. "Do you think he's getting sick?"

"I don't know. He never acts like this. I just changed him but maybe I should check again. You'd almost think something was pinching him or poking him, he seems so uncomfortable—"

Her voice trailed off. My hand had closed over the flint, so now I could start the fire, but first I looked back at her, straining to see in the dark.

"What is it?"

"The moonstone," she said in a quiet voice. "Against his skin."

"Bare? Did it come out of its covering?"

"No," she said. "But it's warm. Come touch it."

I scrabbled over on my knees. Sure enough, when I laid my hand over the bunched scrap of fabric in Annie's hand, I could feel a fever heat pulsing from the covered stone. A shiver tickled its way down my back. "Has it ever been like that before?" I asked, my voice as low as hers.

She shook her head. "Not that I've ever noticed."

I noticed something else, though. "Look. Kinnon's quiet now. It's like the moonstone was bothering him."

"Burning him," Annie said. "His skin is hot where it was touching him."

"But then—"

"Hush," she said. "Do you hear that?"

I froze, still kneeling beside her, and listened to the sounds of the surrounding darkness. Kinnon gave a faint whimper. I saw Annie guide his mouth to her breast, and then he was quiet. Then everything was quiet, the whole world, all the small rocks and winter-bare bushes and weary travelers pausing for one long moment to listen.

A jingle. A hoofbeat. A snort and a whinny. More hoofbeats, more sounds of spur and harness and bridle. A party of horsemen riding in the dark, coming from the northeast as we had. No reason to fear them, no reason to think they would offer us any harm, even if they saw us, and yet . . .

Annie and I drew closer together, wrapping a blanket around both of us and huddling beneath it, the baby still peaceful against Annie's breast. We sat motionless, almost unbreathing, hoping to appear as inanimate as one of those scattered boulders, one of those abandoned bushes. Hoping Kinnon did not finish his feeding and set up one of his inconsolable cries. Hoping he did not realize the moonstone had been lifted from his skin, allowing him to use his power to move any rock or fallen log in the vicinity. Hoping the cavalcade, whatever it was, would pass by and leave us unmolested.

The moon was low in the sky, bright and full. The stars seemed too far away to sprinkle any light on the scene before us. But as the riders pulled into view, moving at a steady, leisurely pace, I felt I could see all of them as clearly as if they had paused before me and waited for me to scan their features.

There were about twenty in the party, some men, some women. The men were dressed in soldiers' clothing, with swords at their sides and battle vests across their chests. All of them wore black relieved here and there with a slash or a circle of silver. Their weapons glinted in the moonlight.

Four of the women wore white and rode white horses and moved through the darkness like river mist on a cold morning, almost too insubstantial to see. What sparkled around their wrists or against their throats was not the silver of a knife blade but the prism of a moonstone, catching the light of the moon and holding it a moment before letting it go.

In the middle of the group rode a lone figure on a magnificent midnight-colored horse. She was solidly built and sat very straight in the saddle, and by moonlight her face looked old, haunted, full of secrets. But her black hair was unbound down her back like a girl's, and she wore black garments as heavily embroidered as a queen's. All the stitching was done in silver, and it glittered and sparkled like snow beneath starlight. She looked like the very personification of a winter night, cruel and beautiful, velvet and diamond, darkness and that rare, breathtaking flash of brilliant light.

I felt the temperature drop as she moved down the road. I felt my bones turn to ice under my skin. I felt frost on my eyelids, snow in my lungs.

She turned and looked straight at us as she rode by.

I did not stir or breathe. Beside me, Annie sat immobile. Kinnon lay against his mother as boneless and silent as a doll.

One of the women in white spurred up to ride beside the woman of silver and darkness. "Lestra? What is it? Do you wish to stop?"

The woman called Lestra seemed undecided. "No—I feel— something," she said, and even at this distance I thought her voice beautiful. "Or maybe not. It's very faint."

"We have another hour of riding at least," one of the men said.

"I know," said the winter-colored woman. "I'm sure it's nothing. Let's continue on."

And she touched her knees to her black horse, and he snorted and increased his pace. In five minutes, the whole caravan was out of sight.

It was another five minutes before Annie or I would risk speaking, and even then, our voices were hushed.

"Who was that?" I whispered. "And why was she so frightening?"

"You heard what they called her," Annie whispered back. "Lestra."

I shook my head. "That doesn't mean anything to me."

"The woman who heads the Daughters of the Pale Mother is called the Lestra."

I was silent a moment. The Daughters had not had much of a presence in our small town, but we had heard of them, of course, from travelers passing through. They worshipped the moon goddess, the Pale Mother, and they all wore her moonstone badge around their throats and wrists.

They hated mystics. They had led the crusade to have mystics turned out of their homes, driven from their places of safety. Stories drifted back to us, from time to time, of mystics tortured at the Daughters' hands, stoned to death, murdered. I had mostly not believed the tales, which had verged on the lurid.

But I had felt so peculiar as this woman, this Lestra, had ridden by. She had looked straight at us. Straight at Kinnon. Kinnon who had fretted and whined and wriggled in his mother's arms as the Lestra drew near . . .

"If she had seen us . . ." I began. I couldn't finish the sentence.

Annie nodded in the dark. "If you had built the fire already."

"If Kinnon hadn't lain quiet."

"She almost saw us anyway, I think," Annie said.

"How? Can she really sense the presence of a mystic? Even one so small and helpless as Kinnon?"

"I don't know," Annie said, her voice a whisper again. Not because she was afraid to be overheard. Simply because she was afraid.

"Where do you think she's going?" I asked.

"I don't know," Annie said again. "I hope it's somewhere we're *not* going."

I shivered in the darkness. I could feel Annie's shoulder, solid and warm against mine, but no other part of my body held any heat at all. "I'm almost afraid to go to sleep now," I said.

"I'm afraid all the time," Annie said. "But we still have to go on."

We slept badly and woke early, sore, cold, and cranky. Kinnon screamed with such rage and hunger that small stones rolled all around our campsite, bouncing against the larger boulders. I was actually grateful for the lack of trees, picturing what might happen if he decided to uproot one on top of his mother's head. We had no choice; we had to tuck the moonstone inside his blanket again. But this morning it was cool. Its filtered touch calmed him, or at least denatured his fury. Thirty minutes after rolling out of our blankets, we were on our way again.

Come nightfall, we were almost dead.

Two

ANNIE AND I HAD BEEN PLEASED TO
come upon a little town just as the sunlight was fading.
It was much bigger than our own village, but hardly the
size of a market city—just a lively, bustling crossroads
town where a traveler could satisfy most needs and be on
his way again. And we had plenty of needs. Annie had
worn a hole in one of her shoes, and we were all out of
bread. We had a good amount of cured meat left, but I
hoped we could pick up some dried fruit. And, oh, just
the thought of paying for a bath at one of the local inns!
We probably couldn't risk our money renting a room,
but I thought we might spare the coins it would take to
indulge in wash water. And perhaps some good-hearted
soul would let us sleep in his stables that night for free.

We stepped into the front room of a small inn, and I
conferred with the proprietor, wanting to know what
services he could offer. Annie was holding Kinnon and
leaning against a supporting beam, grateful for even that
poor substitute for rest. I heard the door open behind

me, footsteps file inside, but I paid no attention until a man spoke.

"There they are. Two women and a baby."

At almost the same time, the proprietor spoke. "Were you asking about a bath?"

"Yes, I thought you might—"

Then I realized what the other man had said. Or maybe his words only registered because, at that moment, Annie screamed. I whirled around, but it was already too late. Two men were hunched over Annie's shrinking figure, catching at her flailing arms; one man was right beside me, a dagger in his hand. I gasped for air but could neither breathe nor speak.

"Two women and a baby," repeated the speaker, the one who was facing me. "Seventeen and eighteen years old. Dark-haired. Been traveling a while. I think we've found them."

"Let me go!" Annie shrieked, putting up a pretty good fight. I started in her direction, but the man next to me grabbed me and pulled me hard against him, my back to his chest. I could feel bruises form everywhere his body touched mine.

"No, you don't," he said. "Don't cause us any trouble, now."

"What have they done?" the proprietor asked. He looked uneasy and a little fearful. I knew he would not risk himself to save us, but I asked anyway.

"Help us," I begged him, twisting in my captor's arms and giving him a hard kick on the shins. He winced and tightened his grip to the point of pain. "Help me—we've done nothing wrong."

"They're mystics," said the man holding me.

The innkeeper looked even more frightened, though part of me thought he was afraid *for* us and not afraid of what we might do. "I didn't know," he breathed.

"We're not!" I cried, still struggling desperately to get free.

"Little one is," my captor said. "So they say."

"Who says? Who accuses us?" I demanded. I kept trying to break his hold or at least slew around in his arms. I could not see Annie, but

I could hear her screaming and crying and begging. Then she howled like murder when someone pulled Kinnon out of her traveling pouch. I only knew that because I could hear her crying, *"Give him back, give him back, give him back."*

"Doesn't matter who says it," said the man holding me, dragging me toward the door. "We'll check to see if it's true, and then we'll deal with you."

I fought him even harder, turning into a wild animal in his arms, but he forced me outside. I could hear Annie being dragged out behind me; I could hear Kinnon set up a furious bawling. All the while I kept wondering: *Who betrayed us? The woman at the tavern where we stayed two nights? One of the travelers who saw us there?*

Our father?

Outside, I gathered breath to scream, and my captor struck me on the head to quiet me. I writhed in his arms, grunting and twisting. I had the impression that a small group of spectators had gathered to watch, but I could not pause long enough to see. My captor hit me again, harder, and for a moment my sight went dark. I could hear Annie's long, hopeless wail and thought, *Someone has strangled Kinnon.*

Then, most unexpectedly, I heard a clatter of horses' hooves, the ringing of swords, and a man's voice lifted in an imperious shout. "Stop this instant! Release these women! Tell me at once what's happening here!"

I wasn't released, of course, but I could tell immediately that this new arrival was someone to be reckoned with. There was a shift in the way my attacker held me; there was silence from the other men. Silence from the entire crowd.

"Well?" Impatient now. "What goes here? Why have you assaulted these women?"

"We have business with them, ser," one of Annie's assailants said in a stiff voice. *Ser?* It was the title used to address serramar, sons of the highest nobility of the realm. Why would a nobleman interest himself in our plight? "They're mystics."

"We have no magic!" Annie cried, desperation in her voice. "Please, please, if you can help us—"

"Release them," the nobleman said.

"*Mystics*, ser," the other man repeated in an urgent voice. "Or at least the baby is. The women—"

"I have no quarrel with mystics," the nobleman replied. "Nor does my mother. They are granted safe passage through Rappengrass lands."

"Yes, but—"

"Release them," the serramar said, his voice very cold. "I have eight men behind me. I think that is poor odds for the three of you."

Another moment the tense standoff continued, and then with an oath, my captor flung me to the ground. I saw Annie stumble to her knees, then, with a cry, snatch up the screaming bundle that was Kinnon. There was a flurry of sound and motion, as our three attackers stormed off and the eight men still on horseback moved forward to form a circle around us. For a moment, I paid them no attention. I had crawled over to check on the others.

"Is he all right? Did they hurt him?" I demanded, trying to peer through the dark curtain of Annie's hair as she huddled over the baby. I could hear Kinnon crying and hiccupping, so I knew he was at least alive.

"I don't know—I don't think he's hurt—I don't know," she stammered, swaying back and forth where she knelt on the ground. "He's breathing, he's alive." And she clutched him to her more tightly.

I became aware of a shadow standing over me, and I glanced up through hazy twilight to see that a man had dismounted and stood beside me. "How is the baby?" he asked, in the serramar's voice.

Slowly I came to my feet and stood there staring at him. He was of average height, brown-haired, with a pleasant face and warm brown eyes. Not particularly remarkable in looks, except that he had that well-groomed, well-cared-for appearance that the wealthy always possess, and the poor never do. "Thank you," I said, my voice breathless. "But why did you save us?"

He gave me a quick smile, practiced and easy. "Because I abhor the men who hunt mystics, and I will not tolerate it in Rappengrass."

Rappengrass. We were headed to the house of a mystic who lived on those lands. This man must be the son of Ariane Rappengrass, who owned most of the vast property in this territory. "You saved our lives."

He was frowning down at Annie, who was smoothing the hair from Kinnon's face and murmuring into his tiny ear. "Yes, but for how long? I had not realized Coralinda's men had traveled so far from home. Where are you going? Have you some place to seek shelter?"

"Who's Coralinda?" I asked.

His patrician nostrils flared in an expression of extreme displeasure. "Coralinda Gisseltess. The woman who heads the order known as the Daughters of the Pale Mother. It is she who leads the crusades against creatures such as you."

I remembered the queenly woman in black and silver, the winter-colored rider. "Coralinda Gisseltess," I whispered. "The Lestra. We saw her last night."

"Coralinda Gisseltess is riding through Rappengrass lands?" the serramar asked sharply. "Then you are certainly not safe. Where are you headed?"

"To the house of a mystic who lives nearby," I said cautiously. He had intervened on our behalf, true, but there was no proof he could be trusted with other people's names. "We were told we could seek shelter with her."

He thought a moment. "Aleatha? Yes, her house is as good a place as any. But you won't make it there without trouble if Coralinda's men are still patrolling the neighborhood. And you don't look as if you could travel another yard today." He raised a hand in a signal, and one of the riders nudged his mount closer. "Stable the horses and find accommodations for the men," the serramar said over his shoulder, not even looking back at his soldier. "We're spending the night. We'll push on in the morning."

HALF AN HOUR LATER, I WAS IN A PRIVATE ROOM OF the inn, taking dinner with the serramar of Rappengrass. I was still amazed that events had turned out this way. But the serramar arranged everything, paying the proprietor for rooms for himself as well as Annie and me, demanding that bathwater be brought up to our room immediately, and inviting us to join him for the meal. Annie instantly refused, saying she had to lie down, she had to care for the baby, but I had gone beyond the point of shyness or propriety.

"I'll meet you as soon as I've cleaned up," I said.

And so there I was spooning up soup and chewing on excellent bread and thinking perhaps I'd gotten one too many blows to the head. For certain, it seemed likely I was dreaming the entire scene.

"I want to hear your whole story, but first I need to know your name," the serramar said, giving me his attractive smile. "Wine?"

"I'm Sosie. My sister is Annie, and her son is Kinnon," I replied. "No wine, thank you, ser. I have a headache already."

He laughed and poured a glass for himself. "I'm Darryn," he said. As if I would ever be bold enough to call a serramar by name. "Is Sosie short for something? Sosinella, perhaps? Sosette? Sostique?"

I could not help laughing. "Nothing so fancy," I said. "I'm just Sosie."

"And you are traveling, why? Endangering all the members of your family?"

I turned instantly sober. "Annie got pregnant by a boy who passed through town. She never talks about him—he was a juggler traveling with a caravan of peddlers. When my father realized the child inside her was mystic, he—well, he wanted to kill the baby, and maybe Annie. Instead, we left."

Darryn sipped his wine. "I can see why Annie would be forced out of your father's house," he said. "But you, too? You have no mystic blood or mystic baby. Surely you could have stayed."

"Not in that house," I said quietly.

"I'm guessing your sister would not have made it very far without you," he said. "She looks frail to me."

I nodded. "She's weak. Sometimes I'm astonished she's made it this far. But she is determined to live, to care for Kinnon." I toyed with my food. "I can't imagine what I would do if she . . . if she gave up. If she died. I don't know how I'd go on, caring for Kinnon and—and living without my sister."

Darryn nodded. "I have sisters myself," he said, "and I cannot imagine either. None of them are mystics, though—the sisters or their children."

"And would you love them if they were?" I asked.

He laughed. "Oh, I think so. Why do we love anybody, after all? Because they have some connection to us. Because they are a part of us. Because their shapes and faces are familiar, and we are not happy if those shapes and faces are missing from our lives."

He sighed, and now his practiced smile went a little awry. I thought that this was a man who chose to show the world only his sunniest face. My guess was that the part of him he kept concealed was probably more interesting. He said, "My oldest sister's daughter has fallen ill. I think, *What will I do if that girl dies?* I can't figure out how to practice the emotion. I can't guess how deep the grief will go. But my fear is that it will go so deep it will never leave me."

"Yes," I said. "Kinnon has only been in my life a month, and that is exactly how I feel. And if something happened to Annie . . ." I shook my head. "I would keep on living, if Kinnon was still alive. But I don't know how I'd go on otherwise."

He smiled again. "This is grim talk! Let's find other topics."

"I don't know that I can provide very interesting conversation, ser."

"Darryn. And I am sure you can."

Oddly enough, he was right. Or perhaps he only pretended the things I said were interesting—I was certain it was a gift he had, of charming young women, old women, whoever happened to be in the room. He asked me questions about my family and my life, nodded encouragement when I told a tale, laughed in the right places, exclaimed aloud if the story required indignation. After all, I decided to have a little wine, and that made the telling easier, the laughter more frequent. We passed nearly two hours in conversation, the serramar and the poacher's daughter, and no one who knew either of us would have believed it.

"Well! A fine night this has been, but dawn will come soon enough, and we'll need to be on the road," Darryn said at last, coming to his feet and stretching his arms over his head. "Up to your room with you. I'll see you in the morning."

A few minutes later, I had slipped into bed beside Annie, Kinnon between us. I thought they were both asleep, but Annie stirred and whispered. "Back so soon?"

"Soon?" I repeated with a laugh. "I think it's nearly midnight."

"I thought he might want you the whole night. But perhaps he does not like girls sleeping beside him."

It was a moment before I realized what she meant, and then my cheeks went crimson in the dark. "*What?* No! He—how can you think such a thing?"

I heard her shoulders shrug against the bed clothes. "When a nobleman rescues a pretty girl of no particular parentage, she only has a few ways to repay him. And since he bought the room and invited you to dinner—"

I was outraged and embarrassed. Had seduction been his intent, and I too stupid to miss the signals? Had it been his *original* intent, which he abandoned once he decided I was not up to his standards? Humiliating no matter which way you looked at it.

"Is that why you slept with your juggler boy?" I said spitefully. "Because you owed him a favor?"

She was silent a moment. "I lay with Ned for love," she said. "But if it would keep Kinnon safe, I would lie with any man in the kingdom."

I turned my back to her, to the baby, to my own mortification and rue. "I would find something else to sell before I sold my body," I said in a muffled voice.

She spoke in a whisper, but I heard her nonetheless. "I have nothing else left."

Needless to say, this conversation left me feeling rather awkward the next morning as we resumed our journey in the company of Darryn Rappengrass and his men. They had no extra horses among them, so Annie and Kinnon rode with a fresh-faced young soldier who announced that he had seven younger brothers and sisters, so he didn't mind holding a baby. I rode behind the serramar, my dress bunched up around my knees and my ankles showing. My arms were around his waist because there was no other way to stay on.

We rode in silence for the first half hour, though I could hear the others behind us making idle conversation. Even Annie's voice floated over to me from time to time, so I could tell the young soldier was making an effort to be agreeable. *Wonder if she'll feel she owes* him *any favors by nighttime,* I thought sourly.

Darryn turned his head and spoke to me over his shoulder. "You're quiet," he said. "Tired? Uncomfortable? We can stop if you need to take a rest or walk off a cramp."

"No, thanks, I'm fine," I said rather shortly.

"Is it that you don't like the company?" he said, sounding amused now. "You can ride with one of my men if you'd rather."

I took a deep breath. "If *you'd* rather," I said. "I don't want to be a burden."

"Do I act as if I think you're a burden?"

"No, but Annie said—and I know you were planning some other journey. We're taking you out of your way, and I'm sorry for it."

"We were just riding. I had no destination," he replied. "What did Annie say?"

I hesitated, but I had the impression he would ask, and ask again, until I answered. "That I disappointed you last night by not offering you something—myself—in return for your kindness."

He burst out laughing, and I didn't know whether to be relieved or offended. "No, indeed, I was not disappointed at all in how the evening proceeded," he said. "I am not in the habit of making conquests of all the pretty girls I meet along the roadside, whether or not I have rescued them from death. And do not take it into your head to start brooding over my answer and wondering if that means I did not find you to my liking," he added, as if he could read the thought even now taking shape in my mind. "Merely, I am not the kind of man who gets much pleasure from casual encounters. Nor am I the kind of man who takes advantage of his station or his very occasional good deeds to make girls tumble into bed with him. I should scold your sister for having such a low opinion of me."

"Oh, no, please, don't," I begged, before I realized he was joking. Then I sighed. For a moment I rested my head against his back, covered in a very fine leather jacket. "I thought the hard part of our journey would be the travel itself," I remarked. "I didn't realize it would be so difficult to sort out how I was supposed to behave around strangers."

"Well, I, for one, have no complaints about your behavior," he said cheerfully. "Or I won't if you will keep talking to me, now that you've started again. I feel certain you can entertain me for the rest of our journey."

So once again we fell into easy conversation, or as easy as it can be when one of you is shouting over the other's shoulder and the other is half-turned in his seat to make his own remarks. He was quite talkative, telling me about his siblings, his nieces and nephews, some of the grand balls he'd attended, the beautiful mansions he'd visited. I sighed once at his description of a great hall in Coravann.

"What? You don't like my tales?" he demanded.

"Oh, I love them! It is just that I am remembering. Your stories make me forget, make me feel like I don't have a single care. And then suddenly I hear Annie's voice, or Kinnon crying, and I realize all my cares are still piled on top of me."

He looked over his shoulder. "Is the baby crying? I didn't hear."

But indeed, some of the other men were crowding over to the side of the road and pulling to a halt, and Annie was already out of the saddle. She sat on a fallen log and threw a shawl over her shoulder and began to feed Kinnon.

"Water down that way, ser," one of Darryn's men called. "I'll go fill our containers."

Since we were stopped, I took the opportunity to get down, find some privacy behind a dead tree that leaned drunkenly in the woods, and relieve myself. Not a pleasant task when the bare ground is covered in snow and the cold air finds its way instantly to your backside. When I hurried back to join the others, I saw Darryn standing with four of his men, apparently deep in conversation, so I stayed well back. Kinnon had paused in his nursing and now he lay on Annie's knees, his tiny hand grabbing at the amulet she wore. It was a blue silk bag tied with a black cord, and inside she carried a chunk of fool's gold. She laughed and shook the bag above his head. His tiny fingers closed over the silken pouch.

The dead tree shuddered and came crashing to the ground.

Clumps of icy dirt flung themselves across the hard road. Loose stones clattered together and went spinning off into the woods. A carelessly buckled saddlebag whipped upward from a horse's back and then tumbled down, breaking open on the road and spilling out a welter of clothes and coins.

"Annie!" I cried, and darted across the road toward her. She was sitting rigid with shock, glancing around in sudden fear, her hand clenched on the black cord as Kinnon tried to tug the amulet from her hand. "Annie! Pull it away from him! *Pull it away!*"

With a jerk, she freed the amulet from the baby's hands. Rocks stopped careening; the trees stopped dropping their stores of nuts and dried fruit. It was as if the whole world grew ominously still.

The Rappengrass men all stood frozen in the middle of the road, staring at us. Kinnon waved his little hands and chortled.

I knelt beside my sister. "It's the amulet," I said, low and fast.

"That's the rock Senneth enchanted for you. She put some of her power into it."

"He can draw on that power," Annie whispered. "When he touches the stone—"

"Apparently so," I said. "The moonstone dampens his ability, but this one makes him stronger. Or so it seems. You need to keep that away from him."

She stared at me, her eyes an intense and fearful green. "How can he do such things?" she asked in a wondering voice. "My little baby?"

"And what else is he capable of?" I replied. "We need help from someone who can show us how to deal with him."

Darryn strolled up, his face showing no trace of the alarm all his soldiers were trying to erase from their features. "That was impressive," he said lightly. "A demonstration by Kinnon?"

"I'm sorry, ser," Annie said, her voice subdued. "I cannot entirely control him."

"I'm surprised you can control him at all," the serramar replied. "But I think it is best we go on our way before he brings down the whole forest."

So we mounted up and headed out, and for the first few minutes, no one in the whole party spoke at all. I heard a few of the men behind us begin exchanging occasional observations, but Darryn was silent for a long time.

"Are you angry?" I asked at last.

"Angry? No, why should I be? Concerned, more like. You said the baby was a mystic, but I didn't really see how he could . . . But power such as that, so randomly deployed, puts you at decided risk. There are many, many people who would see a sight such as we just witnessed and think the baby was too dangerous to be allowed to live."

"You are not one of those people, I hope."

"Of course not. It's just—I was worried about your safety before, and I'm even more worried now."

"We'll be safe at the mystic's house."

"Maybe! If Coralinda's men don't come calling, if little Kinnon there doesn't bring the roof down on all your heads! But I think you will be safer there than you would be if you rode all the way to Rappen Manor with me. There are a few mystics in the town surrounding my mother's fortress, but if Kinnon is going to try such tricks often— well, you'd be better off out in the woods, maybe, where very few people are near enough to watch."

"Oh, yes. I think we want to avoid towns and anyplace where a lot of people gather," I said. "We will go to Aleatha's. I do not see that we have much choice."

"No," he said. "And we are very close. You can walk to her house inside of twenty minutes, I believe."

"Then you must pull over now and send us on our way."

My arms were around him still, and I felt him shrug. "I find myself curiously reluctant to set you down at the side of the road," he said. "I am afraid of what will happen to you when you are out of my sight."

Yes, and I felt an unaccountable depression at the thought that, within a few moments, he would disappear from my view and I would never lay eyes on him again for as long as I lived. *Serramar and poacher's daughter*, I reminded myself. "What will happen is that we will find the mystic's house and we will take shelter," I said. "It will be a relief to get so far after all our adventures."

He half-turned in the saddle, as if to tell me something important, but at that moment the young man riding with Annie called out. "Ser! I think this is where the mystic lives! Just off to the right."

Minutes later, the small cavalcade had come to a stop, Annie and I had dismounted, and our escort was ready to move on. Darryn Rappengrass had slipped to the ground so he could help me out of the saddle, but now he was astride again and looking down at me from horseback.

"Do take care of yourself, Sosette," he said with a little smile. "And your sister and your nephew. May you all stay safe."

I was not sure how to say good-bye to a serramar, if I should curtsey, or place my hand against my heart, or merely bow my head. I opted for words, inadequate though they were. "Thank you so much for all you have done for us," I said. "I will never forget you."

He laughed and wheeled his horse around. "Well, I should hope not," he said, and waved good-bye. Five minutes later, the man and his soldiers were out of sight.

"That way," Annie said, pushing off the road into the undergrowth. If you looked closely, you could see a sort of path there, leading toward what we had been told was the mystic's property. "It should not be far."

An hour later, it seemed we had finally come home.

Three

❋

ALEATHA WAS AN ANCIENT, SERENE, white-haired woman who exuded such warmth and kindness that you felt like you were being embraced even when she did not have her arms around you. As soon as she heard Senneth had sent us, she hugged us both and drew us into her house, a snug place of soft furniture and enticing scents. She settled Annie in an overstuffed chair, pulled Kinnon from his mother's arms, and cuddled him against her like a grandson she was meeting for the first time.

"Oh, you're powerful. I can feel the magic in you," Aleatha cooed, the tone of her voice making Kinnon smile. "You'll be trouble, won't you, little one?"

Annie laughed softly. "He's already trouble. I don't know how to raise a mystic baby."

"Oh, what can you possibly know about raising any baby at all?" the old woman exclaimed. "You're practically a child yourself."

"I'm eighteen!"

"A child," Aleatha repeated. "But I can help you with this one. I can teach you to control him."

"I don't have any magic in me," Annie said.

"Maybe not," the mystic replied. "But you have some power nonetheless." She smiled over at Annie, who looked tense and a little frightened, and her very expression, her very existence, soothed my sister back into calm. "Everybody does."

I was looking around the room, my practical mind bent on practical matters. "Where will we sleep? Do you have space for us? We had planned to stay for as long as you would let us, but I'm not sure we will fit."

Aleatha was still smiling. "I hope you will stay a long time. I have a bedroom in back. You may all sleep here in the front room, if you don't mind lying on the sofa and the floor. Lara can sleep in my room, if she wants, but often she doesn't come home at all."

Annie and I both looked up at that. "Lara?" I repeated. "Someone else lives here with you?"

Aleatha made an indecisive motion with her head. "She has been staying with me now and then for a few months. One day she'll move on."

Well, that wasn't particularly revealing. "Who is she?" I asked. "Is she a mystic? Will she mind that we have come?"

"Oh yes, she's a mystic," Aleatha replied. "She has a gift for growing things. Every plant will flower under her hand. Gardens spring up behind her when she walks." The old witch smiled, and I realized she was being fanciful. "She will not mind you at all, but she is . . . you might find her strange. She rarely talks, and she will sometimes slip away in the middle of a conversation as if she hasn't even realized you are speaking. It's not that she means to be rude. I think she is just not—just not very aware of other people. She is listening to the earth, perhaps. She is listening to the dialogue of the trees. Much more interesting discussions than ours."

I shared a look with Annie, and it was clear we were both thinking the same thing. *What kind of crazy people have we fallen in with? Is it the girl or the old woman who is mad?* But we were in no position to be choosy. We would have to deal with their lunacy if we wanted the haven of this house.

"But there! I'm rambling on, when you must be both exhausted and starving," Aleatha said. "Put your bags in the corner there and come to the kitchen. We'll have a little dinner, and you can tell me the rest of your story."

WE WERE AT ALEATHA'S HOUSE THREE DAYS BEFORE we met the mysterious Lara. In those three days, I was as content and at ease as I could ever remember being in my life, and both Annie and Kinnon seemed as relaxed and happy as I was. We slept deeply and late; we ate the most delicious meals; we basked in Aleatha's unstinting affection. She was the sort of mother you would choose, if you could fashion one to suit yourself. Once inside her circle of care, you felt wholly protected.

I spent most of the days trying to make myself useful, gathering firewood, tending a tiny herb garden she kept in the kitchen window, hauling up water from the ice-encrusted well, and cooking according to Aleatha's instructions. Our hostess spent long hours every day with Annie and Kinnon, showing my sister tricks that I did not understand. She told us she was a reader, which meant nothing to me, even when she explained she had the ability to sense the moods and sometimes even the thoughts of other people.

"It seems like it would be more useful to be able to shift shapes or call down rain or heal people's hurts," I remarked.

Aleatha smiled. "Some people are afraid of mystics with my sort of power. They don't like to think someone else could scan their minds and pick up their thoughts."

I laughed. "Well, I'm never thinking anything very interesting, so go ahead and pick mine up," I invited.

But she had some kind of gift, at least when it came to Kinnon.

She took away the moonstone the very first night we were in the house, but he didn't fling vases across the room or cause books to fly from their shelves. She held him on her lap and gazed down into his wide baby eyes, and some sort of knowledge seemed to pass from her into him. He lay quiet in her arms, and even when he grew restless, kicking his feet and balling up his fists, nothing around him moved or broke.

"You really can control him," Annie breathed.

"Yes," Aleatha replied. "And soon you will be able to as well."

I WAS OUT BEHIND ALEATHA'S SMALL HOUSE ONE cold afternoon when Lara came home. The day was clear and sunny, and I had been chopping wood and gathering odd bits of kindling just to be out in the crisp air. I was stooped over, pulling thin dry sticks out from under a shivering bush, and I had the oddest thought. *It will be spring soon,* I found myself thinking, though nothing, not the bare brown branches of the bush or the stark sunshine or the restless chill of the day, would seem to indicate that winter would ever end.

And then I looked up, and I saw Lara.

She was walking up from the untended acres behind Aleatha's house, a broad, sturdy girl with waist-length brown hair and a round, impassive face. I had bundled up against the cold, but she was wearing only a simple dress with a plain cut and indeterminate color. She moved with a long, smooth stride, her head bent down a little as if she watched her feet or listened to interior melodies. In each hand she carried a basket, carefully covered with cloth as if to protect the contents. When she got close enough, I could see her feet were bare.

I stared at her as she walked past me, only a few feet away, but she did not seem to notice me. She opened the back door by pushing against it with her shoulder, and she disappeared from view.

Where she had placed her bare feet, the dry winter grass had flushed with a delicate green. I could see her footsteps all the way across the garden and down the hill. The bush where I had been laboring was suddenly heavy with dark buds. The scent of the air had richened somehow; it smelled of rain and promise instead of snow and privation.

What kind of mystic was this? She seemed to be spring herself, a restless girl moving across the land, ready to paint each leaf and blossom with its own individual tint. I thought of the woman named Coralinda, the Lestra, the one who had passed us on the road. She had seemed to me the embodiment of winter; maybe it was not so strange that this girl would remind me of a gentler season.

I decided I had gathered enough kindling. I tied up my twigs and sticks and followed Lara into the house.

LARA HAD DINNER WITH US THAT NIGHT, AND OCCAsionally shared a meal with us over the next couple of weeks, but she remained a strange, shadowy presence, impossible to understand. It was not that she was shy, for she would meet your eyes boldly on the rare occasions when she realized you were in the room with her. She was not hostile, for her expression was always pleasant, and she often smiled. Indeed, Kinnon made her laugh. She loved to rock the baby, or slide to the floor to play with him on his blanket, but even then, she rarely spoke. Her communication with him consisted of wordless, happy sounds that sounded so much like the sounds the baby made that, unless you were watching, you could not tell who had produced them.

She was never around for long—an hour or two, maybe a day. She didn't sleep in the house or, as far as I could tell, in Aleatha's barn out back. I didn't know where she put her head down. But now and then when she appeared at the breakfast table, she had twigs in her hair and dirt between her bare toes, and I had to wonder if she hadn't just bedded down on the hard, cold earth.

She was silent, she was strange, she was hardly a woman you would consider turning into a friend. But when she was in the yard, working beside me, the air felt warmer against my skin; when she moved from room to room inside the house, she left behind a floral scent. And whenever she returned from an absence of a few days, she brought baskets filled to the brim with winter treats—nuts or mushrooms or the occasional apple, sweeter and fresher than you could expect any piece of fruit to be at this time of year, no matter where she had discovered it. I found myself wondering if she went off to the woods and hunkered down under some spreading apple tree and laid her palms against its trunk and used magic to bring its bounty to bear a season too soon.

Surely not. Surely no one could do such a thing.

But I was beginning to think there was nothing a mystic couldn't do.

By THE TIME WE HAD BEEN AT ALEATHA'S A MONTH, we had almost forgotten what it was like to be hunted and despised. We were rested, well-fed, loved, and lazy. Even Annie, who had been so close to death only a couple of months before, had regained her energy and normal vitality. Her dark hair was lustrous again, her skin no longer so pale. She was gaining weight even as Kinnon did, and she laughed and smiled and acted like my sister again.

"I like to see Annie outside playing with Kinnon," Aleatha remarked to me one day as the two of us worked in the kitchen, making pies for dinner. It was one of those rare, perfect days of warm sunshine and drenched blue skies, and that morning we had discovered new grass growing out behind the house. Annie had spread a blanket near a tree and called out to tell us that a crocus was pushing its green head up out of the packed dirt. Almost spring, almost. "I think of how dreadful she looked when you girls arrived at my door, and I see how beautiful she is now. And I think, *Yes, that's the Annie that was. That's the Annie that's meant to be.*"

"Kinnon's getting so big now," I said. "Think how heavy he'll be when we start traveling again!"

"Are you thinking of moving on, then?"

"We can't stay here forever."

"I wouldn't mind it if you did."

"That's very kind. But we need to find someplace to live where we aren't sleeping on the floor of someone's house. A place I can get a job. A place Kinnon will be safe."

"Annie can handle him now, or mostly," Aleatha said. "So you could pass for normal, go into any of the bigger towns and not stir up attention."

"Senneth said mystics are fairly safe in Ghosenhall. The royal city. It's so far away, but Annie's stronger now. We can make it there if we travel in easy stages. And the weather is so much better." I laid a flat circle of dough into a dented metal pan and carefully unfolded it. "I have to confess, I've been surprised by the warm days we've had lately," I added. "I thought it would be winter forever."

"That's what you always forget, when it's so cold for so long," Aleatha said. "You forget that winter can be banished. You forget that spring never fails."

I glanced out the window to see that Lara had joined Annie and Kinnon on the blanket. She was holding Kinnon over her head, and he was laughing down at her in screaming delight. All around the edges of the blanket, unexpected clover offered a fringe of pink and white.

"Easier to remember that when Lara's around," I said.

"Yes," Aleatha said. "That girl always gives me hope."

OVER DINNER THAT NIGHT, THE CONVERSATION continued, this time with Annie's input. "How long would it take us to get to Ghosenhall?" my sister asked.

"On foot?" Aleatha responded. "Weeks, I think."

"But at least it's mostly flatlands between here and the city," I said. I had been studying an old map I had found among Aleatha's things. Until I had left on this journey with Annie, I had never been more than thirty miles from my father's house, and I did not know much about the countryside in any direction.

"And you'd be passing through Helven country," Aleatha added. "They say that mystics are mostly tolerated in Martin Helven's land. Though that means nothing, of course. Ariane Rappengrass is friendly to mystics, and you see that they are not entirely safe even here."

"We should wait until it's a little warmer before we try for Ghosenhall," Annie said.

Aleatha nodded and then she sighed. "Ghosenhall is so far for two women on foot," she said. "I wish there was someplace closer you could go."

Lara looked up from the food on her plate. "Carrebos," she said.

She spoke so seldom that we were always startled to hear her voice, throaty and low-pitched. I, at least, never understood what she had to say because I was always so focused on my astonishment that she had spoken at all. "I'm sorry?" I said. "What?"

"Carrebos," she repeated.

I saw Annie's expression sharpen and her face grow alive with interest. "Yes, Carrebos," she repeated, and I wondered when she had heard the word spoken before, because *I* surely never had. "Let's go there."

Aleatha looked thoughtful. "Yes, that might do," she said. "You'd have to take care you didn't pass too close to Fortunalt lands, though, for no inch of that property is safe for mystics."

"What's Carrebos?" I demanded.

"A small town on the western coast," Aleatha said. "There is some talk that it is being settled by mystics. That there are more there than can be found in Ghosenhall, even, and that there are enough of them that no one bothers them. Not the Lestra's men, not the soldiers from Fortunalt, not the ordinary folk who distrust magic in all its forms."

"So we'd be safe in Carrebos?" I said.

Aleatha shrugged. "I haven't been there myself. And it is still a town, with many a back alley and dark tavern for a man to disappear into. I have to think there are some people in Carrebos who aren't so happy to have their streets filling up with odd folk flaunting strange powers. But you might find others there like yourselves—make some friends—it might not be a bad alternative. And it's much closer than Ghosenhall."

"Yes," said Annie. "That's where I want to go."

"Well, let's look at the map after dinner," I said. "And we can plan the best route for our trip."

THERE WAS NO HURRY, THOUGH. WE MIGHT NOT leave for another few weeks. Indeed, just the idea of packing up our belongings and setting out on the road again left me almost too weary to move. I would have expected Annie to feel the same way, but, to my surprise, the thought of the journey seemed to energize her. She spent days mending holes we had worn in some of our traveling clothes, and she took an afternoon to make a list of the food we might want to bring with us when we set out. She even helped in the kitchen from time to time, drying meat, listening to Aleatha's instructions on the best way to cook on the road. We would at least be well-provisioned this time as we set out on the second stage of our journey. We would have no more money than we had had before, but we would have plenty of food and blankets and supplies with us this time. And we would be stocked full with well-wishes and remembered affection. That would carry us some distance, I thought. That would buoy us and light our way.

"Now, if you had some more dried fruit to take with you, that would be good, but I've only the one barrel in the barn, and it's running low," Aleatha said one afternoon. We were all in the main room, stitching the edges of a baby blanket the old mystic had made for Kinnon. "Still, if you're on the road for long, it will truly be spring, and you'll be able to live off the land a little more than you could before."

Lara rose to her feet. "I can take them," she said. "I know where some is."

I was bewildered. "Some what?"

"Fruit," Lara said.

Aleatha looked pleased. "Ah, I thought you might. I have some old sacks you can fill. Bring back as much as you find—I'll make preserves of whatever you don't take and I can't eat."

"Let me get Kinnon's carrier," Annie said.

"Oh, you can leave him with me for the afternoon."

Annie looked undecided for a moment, but I knew she would opt to bring him with us on our little expedition. Not since the night he'd been born had he been out of her sight for a minute. "No, I like to have him with me," she said. "You enjoy a quiet hour or two while we're gone."

"Plenty of quiet after you've left," Aleatha said. "I'll see what we've got on hand for dinner."

In a few minutes, Annie, Lara and I had flung a few burlap sacks over our arms and set off down the hill away from Aleatha's house. I thought, as I followed Lara's green footprints, that she could have outdistanced us by a mile or more and we would still be able to find her just by her verdant tracks. Still, spring really had arrived, gentle and tempestuous by turns; the grass was green almost everywhere. Even so, the places where Lara set her bare feet were more lush, ripe with color. If you knew how to look, you could always tell what direction she had taken whenever she left the house.

We spent nearly three hours on our jaunt. Lara led us to a dense, cool grove of thin trees—a wild orchard—where withered plums and cherries and apples still clung to the thin brown branches. Fruit that had inexplicably survived winter and had somehow failed to be harvested by squirrels and crows. Under foot, buried beneath a froth of leaves, we found occasional piles of dried apples, as well, and small pyramids of cherries. I bent to scoop them from the ground, stretched to snap them from the trees.

Once or twice I plucked a round apple from its branch and then paused, feeling it plump in my hand. Not old fruit, this one, perhaps, but new, brought to term very early by a loving but impatient power. Once, hungry from the work, I paused to eat one of my rescued plums, and found it sweet and juicy under its stretched purple skin. I glanced sideways at Lara and found her watching me, a smile on her face.

"It tastes wonderful," I said.

She ducked her head and turned away, not answering.

We filled our bags till they were so full we were not sure we could carry them back, and then we began the long trek homeward. Kinnon slept in his traveling pouch, Annie was too tired to talk, and, as usual, Lara was never inclined to make conversation. So we walked back in virtual silence. The air had cooled and the sun was about to set as we came into view of Aleatha's house.

And then Lara came to a dead halt and fell to her knees. The motion of her hand brought Annie and me down with her, Annie clumsy as she tried not to jostle the baby. Lara turned her head from side to side, as if listening. The scrubby bushes nearby rubbed their new leaves together as if wringing their flat hands; the trees closer to the house seemed to shiver in a breeze that only they could feel.

Lara looked back at me as I crouched between her and Annie. "Aleatha," she whispered.

"What's happened?" I was so afraid it was hard to get the words out.

Lara shook her head. "They're gone now."

"What? Who's gone? What happened?"

But she shook her head again and came to her feet without saying another word. She took off running toward the cottage, so swiftly that the grass didn't have time to change color beneath her toes.

"You and Kinnon stay here," I ordered Annie, and I darted after Lara.

We found Aleatha in the front room, on the floor, lying in a jumble of overturned furniture and smashed crockery. I could see blood on her clothes, blood on the floor, and for a moment my ribs squeezed down so painfully I almost fainted. Lara dropped to her knees beside Aleatha while I looked dumbly around. Chairs had been broken, curtains ripped from the windows, holes hacked into walls. A pile of kindling smoked in the middle of the room, as if someone had lit a hasty fire, intending to burn the house down, then left before the flames truly caught.

Someone who hated mystics had found this house.

What if we had all been here? We might all be dead now. Worse, what if we had left Kinnon behind while we went apple-picking? If he had died while she still lived, Annie would have perished soon after.

Lara turned her head and looked up at me. "She's alive," she said. "But I need your help."

I caught my breath. I had seen the blood and the stillness of the old mystic's body, and I assumed the worst. I knelt beside her. "What? What can I do?"

"Untie her," Lara said. "I can't touch it."

It was then I saw that Aleatha's hands had been bound with a thin chain of moonstones. Already I could see her wrists turning red where the opalescent gems touched her skin. Uttering a small cry, I dug my fingers through the delicate binding, untwisted it, and flung it across the room. Aleatha sighed and her body seemed to slump, but she did not open her eyes.

"How bad is she?" I asked.

Lara shrugged. She was running her strong, capable hands over Aleatha's cheeks, stroking the tangled white hair, resting her palm against Aleatha's heart.

"Will she—will she survive?" I whispered.

Lara glanced over at me. Her eyes, always a strange mix of green and brown, seemed dark and knowing. "I can mend her," she said.

"You're a healer? That's your magic?"

Lara dropped her eyes and moved her hands again, touching Aleatha's ribs and hips. "I make things grow," she said. "I give them life."

A spring goddess, indeed, or maybe a mystic whose power was rooted in the fertile earth. Senneth's power had been fire, after all, and Kinnon's seemed to draw from the air. I had no idea how magic worked.

"What can I do to help?" I asked.

She looked at me again. "Leave. You and your sister. Go to Carre-bos now."

"*Now?* When she needs us? We won't!"

Lara seemed to struggle a moment to find words, since words were something she rarely needed. "I can hide her," she said. "If they come back. I can't take care of all of you."

If they come back? "We can't just leave," I said. "Not while she's like this."

"Soon, then," Lara said, and returned her attention to Aleatha.

I went to fetch Annie and Kinnon, and my sister and I worked to put the house to rights while Lara tended to Aleatha. Eventually, we laid the old mystic on the bed in her own room, once Annie and I had tidied it. We ate a somber meal that was mostly silent, and we went to our beds uneasy. What if they came in the night, these people who hated mystics? How would we defend ourselves then? Even this haven, welcome as it had been, was not safe any longer. We must move on.

In the morning, Aleatha was conscious, though still weak and in a great deal of pain. "Coralinda's men," she whispered when we asked who had hurt her. "There were three of them."

I wondered if they were the same ones who had assaulted Annie and me on the road. The day that serramar Darryn Rappengrass had saved our lives.

Darryn Rappengrass.

Well, he was not here to save us now, or even give his advice.

"You have to leave," Aleatha whispered. "Today. Now."

I looked down at her in dismay. "That's what Lara said. But to run away while you're in such straits—"

"You must go," she repeated. "It is more dangerous if we are all together."

Perhaps she just said that in an effort to convince us to leave, whether or not it was true. But it was clear that Lara could care for her—indeed, Lara was the only one of us who really could do much for her, besides feed her and clean her, and Lara could do those tasks as well. And Annie, I could see, was desperate to be on the move, to find safety for her son.

Despite the fact that it was clear there was no safety to be found.

We spent that whole day getting ready, packing our cart and organizing our gear. I also chopped wood and worked in the kitchen, preparing meals for the days ahead so that Lara had fewer chores to do. But it was clear, by the end of the day, that Aleatha was getting stronger. Her color was good; what wounds I had been permitted to see were well on their way to healing. The magic in Lara's hands was powerful indeed.

One last dinner in the mystic's house—one last night sleeping on the floor. We rose early, ate a quick breakfast, and made our subdued good-byes to our hostess and her mysterious friend.

"And you are going to Carrebos?" Aleatha asked, holding my hand in hers for the longest time. I nodded, and she squeezed my fingers. "Lara and I will try to join you in a few weeks. When I am well enough to travel."

I leaned down to kiss her soft cheek. "Then we will see you then. Aleatha, I cannot thank you enough for all you have done for us."

She gave me a wavering smile. "You have kept an old woman company on a cold winter night," she said. "You brought a baby into my house. What is a baby but hope, after all? That is a gift that is welcome at my door any day."

So Annie held Kinnon up for Aleatha to kiss, and we said our good-byes once more, and it was time to go. Our bundles and the two-wheeled cart were packed and waiting for us on the front walk. Lara stood in the door and waved to us as we left, and we turned around two or three times to wave back.

But eventually we were too far away to see her, to see even the smoke coming from the chimney of the small house. Back on the road once more. Back into the unfriendly world.

Four

THIS LATEST TRIP WAS IN EVERY WAY AN improvement. The weather was warmer, Annie was stronger, and Kinnon was much better behaved. He still fussed and cried when he was tired or hungry, as a baby will, but he no longer flung items around at will. We never woke to a bombardment of acorns or saw my cart get overturned when he was in a rage. Aleatha had somehow managed to train Annie to control the baby's magic—at least most of the time.

Oddly enough, these days it seemed that Kinnon's magic was strongest when he was happiest. One afternoon we had paused to eat lunch on the side of the road. Annie had nursed Kinnon, and changed him, and now he lay on a small blanket, kicking his legs and laughing up at her. He waved his hands above his head—and Annie's half-eaten apple lifted itself from the ground and hung in the air right over the blanket. Kinnon burbled with delight when he saw it, and the apple bounced in the air but did not tumble to the ground. Annie looked at it, looked at me, and looked back at the apple. She plucked it from whatever invisible hand held it aloft and took a big bite out of it. Kinnon laughed even harder.

Such tricks as that, I thought, might make it more difficult for us to pass as normal if we ever fell in with other travelers.

At first we did not. We moved in slow stages, camping out, hoarding our supplies, skirting Fortunalt lands. When we passed farmhouses, I would often bargain with the farm wife for cheese or fresh bread. We still had a few coins, and I could pay a little. A couple of times, if the people seemed friendly, I would ask if we could sleep overnight in the barn, and then I would help with the morning's chores to pay our way. Annie, who was a skilled seamstress, also offered to do mending or finish sewing curtains, and this sometimes earned us additional food or the occasional pile of coppers. I cannot describe how relieved I was that Annie was now strong enough to help support us—that the entire burden of choosing our route, negotiating with our hosts, and earning our way no longer fell entirely to me.

"It's like you're Annie again," I whispered to her one night as we bedded down in a particularly tidy barn. Well-fed, warm, and even clean, I realized sleepily that I was entirely content.

She was silent a moment. "Do you think so?" she said at last. "I feel so changed. I feel as if I'm moving through the world almost as new to it as Kinnon is. As if I don't know what things are important, what things are good, what things are frightening. As if I have to learn all of that over again—or as if all of those things have changed, and I have to learn what each of them means now, no matter what they meant before."

I turned on my side to face her in the dark. "Is that because of Kinnon?" I asked. "Is he the one who makes you judge everything differently?"

"I don't know," she said. "Maybe. Certainly things I used to care about, before I had a baby, seem silly and useless now. And things that didn't scare me before now have me terrified, because of Kinnon. But sometimes I wonder if . . ." Her voice trailed off.

"If what?"

"If some of this feeling comes from almost dying. From having my life saved by a mystic."

"You think the magic has rubbed off on you."

"No. Yes. I don't know. Her hands were on fire when they touched me. Maybe they set part of me on fire, inside. Maybe part of what used to be inside me has burned away, and now something new has to grow there. I don't think I can explain."

"Are you sorry, then? That she saved you with fire?"

Her hand dropped to Kinnon's head, for he lay sleeping between us. "Oh, no," she said softly. "I could never regret anything she did to me, if she kept me alive to raise my son. It's just—I am different, that's all. And I know I haven't been much use to you."

"Don't talk like that," I said.

"It's true. You are the one who kept us alive once we left our father's house. But I'm better now. I'm stronger. Everything will be different when we're in Carrebos."

WE WERE PROBABLY FIVE DAYS OUTSIDE OF CAR-rebos when we came to another small town, one of those crossroads settlements that dotted the major trade roads and primarily served travelers. We were low on food, and both Annie and Kinnon had developed slight coughs from too many nights sleeping in open air. I left the two of them some distance back on the road and strolled down the main street, considering my options. There were two taverns, which looked quiet enough during the day but might turn noisy at night. One of them looked dilapidated and disreputable, but the other was fairly well-kept and featured a second story which might very well consist of rooms to rent.

I had nothing to lose by asking.

I stepped inside and took a deep breath. It's always been my belief that you can tell a lot about a place by the way it smells. The scents of fresh bread baking and hearty soup bubbling are good signs; an odor of moldy cheese and unwashed floors and spilled wine is not so promising. This place smelled of yeast and onions and soap.

A man worked behind the counter, and four or five other men were scattered throughout the dark room, hunched over their meals or talking idly with each other. They all looked up when I entered, but only the man behind the counter continued to stare as I stepped across the floor to approach him. He was dark-haired and solidly built, and his face was watchful.

"Looking for something?" he asked.

I nodded. "I'm traveling with my sister and her baby. We'd like to spend a night or two indoors, but we don't have much money. I'm wondering if you have rooms to rent and if you'll let me work for our keep."

"I have a room open," he said. "What kind of work do you do?"

A man sitting at the counter sniggered, indicating what kind of jobs *he* expected a nameless, unaccompanied woman to undertake. The barman grinned briefly, but his look was speculative, not lascivious, and he waited to hear my answer.

I'd known men like this my whole life. Coarse, not much impressed by women, but willing to respect you if you did your best and didn't knuckle under to their teasing. I tossed my hair back and tried to look sassy.

"I can cook and I can clean and I can wait tables if the customers aren't too grabby," I said, and both men laughed. "My sister sews, if you've got piecework you need done, but she has to be able to do it while she tends the baby."

"Can you count?" the barman asked. "Last girl who worked here couldn't keep track of the coins and lost me all sorts of money."

"I can count," I said. "I can read, too."

"And you and your sister are willing to share one room?"

"If we can have a bath, too."

"You'll have to haul and heat the water yourself."

"I'm willing."

"Then you can stay a few days. I need the help at that."

WITHIN THE HOUR WE WERE SETTLED INTO THE tavern, which was called Jilly's after the man who owned it. The upstairs room was small, passably clean and situated over the kitchen, so it was both warm and fragrant. I left Annie and the baby there to sleep off the exhaustion while I went downstairs to begin my shift.

Within a few days, I was as comfortable there as I'd been when I worked at the tavern close to my father's house. Jilly expected hard work and strict accounting from anyone in his employ, but other than that he didn't care much about personality traits. It didn't matter to him if I was friendly and flirtatious or grim and sulky. His customers, mostly men, would sometimes try to pat my bottom or catch a kiss, but that was a common thing at a tavern and I could hold my own with them. I actually sort of liked the occasional fresh remark, the implied invitation. It made me remember that I was seventeen and not bad to look at. It reminded me that I had once had a life that was not compounded of flight and fear.

I liked the attention less when it came from Jilly's brother.

Jett was a big man, bearded and mean-looking, and he usually dropped by the bar early in the evenings or late at night, most often with a few villainous friends in tow. No one ever mentioned his line of work, but my suspicion was that he was some sort of brigand, for he sometimes paid in gold coins that I couldn't imagine he had earned through honest labor. He was often drunk, usually loud, and no one seemed to like him much, not even this brother. But Jilly would serve him food and drink, his face set and his mouth shut, and never say a word against him. I couldn't entirely say I blamed him. I knew what it was like to love a sibling even when it was difficult to do so.

Jett was the only thing I didn't like about our new situation. Kinnon and Annie had mostly recovered from their coughs, and Annie had started doing some work for a dressmaker across the way. We all slept on the same narrow mattress at night, on a bedframe so old and creaky that Annie remarked she hoped she was never induced to take a lover while we stayed there. Kinnon was remarkably well-behaved, only knocking over the water pitcher once or twice during the middle of the night and otherwise displaying a sunny temperament. We were dry, we were stationary, we had plenty to eat. I, for one, was almost happy.

"We might think about staying here a few weeks, a few months," I said to Annie one morning as we were getting dressed. "I like Jilly. I like the town. And it's such a relief not to be traveling every day."

She looked up, a shade of alarm on her face. "But—we have to get to Carrebos," she said.

I shrugged and fastened the top button of my dress. "I don't see why," I said. "No one appears to be hunting us here. The whole point of getting to Carrebos was to find someplace safe. I feel safe enough."

I couldn't read the expression on Annie's face. She seemed to be struggling to decide how to phrase something. "But . . . how will we know . . . if Lara and Aleatha escaped?" she said a little breathlessly. "They were to meet us in Carrebos. Won't they be worried if we don't show up?"

"I think they, like us, will hole up in any shelter they happen to find," I replied. "They might never get so far."

"Oh, I think they would worry," she said, shaking her head. "I think this place is fine for now, but we need to be moving on in a week or two."

I didn't ask more questions out loud, but in my mind I asked plenty. Until this point, Annie had never shown the slightest interest in our travel plans or our destination. She had followed where I led, slept where I directed, and obediently set out again when I said we must. Why did she suddenly feel such determination to make it to Carrebos, a place that had seemed to take hold of her imagination the minute Lara mentioned it? What did she expect to find in that little coastal town?

I supposed we must go there if I was to find out.

This day, our sixth at Jilly's, went much as the other five had.

In the morning, I cooked and cleaned. In the evening, I served customers and counted money. Jett came in alone fairly late, when only three or four others were still in the tavern.

"Bring me a pitcher," he snarled at me. "And some meat."

Expressionless, I fetched the requested items and set them on the table. He caught my arm before I could turn away.

"You," he said. "What's your name?"

He'd asked me this three times in the past five days. "Sosie."

"What's my brother pay you?"

"That's not your concern."

He squeezed my arm uncomfortably in his dirty hand. "What do you do for him, hey? Give him extra service after hours?" He laughed.

I tried unsuccessfully to jerk my hand away. "Not to him, and not to you, if that's what you were asking."

His smile vanished abruptly. "You think you're too fine for the likes of us, do you? And you with no prospects of your own."

"You have no idea what kind of prospects I have," I replied.

"Oh, certainly, a great lord in his fine house is somewhere pining after you," he sneered. "I'll give you a kiss for him, seeing as he's nowhere near to kiss you for himself."

And he yanked me halfway over the table and tried to force his mouth on mine. I hauled myself back, grabbed at the beer pitcher with my free hand, and dumped its contents in his face. He choked, released me, and started coughing, wiping wildly at his clothes and face.

"Not interested in *your* kisses," I said in a taunting voice, and stalked on back toward the kitchen. I could hear the other patrons laughing, but Jilly gave me an unsmiling look from behind the bar as I passed by. The look I gave him in return was smoldering.

Two minutes later, Jilly followed me into the kitchen, where I was trying to blot the beer stains from my own clothing. "If you've come to tell me to be friendly to your brother, I'll give my notice right now," I told him.

He gave me a rueful smile. "No, I think you handle him about as well as anyone could. I just came to see if you were all right."

I gave him a sharp look. "And if I wasn't? If he had overpowered me out there in the bar? Would you have stopped him? Would you have helped me?"

Now his smile widened. "Tell me this, Sosie," he said. "When's the last time you ever really needed help? Never saw a girl so able to take care of herself."

For a moment, I felt utterly exhausted. Lost, abandoned, alone. I was so tired of taking care of myself. Of taking care of everybody. "Just because I can do it doesn't mean I always like it," I said shortly.

He came a step nearer. "Well, now, a man like me hesitates to try to get close to a girl like you," he said, and I couldn't tell if he was joking or if he was serious. "Seeing as how you've got some high-ranking lord dangling after you."

Joking. Well, surely joking about the lord. Possibly not joking about whether or not he'd like to get closer. There was a thought to take to bed with me and consider for a while. "Well, one day maybe I'll start looking a little nearer to hand," I said.

Jilly grinned. "Let me know when you do," he said, and turned around and left the kitchen.

I was actually smiling that night as I went up to bed.

In the morning, I was still smiling. Till I rolled over and saw a small, ragged pillow—Kinnon's favorite toy—floating over the bed. I glanced down at my nephew, snuggled between his mother and me. His eyes were wide open, his little hands waving in excitement as he watched the pillow dip and sway above him. I closed my eyes again briefly, opened them, snatched the pillow from the air, and handed it to Kinnon.

"No magic," I said in a cross whisper. "Do you want to get us run out of town—or worse? Behave."

Then I got up, dressed, and headed downstairs to start my day. Which was much the same as my other six days—until the early shift of diners came in just after sundown. We were busy enough that both Jilly and I were waiting tables, me on one side of the room and Jilly on the other side. I didn't see the man at the back booth when he gave his order to Jilly, I just heard his voice.

"I'll have the roasted pig, thanks," he said in Darryn Rappengrass's voice. "And a glass of ale."

Darryn Rappengrass! What was he doing here? Had he seen me? Would he want to see me? Surely he would like to know that we were safe, my sister and my nephew and I, but would he feel a twinge of responsibility and decide he had to look out for us again? We were not far from Rappengrass territory; in fact, we might still technically be on the lands owned by his mother, so perhaps it was not surprising that he was in this locality. Well, surprising to *me*—astonishing, unnerving, breathtaking—but a perfectly ordinary visit for him.

I could not bring myself to go speak to him. I could not force myself on him again. He had saved my life once; he owed me nothing else now, not even courtesy. I worked my side of the room silently, keeping my head averted and my eyes down, and slipped back into the kitchen without being noticed.

Darryn Rappengrass. I'd believed I'd never see him again.

And if I was careful enough tonight, that might still be true.

I was in the middle of fixing a platter for a table full of diners when there was a crash and a commotion out in the bar area. Someone screamed and half a dozen people started yelling, and I heard a loud thump as if a table had been overturned. All of this was followed by an ominous silence. I ran to the kitchen door and stood there listening, my heart pounding. I had already learned that violent strangers arriving unexpectedly usually meant bad news for mystics and their kin. Had Coralinda's soldiers tracked us down again? Where was Annie—safe upstairs? Did anyone here know who we really were?

But the first voice I heard belonged to no soldier. It was Jilly's brother Jett, and he sounded angry and dangerous.

"So! What's a fine lord like you doing in a backwater tavern?" he growled. "Come to look for trouble, hey? I'll give you plenty of that."

"I just stopped in for dinner." Darryn sounded at ease, pleasant, unafraid. "I can go if you'd rather."

"You're going nowhere till I've found out a few things."

"Jett." I heard Jilly's voice, cold and commanding. "Leave him alone."

Jett's voice came in quick response. "I'll leave him alone when he tells me what he's come for. And if I don't like his answer, well, I'll slit his throat."

No time to think. I took a deep breath and burst through the kitchen door into the taproom, sashaying down the middle of the room like a wanton. It took some courage to keep a triumphant smile on my face when I saw the scene before me: Darryn pulled out of the booth and into Jett's cruel embrace; Jett with a bared knife to the serramar's throat. Darryn looked pale but still unruffled. I could tell he was thinking hard, trying to decide what he should say to free himself from this predicament. His hand hovered near his belt, no doubt ready to snatch at a hidden dagger, but that wouldn't do him much good if Jett sliced deep enough and quick enough.

I came to a stop a few feet away and rested my hands on my hips. "So! You came looking for me after all, didn't you?" I crowed, tossing my hair back and sounding most pleased with myself. "You said you didn't care if I left, but you found you missed me, didn't you? Fine lord like you is too good for a girl like me, you said, but maybe that's not true, is it? Your pretty ladies and your fancy serramarra don't give you what I can, is that right? I knew you'd be here sooner or later. I knew you couldn't keep away."

A small crowd had formed to watch the fight, and now I heard some of the men start laughing. "*I'd* give up a fine lady for Sosie," one of our regular customers muttered, and there was another general laugh.

Darryn and Jett were both staring at me, comically dissimilar expressions on their faces. Jett looked wrathful and suspicious, Darryn astonished and blank.

"You're saying this fellow came here for *you*?" Jett demanded, but he had relaxed his grip on Darryn. He still had one arm around the serramar from behind, but the knife hand had dropped.

I flounced closer. "I told you I had a great lord who loved me," I said. "I knew it wouldn't be long before he found me."

"He came here looking for trouble," Jett said, but he sounded less sure.

I laughed. "Well, he certainly found it."

Everyone else laughed, too, and Jett suddenly released Darryn, shoving him from behind. "Faugh," he said, turning away. "Lords. When they aren't taxing your goods, they're stealing your women," he growled. "Somebody bring me something to drink."

The crowd dispersed, chuckling and joking, and one of Jett's friends handed him a pitcher. I could still feel the weight of a lot of people watching me, so I minced a few steps closer and batted my eyes at Darryn. "Well?" I said, loud enough for anyone who was interested to hear, even though I tried to make my voice sound sultry. "You've come all this way to see me and now you're not going to say anything?"

"Sosie," he said. He kept his gaze fixed on my face, but I had the sense he was as aware of our audience as I was, and playing to the others in the room. "I told you I'd find you. I told you it was no good running."

I gave him a smile, all insolence and promise. "Maybe I liked the running," I said. "Maybe I liked seeing how fast you'd follow."

"Well, neither of us is running now," he said.

From the corner of my eye, I could see Jett chugging a glass of beer and watching us balefully over the rim. He might rethink his decision to allow two lovers to reunite. I had to get Darryn out of the bar. I came a step closer and, with a little simper, took Darryn's hand. His fingers closed tight on mine.

"I've got a room upstairs," I said in a low voice. "Come with me and we can get a few things settled." And like the most brazen of women, I led the serramar through the roomful of snickering men, past the expressionless Jilly, and straight up the stairway to my room.

Annie looked up in surprise when we entered. She was sitting on the bench by the window, bent over a pile of sewing. Kinnon lay on a blanket on the floor, drowsing. "Sosie, what are you—oh, my goodness, is that ser Darryn?"

I closed the door behind us and locked it with a snap. "It is," I said, pushing Darryn in the general direction of the only other chair in the room. "Jett took exception to gentry in the bar, so I pretended he was my lover. I don't think anyone will follow us upstairs. Have a seat, ser, we'll have to spend a little time here or they won't believe our story."

But he stood in the center of the room and merely stared at me. "Give me a moment," he said. "I'm still absorbing the fact that you and your sister are here—and so providentially for me! Why aren't you at Aleatha's?"

I sat on the edge of the bed and began bouncing up and down. The springs made a rhythmic creak that I was pretty sure could be heard downstairs if anyone was listening, and now and then the headboard hit the wall with a tired *thump*. "We left Aleatha's a couple of weeks ago," I said grimly. "We were out one day and came back to find her beaten and bloody. Alive, though. We left her with a friend and came this way." I glanced at Annie. "Heading toward Carrebos now."

"Who attacked her?" Darryn asked, looking both angry and sad. Aleatha's cottage was in Rappengrass proper; he no doubt felt some responsibility for what occurred on his mother's land. "Coralinda Gisseltess's men?"

"Aleatha thought so," I said. "No place for mystics."

Darryn began to pace slowly through the room as if he could not stand still. I continued working the bed. "It worries me to think there is no place of safety for you," he said.

"Nor for any mystic," Annie said.

He gave her a brief grin. "I don't know too many besides you."

"We think we might be safe in Carrebos," I said. "Apparently that's where a number of mystics have made their home."

He continued as if I hadn't spoken. "I wonder if, after all, you should come with me to my mother's? The city around Rappen Manor is still secure, no matter who ravages the countryside."

"I don't think we belong at Rappen Manor," I said gently.

"Yes, but—"

"Anyway, what makes you think you can protect us?" I said with a little grin. "*I* was the one who had to save *you* a few minutes ago."

"And I can't tell you how grateful I am! Though I am sorry you have had to ruin your reputation to save my life."

I tried to toss my hair in a flirtatious way, though it was flying about my face from my exertions. "Oh, it doesn't ruin a girl's reputation for men like these to think a lord desires her," I said airily.

"Well, I know *that's* not true," he said. "And I am so sorry for it. And for this distasteful charade."

Annie spoke up. "How did you come to be here by yourself?" she asked. "Where are your men?"

"They're to meet me here in the morning. I must say, my captain was against the idea of me coming here alone, but I thought I would draw less attention that way." He shrugged. "I see I was wrong."

"But why come by yourself in the first place?" I asked.

Darryn laughed and stopped his pacing to look at me. "For exactly the reasons that ruffian suspected," he said. "There's been talk of brigands on the road, and a couple of people have suggested I might find them in this little town. I thought to sit quietly in the tavern and hear men gossip and brag. I would identify the culprits myself, and my men would apprehend them when they arrived." He shook his head. "Like many plans, more flawed in execution than design."

"Well, I wouldn't be surprised to learn Jett is an outlaw," I said. "But I don't think you'll be arresting him any time soon. He often sleeps here, but is gone by morning."

"If I leave now, I could be with my men in a few hours."

Annie and I exchanged glances as I continued my up-and-down motion. "I don't know that you should plan on leaving while Jett's still here," I said quietly. "My guess is he'll be watching for you to go. If he follows you out of here at night, well, nobody will ever find your body."

Darryn looked frustrated. "So, what? I stay here till dawn while you keep that bed squealing? Aren't you getting tired by now?"

Annie stood up and came over. "I'll take a turn," she said, and landed on the bed with one hard drop. I laughed and sprang to my feet. It took me a moment to catch my balance. Annie continued bouncing.

"I'm impressed at my stamina," Darryn said dryly.

Annie and I laughed, but she at least was thinking about something else. "Do you remember when we were little girls?" she asked me. "And sometimes at night we would hear the creaking from our parents' bedroom? We thought they were jumping up and down on the mattress."

"And we were so mad because *we* were never allowed to do that," I said. "It seemed so unfair."

We both laughed again. I reflected that it was the first time in months that either of us had had a happy thought about our parents, particularly our father.

"Once I got older, I started to believe she never loved him," Annie said, sighing now. "I thought she only stayed because she was afraid of him. But when we were little, oh, I thought she just adored him. He would come home sometimes and pick her up off the floor and kiss her so hard she couldn't breathe. Do you remember that?"

"I remember," I said.

"But maybe she didn't like it," Annie continued, a little sadly. "Maybe she was afraid he would hold her so tight he would break her."

"She was the one who didn't hold tight enough," I said. "She didn't hold on to us."

Annie's eyes were on Kinnon, who must appear from her vantage point to be bobbing up and down. "I will," she said quietly. "I'll never let go of my child."

There was silence a moment, all of us thinking about different things. "So what happens now?" Darryn asked. "If I can't leave this room—"

"I've got to go downstairs and finish my shift," I said. "Annie will fetch both of you dinner when it's slower. But *you* shouldn't go out of the room. Not till morning. You'll have to sleep on the floor, but I just don't think you can risk leaving."

"I hate to be so much trouble," he protested.

I smiled at him. "Our turn to help you," I said. "We're both happy to do it."

Eventually, Annie judged Darryn had demonstrated his ardor long enough, and she stopped bouncing and came to her feet. "Oh, I feel a little dizzy," she said with a laugh. "Here, Sosie, let me take a look at you. You look entirely too calm for someone who's just bedded an impatient lover."

So I let her muss my hair while I bit my lips to make them appear red from kissing. "You might undo your top button," she suggested, so I did, and then I dashed water on my face so that I would look as if I had just rinsed away a film of sweat. "You'll do," Annie decided finally. "I'll come down in an hour or two to get our meals."

Darryn said nothing, just stood by the window and watched me. His face was troubled and I knew he didn't like the position I had put myself into—and the fact that I had done it for him. I have to say, I was a bit apprehensive myself about the reception I would get when I returned to the barroom, but I just gave them both a cheery smile and headed back downstairs.

"Well, there's the lord's strumpet," Jett greeted me the minute I set foot in the room. There was a chorus of jeers and catcalls, but the overall tenor was friendly. I supposed men thought that now I'd shown myself to be willing, they might have a chance at winning me for themselves.

Jilly gave me one quick, serious look as he brought in a tray of food from the kitchen. "You're just full of surprises, aren't you?" he said.

I shrugged and brushed past him to see what portion of the meal might have been ruined while I was off pretending to make love. "I guess everybody is," I replied.

The teasing never got worse than that all evening, for which I was grateful, though I did have to endure a few more pinches on my bottom and even more suggestive remarks than usual. I just laughed and acted as if I didn't care.

To tell the truth, I didn't. *Darryn Rappengrass*. Here, in this building, in my very room. I had been so sure he would never wander through my life again. And I had had the chance to save his life—or at the very least rescue him from a brutal beating. I would have dared any amount of ridicule for a chance to give Darryn Rappengrass such a gift. I would have endured the beating itself, if it meant saving him.

We were busy enough that the evening flew by, despite the fact that I was not much interested in the work. It was not far from midnight when Jilly jerked his head to motion me over.

"I'll clean up here," he said. "You go on upstairs. Man risked death to court you, you might as well give him a little of your attention."

"That's kind of you," I said.

"Will you be leaving with him when he goes?"

It hadn't occurred to me anyone would think that was an option. I schooled my face into a pout. "He's got a fancy lady who thinks he's going to marry her," I said, very put out. "He won't be taking me with him anytime soon."

Jilly grunted. "You could do better than a man who keeps you on the side," he said.

"Some days I think so," I agreed, heading toward the stairs. "But it's hard to convince my heart."

The room was dark when I stepped inside, and all the occupants appeared to be sleeping. I saw Darryn's shape on the floor, Annie's and Kinnon's bodies making appropriately sized bumps under the covers of the bed. I undressed quickly and lay down, expecting to be so keyed up that I couldn't sleep. But, in fact, my eyes closed immediately and I was dreaming in minutes.

Something woke me an hour or two later and I was instantly alert, heart pounding. Was Jett creeping up the stairs, hoping to catch Darryn undefended in the middle of the night? I sat up, wondering what in the room might serve as a weapon.

Then I noticed a shape sitting on the bench in front of the window. Darryn. He turned to look at me as I rustled in the dark. "I'm sorry, did I disturb you?" he asked in a low whisper. "I just got up to look outside and try to guess what time it is."

I glanced at Annie and Kinnon, peacefully sleeping. I didn't want to wake either of them. I slid from the bed, taking the top coverlet with me, and crossed the room to perch beside him in the window seat.

"A couple of hours after midnight," I said quietly. "Jett's either gone by now, or sleeping off a drunk. You can safely leave at first light."

"I wish you and Annie would come with me."

"And where are you going, that you could guarantee our safety?"

He sighed and made a face. "Such strange times we're living in now," he said, and even his whisper sounded weary. He leaned his head back against the wall. "A few years ago, I thought I understood the world. Whom to trust, where I belonged, what mattered to me. Now Coralinda Gisseltess is hunting mystics, the king sits insecurely on his throne, my mother is making desperate alliances, and I spend all my time worrying about a girl I hardly know. I no longer understand the world. Maybe who I am and who I'm supposed to be with have completely changed."

"A few months ago I thought I understood my life, too," I said. Wondering. Was I the girl he spent his time thinking about? "And then Kinnon was born and I had to choose. My sister or everything else I knew. I chose my sister. And I have understood nothing that's happened to me since."

For a moment he watched me in silence, though I was not sure how much of my face he could see by the light of the half moon. "Are you sorry?" he asked. "That you picked Annie over everything else?"

"No," I said. "But I am so tired."

"I spent the afternoon talking with her," he said. "But I cannot get much of a sense of her. She is not easy to read."

Now I was the one to stay silent for a little bit. "No," I said at last. "She has changed, too. I don't think I understand this new Annie yet."

"What was she like before?"

"Oh, the sweetest girl. Everyone's favorite. The pretty one, the shy one, the one who would stay up late with you if you were sick and work through the night to make you a present. You could not imagine anyone ever turning against her, ever throwing her out of the house."

"And you? What were you like?"

It was a moment before I could remember. It seemed so long ago. "I was the one who behaved, who did the extra chores, who never caused a fuss, so that no one would bother to watch me too closely," I said at last. "I was the one who always did what I wanted, but I was careful about it. I did what everyone else wanted, too."

"It doesn't sound like you would have been thrown out of the house, either."

I looked at his face, a black cameo outlined by white moonlight. "I wasn't thrown out," I said. "I did what I wanted to do."

"You're the strong one, of the two of you, that's clear to see," he said. "But you're younger, aren't you?"

"By a year. The youngest of four."

"So am I!" he exclaimed. "Though the youngest of five."

"And what are *you* like when you're with your family?"

"Oh, I am the one they all love. I am the one who can make them happy just by appearing at the door. I know that such treatment can sometimes make a man vain and demanding, and I know that at times I seem too sure of myself, too certain of a welcome. I have acquired the kind of ease and polish a man sometimes gets when he has grown used to being loved. But I have tried to be a deeper man than that. I have tried to earn the affection I receive, at least from my family. I have tried to be a good man, an excellent brother, a kind uncle. I have tried to live up to their faith in me."

"And have you succeeded?"

A quiet laugh. "Some days I think so. I suppose you would have to ask them."

"And your parents? What are they like?"

"My father died when I was about five. People who knew him say I am like him. My mother married him when she was already named heir to Rappengrass, and the way the story is told, she chose him because he was smiling and pleasant and would not get in her way. My mother is a very headstrong person, you understand—forceful. Not many people ever get the better of my mother, and certainly no one expected my father to be able to stand up to her. But then a strange thing happened, or so everyone says. She fell in love with him. His opinion mattered to her. She sought his advice and his approval. By all accounts they were deeply happy for more than twenty years. If you were to meet her today, you would find the story hard to credit. But there is still a softness to her when she speaks of him, and she loves all her children very much, in part, I think, because he gave them to her."

"That's a nice story," I said.

"I think so, too," he answered.

Before I could speak again, Annie stirred on the bed and sat up. "Sosie?" she murmured. "Is something wrong?"

"I'm sorry, did we wake you up?" I said, standing and pulling the blanket around me more tightly. "We were just talking."

"Oh. No, I just heard voices and I—go on talking. I'll fall right back to sleep."

But I was yawning, and Darryn's face looked exhausted by moonlight. "No, I think we all better get back to sleep while we can," I said. "You, ser, should be up and out of here early in the morning."

"I'll try to be quiet as I go," he said.

Annie had put her head back on the pillow. "Oh, no," she said drowsily. "Don't even think of leaving without saying good-bye."

As it turned out, all four of us were awake in the morning, as Kinnon roused us with a petulant wail. Annie nursed him as Darryn and I got dressed, turning our backs on each other to offer what pri-

vacy we could in these cramped quarters. I reached the door just as
Darryn did.

"You don't have to come downstairs with me," he said.

"I think I'd better," I said. "In case anyone's watching."

In fact, for the first time since I'd known him, Jett had spent the
night at Jilly's and was stumbling through the taproom downstairs,
growling about wanting breakfast. Jilly, who never seemed to sleep,
was also awake and sweeping out some of the mess from the night
before. They both paused to watch me as I led Darryn down the stairs
and out the front door. I took his hand in mine as we stepped into the
brisk sunshine. Cool out, but with a promise of warmth before noon.

"Where's your horse?" I asked. It hadn't occurred to me to wonder
before.

"I left it with my men and came the last half mile on foot."

"Then I suppose you—"

But I didn't have a chance to finish speaking. There was a drum of
hoofbeats not far away, and within seconds, a phalanx of soldiers
swept into view. They were wearing the maroon sash of Rappengrass,
and the man in the lead looked relieved when he saw my companion.

"Ser!" he called, reining up beside us. The others came to an
orderly halt behind him, though a soldier from the back continued
moving up the line, leading an extra horse. "All is well?"

"All is well," Darryn confirmed. "You see I survived a night without your protection."

"But barely," I said under my breath. I had made to drop his hand
when his soldiers rode up, but he had unexpectedly tightened his grip
on my fingers.

"And did you discover the men you were looking for here?" his
captain asked.

Darryn shook his head. "Not to be sure of. There's no one to
arrest."

"Then we'd best be on our way, ser."

"I suppose so." Darryn smiled down at me; he pulled me closer by
the hand he still gripped in his. "Do you think anyone is watching us

from the tavern windows?" he asked. "Do you think they wonder how a lord says good-bye to his woman?"

I felt a little breathless. "I hardly think so," I replied, trying to keep my voice steady. "They don't seem like very curious men."

Darryn laughed out loud, and then he bent down and kissed me. He was rougher with the kiss than I would have expected, his free hand coming up to press against the back of my head, the stubble of his beard scrubbing hard against my skin. I kissed him shamelessly in sunlight, in full view of his men, the tavern-master, the tavern-master's outlaw brother, and my sister, if she happened to be looking out, and wished the moment might stretch on forever. It didn't, of course. After a moment, Darryn released me and stepped back, finally dropping my hand. He was smiling, but I thought his eyes looked shadowed.

"Good-bye, Sosinetta," he said. No one else spoke or, indeed, showed much expression. Darryn took the reins from his soldier and swung himself into the saddle. From there he looked down at me, his expression unchanged. "I always have the most interesting experiences when I'm with you."

I forced myself to smile, to appear nonchalant, as if the kiss hadn't broken my heart. "I'm glad I could share some of my adventures with you. Travel safely."

"You as well," he said. And before he could add anything else, if he was planning to, his captain shouted the order to move out, and the whole troop was in motion. Darryn waved and spurred his horse forward. In minutes he had disappeared.

Five

A WEEK LATER, ANNIE AND I WERE ON our way to Carrebos.

I would have stayed at Jilly's longer, but Annie, who had been so docile up to this point, was restless, uneasy, and fretful. Kinnon caught the mood from her and was hard to comfort, hard to control. The heavy pewter water pitcher was knocked over so many times in the night that we finally just gave up and placed it on the floor, empty, before we went to bed.

My own lot was decidedly less comfortable after Darryn left, as well. More suggestive comments from the customers, more speculative interest from Jilly. I never actually felt at risk, but I did feel watched all the time, as if the bar's regular customers were waiting to see what I might do next: which man I might bed, which patron I might turn on with a furious tirade. I had the sense that they had placed wagers on my behavior and thought I was a huge entertainment.

I wasn't entirely sad to leave.

Still, after two weeks of relatively easy living, it was hard to go back on the road, camping out at night, hoarding food, watching for soldiers. Mercifully, the weather was good—never entirely warm, but mostly dry and usually sunny. We walked west and slightly north, toward the sea. Annie made up a song that she sang to Kinnon as we strode along. "Bos, Bos, Carrebos . . . the magical home for those who are lost . . ." I wondered if she could truly think we were safe even there.

We reached Carrebos after five days of walking. It was an appealing town, full of narrow cobblestoned streets that seemed to be perpetually wet with sea spray, a mismatched collection of buildings whose weathered fronts gave them a friendly air, and more people than the place could seem to comfortably hold. But something about the overcrowding gave the town a happy atmosphere, as if it was fair day every day. Caravans came and went from morning till night, bringing in farmers and peddlers and anyone with necessities to sell. Families camped all around the fringes of town, their wagons and campfires visible from almost any vantage point in the city. Tall-masted ships bobbed and ducked along the narrow harbor, and the salt of the ocean flavored every breath you inhaled, every bite of food you ate.

We camped our first night a stone's throw from a family of eight whose rambunctious children were soon squatted around our own fire, pelting us with questions. I wondered if anyone in this group was a mystic. Why else come to Carrebos? But I didn't inquire. When you ask a question of someone, even a child, that person then has the right to pose a question in response. And I wasn't sure that, even now, we could afford to be truthful.

The second day, I went into town and looked for work and a place to stay. There were more jobs than lodgings available, so I took my time, refusing two offers when my prospective employer couldn't promise us accommodations. But finally I found a situation that seemed to suit us all. Another tavern, of course—when this trip was done, I'd be able to run my own taproom, I thought—owned by a young couple with one-year-old twin boys. Annie would watch the children while I cooked and waited tables. There was a storeroom connected to the kitchen where Annie and Kinnon and I would live, once the owners moved most of the goods stacked inside to the lean-to out back. The room still smelled of herbs and spices and onions and dried meat, but that wasn't going to bother anyone in my little family. A narrow mattress for Annie and Kinnon, a pallet on the floor for me. No complaints there, either. It was a job, a roof, a place to settle. All we needed.

We moved in, and life assumed a certain reassuring rhythm. Annie and Colette, the mother of the twins, quickly became friends as they shared child-rearing tasks and traded advice. Eddie, a thin and somewhat anxious man, veered between being grateful for my help and vexed when things didn't go perfectly, which made him a not entirely easy man to work for. But I liked him, or at least liked him in his calmer moments, and we soon understood each other's style. The storeroom-turned-bedroom was crowded but comfortable, and Kinnon didn't use his power to knock over too many barrels of seed or baskets of nuts. We were content.

Naturally, from our first day in Carrebos, Annie and I began looking around for signs of magic. Colette and Eddie didn't at first seem rife with it, and Annie told me within two days that she thought the twins were entirely ordinary. I wasn't even sure how magic manifested itself in most people. Surely they did not all, like Senneth, set people on fire? Or, like Kinnon, push objects off shelves and dangle them in the air? Surely most mystics could hide their power, if they wanted to, control it, at least most of the time. So how did anyone know?

We saw the first evidence of magic after we'd been in Carrebos a week. Colette and Eddie and I were in the middle of serving lunch when bells began clamoring up the street. Within seconds, bells were ringing all over the city, urgent and melodic.

"Fire," Eddie said. Yanking off his apron, he snatched up a bucket and ran out the door. Most of the patrons in the bar laid down their forks and followed him. Curious, I headed out behind the others. As soon as I stepped outside, I could see the flames dancing through the wooden roof of a building not a quarter mile from us—and I could see the bucket brigade that already stretched from the wharf to our street. Townspeople mobilized quickly to put out a neighbor's blaze, since one rogue fire could bring down a whole city in a matter of hours. As I watched, the first buckets of saltwater were thrown on the fire, causing it to hiss and sizzle.

Moments later, a young boy—he looked to be about twelve—darted through the crowd and ran into the burning building. I heard one woman scream and a number of people murmur, and two more buckets of water were splashed onto the blaze. But then suddenly all the flames went out. They sighed and settled like a dog dropping at his master's feet after a hard run. The men put down their buckets; the watchers held their breath. A minute later, the boy strolled out, unharmed and nonchalant. I was too far away to hear what he said, but the people closest to him laughed, and someone came up and slapped him on the shoulder. A handful of onlookers surged forward to see what damage had been done by fire and water. Everyone else began to slowly disperse, clumps of people walking and talking together, a few nodding, a few pointing.

No one seemed ready to stone the boy for a display of magic. Which was clearly what it had been. He obviously had the power to control fire, to bend it to his will, and he had used that power to save the town.

Why would people like Coralinda Gisseltess be afraid of a boy like that?

I returned to the tavern, as did everyone who had deserted it, and we continued serving our midday meal as if nothing particularly exciting had happened. But that afternoon, when there was a quiet spell and I was alone in the taproom with Eddie, I finally got the nerve to ask him.

"That boy," I said, as I dried glasses and handed them to Eddie to put away behind the bar. "The one who ran into the burning building. He's a mystic, isn't he?"

Eddie nodded and took another glass from my hand. It wasn't

quite dry enough to suit him, so he wiped it with his own towel before putting it away. "Good thing, too," he said. "Wind's strong enough today to send a spark right to my roof and burn this place down."

"Is it true?" I asked. "That people in Carrebos don't mind mystics?"

He shrugged. "Most of us don't. Those who do have pretty much moved out, as more mystics started arriving. It's an odd place, special. Why would the people of one town decide that they would welcome magic? Why would one particular city become a haven? But the more mystics arrive, the safer the town becomes. Now I think if someone in the town decided to start persecuting mystics, *he's* the one who would be stoned or at least run out. There are enough of us to protect our own."

I thought this over a moment. "You're a mystic?" I asked cautiously.

He shook his head. "Not me. Colette. She's a reader."

Aleatha had been a reader, so I could guess at Colette's abilities. "She can tell how people are feeling," I said. "She knows if they're good people or bad ones."

Eddie nodded. "She can't hear thoughts but she can pick up emotions. She knows your little one is a mystic."

"Yes, but I don't know what to call him," I said. "He can fling things in the air just by wanting to. Knock things over."

Eddie looked interested. "Now that could be useful if you could harness it. Your sister a mystic, too?"

I shook my head. "We're guessing the baby's father was. Annie says he traveled with a caravan of peddlers but that he could do amazing tricks. Juggle plates and balls. Keep them in the air."

Eddie laughed. "Wouldn't you like to see someone like that do magic tricks? There's an acrobat troupe came to town last week. I think they've got a couple jugglers with them. Wouldn't it be funny if they were mystics?"

And just like that, I knew.

Annie had wanted to come to Carrebos because Kinnon's father was here. He must have told her about the place, mentioned how it was a refuge for people like him. She had forgotten it existed, or forgotten its name—she had plenty of other things to occupy her mind—until Lara mentioned it. But once she remembered, she had had a good reason for coming to Carrebos. She wanted to see her lover again. To melt in his arms or scold him like a harridan, I had no idea. But that juggler boy was the reason we were here.

"Acrobats and jugglers," I said, keeping my voice light as I dried the last of the glasses. "I bet Annie would enjoy a chance to go see them perform."

"Why not go tonight?" Eddie said. "You can have the early shift off."

AND SO THAT NIGHT, ANNIE AND KINNON AND I went to see the acrobats. They had set up a big tent to the north of the city, musty and smelling somewhat of stale bodies. There was one riser that ran all around the rim of the tent, and some patrons stood on that to see over the heads of all the other people who were standing on the ground itself. Wires were hung from the outer tent poles to the main one in the center, and from these, lanterns hung and swayed, lending a somewhat unsteady light to the whole proceedings. Maybe two hundred people were crammed inside.

Ten acrobats performed tricks. They jumped and cartwheeled and balanced and flipped in such amazing combinations that I knew my mouth hung open. Seven of them were boys or men. The three girls were young enough to not be shamed by the outfits they wore: close-fitting leggings and flowing shirts for the girls, leggings and nothing else for the men. They all had powerful muscles in their legs and a look of rapture on their faces.

It was easy to pick out the two who must be mystics, for they did impossible tricks. They jumped in the air and stayed there, almost floating, turning this way and that, doing handstands on nothing, drawing themselves into balls and bouncing around the perimeter of the tent. All this before unfolding, descending, and coming gently to their feet. One of the mystics was a girl, probably eight or nine, with lively blue eyes and flying black hair. The other was a young man, perhaps twenty or twenty-one, with long pale hair, dreamy dark eyes, and hands that seemed shaped to tame the wind. Annie could not keep her eyes off him, even when he was not performing. She clutched Kinnon to her chest so hard he squirmed, but she paid no attention. She was watching the beautiful man make his beautiful patterns in the air.

When the performance was done and people began streaming out of the tent, I waited for her to make some excuse. I thought she might say, "Oh, I enjoyed that so much! Let's go tell the acrobats how wonderful they were." But she said nothing, merely turned to follow the rest of the crowd out into the cool night.

We were halfway back to the tavern when I could keep quiet no longer. "Well?" I demanded. "Why don't you go talk to him, then? We've come all the way to Carrebos just so you can see him and show him your child. Why hang back now?"

She looked at me, and her face seemed shocked by starlight. "Why do—what do you mean?" she stammered.

I waved my hand impatiently toward the tent. "That young man! He's your juggler, isn't he? Kinnon's father. That's why you wanted to come to Carrebos."

She was silent for a few more steps. "I wanted to come to Carrebos because I thought Kinnon would be safe here," she said at last. "But I did know—I did think—Ned might be here. I didn't mean—I never thought—it's not like I want to talk to him, I have nothing to say to him. But I just—at least now he's—I had wondered if he was still alive. And now I see he is. And that's all I need to know."

"Nothing to say to him?" I repeated in a rude voice. "How about, 'Oh, by the way, when you left me I was carrying your child. And here he is, do you think he looks like you?'"

"I couldn't say that to him!"

"Well, I could," I said. "I think he needs to know."

But Annie was shaking her head and walking even faster. "No. I have made my choices, and Ned does not figure into them. And you will only hurt me if you do not respect my wishes."

Well, what was there to say to that? I sighed and followed her home. She took Kinnon off to bed, while I tied on an apron and went to work. I would never understand my sister. I would never understand anyone in the entire world.

Although later it occurred to me that my own behavior might not have been so different. If Darryn Rappengrass were doing magic tricks in a tent outside the Carrebos city limits, I would go watch him perform. And I would stand in the back row, and keep my face averted so he would not see me, and I would be happy just to know he was alive.

But secretly I would wish he would notice me.

And I would go back every night.

In fact, Annie *did* return to the acrobats' tent the next evening and the next. Once she went alone, except for Kinnon; once Colette went with her, bringing the twins. The third night she stayed home. The fourth night she readied herself to attend again. I'd already asked Eddie if I could accompany her. He'd looked worried, calculated the loss in revenue if I was not there to wait on tables, sighed, and nodded.

"Have you talked to him yet?" I asked as we stepped inside the tent.

"No," she said. "Stop asking me that."

Inside, I looked around. Tonight there were chairs set up a few feet in front of the risers, so now there would be three ranks of viewers. Business must have been good for the acrobats. I insisted we take some of the chairs, so the baby could sit on Annie's lap; otherwise, I knew, he grew very heavy in her arms before the night was over. She finally agreed, but then put a shawl over her head to hide her face. Sometimes she could be the most contrary girl.

The show was even better this night. Not only did we see acrobatics, but Ned and his fellow mystic performed a juggling routine that was truly amazing. They kept at least thirty objects in the air all at once, tossing them to each other across the width of the tent, whirling them in patterns through the air. Meanwhile, the boy who had put out the blaze the other day had joined the troupe. He worked in tandem with Ned to set objects on fire just as the juggler threw them into the air, cooling them to cinder as they fell back into Ned's hands.

We were all on our feet applauding this neat trick when about twenty men came streaming in through the two main doors of the tent. I don't know what everyone else thought, but at first I believed they were just a new part of the show, more acrobats from a rival troupe come to show off their skill. They were dressed all in black and silver, and moved with a deadly grace. Before I realized what was happening, they had advanced into the center of the tent and flung glittering nets over all of the performers.

Glittering. With moonstones.

Black-and-silver riders.

Coralinda Gisseltess's men. Here to hunt down mystics.

Everyone seemed to realize the truth about the same time I did, and there was such a confusion of shouting and stamping! Half the crowd in the stands tried to flee, and the very ground was rocked with the sound of their panicked footsteps. Others pushed forward, yelling invective. Most were afraid to get too close to the Lestra's riders, who had drawn their swords and now stood in the middle of the tent, prepared to battle all comers. I saw Ned on his knees writhing inside his sparkling cage, probably from the pain; I saw the fire-taming boy and the acrobat girl lying on the ground, twisting inside their own nets. I could not think what to do. I was frozen in horror and despair.

Beside me, Annie dropped back into her seat, and for a moment I thought she'd fainted. But no—with quick, decisive movements, she pushed back the collar of her shirt, pulled out the cord that held her amulet, took Kinnon's hand in hers, and wrapped his fingers around the silken bag.

Instantly, the whole world came apart.

The lanterns swung wildly from their thin wires—the perimeter tent poles pulled themselves from the ground and danced on the grass. The canvas itself folded back from its central stays and then *whumped* back down with a great gush of wind. I heard Kinnon shrieking with laughter just as two of the lanterns fell. A thin ribbon of fire shot out from the broken glass of one and began rolling down a line of dead grass. The main tent pole swayed and looked as if it would crash any minute.

The soldiers themselves started yelling, looking about them in fear and superstition. Two of them threw their swords down—or, no, I realized, Kinnon's magic ripped the swords from their hands. Was Annie directing his movements or was his power just grabbing at anything that might come loose? Two more soldiers lost their weapons. The fire on the ground crept steadily across the grass, gaining brightness, gaining height.

Now there was even more of a melee around us: bodies shoving, people shouting, the risers thumping against the ground as they lifted and dropped. "We have to get out of here!" I shouted in Annie's ear. "This place is going to go up in flames!"

"We can't!" she cried. "Ned—and the others—"

But I could see more clearly than she could what was happening in the madness at the center of the tent. Some of the townspeople had managed to fight free of the crowd, and all the acrobats who weren't seared by moonstones had escaped their restraints. They knew magic when it was being worked on their behalf, and they were not, like the soldiers, paralyzed by the whipping canvas, the diving lamps, the dancing poles. They had formed quick, murderous groups, each assigning itself to one of the Lestra's men. Even now they were wrestling the soldiers to the ground, taking away their weapons, turning the swords upon the attackers. I saw blood spilling onto the grass now sparkling with fire.

I grabbed Annie's arm. "Out!" I shouted again. "Come with me—come *now!*"

I pulled her to her feet, dragged her toward what might have been a door in the tent and might have been a hole pulled open by Kinnon's magic. She resisted for the first few steps, but then I felt her sort of sigh and acquiesce, and I had to look back to see what she had witnessed. Ah! One of the acrobats had released the mystics from their moonstone nets. I saw the fire-taming boy spread his fingers and then all of the flames lay meekly down.

I jerked Annie out of the tent, into the frenzied darkness. People were milling around outside the tent, calling out questions, huddled together, making plans of assault. I saw the shape of more than one knife lifted in the darkness.

"I hope you've taken that charm out of Kinnon's hand by now," I said crossly, towing Annie behind me. "We don't want him bringing down every shutter and sign in town."

"I have," she said absently. "It's in my pocket." Her voice was muffled; her head was twisted to watch the scene behind us. "He got free, didn't he? You saw him get loose from the bindings?"

"I saw. And that boy put the fire out. I don't think the tent will burn. That's what I was worried about."

"I didn't know what else to do," Annie said in a worried voice. "I thought they were going to kill him. I thought those soldiers would kill all the mystics. I didn't know what to do. I gave Kinnon Senneth's stone. I didn't think—I didn't know what to expect."

All of a sudden, I laughed. *What* an interesting life we had ahead of us as Kinnon learned how to control and direct his considerable power! We could only pray he was a good boy who would not turn his magic to malicious purposes. Pray and do what we could to teach him in the ways of virtue and kindness.

"I think you need his father's assistance," I said as we pulled within sight of the tavern. Colette and Eddie were standing on the doorstep, staring out toward the noise and excitement of the acrobats' tent. The street was full of people dashing to and from the disaster, spreading the tale, going to help. "You need to talk to Ned. Tomorrow. There is no way you can raise a mystic baby by yourself."

"Maybe," she said. "We'll see."

Colette was running out into the street to greet us. "Sosie! Annie! What happened? Were you there?"

"We were there," I said. "Let us come in and sit down, and then we'll tell you the whole story."

Six

THE FOLLOWING DAY, THERE WAS NO conversation except that revolving around the events of the night before. Much had happened once Annie and I left the scene. Half of the soldiers had been killed, while the others had escaped. A dozen townspeople had been injured—trampled, burned, or wounded in combat—but all of them survived. Those who had been badly hurt were being cared for, we were told. A healer had arrived in town that very afternoon, most providentially, and was making her way from sickbed to sickbed, chasing away pain.

Next we learned there was to be a series of town meetings as the citizens of Carrebos determined how to prevent such a catastrophe from occurring again. Should they post sentinels? Institute a civil guard? Might there be some way they could use the mystics among them to give early warning when hostile strangers gathered nearby? I would have thought the answer to that was a decided *yes* and should have been thought of before.

Three visitors came to the tavern that day, looking for Annie and me.

The first one came drifting in through the kitchen door while I stood at the stove, cooking lunch. I suddenly realized the room smelled like flowers; I felt warm air brush across my skin. I dropped my ladle and spun around.

"Lara!" I exclaimed, crossing the room to hug her. Her round face softened to a quick smile and then she resumed her usual impassive expression. "How long have you been in Carrebos? Is Aleatha with you? How is she?"

"She's recovered. Not here. I left her with friends," Lara said.

I remembered that a healer had been busy last night, tending those hurt in the disaster. "Have you been here since yesterday?" I asked. "Did you see the tent? And the fire? Did you heal the people who were wounded?"

She nodded—a yes to all those questions. I saw a bit of bark in her long brown hair and reached up to pull it out. "And are you staying in Carrebos?" I asked.

She shook her head. "Just passing through. Checking on you."

I smiled and waved my hand at the kitchen laid out around me. "We're settled here. We're doing well. I think we might finally have found a place we can stay for a long time. But we have been worried about you and Aleatha. It is such a relief to see you! Can I give you some lunch? It's almost ready."

She shook her head again. "I have more to do," she said. "Kiss Annie for me."

And with that, she turned on her heel and ducked out the back door. I couldn't help myself: I crossed the room and stepped outside, just to watch her go. I swear, as she passed through the kitchen garden, the stalks straightened and shot up a few inches; the stubbly grass on the side of the road grew rich and green. The sun beat down on my head with some force, reminding me that summer was not that far away. And, oh, the sweet flavors in the sudden, faint breeze! Rose and hyacinth and lilac. I lifted my head and inhaled deeply.

Coralinda had sent her winter-colored soldiers here the night before, and spring had followed after.

THE SECOND VISITOR ALSO CAME TO THE BACK DOOR. I had cleaned up the lunch dishes and was now thinking about dinner. Annie was in the kitchen with Kinnon and the twins, all four of them underfoot. I was about to send them into the garden to play when I heard a decisive knock. The delivery from the butcher, I hoped.

"Come in!" I called.

In walked Ned the juggler. Close up, his dark eyes were even dreamier, his serious face sensuous under the pale blond hair. I could see some of Kinnon in the shape of his chin. "I'm looking for someone," he said, and his voice was both polite and determined. "I was told I might find her here."

"Them," I said, and pointed to where Annie sat on the floor. Kinnon was in her lap and Colette's twins were climbing on her outstretched legs. Her dark hair was down and unstyled, and she looked about fourteen. "You can find *them* right here. Annie and your son."

Ned stared, then dropped to his knees right there in the kitchen. I scooped up the twins and went into the taproom, looking for Colette. "Annie's got a visitor," I said, depositing the boys in one of the back bar booths, where Colette sat counting money.

She looked pleased. "That acrobat? I know she still cares for him. I wonder what kind of man he is."

"Handsome enough, that's for certain," I said.

"Still, he left her to raise a baby on her own—a mystic child at that."

I took a pile of coins and started dividing them into stacks. "Not so sure he knew there was a baby on the way," I said. "I'm wondering if he figured it out last night when objects started flying around the tent. 'I thought only *I* had that kind of power,' he might have been thinking. 'Could it be I fathered a child sometime? But I have loved no one but Annie for this past year.' I don't know. Maybe he just saw her face in the crowd last night and decided to come looking for her today."

"That speaks well of him," Colette decided. "He could have run the other way."

When I returned to the kitchen twenty minutes later, Annie, Kinnon, and the juggler all were gone. I smiled, then I sighed. Then I went back to work.

The third visitor came to the front door, looking for me.

Eddie and I were giving all the tables a last wipe-down before the dinner patrons arrived and checking to make sure all the silver was clean. A man and his wife were already sitting at the back table, arguing about something, and I was wondering if a second glass of ale would make them more agreeable to each other or less so. The door opened, and a solitary man stepped in. I automatically looked up to assess him, and then I dropped my cleaning cloth to the floor.

Darryn Rappengrass.

He saw me and, smiling, came strolling over. "I knew I would find you hard at work somewhere," he said. "Taking in laundry or waiting tables or hiring out as a maid. Never saw a girl who kept herself so busy all the time."

I looked at him, looked at Eddie, looked back at the new arrival. I could tell that color had scrawled embarrassment and excitement across my cheeks. "Ser Darryn," I said and would have bobbed a curtsey except I was pretty sure any sudden movement would have sent me toppling to the floor. "Would you like something to drink? Something to eat? Let me find you a table."

"I'd like to talk to you," he said. "Can you come outside for a bit?"

I looked at Eddie again. His thin, nervous face was drawn into an expression that might have been a scowl and might have been an attempt to disguise intense curiosity. "Just a few minutes," I pleaded. Eddie nodded. I retrieved my cloth from the floor, tossed it to the counter, and followed Darryn outside. There was a wooden bench set invitingly right in front of the tavern. We sat. I tried not to think that anyone standing just inside the door would be able to overhear our conversation.

"So! How have you found life in Carrebos?" Darryn asked in a genial voice. "You look relaxed and rested, so I'm assuming the life agrees with you."

"I'm hopeful," I said. "We feel both safe and comfortable here. Eddie and Colette—the people who run the tavern—have been good to us. There are enough mystics here that I think they can all take care of each other. And today Kinnon's father came looking for Annie."

"That *is* good news," Darryn exclaimed. "I didn't know he was here."

I laughed. "Neither did I, but apparently Annie did. She's off with him right now, and who knows how that conversation is going? But she's been gone more than an hour, which I think is promising."

"Maybe he'll step up and take care of her and the boy," Darryn said. "Maybe she won't need you anymore."

I turned my head to look at him. He hadn't meant it cruelly, but it was still a hard thing to contemplate. "What would I do with myself if I wasn't taking care of Annie and Kinnon?" I said. "Until a few months ago, my life was my own. And now I can't even imagine having my life back. What would I do with it?"

"What would you want to do?"

I shifted a little on the bench, so my whole body was turned toward Darryn. He was dressed in plain clothes today, but there was still no mistaking the fineness of the cloth, the excellence of the cut. "What are you doing here?" I asked softly. "Why have you come looking for me?"

He smiled a little and took my hand in a gentle hold, easy to break if I tried. I did not. "I wanted to see what it might be like to have a conversation with you when one or the other of us didn't have a knife to the throat," he said.

"You're a serramar. I'm a poacher's daughter," I told him. The words were easy to say; I'd said them in my head often enough. "It doesn't matter whether we can have a conversation or not. We have no place in each other's world."

His fingers tightened a little. "Oh, but the world is changing," he said. "I am very much afraid we are going into a war that will turn this country upside down and inside out. Old alliances will break, new associations will form. Nothing will be as it once was."

"Who will be fighting this war?" I demanded.

"Coralinda Gisseltess and her brother on one side, joined by a whole host of ambitious landowners who want to expand their borders," he said. "The king, his loyal subjects, and the mystics on the other." He squeezed my hand again. "So you see, you and I will be on the same side. When the world changes. When impossible things become possible."

"I wish that were true," I said. "Not the part about war. The part about the world being different."

He lifted his free hand and brushed a strand of hair from my face. His touch, and his smile, were both so gentle that I shivered a little. I was already more than half in love with this man. It had not seemed to me a remote possibility he could fall in love with me in return. "I think we're about to enter a period of great turmoil," he said solemnly. "And to get through it, all of us are going to have to hold on to the things we cherish most. The things that make us happy. The things that make us strong. You're so strong, Sosinetta, so capable, so impossible to defeat. I think if you are standing beside me, I will not break."

"I'm only strong when I have something to live for," I said.

"I can give you that," he said.

He pulled me closer, put his arm around me, and there, on the public bench, in front of every passing soul in Carrebos, I leaned my head against the serramar's shoulder. Our hands were still locked together; I felt him kiss the top of my head. "So Coralinda Gisseltess is leading the country into a war?" I murmured. "She was here last night. Or some of her men were, trying to kill mystics."

"I heard the tale," Darryn replied. "She has sent similar men to

towns and villages all over the kingdom, attempting to destroy anyone with a trace of power."

"I'm afraid of her."

"You should be."

It was warm out in the late sunshine, but I shivered a little against
Darryn's hold. "She's so elegant and cold," I said. "She reminds me of
winter."

"Yes," he said, "and like winter I think she will bring darkness and
death to the land."

But Coralinda's snow-and-midnight soldiers had come here last
night, and been beaten back, and all their damage had been healed by
Lara's sure touch. I stirred and sat up. Darryn kissed me lightly on the
mouth. I smiled, and he kissed me again.

"Winter may be upon us soon," I said, "but spring never fails."

The Kiss
of the
Snow Queen

✺ ✺ ✺

CLAIRE DELACROIX

One

✳

THE STIRRING OF SHADOWS IN THE BRONZE mirror would have awakened Gerta, had she slept. She had been awake all the night, so she was immediately aware of the motion within it. She watched it warily, reluctant for once to heed its summons.

She had done wrong, and she knew it well. She had used the mirror against its purpose, against her mentor's counsel, and it had been three days since her transgression.

Gerta feared to see what reckoning the mirror conjured. Such forces could be willful, perhaps as willful as she had been in trying to bend the mirror's power beneath her own inexperienced hand. She had been warned, when the heirloom mirror had been entrusted to her care, that it could be capricious. Vengeful, even.

But what choice had she had?

The mirror in question was a bronze disk, one face of it polished highly. Most people saw their own reflection within it, but Gerta, as a seer, saw distant events and portents displayed upon it. Her gift was rare and, as soon as it had become evident, she had been apprenticed to another seer. Isold had been her mentor from childhood until that woman's death five years past.

So much had changed with Isold's demise. Gerta still yearned for the days before the arrival of the Cath Palug in her father's realm, for that fiend was the root of all evil that had followed.

The mirror tickled her thoughts, persistent as it seldom was. Still Gerta lingered abed. Her training was not complete, but she had the wits to know trepidation.

Gerta's chamber was at the summit of the sole tower in the abode of Gundobad, the king of Burgundy. She had long thought its location befit a seer, for it would protect her chastity, but now she understood that her chastity had been protected for another reason.

Her chamber was still dark, for it was not yet dawn, and the hall below was blessedly quiet. She could have slept in her exhaustion, had she felt confident that she would not be assaulted in her slumber. The trunk pushed against her door was no guarantee, nor was the dismissal of all maids who might have betrayed her while she slept. Gerta rubbed her eyes, exhausted and hungry from three days secured here alone in her defiance. She looked toward the mirror, hoping fiercely that her summons would bring relief.

There was only one way to be certain. Gerta rose to heed the mirror. She had best know the worst of what she had done.

She was still dressed, wearing her favored plain robe, the one that did not look like the choice of a king's only daughter. The robe was blue, the pale blue that came from woad, woven finely from wool and devoid of embroidery. It covered her from chin to toe, the sleeves hanging modestly over her hands. To leave her hair unbound but cover all of her skin, with the exception of her fingers and her face, was the modesty Gerta had been taught to better protect her gift—though such modesty had served little in this place.

It was when Gerta bent to pull her leather shoe over her heel that she noticed the odd shimmer in the air. There was fog in the valley beyond her window, which was not uncommon in itself, but this fog was strange. It had slipped over her sill like quicksilver and now pooled on the floor of her chamber. It seemed to swirl there, glittering, as if an unnatural wind stirred in her chamber.

As if it moved by some force of its own.

As if it awaited her.

The mirror tugged at Gerta, but the fog both fascinated her and made her afraid. This was a fog wrought of shadow: there was darkness within it, a foreboding darkness.

Instead of going to the mirror, Gerta glanced to the window. All souls in the valley slept, thanks to Gundobad's generosity with thin ale these three days, but the current of fog was in motion. In contrast to the stillness, it wound like a river, moving sinuously between the quiet huts below.

Gerta frowned, for this fog showed purpose as natural fog never did. It unfurled across the valley like a ribbon, a ribbon with a clear destination. It did not trouble itself to fill the furrows or coil around the mountains that framed the valley: it made directly for its goal. It had cut a path straight to Gerta's window. She leaned out and saw that it ascended the wall with that same purpose.

It hunted her.

Or it replied to her unorthodox summons. Gerta turned to regard the rising mist on her floor warily, her heart skipping with the surety that she was prey.

The fog drew closer as she watched, slipping around her ankles, for all the world like a possessive caress. Her skin chilled immediately, as if she had plunged her foot into ice water.

Gerta leapt out of its clutch and imagined that she heard faint laughter. She crossed her plain chamber hastily, lifted the bronze mirror, and turned its polished face upward. Within the circle of bronze, shadows swirled and churned, echoing the motion of the fog. She stilled her breathing, ignored the strange sense that she was being watched, and opened her thoughts to the mirror.

The shadows resolved so abruptly that Gerta jumped. A face was suddenly before her, a face so clearly shown that she was startled. It was a man's face, radiant with virility, tanned and golden and as confident as the midday sun.

It was more than his face shown in the mirror—the mirror had *become* his face. Gerta might have had her hand upon his throat rather than the handle of the mirror. Indeed, the handle felt warm and had the feel of flesh beneath her fingers. She felt a pulse beneath her palm and her own heart leapt in fear. She had never had such a vivid vision and some part of her wished that had never changed.

She was in the presence of a potent sorcerer, to be sure—and he had replied to her summons. Gerta's mouth went dry.

He was sufficiently handsome and sufficiently close to disconcert a maiden like herself. His eyes were blue, a clear vibrant blue, and lit not only with shrewdness but with an appreciation that could make a woman lose whatever inhibitions she held.

"I come, at your summons, to serve your will," he said, his voice a pleasant timbre that sent a shiver through her.

Gerta shook her head, for she should not have been able to hear him. "What you have done to the mirror is not possible . . ."

He smiled, as if bemused. "Many things are possible, if we have the will to believe them so."

He seemed to be surveying her, which was also impossible: the mirror granted views but did not allow for communication.

All the same, this man heard her and she heard him. Gerta caught her breath, wary of his power even as her thumb moved across the handle of the mirror. She could feel his flesh, feel his pulse and the heat of him, and seemingly could not halt the motion of her thumb. She had never touched a man, and no man had been permitted to touch her—this caress was forbidden, stolen and beguiling all the same.

That must be why her heart raced. It could have naught to do with the warmth of his gaze.

"You are a sorcerer," she guessed, for Isold had told her of such men.

He nodded. "As are you, for this is no small spell you wove."

Gerta felt herself flushing. "I know naught of spells . . ."

"Yet you cast a fearsome one all the same." His fair brows pulled together briefly. "Such talent is not unknown, but it has need of a mentor, the better that it can be tamed." Then he looked upon her, both assessing and appreciative.

"That is not why I sent the summons." Gerta averted her gaze. "My mentor is dead these five years, and I knew not what I did," she confessed, then could not help but look for his response.

He smiled, a smile that lit his eyes. "Then you have need of another mentor. Perhaps that is why your summons found me. I have need of a pupil, and perhaps of a partner."

He put a slight weight upon the last word, sufficient that Gerta understood his meaning. She had guessed that there would be a price to be paid for her audacity, but she had not expected such a high one.

"You should know that I am a maiden, once and always," she said with breathless haste. "The loss of my chastity will be the sacrifice of my gift as a seer. So I was taught and so I believe."

"That cannot be true," he said patiently, "for then we should have no wager."

She could not dismiss him, nor could she pledge what he asked of her. Gerta wished ardently for counsel, but knew she would find none in Isold's absence. Worse, she felt herself slowly blush beneath his regard, her face suffusing with heat.

She knew she should tear her gaze from his, but despite herself she was intrigued. Her pulse quickened that there was another of her kind who breathed, at the prospect of having a tutor again—and she was honest enough to acknowledge that it quickened for another reason, as well.

"Who is to say what gift will come in the place of the one you have?" He regarded her warmly, clearly undeterred, and a treacherous part of Gerta was glad of this. His voice was filled with both confidence and compassion. "A whole is wrought of two halves, Gerta, and is greater than the sum of its parts. You must trust in the way of things, in the fact that your summons came to me, of all men." He winked at her then, silencing whatever she might have said. "But before we speak of this and much more, there is a task I must perform for you. Your request must be fulfilled."

Before Gerta could protest, he became smaller and the mirror became its usual self again, the handle reverting to cold metal. It was as if he stepped back, and she felt the loss of his attention.

Then she cried out. She recognized the place where the sorcerer stood and understood with sudden clarity the fullness of what she had done. He stood before a cave, a cave that was as familiar to Gerta as the lines in her own hand.

The mirror often showed her warriors who met their end at this stone portal: this was the abode of the Cath Palug, the beast that had ravaged her father's land and people, the fiend that had destroyed her father's kingdom and driven them into exile.

The mirror had found a trick to resolve her request, for the demise of the Cath Palug would defeat Gundobad's intent that Gerta should wed his son, Sigismund.

But no man could defeat the Cath Palug. Those who fought the great cat paid with their lives. She had cast into peril someone who aided her.

Again.

"Do not do this thing! Do not face the Cath Palug!" she shouted, but the sorcerer strode to the opening of the cave, apparently unable or unwilling to hear her any longer.

Gerta felt sickened by her deed, impotent as never she had. She had called for aid: she had used the mirror to make a cry for assistance to selfishly secure her gift.

And now this sorcerer would die, for answering her call.

As she watched, the sorcerer laughed, raising his voice in a whistle of summons. He even called the beast! Gerta caught her breath at his daring. Daughter of a warlord, she admired that this sorcerer was a warrior as well: she liked that he did not flinch from a foul deed. And she admired his boldness, to be sure.

She did not like that he would pay for his valor with his life.

She saw the cat's profile appear against the darkness of its hovel, saw its eyes glint. It was large, larger than a man, and possessed of a hunger that could never be sated. It had grown larger since last she had glimpsed it, grown by feasting upon the meat of the warriors it ruthlessly slaughtered.

It crouched. It snarled.

It leapt.

The sorcerer raised a massive spear against the beast and made to drive it into the beast's breast. The Cath Palug snapped the spear as if the weapon were a mere twig, then roared in fury. The sorcerer drew his sword with startling speed, but the cat caught him around the throat, closing its powerful jaws around the pulse of his life.

Gerta cried out. The Cath Palug was strong and fast, stronger and faster than most warriors anticipated. Those who faced it had little chance to learn from their errors.

To Gerta's astonishment, the sorcerer bellowed and smote the beat with a blow that should have killed it. He was strong! Gerta thrilled at the evidence and dared to hope that he might triumph. The cat retreated snarling, its wound flesh-deep only, its blood staining the snow.

The sorcerer swore under his breath and the pair circled each other warily. Gerta's grasp upon the mirror was so tight that her knuckles were white.

But truly, what difference if this sorcerer claimed her or Sigismund did? Her gift would be sacrificed either way. She had never feared so much for the life of any man who faced the Cath Palug, and there had been many, some even as valiant as this man.

What had changed?

The answer came most unexpectedly, so unexpectedly that Gerta dropped her mirror.

"WELL, IT'S NOT THAT COMPLICATED," A MALE voice said immediately behind her. His accent was as unfamiliar as his voice. "Work with me here, Gerta, my girl; you're clever enough."

Gerta pivoted in terror as the mirror clattered to the floor, but her chamber was empty. Her gaze darted to the portal, but the trunk still barred entry. The light was turning pearly with the promise of the dawn and there was no corner in her chamber in which a man could hide.

She was alone, to be sure.

When Gerta could not summon a coherent word, the voice continued. "He's your destiny, of course."

She peered out the window, thinking there must be someone outside, hanging from the sill or the roof with uncommon agility. Nay. She leaned her ear against the portal, thinking some bold soul assailed her from the corridor beyond. Nay. No man crouched in the rafters, either, and the trunk held only the few garments of her own that always it held.

She stood in the middle of the room and turned slowly. She was losing her wits.

A man she could not see whistled low and Gerta jumped. "Some girls have all the luck. He is one handsome piece of work, Gerta, and that smile . . . mm mmm mmmmmmm."

"Who spoke?" She drew her small eating knife and held it before herself. "Who are you? Show yourself."

"Oh, baby, I'd do it in a minute if I could. Give me a kiss and help me out."

Gerta felt a caress across the back of her neck, in the shadow beneath the weight of her hair. A stroke of strong fingertips that made her tingle in a new way. She gasped and turned, but there was only the shimmer of the fog behind her.

"Who are you? What are you? And what do you desire of me?"

Rich male laughter echoed in her chamber, so resonant that it could not have been her imagination. This was no trick of the sorcerer in the mirror, for the voice differed. This one was deeper, darker. Older.

Undoubtedly more skilled than she. Gerta's breath came quickly in her fear. There was only the sinuous fog in her chamber, the fog that was like no other fog she had ever seen, a force she did not know how to conquer.

She straightened with bravado. "You must depart immediately.

Your voice reveals your gender and it is forbidden for a man to enter my chamber."

There was a smile underlying his response. "Fortunately for you then, I'm not a man. This must be your lucky day."

Gerta did not have the audacity to ask what he was. "Fortunate for me? How so?"

"Isn't the woman the one who pays the price for tempting a man's lust? A strange custom to my thinking, but not an uncommon one in mortal societies. Take Sigismund, for example."

"I will not take Sigismund!" His words struck a bit too close to the bone for Gerta's taste and she raised her knife higher as he laughed. How could this strange intruder know such details of her life? "I command that you show yourself!"

He chuckled, as if the idea was absurd, the sound coming from no distinct source. Perhaps she *was* going mad. The prospect of being tied to Sigismund for the remainder of her days, of being trapped in this violent household with no hope of release, perhaps could do that to a woman.

"His name is Cai," the voice continued confidentially. "Cai the Tall, one of the nine enchanter kings of England. He's from Wales, actually, but details, details."

"You evade my demand."

"I'm telling you what you really want to know, Gerta, what you *need* to know. Why else do you think I'm here? This Cai guy has some pretty serious credentials. Companion of kings, slayer of giants." He cleared his throat softly and Gerta hated how avidly she awaited his words. "I'm thinking you two kids have got something in common. Face it: you could do a lot worse, my girl."

"I am no girl but a woman in truth . . ."

"You won't be a woman until you are claimed by Cai and you know that as well as I do."

"No man may touch me," Gerta began to protest, but the intruder's voice dropped to a whisper, a current of low sound that seemed to slither into her ears.

"So, how do you think Cai will be in bed, Gerta? Rough? Wild? Tender?"

The treacherous whisper left a warm course over her lobe and into her ear, leaving a heat of speculation in its wake, one that reached all the way to her heart. Gerta felt as if she had suddenly stepped into a beam of bright sunlight, as if her very flesh was aflame. Gerta could feel the course of her own blood, could not evade the thunder of her own pulse.

She was awakened.

She seemed to feel a caress, one that slid down the length of her arm. A man's fingers might have entwined with her own, his palm over the back of her hand, though she could see nothing. She stared at her arm in mingled astonishment and dismay, unable to account for her response to the leisurely caress. It could not be called anything else, and her mouth went dry as she thought of Cai touching her thus. Such a gentle caress could not have been from any other man she knew.

Her hand was then lifted by an unseen force, a kiss planted on her palm. She could feel the press of a man's lips against her flesh. She stared at her hand in marvel as tingles spread through her from that point.

Then she cried out at the flick of the tip of his tongue across her palm. "Do not do that!" She backed away, wiping her palm upon her skirts.

"Listen to your pulse, Gerta. How about that warmth in your belly?" The voice might have been whispering in her ear then, the feel of breath against her throat making her shiver. "How about that heat down below there?"

"Leave me be!"

"Cai will certainly be lusty. Men like their earthly pleasures, sorcerers even more so, not that there's anything wrong with that. And he wants you, I can tell." He chuckled. "But then, who wouldn't?"

Gerta felt herself blushing crimson. "Who are you? What are you? What do you want with me?"

"What everyone wants, pretty much, except that I can't do much about it." He laughed then, although Gerta did not see the humor in his words. "Consider me a catalyst."

"I do not know this word. Your speech is strange, as if you are a foreigner."

"You could call me that, for sure." He sighed. "How about a matchmaker? Do you have those? Someone who smooths the way, so that everyone gets what they want?"

"I do not desire to be claimed by a man."

"But you called . . ."

"To keep Sigismund's hands from me! What else could I do?"

The voice interrupted her. "And don't you think it's fair that if Cai defeats the Cath Palug, he gets the bonus prize?"

"I will be no man's prize."

"Will your father see matters your way? I think not. If our friend Cai there kills the Cath Palug, I'm thinking Daddy-O will have a little reward for him." He paused. "Like you, for example. Prize, bride, it's all pretty much the same in a barbarian culture, don't you think?"

The voice was right, much to Gerta's dismay. Her current situation revealed that her father would be glad to trade her for his own advantage—he had not fought Gundobad's decree.

"And think about it." The voice surrounded her again, sliding into her own thoughts as if it would mingle with them. "A warrior's hands upon you, a partner both strong and gentle. Two minds as one. Haven't you felt a bit lonely since Isold left? You've got to believe it could be worse, Gerta."

"He will not win." She folded her arms across her chest. "This discussion is of no import. No man defeats the Cath Palug."

"Someone's got to do it sometime. All good things come to an end, and all that."

"Nay, the Cath Palug is invincible."

"No one is invincible, babe."

Gerta caught her breath. She could feel the weight of a man's hands on her shoulders, as if he stood behind her and nuzzled her neck. Despite herself, her body was responding to this strange intruder, a part of her mind considering the pleasure that might come of a man's touch. If he had tried to force her, she could have spurned him; if he had been substantial, she could have struck him. But he seduced her and his touch was dangerously persuasive. As it was, her feet seemed rooted to the floor.

"Not even you," he breathed.

"I will succumb to no man's touch."

"You've done pretty well so far. Doesn't ol' Sigismund call you the ice maiden?"

Gerta glanced over her shoulder and almost caught a glimpse of a man. She blinked and whatever she had seen was gone. "How do you know this?"

He chuckled. "I know a lot of things. Think: you and Cai would be two of a kind," he whispered, seemingly leaving a line of kisses along her throat. Gerta swallowed, trying to fight the allure of his caress and not doing as well as she would have liked. She stood straight, hoping she appeared to be unresponsive.

"Aren't you lonely, sometimes, Gerta?" The words were so softly uttered that they might have been her own thoughts. "Wouldn't it be great to have someone to talk to, someone who understood the burden of your gift, someone who knew how best to use it?"

Gerta's eyes flew open. This was sorcery! She had to flee such a persuasive spell! She darted to the door and shoved the trunk aside, only to have it slid back into place before she could open the portal.

"Oh, no, you don't want to go out there. Do you really think Sigismund isn't watching the door?"

Gerta fought the weight of the trunk without success. It seemed to be fixed to the floor and had the same dark shimmer about it as the fog. She guessed that she would never move it.

"I won't be able to do much if he gets his hands on you, and no one else will help you here."

There was truth in that, truth that halted her. Gerta looked around herself in panic, knowing she was captive. Never had she felt so trapped by a lack of choices. Her breath came quickly but she could not slow it.

"Your arrival in his bed is three days past due, and I'm thinking the boy is getting a bit restless. It's not going to be fun, Gerta, when Sigismund takes what he thinks is his to have."

The fog, Gerta realized, had piled itself in the corner where it shimmered like a dark opal. If she squinted, its shape might be similar to the silhouette of a tall and well-muscled man.

She straightened, liking that there was something to confront. "What do you desire of me?"

"That would be the million-dollar question."

"I do not understand all of your speech."

"A kiss would be a good start."

"You will not have one, so long as the choice is mine whether to surrender it."

He sighed, then his tone turned chiding. "Ah well, then, don't miss the good bits on my account. Cai conjured up this show for you, after all, though even he never guessed how it would end. You should at least have the courtesy to watch."

Gerta felt her eyes narrow. "How can you know what the mirror will show before it does?"

"Oh, come on, Gerta. You could guess if you wanted to. It's not rocket science. Go on, give the man the grace of your attention. It cost him big to work this spell."

Would Cai defeat the Cath Palug? Gerta glanced at the mirror, curious but uncertain whether it was wise to turn her back upon this strange intruder. She prickled, though, with the surety that the mirror's turmoil still unfurled.

The intruder chuckled again and Gerta knew he had guessed her thoughts. Odd, she had always thought herself adept at hiding them. She snatched up the mirror and looked within it, willfully ignoring her unexpected and unusual guest.

To her surprise, the mirror had waited for her. This had never happened before, and she felt a grudging respect for Cai's abilities. She could learn much from a sorcerer of such power, and a part of her yearned for such knowledge. Had this occurred already? Or was it yet to occur?

Could her choices affect Cai's survival?

"Now, you're thinking," the voice mused.

She thought no further before the beast sprang again. It buried its claws in Cai's hauberk. They were black, those claws, long and sharp and gleaming like obsidian. Gerta had seen them slice men open like knives. Cai bellowed in pain and fury. His blood ran crimson, the Cath Palug's claws buried almost their full length in his shoulder.

There was too much blood. Gerta bit her knuckle and could not so much as blink lest she miss something of import. Cai stumbled as he bled, and then he fell.

To Gerta's dismay, no soul came to his aid. Surely he had not embarked upon such a quest alone? But sorcerers oft labored alone, especially when they believed their success inevitable.

A lump rose in Gerta's throat as the cat, the cursed Cath Palug, grasped Cai's hauberk with its teeth. The sorcerer murmured but could not rouse himself to fight off the fiend, so fearsome were his injuries. The growling cat dragged the warrior into the yawning darkness of its lair.

There was naught left but a trail of the sorcerer's blood, brilliant red against the snow, marking the path to the cavern.

Cai was still alive, Gerta knew it, and she guessed that the beast would torment him before killing him. The prospect sickened her. Such nobility of intent deserved better reward than this. Gerta put the mirror down with force, more angry than she ever had been, and turned away.

This was her fault.

She looked to the shimmering shadow, disliking that she would be fulfilling his expectation. "What must I do to aid Cai?"

Two

"THAT'S THE SPIRIT! SEE? TWO OF A KIND," the intruder said with such surety that Gerta longed to do him injury. "That's some kind of connection. So tell me, what changed your mind?"

"He is not yet dead," Gerta said, her words thick. "The cat will torment him before killing him."

"Compassion is good. It could come in handy."

"I do not understand."

"You don't need to. Yet." The intruder cleared his voice, and Gerta wondered if he meant to say something unpleasant. "You know, I hate to raise the possibility, but the Cath Palug might not kill him at all."

Gerta's lips tightened. "He will die eventually."

"Maybe not."

"I do not understand your meaning," she said with impatience. "I thought you intended to show me his triumph."

"Ah, well, you can't have everything. Besides, you didn't want him to succeed."

"I did not condemn him!"

"Not like you've done to others," the voice mused.

Gerta strode across the room, trying to put distance between them. "I do not know what you mean."

"Then you're dumber than you look."

"I . . ." Gerta silenced her angry response with an effort, for she sensed that the intruder simply wanted to rouse her ire. "What must I do to aid Cai?"

"Obviously, you're going to have to go to the cave of the Cath Palug and intervene."

Gerta stepped back in shock. "I cannot do this!"

"Why not?"

"I am a maiden. I am not a warrior. I cannot defeat the Cath Palug when a man such as Cai cannot do so." Gerta's protests sounded like excuses even to her own ears. "My father would forbid it!"

The shadow laughed. "And why would you care about his perspective?"

"And it is three days' walk to Lake Lausanne. Cai will be dead before I can arrive there."

"Gee, and I thought you felt a little responsibility, maybe a bit of guilt."

"I cannot do what you decree. It is beyond my abilities."

"So, you're afraid." The voice made a clucking sound. "What happened to good ol'-fashioned nobility?"

"I cannot do this!"

"You mean that you *will* not do it. There's a world of difference."

He was right. Indecision warred within Gerta and she turned to pace the chamber. She dreaded what Cai would endure in that cave, yet at the same time, she knew what would be demanded of her if he survived.

Did her compassion extend to the sacrifice of her gift? What would Isold have done? Gerta knew, which only fed her guilt.

The shadow spoke with easy confidence. "So, let's walk through this one. The sorcerer from whom you could learn a million things— give or take—could very well die because you didn't do anything to aid him, and it would be your fault because you summoned him in the first place. That would be dirty pool, no matter how you look at it."

"I cannot be responsible for every event!"

He ignored her outburst. "So, Cai dies, the Cath Palug continues to kill, and your father remains in exile, which means that the deal he's already struck with Gundobad will stand. You'd get to stay in this fabulous place for the rest of your life, with Sigismund on top every night. The thing is, you might not live that long, so maybe it's worth it."

"Cease your chatter!"

"How long do you think it's going to take Sigismund to figure out how to get in here? He's not the sharpest tack in the box, but it's not a really tough problem. He should be able to manage a rape pretty soon now, and that would pretty much end the stand-off. You can only lose your chastity once, after all, and once it's gone, it's gone."

"You are impertinent!"

"Oh, come on, Gerta, why else did you bar the door?"

"I must protect my chastity."

"Yeah, from Sigismund. Tell me, did those bruises heal?"

Gerta's hand rose to her upper arm of its own volition. "You cannot know this. It was resolved between my father and Sigismund's father, Gundobad. The wergild was paid for the insult Sigismund made to me."

"And then the deal was cut. He's going to have you, probably tonight, unless the Cath Palug dies."

Gerta turned away. "Cai might triumph over the Cath Palug."

"Okay, I can work with that. Let's imagine that Cai does win, but he's in pretty rough shape, isn't he? He'd probably be so damaged that some other guy could beat him to the punch, could come trotting to your father and pretend that *he* had killed the Cath Palug, and your father would then give you away to an impostor. Much as I admire a little opportunism, you're selling yourself short here."

Gerta felt the color drain from her face. It was all too plausible.

"But you're right, Gerta, it's a much better plan to just stay here, to just wait for Sigismund to take down the door."

"You are sardonic."

"You're forgetting that power comes from making your own choices and then doing something about them." His voice lowered. "You're forgetting that redemption has to be earned."

It was unthinkable that she could confront the Cath Palug and win, but then, maybe there was something unnatural about the beast. She had conjured a spell of power, Cai had said so. Did she even know the fullness of her abilities?

Gerta turned to the window, her eyes widening when she saw the frost that had inexplicably filled the valley. She clutched the sill with cold fingers, astonished at the scene before her.

"Well, I'll give you the inside story, Gerta, since I can see the proverbial writing on the wall here. The only man who can kill the Cath Palug is our pal Cai, but he can only do it with your aid. You've got to do it as a team, and I'm here to coach."

Gerta's gaze flicked over the valley, distracted by the sight. The fog was inexplicably gone, the valley garnished with hoarfrost. Every branch glistened, every tree had become a jewel, and the very snow sparkled as if strewn with gems. Icicles hung on the edges of the roof, the first blush of daylight making them tinkle and twinkle. It was both beautiful and unnatural.

Treacherous.

"But it is May," she said, almost to herself. "It is too late for such cold." It should have been a magical sight, the glitter of all that ice, but there were shadows within it that made Gerta dread its intent.

Could ice have intent? Could ice have malice? She would never have given such a thought credence, not before this morning. She would never have thought fog could speak with her, either, or that the mirror could be used by another to address her.

"It's the ice, you see," the intruder said, as if that was a reasonable reply and indeed, it made a certain sense. "Ice is at the root of everything, and the Cath Palug is just one of its instruments."

Menace carried from the ice as surely as the scent of wood smoke assails the nose, as surely as the unseen presence of the Cath Palug made men's hearts beat in fear. Gerta felt the intruder join her and glanced sidelong, barely catching the glimmer of his silhouette.

The hairs on her left side, those closest to him, stood slightly and prickled, as they would when changing garb in midwinter, as if there was something about him that could quicken her very flesh. She had a definite sense that she stood too close to something she should not approach at all.

Yet like a moth lured to the flame, she was tempted to move even closer. What she did was hold her ground, savoring the tingle that danced through her body. "You brought this ice," she accused, recalling the dark shimmer of the fog and seeing a similar shimmer in the hoarfrost.

"Not exactly," he said. "It followed me. Unfortunately."

"From where?"

A smile filled his words. "Well, that would be the point, wouldn't it?"

She could almost see him, leaning his elbows on the sill. He was handsome in a darker way than Cai, but cocky in much the same way. He was sure of himself and sure of his own allure. He smiled at her and there was something wicked in that expression, something so alluring that Gerta recognized it as dangerous.

Then she blinked and could not see him clearly any longer.

Her breath caught in her throat. She could smell him beside her, though, the warmth of another presence, the heat of a man in her own chamber. She could feel the leap of her pulse, the awareness of his presence in every fiber of her being, and she knew that the spell he wrought was one to which all women were susceptible.

Surely she was more clever than that?

"You are more substantial than you were," she said.

"You're yearning. Lust isn't as good as the real thing, but I can make it work."

"I feel no lust for fog!"

"What about Cai?"

Gerta shivered and averted her gaze.

"You've got to realize that a fear unfaced is one unvanquished," he said gently. "And a foul deed for which you have not done compense is a burden of guilt upon your back. I should know."

Then he moved away, the fog dispersing around the floor of her chamber, as if granting her time to consider her course. He could well afford to grant her that time, for he was right. As much as she would have liked to deny it, Gerta truly had no choice but to aid Cai.

Perhaps she would fail.

Perhaps she would not lose her gift in the end.

It did not matter. She had to aid him, even knowing what the price to her might be.

GERTA HAD NO IDEA WHAT SHE MIGHT NEED TO vanquish the Cath Palug, but there was little she had to take. Her father had sold what few trinkets they had had to maintain a vestige of his kingdom for as long as possible after the arrival of the Cath Palug.

It had not been sufficient to keep them from becoming exiles, from seeking Gundobad's hospitality. Gerta opened the trunk and removed the fur-lined cloak she had stored there for the summer, donning it with impatient gestures. She belted it around her waist, then pulled on her thick boots. She had two knives and took them both, placing them in a sack along with a few other belongings, a comb, another shift, a partial loaf of bread she had not eaten yet. She lifted the mirror, intending to take it, and the intruder cleared his throat.

"Not that. Don't take that."

"It is my tool."

"It can be used against you."

Gerta gave the fog a quelling glance, then shoved the mirror into her sack. She did not imagine his sigh of forbearance. "You must tell me of this ice, so that I understand it better. A foe cannot be defeated which is not understood."

"The ice is only a tool, or a weapon at best."

"To understand a weapon is to better understand the one who

wields it." She granted him a glance. "And perhaps it can be turned against the one who wields it."

"Fair enough." There was a smile in his voice that made Gerta feel proud of herself.

Despite the lack of a clear plan, she felt a shiver of anticipation at the boldness of her quest. She would depart with no more than a shadow as her companion, albeit a male shadow, to aid another seer. She had undertaken no deed so daring since Isold's demise.

In the absence of Isold, Gerta had not known who might have aided her if she overstepped herself. She wondered if Cai had summoned her because he had suspected he might have need of aid. But she could not reconcile that with his complete confidence.

Nay, she believed that he had summoned her so that she could witness his triumph. Had the battle gone awry because he had expended too much of his power to command her mirror? The prospect of her own apparently infinite culpability gave haste to Gerta's gestures.

She turned to the portal with more determination than she might have expected, but the voice sounded suddenly close by her ear.

"Not that way. The last thing we need is Sigismund to tag along."

"But there is no other way."

He laughed. "Isn't there?"

Gerta felt herself caught around the waist, as if a man pulled her fast to his side with one strong arm. In a heartbeat, she was aware of the intruder's height, of his heat, of the pulse of his own heart so close to her own.

A man held her against his body! His strength was undeniable as was the curious rush of pleasure that slid over her flesh. Her breast was crushed against him, and the sensation was not unpleasant. Indeed, her body responded to the feel of him with enthusiasm.

"Unhand me! It is forbidden for a man to touch a seer. You will be compelled to pay the wergild . . ." Gerta struggled to no avail. Her captor carried her easily to the lip of the window, caught her knees beneath his other arm, then leapt into the very air.

They plummeted like a pair of stones.

He would see her killed! Gerta parted her lips to scream but made nary a sound.

For her captor's lips closed over her own in a possessive kiss.

For a dangerous moment, Gerta was shocked into immobility, which only granted her assailant the chance to deepen his kiss. His embrace fanned the flame that Cai had awakened. His tongue found its way between her lips and Gerta gasped, then was amazed at the pleasurable sensation he granted with his caress.

Then she pushed him away, realizing her own weakness. She had but a moment to hate his low laugh of triumph before she realized that they did not fall any longer.

They moved parallel to the ground, over the roofs of the huts clustered outside Gundobad's portal. Gerta frowned. She heard the beat of leathery wings and looked up. She could see her captor faintly, mischief gleaming in his eyes, his smile flashing white. She dared not look long upon him, for there was something in his avidity that stung her eyes.

It was when she looked down, to the shadow they cast upon the ice, that her heart fairly stopped. A shimmering dark shadow possessed of massive wings held her captive. Gerta thought of predators returning from the hunt, of owls and hawks.

What manner of monster had claimed her, and what was his intent in truth? She did not even know his name, much less his nature.

Suddenly, her choice to aid Cai seemed wrought of folly alone.

GERTA FOUGHT WITH RENEWED VIGOR IN HER terror, though to no discernible effect. In fact, her captor held her more tightly, which only reminded her of Sigismund's recent assault. Gerta twisted and writhed, nigh mad in her fear. Her captor swore mightily, and their course over the valley dipped low, but he held fast to her waist.

"Unhand me!" Gerta cried. They had already flown past the cluster of huts and ascended rapidly to the pass at the far end of the valley.

"Remarkable as it may seem, you're more useful alive." He sounded as if he spoke through gritted teeth.

"I demand that you release me!"

"I think you're right," he agreed with sudden amiability. Gerta did not have time to distrust his new tone. "You're too much trouble."

And he let her go.

Gerta screamed as she fell toward the earth. There was no one this far from the village to hear her, no one who might aid her—even if it were possible to do so. She tumbled earthward with fearsome speed, her hair whipping around her face, her skirts blowing above her knees. She had no care for modesty, for she knew that she would be broken in a thousand places upon impact.

She screamed for it was all she could do.

Suddenly she heard a swish of wings and, not the height of two men from the ground, her captor plucked her out of the air. She clung to him, her breathing ragged and her pulse racing, and he carried her ever upward.

"Appreciate me now?"

"You did that apurpose," Gerta accused, once she had recovered her breath. "You meant to put fear within me . . ."

"You've got to admit, it's got its uses."

"You are a wretch, and a cur. You are a scoundrel and . . ."

"Look, Gerta, babe, not to be rude, but that's all old news."

Gerta closed her mouth, fumed and hung on to him in silence. Her captor eventually landed, stumbling only slightly on the shimmer of ice, and set her on her feet. They were at the end of the valley; the castle and village no more than distant shadows. He exhaled mightily and might have made some unwelcome comment, but Gerta swung her fist in his direction.

"Cur!" she cried, but her hand swept through the cloud that was her captor with no resistance. At most, she felt a chill on her flesh.

He laughed.

"No man shall touch a seer! No man shall embrace a seer, lest her gift be sacrificed. So is it decreed within the laws of every land."

"Gerta, hon, we've been over this. I'm not a man, so you've got nothing to worry about on that score." He sounded tired and Gerta felt a prickle of concern for him, one that she quickly dismissed. He exhaled mightily and seemed to dim slightly. "Gotta rest a minute, Gerta. I haven't manifested in a long time. It's a lot harder than I remember." He sighed. "Or maybe I'm just getting too old for this intervention crap."

As she was coming to expect, Gerta did not fully understand him and that did little to reassure her.

He seemed to peer at her, though his features faded in and out of view. "You've got to weigh, what, one forty? One fifty? There's a lot of you to love, Gerta. No wonder I'm bagged. Trust me to glom on to the substantial ones."

Though she did not understand his measure, his tone told her that he did not truly flatter her. Gerta straightened. "I am robust, which is a mark of health. The feeble do not survive."

"I guess they wouldn't in these conditions."

Gerta frowned, for she saw naught amiss with her living conditions beyond the presence of Gundobad and Sigismund.

He continued. "Being a robust woman, don't you think you should see your royal lineage continued by having kids yourself?"

"To be a seer is a greater calling."

"Yeah, I see that your father believes that. I don't think everyone's onboard with this rationale, Gerta, and if you're going to give it up, why not give it up to one of the good guys?"

He did not seem to expect a reply and truly Gerta did not have one. She looked around herself, felt her belly grumble, and had a thought. "It is three days' walk to Lake Lausanne, where the Cath Palug holds Cai captive. If you fly us there, we could arrive more quickly to assist him."

"Assuming I could fly that far. Unless, of course, you wanted to do the horizontal mambo. Maybe a couple of times. That would give me the stamina for a long flight."

"I do not understand."

"I told you, Gerta, I get power from lust. Your lust. Kisses are well and good, but for that kind of effort, I'll need sex. With you. Multiple times."

Gerta took a step backward in shock. "Nay!"

"Then do me a favor and at least fantasize a bit about our boy Cai. You're going to need me when we get there, and the stronger I am, the easier this whole thing will be.

"But Cai . . ."

"Will have to hang on, all by himself. Give him some credit. I think he can do it. And unless you put out, we don't have a lot of choice."

Gerta turned away, unable the accept the burden demanded of her to right her error.

Meanwhile, her companion straightened. She found it was easiest to perceive him from the periphery of her vision, as if glimpsing him from the corner of her eye. He was taller than her, those large black wings arching high over his shoulders. He patted her shoulder companionably. "If it makes you feel better, I didn't expect otherwise. I think we should arrive in time."

"And you?"

"I'll drift along. Don't mind if I fade in and out. I'll be here." He grinned at her. "And remember, you can always make this easier for both of us."

"Willingly? Never!"

He chuckled. "Too bad you're so cute when you're outraged. It makes it tougher for me to behave myself."

She felt a fingertip flick across the tip of her nose.

Gerta took a step away from him, disconcerted. "What are you? Who are you?"

"Well, that's a long story."

He did not seem inclined to share the tale. He was a sorcerer,

Gerta decided, a sorcerer who could depart from his body. Isold had told her of such power. Gerta had always suspected that it was no more than a tall tale, but here was evidence of its truth.

Perhaps she could persuade him to teach her this trick.

"The ice then," she said with resolve. "You must tell me about the ice as we walk, as you insist it is at the root of everything."

"I thought you might have more interesting questions now." ·

Gerta did not misunderstand the undertone of his comment. His voice was low, teasing, as if he deliberately coaxed that new flame within her. Her lips were burning yet from his audacious kiss, and though she had fought his embrace, she felt a heat within her that she had not possessed before.

He had stirred something to life, with his words and his touch, and Gerta doubted it would ever be fully quelled again. It had been easier to reject intimacy with conviction before she had sampled the pleasure it could bring. True to his earlier comment, her companion seemed to have gained vigor from their embrace, for he was more clearly discernible than he had been yet.

He seemed to float beside her, a dark shimmer just beyond the edge of her vision. Gerta strode toward the summit of the pass with confidence, ignoring the weight of his gaze and the resulting heat of her flushing cheeks.

"The ice. How is it at the root of everything?" she asked. "And what does it mean for Cai?"

"I don't suppose you might be Christian?"

"Of course, I am Christian. We were immersed in the river at my father's command, after our arrival at Gundobad's court and his insistence that we join his faith before joining his household."

"Baptized," her companion provided. "You were baptized."

"Aye, that was his word."

"Don't suppose you had catechism class?" Gerta waved a dismissive hand. She had never been very interested in the teachings of Gundobad's bishop, and to be fair, he had never been interested in what she might have taught him. "The bishop didn't tell you any stories?"

"Oh, he told one, but I thought little of it." She felt her companion's expectancy but shook her head. "It is your task to recount a tale first. There will be time aplenty for mine."

He laughed lightly. "Fair enough. You sure it's this way?"

"Do you suggest that I do not know the way to my father's abode?"

"No, no, it just looks like a rough road."

"All journeys of merit are arduous."

"Well, ain't that the truth."

Gerta was glad that she was young and strong. She could walk two days with little food, for they would cross mountain streams where she could drink fresh water. And by midday on the morrow, they would reach the hut of the old woodcutter. Gerta could walk far on the promise of Egan's company, his savory cooking and his warm hut. There was a man who had served her father well, a man with a heart filled with kindness. It would be good to see him again.

Gerta walked more quickly at the prospect.

I T TOOK A WHILE FOR HER COMPANION TO FIND THE thread of the beginning of his tale, but Gerta did not prod him further. She concentrated on keeping to the path and keeping her footing, for the ice was spread thickly and the slope inclined.

"You see, your bishop could have told you stories that would have answered a lot of this, but since he didn't—you know, you could report him to the big guy for that—I'll have to start at the beginning. Or close to it."

Gerta walked in silence, fairly hearing her companion think. The tale the bishop had told had supposedly been of the beginning, and she wondered whether her companion would tell the same tale.

"Once, there were beings, let's call them angels for the sake of argument."

"Angels," Gerta echoed, trying this strange new word upon her tongue. This could be no tale she knew.

"These angels existed at the beginning of all time. For a while there, God considered them to be his first and greatest creation."

"God?"

"The force that or being who created everything, the world and everything in it, the stars and the sun. The force that exercises supreme authority. Your bishop called him God, didn't he?"

"I paid little heed to the bishop. Though it is courteous to acknowledge the gods in which other peoples believe, but I do not believe in this God." Gerta studied the frozen ground. "I believe in the sun and the moon, the earth and the sky, the power within us and some power without, the cycle of death and birth that occurs every year."

"Fair enough," the voice agreed. "What about good and evil?"

Gerta shrugged. "There is good and evil in all of us and in all things. The balance or lack of it is part of life."

"Phew! I could really get to like this non-Abrahamic religion thing, you know? The whole polarization of good and evil has always been a bit tough for me to swallow. Dualism is too simplistic, too straightforward to have much to do with the real world. I've never liked it."

Gerta said naught, for he might as well have been speaking the language of a foreigner.

"I'll guess that the Burgundians are Arian Christians, isn't that right?"

Gerta frowned. "It sounds familiar. Would some Arius have been their leader?"

"Bingo! Well, consider yourself smart to have not bought into their whole game. They're going to be ousted as heretics soon and it won't be pretty."

"I see," Gerta said, although she did not.

"Okay, so back to our story. Essentially, the bloom faded from the rose and God decided to go with another creation. People. He made men and women."

"I know this tale of God's creation of men. Adam and Eve were in the tale recounted by the bishop."

"Ah, so he told you about the Garden of Eden."

"'In the beginning, God created the heaven and the earth,'" Gerta recounted, then shook her head. "But God wished for people to be serfs in service to him, as if they had been conquered in battle."

"Why do you say that?"

"Because he refused them knowledge and the understanding of good and evil. He wished to keep them in ignorance of their own nature and their place in the world. It is not natural for people to refuse to learn or to be denied the opportunity. It is what one does with serfs, to keep them from lusting beyond their place." She could not keep herself from sneering. "This bishop blamed women, blamed Eve . . ."

"That would be temptation. You know, I always liked Eve. It was more than her being such a hot babe; she had what the French are gonna call a certain *je ne sais quoi.*" He made a sound, like the smacking of lips, which Gerta ignored.

". . . for taking of the fruit that was left in her very sight. But why would it have been left before her, if it was not hers to claim? If you do not wish any soul to covet some possession you own, you do not display it to them. You do not show it to them and forbid them to desire it. This is not reasonable. Treasures should be hidden, their merits shared with a select few."

"Sounds like Gundobad's logic to me. His son should get to have you and you should pay for the sin of tempting Sigismund's lust by the sacrifice of your gift. Blame it on the women. It's an old game, almost as old as me, if it makes you feel any better."

But Gerta did not care about this assertion. She spun to confront her companion. "How do you know so much of such details of my life?"

Three

"I KNOW MORE THAN YOU EVER WANT to, Gerta honey. I really hope that you don't have any affection for Sigismund . . ."

"Not I!"

"Good, because this guy's bad to the bone, you know. He's going to kill his own son one of these days." He grimaced. "He's not really a primo catch, if you know what I mean."

Gerta was not surprised by these tidings. "His father, Gundobad, is mad and violent," she whispered, fearing to be overheard even so far from listening ears.

"You've nailed it in one. Not everything passed from father to son is worth keeping." To Gerta's relief, her companion left that notion alone, for it was troubling to find herself in such vehement agreement with him. "So, back to our story. God thought that his new work was a triumph and so he wanted the angels to serve people."

"So, *they* would be the serfs!" Gerta shook her head. "This is some God who desires only such service from his creations."

"Don't all gods desire service?"

"Respect, this they all demand. Flattery and offerings, not slavish obedience." Gerta took a deep breath, seeking the means to explain the difference. "The old gods seek deference, but they do not command mortals. They can do deeds to aid or to plague men, which is why their aid is requested, but they do not dictate our choices."

"What about fate?"

"Who can say? It might be that the nature of a man so shapes his choices that his destiny can be determined from his birth."

"Character and deed perfectly entangled," her companion mused. "But then, who created the character of the individual?"

"Who can say? There are mysteries not ours to examine."

"So, it might have been your destiny to come along with me? This journey might be the culmination of everything you've learned so far in this life?"

"I do not doubt that you have tricked me," Gerta said sternly. "If naught else, you did not reveal your nature truly to me, not before I had no choice but to continue."

"You could turn back. It's not that far to the village. You could be there by sunset."

Gerta glanced over her shoulder, half-tempted. They had climbed almost to the pass through the mountains and she was breathing heavily from her exertions. In truth, they had come farther than she had realized, for she had been so interested in their conversation. The sky was a clear blue, the sunlight making the ice sparkle like gems.

Her father was far behind her, the father who had betrayed her. So as well was her betrothed, the man who would rape her daily once it was his right.

Gerta turned her back upon the valley she had come to think of as her home and began to climb onward. It was surprisingly easy to do. She recalled the blue of Cai's eyes and felt an unwelcome thrill of anticipation. The path became steeper from here and she bent herself to the task of climbing, savoring her own strength. She felt alive as she had never before.

"Not going back?" her companion taunted.

"I owe it to another sorcerer to grant my aid in his distress," she said stoically. "I need to repair what I have set awry."

"And that's your sole motivation, is it?" her companion teased. "You know, I think you just want to know how Cai *tastes*."

Gerta's face burned. She stared at the snow before her and marched onward, ignoring the shadow that drifted behind her. The silence pressed against her ears and she suspected that he knew what she was thinking.

She was thinking of his earlier comments. She was thinking about the surety in Cai's gaze. She was recalling how her mouth had gone dry beneath his perusal; she was recalling how alluring she had felt as he looked upon her. She was wondering about the weight of a man's hands upon her body, the dance of his tongue with hers. The heat in her belly that resulted from this consideration was not unpleasant. She recalled her captor's kiss and was suffused with warmth. That had not been so difficult to endure.

Isold had taught her that the passion kindled by men was a fleeting pleasure, one that would cost Gerta the greater power of her gift. Yet here she strode toward a man intent upon claiming her, a man who understood the price she would have to pay and would demand it of her all the same. Instead of fleeing Cai, she went to his aid.

Was that the true danger of her journey? Gerta did not know, but all the same, she did not feel that she could turn back. She knew that she would dream of Cai being dragged into the Cath Palug's cave. She knew that she would imagine the torment he endured there. She guessed that she would know the moment that he died.

And she knew that if she remained at the court of Burgundy, she would not be able to live with the fact that she had done nothing to aid him. Her gift, it seemed, was forfeit anyway, and she chose to surrender it to Cai instead of letting Sigismund steal it.

She strode toward the pass, undeterred by the deep snow, not sparing Burgundy a backward glance. Her future lay ahead. Gerta was certain of it, though she could not guess what her future might be.

"You spoke of angels," she reminded the companion sternly, wanting an escape from her thoughts as much as his tale. "Continue your tale, if you please."

She half-expected him to deny her, as he seemed inclined to provoke her. Instead he said nothing. She glanced his way and was shocked by how vividly clear he had become. He was even whistling slightly beneath his breath.

He winked at her, a vision of masculine pride. "That's the spirit, Gerta, babe. It's a rotten job thawing you out for Cai, but somebody's got to do it." He seemed to be enjoying himself overmuch, to her thinking. He flicked his tongue at her, both bold and beguiling. "Whatcha going to dream about tonight?" he whispered, eyes shining. "Maybe we can get in a little practice before the main event?"

Cheeks burning, Gerta turned away from him and stumbled onward in the snow.

ONLY A FEW MOMENTS PASSED BEFORE GERTA'S companion resumed his tale. "Well, as I was saying, God wanted the angels to pay homage to man. And some of the angels refused. When he demanded that they bow down, that they kneel to the first man and woman, these angels flat-out refused. They said no."

"And so they were punished," Gerta guessed. "For God did not like to be defied. It is the nature of kings to dislike defiance."

"I guess it is. And so the angels who refused were to be banished . . ."

"They were to be made outlanders, unwelcome at any hearth."

"*Exactimundo.* And as you might imagine, some of them felt this wasn't too fair of a judgment, because after all, they had been created first. It seemed that they should be first in God's affections, and really, comparatively, they were much finer beasts."

"What did they look like?"

"They are large and radiant." There was admiration, even awe, in his tone, and Gerta wondered whether he had seen these beings. "They are made of light, not flesh or the clay of the earth."

"And their language? What does it sound like?"

"They have none. They each understand the thoughts of another of their kind, and immediately."

"Ah, Isold told me of this power. Some men can do this as well."

"I guess they've learned. At any rate, these angels wanted to appeal God's decision . . ."

"Kings dislike a challenge to their authority." Gerta shook her head disapprovingly. "Such deeds lead often to war and bloodshed."

"Well, war is what happened, and to make a long story short, the defiant angels lost so they were banished, as per the original decree."

"And anger burned hot within them," Gerta guessed. "For they believed yet that they had been treated with injustice."

"You're good at this. It's as if you know this story already."

"It is not that uncommon a tale. The angels are different, of course, but men and kings have such battles all the time."

He muttered something that sounded to Gerta like "Isn't that special?" although she could make no sense of such a comment. She chose to ignore it, as she ignored so much of his idle talk.

After a moment, he continued. "So, one of them decided that the problem really was God's, that God had failed to see the weaknesses of his new creation and, in so doing, failed to appreciate the marvel of angels."

"This is rational. Men and women are filled with weaknesses, and we know from the tale of Adam and Eve that this God is not enamored of those who succumb to temptation."

"So, this angel—a fallen angel if you will—created a looking glass."

Gerta shivered, though she could not imagine why, and felt suddenly aware of the weight of her bronze mirror within her bag. "I do not understand this looking glass."

"Think of your mirror, and how it shows what is far away. This glass was similar, but clear."

Gerta struggled to envision such a device and failed.

"Imagine that you could cut water," he suggested. "Imagine that you could cut a slice of water . . ."

"Ah, or rock crystal!"

"Right! Now imagine that you could hold it up to your eye and look through it, and see matters that you could not see without it."

"Sorcery," Gerta said flatly.

"Some called it that. This looking glass showed wickedness where good was only apparent otherwise. It showed the truth, and it showed that men were far less ideal than God imagined. It showed the dark impulses of their hearts, it showed their secret desires, and it showed their envy of each other. It showed the mingling of good and evil everywhere. And so, because the glass showed the truth and the fallen angels believed that it would persuade God of his error, they seized the mirror and flew as one toward God to show it to him."

"Flew?"

"Angels have always had wings."

"You are one of these angels," Gerta guessed. He did not answer her so she assumed she was mistaken.

"The glass was heavy, though, heavier than expected, and the journey was farther than the angels remembered from their fall. And so it was that they dropped the glass and it fell to the earth—much, in fact, as they had done. But unlike them, the glass shattered into thousands of tiny shards and scattered in the wind. In that instant, the glass was spread throughout the domains of men and even beyond, tiny dark slivers of it wreaking havoc wherever they fell."

"How so?"

"Many men had a shard of glass stick in their eye, and afterward, in all that they saw, they perceived only the evil within it. And some people had a splinter of ice lodge within their heart, turning it to ice and making them scornful of their fellows. Some foolishly thought the piece they found to be a pretty treasure. They turned it in the light, looking through it at the world, unaware of how it poisoned their view of all they saw.

"And in the wake of this, men tasted the fullness of their own evil: they killed each other over trifles, they let envy breed within their hearts, they let lust guide their actions. They forgot all they had been taught about compassion and respect for their fellows, and each cared only for himself." He paused. "And they called it truth."

Gerta considered this. "I thought it was the fall of man from the Garden of Eden that was responsible for all evil, that Eve bore the burden of banishing all of us from the Garden."

"And the glass only makes it worse. No illusions about what you're facing, not with the glass."

"Is this glass yet in the world?"

"Of course. It's what followed me; it's what drives Gundobad. The Cath Palug was wrought to serve it . . ."

"Like the serpent in the garden."

"No!" her companion said sharply. "Not at all like the serpent."

"It seems to me to be much the same," Gerta said, simply because the notion provoked him.

"It's not the same at all!" He seemed to take a steadying breath, though precisely what had vexed him, Gerta could not guess. "The Cath Palug does what it does. It doesn't think or weigh possibilities: it was created for a single purpose and it fulfills it. If anything, it has more in common with the apple. It's an instrument, or a vehicle, but not a force in itself."

Gerta struggled with the import of this. "Then there is a greater force, one which created the Cath Palug, just as the apple was created as a tool."

"I tell you, you *are* good at this. Are you sure you don't know this story already?"

Gerta shook her head. "But what purpose does the Cath Palug serve? The death of men cannot be of so much merit as that."

"Well, they're not all supposed to die. It just forgets itself and gets kind of carried away, especially when it's hungry."

Gerta frowned in recollection. "When my father still held his kingdom, the Cath Palug was more inclined to maim men than to destroy them. It killed children and small animals, but oft let injured men escape. We thought then that its power had limits, but this is clearly not so."

"It was doing what it was made to do. The Cath Palug's claws and teeth are fashioned of that dark glass and its purpose is to see that glass spread among men."

Gerta halted suddenly, remembering how the Cath Palug's claws had torn into Cai's chest. "There is a piece of glass in Cai's heart," she guessed with horror.

As much as she hoped her companion would deny this, he nodded. "And another in his eye."

"But why did this not kill him?"

"Because neither the Cath Palug nor its mistress wishes for him to die."

"Mistress?"

"The glass has been claimed by a queen, or maybe she's become a queen by mustering its power. She's gathering all of the shards and piecing together the original glass once again. Most die soon after the shard embeds itself in their flesh, but Cai is stronger than most."

"Because he is a sorcerer himself."

"And that makes him useful."

"How so?"

"She's harnessing his power for her own, and he hasn't the will or even the knowledge to fight her. The glass makes her appear most beauteous to him."

"Surely he cannot willingly serve a woman with evil intent for him?"

"Beauty is its own temptation."

Gerta quickened her steps in her concern, then stopped and pivoted so abruptly that her companion would have collided with her had he been human. Instead, he passed directly through her, leaving her shivering and slightly disoriented.

"Don't do that again, all right?" he said, apparently similarly affected.

"But how do you know so much of this glass?" Gerta demanded. "Does she hunt you, as well?" Gerta's voice hardened. "Or are you one of her minions, sent to beguile me?"

He laughed heartily. "No, she knows little of me, as yet, which is why I can help you."

Gerta's eyes narrowed. "But then, why did the hoarfrost follow you?"

He grinned. "Because it remembers me, as surely as men and angels recall God." He paused, as if willing her to guess, but Gerta did not dare to voice her thought. "Because I made it, Gerta. I made the glass in my desire to show God his error."

GERTA COULD NOT LOOK UPON HIM, NOT WITH such bright pride in his eyes and in his stance, not that in combination with the travesty he had confessed. He was responsible for the glass, and thus for the Cath Palug and the horror that beast had visited upon so many people. He was responsible for Cai's fate, because he had created the means by which Cai could be injured and trapped.

Sickened, Gerta pivoted and made haste to the pass. She could hate her companion for his deeds, but then, had she not made a similar transgression? Or two?

The way became more arduous then and Gerta took the opportunity to cease their conversation. The snow was deeper toward the summit of the pass, deeper than she could have possibly expected so late in the spring. There should have been no snow, even a scattering of flowers. What force seized the land and made it unfamiliar?

Gerta thought that perhaps she could guess.

The valley rose to a sharp divide, high above them. This was the pass proper from one valley to another, and Gerta knew it, though she had not come this way since her father's passage into exile, since they had been driven from their home by the Cath Palug.

The way was steep and slippery. As she put one foot after the other, focusing on each step instead of the sum of the climb ahead, she wondered whether they would have come this way if she and her father had known more of Gundobad's nature.

Would it have been better for her father to have let Gundobad die on that battlefield years before?

Gerta was shocked by the audacity of her thoughts. The sun was mercilessly bright, the sky utterly clear, the air piercingly cold. Gerta imagined that her breath turned to ice as soon as she exhaled, and surely, it made a frosty cloud before her. There was frost upon the front of her cloak, ice formed of her own breath.

"Does it seem colder to you?" her companion asked.

Gerta nodded, grasped the rocks, and pulled herself to the summit of the pass. "I expect no less at this height," she managed to say. She breathed deeply after her climb and the cold air stabbed inside her like a thousand icy daggers.

The view from the high point of the pass was stunning, exhilarating, and she was suddenly fiercely glad that she had made the climb. The valley claimed by Gundobad was spread before her, his abode barely discernible in the distance. The entire valley was covered in a shimmering, glittering blanket of snow, so fresh and so white that it hurt the eyes to look upon it. From here it looked to be untrammeled, pristine.

"Perfect," Gerta said softly, seduced by the sight.

"Bite your tongue! That's what she wants you think!"

Gerta glanced about herself in confusion. "But the snow is beautiful, despite being out of season . . ."

"It is death. You're looking upon death, not perfection, though there's one who would like you to confuse the two."

Gerta frowned. "Who?"

"The foe you go to confront, of course. Some call her the Snow Queen." Apparently contenting himself with that ominous comment, her companion moved ahead. He moved with a lithe grace that was more apparent as he became more substantial, a lean-muscled strength that was appealing. He might have been nude, Gerta could not be certain, for there was a brightness about him that made it difficult to look upon the details of his form for long.

Her lips tingled and she turned her back upon him, feigning a last look at the valley behind them. She licked her lips without intending to do so and found an unfamiliar taste upon her own mouth. That reminded her of his outrageous comment and she wondered how Cai would taste.

How would he kiss? Would he claim her or would he coax her?

How long would it take her gift to abandon her? Gerta pulled her mirror from her satchel hastily, needing to affirm the presence of her gift. Her heart skipped as she turned the mirror upward, for she feared that she would see nothing within it any longer.

A woman's face was there, the sight so clear, the woman so present, that Gerta jumped. The woman smiled at the sight of her, as if in welcome, as if she could see Gerta as Cai had done.

There was something familiar about her, though Gerta could not immediately identify what. Her skin was fair, her flowing hair as white as the snow, her lips as red as blood. She was beautiful in a haughty way, alluring yet distant.

It was her eyes that made Gerta pull back: they were oddly pale, a silvery blue that put Gerta in mind of a wolf, or ice upon a frozen stream. There was something hungry about her smile, something that made Gerta wish she had not looked in the mirror in the first place.

"Begone," she commanded in a whisper, but the woman's smile only broadened.

She raised a finger, beckoned as if confident that she would be obeyed. Only then did she fade from sight.

Gerta swallowed in fear. She knew she had not dismissed or frightened the woman away. The woman had left of her own choice. And the woman had looked upon her, Gerta knew it well, just as Cai had done.

She sat down for a moment in the snow, fetching the bread from her bag to cover the fact that she was thinking. It was impossible for another to command her mirror. She knew this as surely as she knew her own name. Yet two sorcerers in one day—for the woman could be naught else—had seized control of Gerta's mirror.

Perhaps it was not truly her mirror any longer.

Perhaps this was part of how the gift was lost.

Perhaps there was more in this world than she knew. Gerta shuddered, for she did not know that any sorcerer would aid her if she overstepped herself in this quest: Isold was dead and Cai was enchanted, and she knew no others of her kind. Gerta ate the bread, not truly tasting it, then stood and made to climb again.

There was naught for it. What she had begun would only be resolved by continuing, by aiding Cai.

FROM THAT POINT, THE PATH ASCENDED ONLY slightly, winding a course around the rocky outcroppings of the mountains. They would not see the vale on the opposite side until the following morning, perhaps midday. In better weather, this pass was rife with bandits, but that was one threat they would not face. So few used the pass in these days that the bandits had abandoned it as well.

Gerta hastened after the shadow of her companion, half-expecting that he would know what she had done.

"Having a last look?" he asked, and it took Gerta a moment to realize the ambiguity of his question.

"The vale of Burgundy has been my home these past four years," she prevaricated. "It is not so easy to turn away."

"I'd think it would be easy to walk away from Gundobad and Sigismund." His words slowed, deepened, warning Gerta that she might not like his next words. "Or maybe it's your father who's easy to leave behind, given how he's let you down."

Gerta did not answer him, for it was not his affair. "You have not yet told me your name."

"So many names, so much time." His tone was cavalier. "Maybe I should let you pick one from the wide and varied selection."

"You make a jest of a simple question."

"Because it's not really a simple question. But never mind, I'll pick one for you, one that has some resonance for you and your times."

"You make it sound as if you have known other times."

"Well, I have. That's the problem with being immortal. Actually, seeing other times isn't the problem: getting them mixed up is the issue. I'd love to have a reference book, you know, maybe something called *The Evolution of Everything*, so I could avoid anachronisms and embarrassing mistakes. It would have to be a slender volume, so I could sling it along easily on my travels."

"Anachronism?" Gerta repeated the unfamiliar word with care.

"That's referring to things before they've been invented. Like suggesting that we take the train to your father's realm. The Venice-Simplon Orient Express will be a pretty nifty way to get through these mountains, although really, it will go under them. An engineering marvel and a damn fine way to travel. Beats all this tromping around in the snow, hands down."

"You speak madness. There is no other way to get across this pass. Even a horse must be led. And no man travels under the mountains."

"Well, that's my point. This isn't the *time* for the Orient Express, though it's the *place*, or pretty close to it. So, talking about it or even better, taking it, would be anachronistic. I'm good on the big stuff, but every so often something small trips me up. You don't have forks, for example."

"I do not know this word *forks*."

"They're eating implements, like a little spear. Really good for snagging a piece of meat from the stew without getting gravy on your fingers."

Gerta frowned. "My fingers have always sufficed."

"To each his own. The point is that I know better than to ask you for a fork. It'll be Renaissance Italy before anyone has one. The big stuff is easy—salt, for example, is a given, any time in Europe after the Romans."

Gerta's belly growled. "You could cease to speak of food and much associated with it. It would make the journey pass more amiably."

"Hungry, are you?"

"Are you not?"

"There are a few advantages to not being wrought of flesh. Not many, but that's one of them. Never hungry. Never have any results of having eaten, if you know what I mean. That basic biology stuff has nothing to do with me, and that's pretty much okay by me." He heaved a breath. "Sex, now, there's some biology that could work for me. Do you realize what a problem it is to have lust but not have any outlet for it?"

"Nay." Gerta spoke crisply, speeding her steps at this awkward topic of conversation. "Tell me your name."

"Let me finish my point. It's the subtle stuff that trips me up. Like sex. What do people think about sex in these times? What's appropriate? Do you even kiss? Cunnilingus or fellatio or neither or both? It's all so complicated and so easy to screw up—pun intended— inadvertently." He sighed. "And usually, sex is a closed subject, a little socially taboo topic, so it's not as if I can just ask anyone."

"Your name," Gerta insisted, impatient with his meaningless chatter. "What is your name?"

"How about Loki? You could call me Loki."

Gerta halted and stared in his direction. "This is your name? You are named for the Norse god of mischief?"

"I've been called that, that's for sure."

Gerta shook her head in astonishment. "But that is audacious beyond belief. It is blasphemy to call a pers—*someone*—anyone after a god."

"Happens all the time."

"But Loki is not a god whose wrath I would invite with such a jest. He was . . ."

"What?"

"Unpredictable." Gerta deliberately chose a less potent description than "evil."

Her companion chuckled, the sound coming from everywhere and nowhere. "Trust me, Gerta babe, Loki won't take offense. We've got an old connection. I think it's a good name to use here and now. Kind of ties in with the whole Dark Ages motif." He nodded, seeming to assess it. "It's working for me."

"You speak nonsense again," Gerta said with some exhaustion and began to trudge onward.

"You look tired." He sounded sympathetic, which Gerta distrusted.

"This despite my not having carried a woman of one forty or one fifty."

He laughed. "Tell you what, Gerta, here's a little bonus for you. A frequent-traveler upgrade, so to speak."

Gerta ignored him. She was too tired to jest and felt the cold too keenly to find him amusing. Her fingertips were chilled, her toes were cold, and the snow was deeper than her knees with ice beneath it.

She made slow progress through the pass. Worse, it was starting to snow. She wondered whether she truly could walk all the way to the woodcutter's hut without rest. To sleep in this cold would be treacherous, for she might never awaken. A sharp fear lent new vigor to her steps.

"You're gonna like this one, Gerta. You see, just around that corner up there is a little hut."

"There is not."

"Oh, it's there. It's off the path a bit, kind of cleverly disguised. It's not really four-star accommodation—no in-room mini-bar, for example, or room service, more's the pity—but it's *there*. And as an extra bonus, a limited-time offer, the murderous bandits who lived there are gone, scared off by the lack of business. They did leave behind some dried meat."

Saliva gathered in Gerta's mouth. "You lie. Loki lied all the time and if you are his namesake, then you must lie, too."

"Not this time. Remember that Loki lied when it was useful to lie and he told the truth when that was useful, too."

"Loki used others for his own purposes."

He smiled with dangerous charm. "And you wonder how I got this nickname."

"Show me this hut. Prove to me that you do not lie this time."

"There's a small catch."

Gerta regarded him with narrowed eyes.

"A toll, if you will."

"I knew there would be a trick. Loki was a trickster."

"Well, you can guess my price."

"I will not lie with you."

He laughed merrily. "You've got to love smart women! I'll settle for a kiss, Gerta babe, just one smackeroo. What do you say?"

Gerta clenched her teeth for they threatened to chatter. The snow was falling thickly and the sky was darkening. She heard a distant howl that might have been of a wolf. Loki watched her, eyes aglitter, smiling with a confidence that made her long to trick him in turn.

"One kiss," she said, holding up her finger. "*If* you do not lie."

His smile flashed. He darted ahead of her. She was hard-pressed to keep up to him, but then, she supposed he was motivated as she was not.

But when she stood before the hut in truth, Gerta nigh fell to her knees in gratitude. It was here, it was solid, and it was so well hidden that she would have walked directly past it. There was even a piece of dried meat hanging within it, and wood for a fire.

"You did not lie."

"Not this time."

Gerta met the anticipatory gleam in his eyes and felt a tingle within herself. Loki had earned his kiss, and she was not fool enough to deny him his due.

Four

LOKI WAS POSITIVELY GLEEFUL. HE HOV-
ered close as she kindled a fire, blew in her ear as she ate
some of the meat. Fingertips tickled the back of her
neck, the occasional kiss landed like a butterfly upon
her flesh while she felt the cold's grip upon her ease. He
did not leave her be and Gerta knew why: she was
delaying the embrace she owed him and he clearly knew
as much.

Yet he was content to merely tease her. Sigismund
would have cast her to her back already and forced her
to surrender, had he had such justification.

Gerta slanted a glance in Loki's direction, noting
how his eyes shone. Her lips burned in recollection of
his kiss, and she realized that he had not assaulted her:
even when he stole that kiss, he had coaxed her to join
him in the pursuit of pleasure.

"You do not simply seize what you believe to be your
due," she said, appreciating the difference between him
and Sigismund.

"Please," he said, holding a hand over his heart. "I'm not a barbarian." His gaze flicked over her and his smile turned rueful. "Not that there's anything wrong with that."

Gerta poked at the fire, coaxing the flames to burn higher. Smoke unfurled, filling the hut before it found the hole in the roof. "Do you know what occurred in Gundobad's hall?"

"Let's assume that I don't." Gentle fingertips trailed across the back of Gerta's neck, sending a pleasurable tingle over her flesh.

She shoved to her feet and paced. "When the Cath Palug came to my father's realm and proved that it could not be dislodged, we were forced to flee our home. The lands were laid waste; many men had died; the people were dispirited. My father turned to Gundobad, King of Burgundy, because he had once saved Gundobad's life in battle, and so Gundobad owed my father a boon. He agreed to accommodate us, in recognition of that debt." Gerta shuddered. "My father had only fought with Gundobad. He did not know that the man was mad."

Loki watched her closely and she was aware of the heat of his proximity. She strove to not look at his lips.

"Gundobad inherited his throne from his father and was to share authority with his three brothers. He has already murdered his brother Chilperic and drowned Chilperic's wife by tying a stone around her neck. It was whispered that she was witness to her husband's death and Gundobad feared her accusation."

"Murdering your in-laws. Nice crowd you're hanging with."

"We learned this after our arrival, but had no place else to go. No one dares defy Gundobad. His other two brothers might as well be serfs for the fawning obedience they show him."

"They're afraid."

"They are wise to be afraid. My father, too, is afraid of Gundobad, for we are securely within his power."

"Yet you defied him, didn't you? I'm thinking that barred door to your chamber wasn't part of the plan."

His gaze was too bright, too perceptive. Gerta swallowed and looked at the floor. "Three days ago, Gundobad declared that my father and I were in his debt, that any boon he owed my father was well paid."

"I'll guess that he made a specific demand to pay that debt."

"Me." Gerta lifted her chin. "He decreed that I should wed his son, Sigismund."

"Daddy's boy?"

"Sigismund desires whatsoever he sees, and he has no compunction about using violence to possess what he desires."

"Your father did not decline?"

"He dares not defy his host." Gerta swallowed, for what she had to confess was an error on her part. "But I could not tie myself to Sigismund. I could not surrender myself to violence, and sacrifice my gift as well. And so, in my desperation, I did what I had been taught never to do: I used my mirror against its purpose. I tried to summon aid. I sent the call to which Cai responded." She met Loki's gaze steadily. "And in so doing, I summoned the ice, though I never meant to do so, and thus, I summoned you."

"No." Loki shook his head. "News flash, Gerta babe: nobody summons me. They can invoke and I will hear, but I'm no dog that comes every time it's called. Self-determination would be my banner. If I answer, it's because I choose to do so."

"Then why did you come to me?"

He smiled, a smile so filled with intimacy and affection that Gerta felt herself blushing. "Here's a little secret, just between you and me: I usually only come because there's a good deal to be made."

"What manner of deal?"

"One to my advantage, of course." He winked. "Or maybe I came because you needed me. You're kind of cute, in an uptight virginal barbarian way."

"Is this a lie, Loki? Is this a tale to serve your ends?"

His smile broadened. "Not all of it." His gaze fell to her lips, and she felt the heat of his glance as surely as a touch. Her fingertips rose to her own mouth and his eyes brightened.

"I owe you a kiss," she whispered, barely recognizing her own voice so breathless was she.

He nodded, but made no move to come closer. "I'm waiting."

He waited. That was all the encouragement she needed to pay the debt to which she had agreed. Gerta hesitated only a heartbeat before she stretched out her hand. Her fingers passed through him the first time, chilling as they did so, but Loki shook his head.

"Remember how you use the mirror," he advised softly.

Gerta understood. She closed her eyes. There was a way of thinking, a focus that was yet unfocused, which she had learned in order to use her mirror. She let her mind slip, let the smell of wood smoke and the taste of dried meat and the heat of the cabin fade away, let the vision of Loki form in her thoughts.

Then she reached. She smiled when she felt his chin. His jaw had a strong line. His skin felt smooth though she could discern the faint prickle of whiskers. She let her hand slide up to his ear, his throat, the thick ebony waves of his hair. She trailed her fingertips across his brow, felt his dark eyebrows beneath her fingers, traced the line of his nose.

He watched her, eyes brightening when her fingertips came to rest upon his lips. They were firm, curved in a slight but confident smile. She let her fingers move back and forth, caressing him, learning the shape of him.

And he permitted this. Gerta dared to open her eyes, to look into his, and felt that she looked into the depths of the night sky. His eyes were an indigo so dark that they might have been black of hue, and they were filled with stars. The longer she looked, the more dizzy she felt.

More bold than ever she had been, Gerta eased to her toes and replaced her questing fingertips with her lips. She tasted Loki's gasp, she let her hands fall to cup his jaw, and she leaned into his kiss. She opened herself to him, for she owed him no less, and was stunned by the wave of pleasure that claimed her.

To her astonishment, he guided her gently, angling his head, lifting one hand, cajoling her response with his tongue. She understood intuitively that she was being tutored, and she followed his lead, echoing his every gesture and feeling her ardor rise with each caress.

She was trembling when she stepped away, and she did not know how much time had passed. Her lips were swollen and softened, a knot within her had been loosed. The fire had burned down a bit, though the flame in Loki's eyes shone brighter than ever. He was more substantial, as well, and it was more difficult to look through him.

He exhaled mightily and shoved a hand through his hair as he whistled. "You're one quick study, Gerta," he teased then winked.

Gerta flushed crimson and turned to tend the fire, unable to keep herself from smiling as Loki laughed. She saw him flexing from the periphery of her vision, watched him stretch his wings out to their full dimension with a kind of joy.

"Why do you gain so much power from a caress?" she asked.

He turned to her, surprise in his expression. "Because there's a big power in lust, in desire and sex. Some cultures celebrate that; others suppress it. There's a potency in your caress, in everyone's passion. I've taken it upon myself to teach you how to harness it, how to direct it, how to wield it like the weapon it is."

"Why?"

He grinned. "You'll see."

And he would admit no more than that.

Gerta is dreaming.

Gerta stands in her father's court. She knows what will happen, for she has had this dream nightly for five years. She stirs in her sleep, fights against the dream, knows that she will lose.

The dream always triumphs, and so it does this time.

Her father, regal in his vestments, adorned with his crown and surrounded by his courtiers, looks tired. He faces a dire challenge to his suzerainty, and he is losing. The most stalwart warriors in his company have already been conquered by the Cath Palug, and on this day, he has called for all the people who answer to him to gather, to hear his edict.

Gerta stands with Isold, her mentor and friend, and feels Isold's agitation. Isold has seen something in her mirror, though she will not speak of it, no matter how Gerta pleads with her. Gerta feels caught up in a tide of events that she is powerless to halt.

Her father raises his hands for silence. "I have decided, upon consultation with my counsellors, that the Cath Palug is the work of a sorcerer."

Isold straightens and Gerta knows that she has not been consulted. Perhaps she is insulted.

"And the person best equipped to defeat the curse of a sorcerer is not a warrior, as we have witnessed in the loss of our finest and most valiant men. It is another sorcerer." A murmur passes through the company and Gerta's father turns his gaze upon her. She starts, fearful of what he will decree, knowing that she is not ready for such a challenge. "Or a sorceress. Isold, I command you to undertake this task."

Chatter erupts in the chamber, though Isold stands straight and unsurprised. Was this what she envisioned? She steps forward and bows low. "With respect, my lord, I may not succeed in this task. I would not have your court be left without a seer."

"Without a kingdom, I have no need of a seer." At the company's evident dismay, Gerta's father softens his pronouncement. "And there is always my daughter, after all."

"Your daughter's education is incomplete," Isold says with a firmness Gerta is certain her father does not expect of a minion, even a gifted one. "Who will tutor her if I do not return?"

"This is not a question for you to ponder," the king says sternly. "It is your duty as one sworn to me to welcome any command I make of you."

"All know that seers answer to a different code," Isold says with resolve. She turns to Gerta, her gaze hard. "I swore to teach you all I know and the measure is far short of fulfillment. Do you, Gerta, release me from our sworn agreement?"

The entire company turns to Gerta, their manner expectant. Some are hopeful, some are condemning, most are fearful for the ravaging attacks of the Cath Palug have struck terror into their hearts. Gerta sees only the fierce green of Isold's eyes and knows this to be a test, knows that she is not ready to *make such a choice. She shakes her head slightly in confusion, that gesture drawing her father's ire.*

"Gerta! Do not defy my will in this!"

She bows her head, steps away from Isold and lifts her hands high. "I absolve you of your vow," she says in haste, as if the words must be said quickly or not at all.

The company murmurs approval, her father makes a grunt of satisfaction, but Isold's gaze is unswerving. Her steady regard feeds Gerta's certainty that she has erred.

"So be it," Isold says abruptly and turns away. She marches directly out of the hall, and Gerta watches her go in silence, knowing that she will never see her beloved mentor alive again, knowing that she has held the power to save Isold in her own hands yet chosen not to wield it.

Gerta awakened with a cry, her palms sweating and her heart racing. She sat up, shivering, and wrapped her arms around herself, willing the shards of her dream to leave her.

"Guilty conscience?" To her astonishment, Loki was stretched out beside her, not a handspan between them. She could feel his heat and for a treacherous moment considered the merit of being consoled.

Then she moved away from him, stumbling toward the dying embers of the fire to stir them to life. Isold, she had betrayed Isold. Had she similarly betrayed Cai with her summons?

Aware of Loki's amused glance and suspecting that he knew of her dream, Gerta went outside to relieve herself. She forced her way to a place where she could not be seen from the cabin and shivered as she lifted her skirts. The cold nipped at her bare skin, urging her to hasten. She watched the snowflakes falling and was amazed by their size: they were as big as the end of her thumb. No wonder so much snow had gathered during the night. She tipped her head back and studied the pale hue of the sky. Snowflakes swirled downward from the pewter sky in hordes that had no end.

There would be no sun on this day. She would have thought it too cold to snow, but clearly she was mistaken. Newly aware of their predicament, Gerta returned to the hut in haste. "It is cursed cold this morning, colder than last night."

"You could kindle a fire here. There is still a bit of wood."

"Nay. It is snowing with vigor. We must descend from the pass as quickly as we can, lest we are trapped here." Gerta seized her pack even as she spoke.

"Does that happen?"

Gerta shook her head. "I have never seen snow like this in the pass, even in winter. And it falls at relentless speed."

"Almost as if someone or something meant to trap you in the pass."

Gerta looked up in surprise. She thought suddenly of the woman's face in her mirror and itched to look into the bronze disc again. She sensed that her companion would not approve and stilled her impulse, even though it was scarcely his place to dictate her use of her own mirror. "Who is this Snow Queen? From whence did she come?"

"Well, that's a tough one. She's been around for a while, that's for sure, almost as long as me."

Gerta slung her pack onto her back and tightened her belt around her cloak. "Then you can tell me what you know while we walk. Once through the pass, we will head for the abode of a woodcutter. He lives on the edge of my father's realm but has always been kind to me. I am certain that he will see me fed and both of us kept in warmth this night." Gerta sighed and frowned. "I had hoped to make his hut by midday but it will take longer in this storm."

"Then tomorrow will be a long day, with a fight at the end of it."

"There is naught for it."

Loki smiled, as if tempting her to consider other options, then unfurled his wings. They touched the roof of the hut, spanned its width, and were not fully extended.

"It is not so distant from here. Could you fly us in haste?"

"Altitude," he said with a shake of his head. "The air is thinner at altitude and gives less lift. It's heavy work to fly over mountains."

The gleam in his eyes left little doubt of what precise deed he would require to have sufficient strength. An answering heat raged within Gerta, but she denied it.

"Impossible, and you know it well. We walk." Gerta glanced about herself, ensuring that the cabin was as she had found it. She packed the rest of the dried meat, then opened the door. An icy wind swirled around her ankles as she fastened the latch on the door, but she leaned into the wind and strode into the storm.

She glanced back after a dozen steps and could not even discern the outline of the hut any longer. She schooled her panic, knowing it would not serve her well, and strode onward. She could feel her companion's presence, just behind her left shoulder, and curiously, though he was often an irritant, she was glad to know he was there.

"THE SNOW QUEEN, NOW," LOKI MUSED, HIS VOICE so close by Gerta's ear that he might have been sitting on her shoulder. "Well, there's a lot of speculation as to where she originates, but let's go with the Norse theology, as that's most familiar to you."

"There is no goddess of winter in that pantheon."

"Not a goddess but a patroness. There was a giantess named Skadi, a real beauty, a huntress who favored winter. In fact, she was said to be in command of winter, for she preferred it and ensured its grasp upon the land."

"But perpetual winter would mean death to the people."

"Nobody said she was a fun date. Death was her provenance, as well. She was a keeper of dark secrets—a sorceress, if you will—and keeper of men's souls. Now, her father was killed by the gods and so she came to them in a fury, seeking reparation in the death of a god. Loki"—he coughed lightly—"charmed her into making a deal that was less onerous to the gods."

"So you are named fairly as one who seeks to turn matters to your own advantage."

He ignored that, though Gerta had not expected otherwise.

"Skadi was persuaded to marry a god instead of see one killed, but she was given the chance to choose which one. I seem to remember things getting pretty wild and a lot of mead being drunk in the pursuit of Skadi's smile, but at any rate, she did finally smile and further she agreed to pick a partner by his feet."

"His feet?"

"You see, she thought she was clever. She was attracted to Balder, most handsome of the gods, and was certain she could identify him by his feet and thus get herself a handsome god of a husband."

"But Loki killed Balder. Did that occur before or after?"

"Uh, before, so Balder wasn't there. Skadi didn't realize that, so she picked and it turned out that she chose Njord."

"God of the sea."

"And he was one happy camper, let me tell you, because he needed a wife and Skadi was one hot piece of business. Skadi was less impressed and blamed Loki for her situation. We got them a bit drunk and kept them happy and things seemed to begin on the right foot, so to speak."

Gerta noted that Loki seemed to find this amusing, though she could not see the jest. He seemed also to be confused as to whether he had actually been present at the festivities—instead of the actual god—but she supposed that was the god Loki's vengeance for the frivolous application of his name.

"Ultimately, Njord took his wife back to his home, which was on the coast. While she was there and while he coaxed her smile, winter retreated from the land—it's that heat we make in bed, that power I was telling you about. This seemed pretty much peachy, but Skadi couldn't stand the sound of the gulls. The constant breaking of waves drove her crazy, and she insisted that she couldn't sleep. So, the happy couple went back to her father's home, which was in the mountains and completely snowbound."

"And winter touched the land again."

"Right. But there, Njord couldn't sleep because of the howling

wolves and the whistle of the wind through the pine trees. He needed
water to be happy, being a god of the sea and all, and was as restless as
his wife was happy."

"I will guess that they made an arrangement."

"They did: nine months in her home, three in his—that tells you
something about how badly Njord had it for her. And the Norse got
nine months of winter and three of summer as a result of that deal,
the divine rhythm being echoed in the world we know and love. The
marriage didn't work out in the end, though—irreconcilable differences, you know—but the cycle of the year stuck even after Njord
went back to the sea full-time."

"And Skadi?"

"Well, I guess she needed a hobby because that's when she started
collecting souls. They're a hot commodity in the divine realm, you
know. Collect the complete set, and all that."

"I did not know."

"And really, appropriating souls gives her a longevity she wouldn't
have otherwise." He mused, seeking a comparison. "Like rainwater
filling a barrel over and over again."

Gerta understood, though there was little she could say. She began
to doubt herself as the snow rose higher and higher. How could she
defeat an opponent who had devoured souls and assumed their power
for so many aeons?

GERTA STUMBLED OUT OF THE PASS MUCH, MUCH
later that day. The snow had risen as high as her waist and it had been
an ordeal to continue to push through it. She could not feel her toes,
or her fingertips, and the end of her nose and her earlobes were so
cold that she feared they would shatter if she touched them. But she
seized the familiar outcropping of rock that marked the end of the
pass and pulled herself past it.

She stood in her father's kingdom, her breath leaving clouds in the
bitter cold, and shook with relief. The snow was still falling, but it

had been blown from this side of the pass. The mountainside was slick with ice, ice that had been polished to a sheen by the wind, and Gerta was too tired to fight against it.

Truly, there was no need to do so. She sat down on the ice and began to slide on her buttocks, letting the downward slope of the mountain labor in her favor. She crossed her legs, pulling the back of her robe over her knees. With her pack in her lap and her head bent low, she slid ever faster down the mountainside.

The wind snapped at her hair and loosed her braid, tearing her hood back with icy fingers. Pellets of snow stung her face and drove themselves down the neck of her robe. They stung the backs of her hands, but Gerta did not care.

She could see the woodcutter's hut before her, a shadow among pine trees, a welcome haven after her efforts of this day. She knew that the fire would be raging, that there would be a pot of soup or stew hanging over the flames, and that Egan would welcome her with a bellow of joy.

Indeed, she could think of a little else in her anticipation.

But there was no thread of smoke rising from Egan's hut, which was a marvel in this weather. Gerta dug in her heels and slowly eased herself to a stop. The ice had formed in swirls around the trunks of the pine trees and with her last bit of speed, she was flung into one of those swirls. She came to a halt before the woodcutter's door with such a graceful flourish that the storm might have deposited her there apurpose.

Gerta thought about the woman's face in her mirror, then pushed such whimsy from her thoughts. It was coincidence, no more.

She spied the silhouette of Egan himself, a great bear of a man dressed in furs, on the far side of the hut and her heart soared. He had not turned to greet her, but truly, her arrival had made little noise.

"Egan!" she cried, struggling to her feet.

He did not answer, did not so much as move.

He must not have heard her.

Gerta hastened toward him. "Egan! I would beg your hospitality this night, if you would be so kind to an old friend."

Still he said naught. Still he did not turn. A shadow of dread touched Gerta's heart. She seized his arm and he did not jump.

"Egan!" She shook him, but he was still and immobile. His face was yet averted, so Gerta stepped around him, though she gasped when she looked upon him fully.

There was ice in his moustache and beard, ice even across his cheeks and nose. His eyes were open, staring, his lashes frozen into tiny icicles. He did not blink. He did not breathe.

"He is frozen!" Gerta said, taking a step back.

"Like a Popsicle," Loki agreed. "Guess we'll just make ourselves at home."

Gerta stared at Egan, knowing something was amiss. She had seen men who had died in winter's embrace, for men lost in storms and recovered later were oft brought to her, in case they could be healed. They were always dead beyond doubt, their flesh a curious cold hue. But Egan did not look dead. He looked alive, if encased in ice.

He was enchanted. She knew this with sudden clarity and guessed what she must do.

"We must take him with us, into the hut," she said with authority. "We must thaw him."

"Oh, that's a really bad idea."

"It is the only deed that can be done! He is bewitched, it is clear!"

"Are you sure you want to go there?"

"I can do naught else! Egan has been an ally to my father. I cannot abandon him like this."

Her companion sighed with forbearance. "One of these days, Gerta babe, you're going to learn to take my advice."

"I am never deaf to sound counsel, but I must think of others beyond myself."

"Well, don't blame me for the results." Loki sat on the woodcutter's stump, clearly unwilling to lend any aid.

"You are heartless," she informed him. "To not assist another just

because there is no immediate advantage to you is reprehensible."
Loki examined his fingers with apparent fascination.

Gerta exhaled in frustration, then bent to her task. She pushed
and shoved at Egan, but his feet were frozen to the ground. It would
have been easier to move a tree.

After some effort, she discovered the sledge that he used to bring
wood back to his hut and his axe. She positioned the sledge behind
him, then hacked at the ice that bound his boots to the ground. It was
heavy labor and she was already exhausted.

Loki whistled tunelessly. Gerta cursed him soundly and he blew
her an impertinent kiss. Her hair fell into her eyes and the cold
nipped at her, but Gerta persevered.

Finally Egan fell, toppling like a great tree onto the sledge. She
had to scramble to make certain that he did not roll off it. She caught
her breath for only a moment before hauling him toward the hut.

"You could be of some assistance."

"Do you really want me to waste my power on something so
pointless?" Loki straightened. "Now if you were interested in bolster-
ing my power, I could afford to expend an increment here and now."

Gerta hauled on the sledge again. "Nay!"

"The thing is that chastity offers a simple kind of power, but it's
power that comes from denial, from negating the fullness of what you
can be," Loki mused. "Potency, sexual or otherwise, comes from the
positive side of the coin, from not just the awareness of what is possible but of doing it. And you know, if you believe as much, then nothing is impossible."

"Eternal life is impossible."

"Babe, you're in the presence of Exhibit Number One."

"You dream."

"It's not an exclusive club, you know. You could be immortal, too."

"I cannot!"

"Not as long as you believe you can't be. That's how it works.
Whether you believe you can do something or you can't, you'll be
right. Neat trick, isn't it?"

Gerta refrained from comment. She reached the door of the hut, panting from her efforts, then hauled the entire sledge inside. Egan stared unblinkingly at the roof and Gerta shivered at the sight of him.

She set to kindling a fire and soon had a blaze on the hearth. She held her own hands out toward the flames and halfway feared that they would melt rather than revert to their former warmth.

When she looked again, Egan was beginning to drip upon the floor. Gerta knelt by his side, wiping away the ice from his face as it melted. His flesh was cold, but she fancied she could feel his pulse in his neck. She pulled the sledge closer to the fire. Within moments, his cheeks looked more ruddy, though it could have been a reflection from the flames.

Gerta's belly growled and she turned to seek something to eat in his simple stores. There was some smoked pork and a few root vegetables so shriveled that Gerta was not completely certain what they were—or what they had been. She found an onion and was encouraged that they might eat well this night. She took Egan's cauldron outside and packed clean snow into it, then lugged it back into the cabin, intending to hang it over the fire.

She had only just crossed the threshold when Loki yelled a warning.

Five

"LOOK OUT!"

Gerta spun at Loki's cry and found Egan standing before her. She had an instant to marvel that he was revived, before she noticed his unnaturally wide stare.

Then she glimpsed the flash of a descending blow.

Gerta cried out and leapt backward. The axe blade missed her by the barest increment.

"But Egan, but what . . ." she managed to stammer before he came after her, swinging again. She dropped the cauldron and held up her hands, the blade slashing across her palms so that she cried out in pain.

"Egan!" she screamed, but he brandished his axe again. The blade flashed and Gerta ran.

She darted behind one tree and another, horrified by how Egan followed her. He swung his axe over and over again, whenever she was within striking range. He wielded the heavy tool as if it weighed naught at all, so accustomed was he to it.

But there was something amiss. Egan moved at a strangely slow speed, as if against his will. He did not falter but neither did he move more quickly. His features were expressionless, his stare blank. Gerta did not understand what had befallen him but she instinctively knew one truth: Egan would only halt when he killed her.

Unless she killed him first.

Horrified at the prospect, Gerta knew that she had to do something soon lest she be slaughtered. She leapt behind one pine and Egan swung his axe so hard that it was nearly buried in the trunk. The tree shuddered beneath the force of his blow.

That gave Gerta an idea.

"You will never catch me, Egan," she said with a confidence she did not feel. "You move too slowly, it is clear."

There was no anger in his expression, though he followed her. She taunted him, drawing his blows and ducking out of range in the last moment, until she led him to the largest tree.

Gerta held her ground as he raised the axe blade. She stood stalwart as the axe began to descend. She did not move one step as the blade sliced through the air, directly toward her neck.

And just before the blade kissed her skin, she jerked backward. The axe blade whistled past her and buried itself in the trunk of the tree. Egan tugged at it but the force of his blow had been too considerable. He was so determined to retrieve his axe that he seemed to have forgotten Gerta.

Gerta raced back to the cauldron she had dropped. To her relief, when she turned, Egan still fought to free the axe. She crept up behind the woodcutter, hating what she had to do, then swung the iron pot at the back of his head.

He tumbled like a felled tree, and Gerta hit him again in her terror. He twitched and Gerta hit him again and again. It was only when he fell still, when the blood flowed from his wound, that she dared to cease.

Gerta circled Egan's fallen body, panting at the travesty of what she had done, her heart still racing. Her tears welled that she should have to injure a man who had been so good to her. Confusion and exhaustion made it impossible to halt her tears once they had arisen.

"What did I do?" she whispered, as her first tear loosed itself.

A hand shoved her suddenly from behind and she fell, sprawling across the inert woodcutter. Gerta shouted in dismay and struggled, but still her tears fell upon Egan's face.

There was a strange sizzle emitted from the point where the tear touched his face.

Gerta frowned. "What have I done?"

"Another!" Loki insisted, for it was he who had shoved her. "Shed another tear!"

"I do not understand . . ." Gerta made to rise, not liking whatever force ruled these events.

She did not make it to her knees.

"Listen to me for once, Gerta!" Loki raged, infuriated as she had never seen him. "Weep! You must *weep*. It is all that can save him!"

When Gerta stared at Loki without comprehension, he swore, then slapped her face so hard that she gasped. Gerta's tears sprang forth again, a trio of them falling upon Egan's face. Again, there was that odd sizzle, as if something melted beneath them.

"More!" Loki made a growl of frustration. "People think saliva is the universal solvent but, really, it's human tears. You're compassionate, Gerta, use it!" He took a ragged breath. "Think about ol' Egan here and what's happened to him. Think about his fate without a soul. Think of how he must be suffering—and weep for him!"

Gerta surrendered her mingled grief and confusion. The tears fell across Egan's face, until finally a shudder slipped through his body. The hue of his skin changed then, turning gray as Gerta knew dead men should be.

Her last tears made no sound when they fell upon his flesh. Loki bent past her. He pulled Egan's eyelid back, and there, nestled in the socket, was a long sliver of black glass.

"Ice," Gerta whispered, remembering his tale all too well.

"Ice," he agreed. Gerta made to take it, for she was curious, but Loki snatched it away. "I'll take charge of this," he said and she could not see where he secreted it. He then closed Egan's eyes with care.

"He looks peaceful now."

"He is at peace now." Loki looked around them with narrowed eyes. "You can sleep now, Gerta. You'll be safe here tonight."

"Even from you?"

He spared her that wicked grin. "I only take what's offered. You should know that by now." He winked. "But if you're offering . . ."

Gerta looked at Egan, her thoughts churning. "Is this what has happened to Cai?" she asked and saw the answer in Loki's abrupt solemnity.

Before he could answer, feminine laughter sounded across the snow-covered field. The sound rang out from the pack Gerta had dropped. It was the woman in Gerta's mirror, her laughter loud and cruel and yet ringing like a thousand silver bells. Gerta stared at her pack in horror, recognizing that distinctive laugh.

The woman in the mirror was Isold.

"You looked!" Loki said with disgust, clearly not understanding the full reason for Gerta's dismay. "Didn't I tell you that the mirror could be used against you? Did you listen? Nooooo, of course not, it's too easy to heed my counsel and make our lives simple. Nooooo, you had to show yourself to her, so that she would know we were coming." He bent, eyes gleaming, and she felt him seize her shoulder. "One thing, Gerta, one small detail that will shape everything. Maybe you could stir yourself to remember."

"What?"

"Did you tell her about me?"

"We did not speak."

"Were you *thinking* of me? Were you aware of me in any way? Was there a shadow of my presence in your thoughts? Because if you did"—he sighed and shook his head—"then the gig is up, girl."

Gerta did not know. She shook her head, unable to give him the response he clearly desired with any conviction. He released her shoulder and turned away from her, his disappointment in her clear.

"What will she do to Cai?"

Loki barely glanced back. "He has ice in his heart and his eye. You work it out."

Gerta looked at Egan, a humble woodcutter possessed of no magical powers who had nearly killed her. She saw now that the winters had been harsh for him, that he had lost weight and that his face was more deeply lined than she recalled. She touched him, whispered a blessing, then stood on unsteady legs.

There was a lump in her throat at what she had to do to right her own error in summoning Cai but a resolve in her heart beyond anything she had ever known. Loki paced, impatient and displeased, and perhaps not in the best mood to hear any offer from her.

Gerta took a deep breath, for she knew what she had to do. "I will surrender my chastity to you this night," she said, watching Loki turn to face her in his astonishment. "If you will fly us to the Cath Palug's cave in the morning."

There was a glint in his dark eyes. "Out of uncontrollable passion for me?"

Gerta shook her head, unable to lie.

"You're doing this for Cai. A guy could be insulted by that, you know."

"I would do this to right the error I have made. It is often necessary to surrender something precious to oneself to make reparation for the damage one has done."

He sobered. "To earn redemption."

Gerta shrugged, not truly caring about such details. Their gazes locked and held for a long moment, and she feared in his silence that he meant to deny her. He was so changeable, so incomprehensible, that she was suddenly aware that she could not predict his choices.

Then, Loki strode toward her with a confident swagger and cast his arm across her shoulders, guiding her back toward the hut. "We're on the same page, Gerta, don't worry about it. And lucky girl, I'm going to make this worth your while. See, I've had a bit of practice despoiling maidens." He winked. "You're going to like this."

But Gerta was not so certain. Her chastity would be surrendered, surrendered much sooner than she might have hoped and surrendered to a being she would never truly understand.

She did not need her mirror to fear that portent.

GERTA AWAKENED TO FIND HERSELF ALONE IN Egan's hut. Embers glowed on the hearth, and she lay on the hard straw pallet for a moment, savoring the warmth both outside and inside of her. She had the sense of forgetting a dream upon awakening, for she could not precisely recall meeting Loki abed: each whisper of recollection that she pursued, thinking it would lead to a fuller memory, slipped from her grasp and disappeared.

She did feel curiously replete. There was a thrum within her, a new potency that she had not known in herself before. Yet all the same, it was a part of her, and hers to command.

She was more glad to be alive than ever she had been.

She rolled over and saw that Loki had brought Egan into the hut. The old woodcutter lay upon his own pallet, his features composed as if he slept. It was better thus, for no animals would despoil his corpse before he could be buried properly.

Gerta rose to seek Loki, a new spring in her step. She opened the door of the hut and halted in amazement. He stood not a dozen paces away, stretching his great black wings as he had the previous morning.

On this day, however, he was so radiant that she was nigh blinded. He shone, as if lit from within by some dark fire, a light wrought of shadow but impossible to look upon fully all the same. He turned, perhaps at the sound of the door, and smiled. Gerta had to avert her gaze from his brilliance.

"Loki, I do not remember what occurred last night. Is this some kind of sorcery?"

He laughed, a triumphant sound that filled her ears. "It's a gift, Gerta, a little prezzie from me to you. I think you'll be happier not knowing exactly what you've done." She dared to glance at his face and he blew her a cocksure kiss. "You can thank me later, babe."

He savored her discomfiture for only a moment before he stretched again, his massive wings casting a shadow across the white, white snow. It seemed to Gerta that he was twice the size he had been before. Once again, she had the sense that she had summoned forces far beyond her understanding and control, though this time she said as much.

"Loki, I am afraid."

"Sensible reaction, I'd say."

"Loki, do not jest. I fear that going to the cave of the Cath Palug is an error, that we will only make matters worse for Cai."

"You think there's worse than what happened to Egan?"

There was truth in that. Gerta bit her lip. She studied her toe and spoke her thoughts with care. "If Skadi consumes souls and takes their power for her own, how can I ever hope to defeat her? I have not even finished my apprenticeship."

"And . . .?"

She looked up. "What do you mean?"

"And there's something you're not telling me. Cough it up."

Gerta took a deep breath, glad in a way to surrender this secret. "I saw the Snow Queen in my mirror. I looked to ensure that your stolen kiss had not claimed my gift and she was there. I could not name why she looked familiar, for she has changed much . . ."

"But you know her?" Loki did not seem to be surprised.

"She is Isold." Gerta glanced up but Loki did not react to this. "You must understand, Isold was my mentor. She knows far more than I do, for I never completed my study beneath her tutelage. And I did not stop my father from dispatching her to face the Cath Palug, even though I could have done so. She must hate me for what has happened to her."

Loki turned and came toward her. Gerta did not look up and still she had to squeeze her eyes closed for the glory of him burned her eyes. He touched her chin and she noticed immediately how much more substantial he was: he might have been wrought of flesh, so firm was the press of his hand against her face, might have been flesh if not for the slight sizzle that followed his moving caress.

Wrought of light, Gerta remembered, and felt awe.

"You forget your assets in this battle, Gerta," he said gently. "You have the greatest power of all, and you don't even count it."

"What is it?"

"You have purity and innocence of heart. I made you forget last night so that you would still have that in your arsenal." And he bent, against all expectation, and pressed a kiss to her brow. The imprint of his lips seared her flesh and continued to burn after he had stepped away.

"Climb on my back, Gerta," he invited as he crouched before her. "We're late, we're late, for a very important date." He cast her a grin, pleased by yet another jest that she did not understand. Gerta smiled in return, encouraged despite herself.

Then he took flight and she gasped aloud.

HER FATHER'S REALM WAS DESTROYED. GERTA'S HEART broke as she looked over Loki's shoulder and saw the damage to the land below.

"No place like home, huh?" he said and she shook her head.

"Nay, it was not like this. There were vineyards here, and orchards, and gardens outside every hut. The meadows were filled with blossoms and the streams were filled with jumping silver fish. There was abundance in my father's realm before the Cath Palug."

She shivered, Loki's rare silence persuading her that he did not believe her. "It has been five years since winter came to the land and still it has not left. Five years of winter. Look! Even the pine trees turn to brown, for only the larger ones are rooted deeply enough to survive."

"There are no buds on the tree branches."

"The fruit trees are dead. No spring can awaken them now."

"Nothing like the kiss of death," Loki said.

Sadness seized Gerta and she feared their quest was a futile one. Even if the Snow Queen was defeated, even if winter left this realm, would the trees ever break into leaf again?

"Please fasten your seat belts and return all chair backs and trays to the upright position," Loki said then, much to Gerta's confusion. He spared her a grin. "We're here."

She peered over Loki's shoulder in anticipation. The opening to the cave of the Cath Palug was surrounded by trees, curious trees that she did not remember.

Loki flew low and Gerta realized that it was a forest of men. They stood frozen, ice dripping from their helmets and their weapons. Horror was captured in their expressions and Gerta understood that they had been in the act of going to Cai's aid when they had been trapped.

"Cai's companions," Loki said grimly.

"Frozen like Popsicles," Gerta agreed, not understanding Loki's earlier words but recalling them. He laughed under his breath, as if surprised.

He landed gracefully before the opening of the cave, and Gerta imagined that she could smell the blood of hundreds of warriors from within its shadows. She shuddered, squared her shoulders, and glanced to Loki. He nodded, and they stepped into the cold darkness of the cave as one.

To Gerta's surprise, Loki shone like a black opal in the darkness, releasing a faint luminescence that lit their steps. There were bones scattered across the frozen ground, remnants of armor and weapons and men. Gerta's bile rose but she forced herself onward.

To Cai.

They found the Cath Palug not a dozen steps inside the portal, snoring. Gerta was reluctant to leave it alive behind them, but Loki beckoned, then continued into the yawning darkness beyond.

An abyss opened behind the cave, Gerta saw with astonishment.

They followed a path ever downward, a path that offered no choices of direction, then stepped into an enormous cavern. A mountain had been hollowed for this chamber, it was clear. It was so large that Gerta could not see its end in any direction.

The floor shone, like fine polished marble, and the roof was beyond Gerta's abilities to discern. Stalactites hung from that distant roof, Loki's light making their tips glisten in a familiar way.

"Ice," Gerta said softly.

"Got it in one," Loki agreed, his voice barely a breath. "That explains a lot." He knelt and touched the floor with one hand, reverence in his gesture. Gerta followed his move and saw that the floor shone like obsidian. It was cracked a thousand times in a thousand directions, shattered into millions of tiny shards.

And then she realized what it was. Loki ran a hand across its surface and she wondered whether he had expected to ever see his dark looking glass assembled into one piece again.

He lifted his head, then pointed across the ice. Far in the distance, Gerta could just discern a throne. It was massive, twisted in shape and high of back.

"That throne must be on the other side of this cavern!"

"It's in the middle," Loki said with conviction. "And it's made of skulls."

Before he could suggest their course, Gerta gasped aloud. She spied a man upon the ice beside the throne, a man who ran his hands ceaselessly over the surface of the mirror as if he could do naught else.

And she knew without doubt who he was. He would be tall and fair, and possess eyes of clearest green. So great was Gerta's relief to find Cai alive that she ran to him.

THERE WAS A LISTLESSNESS ABOUT CAI THAT GERTA could not reconcile with his earlier confidence. Her footsteps faltered when she noticed this. He traced cracks in the surface of the ice with a fingertip, then apparently forgot what he was doing and began again. Over and over again, he did this, driven by a compulsion Gerta could not name.

She framed his face in her hands and forced him to look at her. His gaze was vacant, his mouth slack. Gerta thought of the proud sorcerer who had confronted her in her mirror, thought of his surety, and found her horror rising at what he had become.

What a travesty that a man of such potency could be reduced to this! There was a mark upon his temple, a mark of silver filigree that resembled the imprint of a woman's lips. Gerta traced it with her fingertips and knew that the Snow Queen held him in thrall with a mere kiss.

Gerta instinctively touched her lips to the wound, and Cai shuddered at her caress. She understood then the purpose of Loki's instruction, understood with sudden frightening clarity. She kissed Cai before she could consider the wisdom of her course.

He did not resist her, nor did he respond to her touch. Gerta used every gesture Loki had taught her, poured all of her passion and hope and desire into her kiss. She understood that she could not have done this deed without Loki's tutelage, and still she feared she did not know enough to save Cai. She felt desperation, then, just before she gave him up for lost, Cai's lips moved slightly beneath her own.

Gerta gasped in joy. She deepened her caress with new fervor, feeling Cai's response increase with every heartbeat. She felt him thaw, felt the ice recede and knew a joy beyond any other. She kissed him, she offered him all she had to grant.

And so great was her relief that Gerta wept, wept a river of tears that flowed over Cai's upturned face.

"WELL-DONE," ISOLD SAID CRISPLY.

Her voice was at such close proximity that Gerta jumped in alarm. She broke her kiss and glanced over her shoulder, aware all the while of Cai's wonderment. She felt his gaze upon her, felt his fingertips touch her chin, but she dared not look to him yet.

She was still dizzy herself, and their woes had only begun.

Isold smiled, though there was no warmth in her expression. She appeared much older, her brows and hair seemingly touched by frost, but the steadiness of her gaze had not changed. "But then, you always were a dutiful pupil." She arched a brow. "If a faithless one."

Gerta was stung to silence by the reminder of her betrayal of her mentor. A waft of cold air assaulted Gerta as Isold swiftly leaned past her. With long fingertips, Isold pulled back Cai's eyelid, taking no care to be gentle. He winced as she claimed the shard of black ice from his eyelid. He moved slowly, like a man awakening from a deep sleep, too slowly to halt Isold's efficient gestures.

"Perfect!" she said when she claimed the shard of black ice from his eyelid. She reached beneath his hauberk, following the same course as the Cath Palug's claws, and extracted a second shard from his chest.

Cai took a shuddering breath and coughed. He shivered, seemingly to his very marrow, then looked around himself as if unaware of where he was. The filigree mark on his temple had turned an angry red. He quickened, even as Gerta watched, and the shrewdness she had witnessed previously returned to his gaze.

"Chaste little Gerta," Isold murmured. "Who could have imagined that a virgin could have stirred a man beneath my power?"

"You bade me remain a maiden," Gerta said cautiously, sensing that there was something of import in this. "The better to preserve my gift as a seer."

Isold laughed. "The mirror is what it is, Gerta, and it shows what it will show. Such vessels answer to a higher authority than a little seer like you."

"You lied to me, then."

"Indeed I did. A sorceress of my potency could see much further in your mirror. I saw myself, reigning upon Skadi's right hand before ever I came here." Isold nodded. "It was my destiny, as evidenced by my own name. 'Rule of ice,' that is the meaning of the name *Isold*, and truly, I do rule the ice as Skadi's trustee." Her smile turned cruel. "I collect souls for her, which sates her, and one day I shall wrest the last vestige of power from her lax grasp."

Gerta had never suspected that Isold had used her!

Isold smiled. "And I saw you, coming boldly to challenge me, burdened by guilt but still possessed of a chance of success. And so I taught you, Gerta, that you must be chaste, that no man must lay a hand upon you, the better that you might have no opportunity to awaken the sorcerer whose soul Skadi desired more than most." She shrugged and granted Cai a skeptical glance. "But who can guess what will stir a mortal man?"

"I do not understand. I sent a summons for aid three days past and Cai came to assist me." Gerta felt Cai claim her hand. His fingers were still chilled but his grip was resolute.

Isold laughed again. "You believe that *you* sent the summons? Gerta, child, your power is not sufficient to command the mirror. I heard your attempt and turned it to my own purpose." Her eyes gleamed with pride. "*I* summoned Cai, though I made it appear that you did so. He would never have heeded me otherwise."

"There be truth," Cai muttered.

"It matters little," Isold said. "Now, you will surrender your mirror to me, and perhaps I will be merciful." Her hungry smile granted Gerta no confidence in that possibility.

Gerta clutched her pack. "But my mirror is as a part of me . . ."

"Have you not realized the truth? How did I find myself such a witless pupil?" Isold sneered. "Have you not guessed from what the mirror draws its power?" She gestured broadly and Gerta's gaze was drawn unwillingly to the seemingly endless expanse of dark ice surrounding them.

Isold leaned close to whisper, "Your mirror shows truth, does it not?"

Such a mirror as this could only be given, entrusted to another seer by choice. Did Gerta even wish to have such a vessel in her possession?

Cai gave her a nudge and a glance, and Gerta agreed with his impulse. She surrendered the mirror to Isold, gladdened to be rid of its burden.

The sorceress clutched it in her hands and closed her eyes. She gritted her teeth as she crushed the bronze mirror in her hands; she arched her neck and exerted such a force of will that Gerta could not look fully upon her. The mirror melted within her grasp, melted to no more than a whiff of dark smoke.

And a long shard of black ice.

Isold smiled in triumph. "This is the last of it," she confided. "Now the glass will be complete, as once it was."

She cast the three shards into the air, and they moved seemingly of their own volition to find their places in the puzzle of the ice. Gerta feared the result when they slipped into their places, though she knew not what to expect. She clutched Cai's hand and he clutched hers and neither of them took a breath.

Naught happened.

Isold frowned and looked about herself in confusion.

"Missing something?" Loki asked and sauntered across the ice toward them.

LOKI WAS MUCH SMALLER AND MORE SHADOWY than Gerta expected. He might have been a kitchen serf, bent under the burden of his labor and faded from exhaustion. She could not even discern his wings.

The flight must have been a greater strain for him than anticipated, and Gerta felt a new fear. He was cocky, though, confident as always, his swagger in marked contrast to his appearance. His smile had a fearsome brightness and his eyes shone with what might have been anticipation.

Loki the trickster. Gerta had little time to consider this, for he moved his hand and something flashed within his grasp.

"You're missing one last piece," he informed Isold with a measure of insolence. "Wanna jump for it?"

It was the piece of glass that Loki had taken from Egan's eye.

"Who is your humble companion, Gerta?" Isold demanded.

"I could not undertake such a journey alone," Gerta said hesitantly. Loki gave her a look and she fabricated a tale, following his silent bidding for once. "He is no more than a minion, pledged to my father. You know that my father surrendered his best men to the Cath Palug years ago."

Loki's eyes widened slightly and Gerta did not doubt that he would have much to say about that description. It sated Isold, though, and persuaded her that he posed no threat.

She extended her hand regally, clearly believing that he was no more than a feeble man. "Give me the shard."

"I don't think so." Loki bounced it on his palm. "I kind of like it. It's shiny, you know?"

"I know not who you are, but your defiance is unacceptable," Isold began to fume. "Give me the shard!"

"We could arm wrestle," Loki taunted, tossing the shard of black ice from one hand to the other. Isold snatched at it when it was airborne, but without success. "Thumb wrestle. Draw straws. Or"—he granted Isold an arch glance—"you could seduce me into giving it to you."

Isold stilled and smiled a cunning smile. "That can be arranged."

"Goody goody." Loki stood his ground and again Gerta had the sense that he barely restrained himself.

Isold leaned forward and kissed his brow, lavishing her attention upon him. Loki whistled, turning the shard in his hand, utterly oblivious to her.

"What is this?" Isold murmured, then kissed him again.

"That's it?" Loki asked when she lifted her lips from him. "That's the best you can do?"

Isold was clearly astonished that he had not readily succumbed. "Once more," she demanded, and he nodded with insouciance.

"Why not? Maybe the third time's the charm, hmmm?"

Isold drew herself taller and caught Loki's face in her hands, bending toward him with purpose. She kissed his brow, clearly funneling all of her power into the embrace.

It was to no avail. She stepped back and regarded him warily. "You are no minion."

"My turn," Loki said. He flicked the shard of ice off his thumb, and it flew through the air, gleaming as it sought its place in the shattered ice. In the same instant, Loki seized Isold and kissed her full on the lips. She managed to make a strangled cry and no more before she began to lose substance. She struggled but Loki did not release her.

Indeed, Gerta thought that he deepened his kiss. His grip was clearly relentless, his kiss consuming. Isold became more and more shadowy, yet he released her when she was no more than a wraith.

"Take that message to my old pal Skadi," he bade her. He snapped his fingers and the wisp of what had been Isold disappeared.

Cai gasped and Gerta felt the last shard of ice snap into place. There could be no mistaking it. The lake of ice lit suddenly, illuminated with that shadowy opalescence along all of its cracks, then shimmered and fused into one glass again.

And Loki began to laugh.

GERTA WATCHED IN DISMAY AS LOKI GREW LARGER and darker. He was more substantial than ever he had been, blacker and bigger and more fearsome. He was exultant. His laughter shook the walls of the cavern and resonated within her very marrow. He looked down upon them in his dark majesty and the radiance of his eyes fairly blinded Gerta.

She feared then that she had erred in truth, that she had been used for a wicked purpose. Had Loki used her as Isold had done?

Beside her, Cai straightened and she admired his fearlessness. "What will you do?"

"No more and no less than what I came to do," Loki smiled and the sight sent fear dancing down Gerta's spine. "No more and no less than Gerta helped me to do."

Gerta and Cai exchanged a glance of trepidation.

"I will destroy it, of course." Loki shook his head as he looked across the expanse of dark ice. "Though it's a damn shame. This is a fine piece of work."

Gerta looked at him in shock. "But, but why? You said you had made it."

He lifted a finger as if to chide her for doubting him. "And I did. But it was wrong to make it, wrong to try to show God his error." He swallowed. "It was pride I showed, not truth."

"And you mean to make reparation?" Gerta guessed, recalling his earlier comments.

"There is only one way to right a wrong, only one way to earn redemption. You've got to fix what you screw up." Loki heaved a sigh. "Destruction is the shadow of creation. Some cultures celebrate this, though most choose to forget it. The bottom line is that I, as the creator of the ice, am the only one who can ensure its destruction."

"But how?" Cai asked. "It has been shattered before and survived in pieces, which was worse."

"Tears!" Gerta guessed.

Loki grinned at her. "Tears."

"You do not weep," Cai observed.

"We seldom weep, but mortals have potent tears. If I take pieces of ice to places of suffering, places where tears of compassion are shed, then it will be melted, one chunk at a time."

"But it is so vast," Cai protested. "It will take eternity."

"Isn't it a good thing that I'm immortal?" Loki commented. "I've nothing but time on my hands." He cried out a command, a word in a language Gerta did not know and never wished to hear again, and raised his hands skyward.

The ice followed his gesture, rising and buckling. Fissures opened upon its surface, and instead of shards, it was broken into pieces about the size of a man. Gerta clung to Cai as the ice beneath their very feet uprooted itself. Loki seized one piece, then ran across the broken ice and bounded into flight.

The remaining chunks of ice, to Gerta's amazement, shuddered, lifted, then pursued him. The cavern was filled with spiraling pieces of dark ice, seemingly caught in a whirlwind. They all moved upward and away, following Loki.

When the storm of their passing had subsided, Gerta realized that she and Cai must have been swept along, for they stood alone in the cave of the Cath Palug.

THE CATH PALUG WAS DEAD.

"I suppose it survived its purpose," Cai said when he bent to examine it.

"Or it could not survive without the ice."

Cai shook his head. "In this cavern was a dark power, to be sure. This is no sorcery I would know." He touched the great beast and it rolled bonelessly to its back.

Its paws had been cut off.

Gerta retched at the sight, though Cai, more accustomed to battle, merely frowned. "Look. Two of them are embedded in my shield," he said, pulling his shield from beneath the beast's corpse.

"And the other pair is there." Gerta pointed to the jumble of bones from other fallen warriors, where the two paws had fallen. She saw now that the ground was stained with the Cath Palug's dark blood. Cai studied the corpse of the fiendish cat, then grinned.

He pulled his sword from its chest with satisfaction. It had been embedded to the hilt in the beast, and its blade was stained with that dark blood.

His eyes narrowed. "The Cath Palug dragged me into its lair," he said, as if his recollection was faint.

"You must have defeated it here," Gerta said. Their gazes met and, for a moment, they both knew that that had not been the case. They stared at each other in mutual awareness of the marvel they had witnessed, of the surety that they would soon forget it, then a cloud passed over their recollection.

"It was ferocious and thirsty for your blood," Gerta said, impressed by the valor and strength of this man. Her father would surrender her hand to him, she was certain, and truly he deserved no less for his noble deed. "Yet you did not falter."

Cai looked at her and smiled, the warmth in his eyes making Gerta flush. "How could I, when such a fair maiden was at stake?"

Gerta's face heated and she averted her gaze, awkward in the company of a man so virile, so attentive. They were alone and she was aware of the scent of his flesh, the heat of his presence, the sound of his breathing.

Cai chuckled, a hearty sound that warmed her heart. He slid his fingertips down the length of her arm, conjuring a faint recollection within Gerta. She caught her breath at his boldness, but admired his tenderness. She watched his hand, shivered when he reached the end of her sleeve and his warm fingers trailed across the bare flesh of the back of her hand. He interlaced their fingers, capturing her hand within his, then lifted her hand to press a kiss into her palm.

His gesture was so simple, yet so potent. Gerta must have dreamed of this moment, of his first caress. She looked at Cai, looked at him fully, seeing her destiny in the bright sparkle of his eyes. Her heart pounded with an awareness of him, his height, his breadth, his gentle manner and his wisdom, and she knew that she would learn much in this man's company.

She knew that she would gain far more than she lost.

"Be my bride," he murmured.

"Prize, bride, it's all pretty much the same in a barbarian culture," Gerta said, then clapped a hand over her mouth. From whence had such words come?

Cai laughed, undeterred by her uncommon speech. "Praise be for that," he murmured, then bent to touch his lips to hers.

They stared at each other in marvel when he lifted his head, then smiled in unison at the sound of birdsong. Gerta took Cai's hand within her own and led him into the garden of her father's realm.

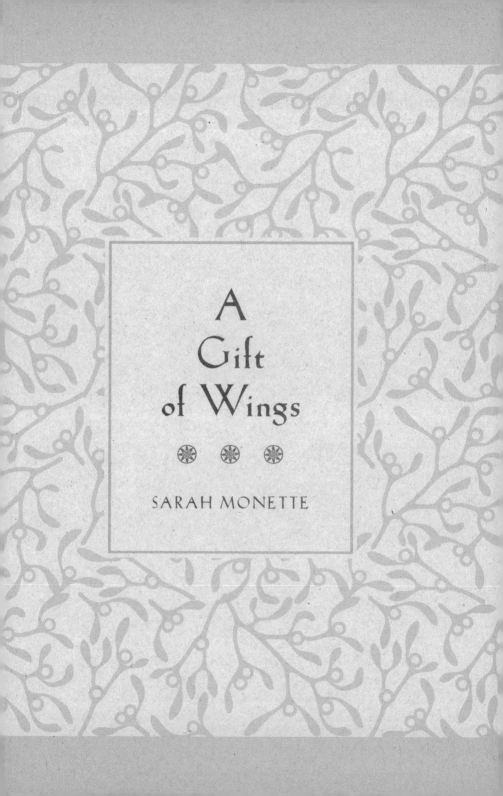

A
Gift
of Wings

✳ ✳ ✳

SARAH MONETTE

They left Karolinsberg on the morning of Queen Anna Theresa's coronation. Snow was starting to fall when they rode out of the city, fat, harmless flakes. Agido tilted her head back to watch their dizzying descent as she had done as a child in Iphigeneia, unimaginably far to the east, so far away that her homeland was little more than a fairy-tale to the people of Norvena Parva, and the color of her hair and eyes marked her as a foreigner, almost a monster.

Maur, slight-boned, pale and fair, rode beside her, huddled in his old black greatcoat like a molting crow. His blue eyes were dull, almost glassy, with none of the brilliance, the vitality, that had first drawn her to him. They had been lovers in the spring, before the war, but when she went to visit him after he was released from the Annamaihopital into his grandmother's care, he made it plain without so much as a word that they were not lovers any longer.

It hurt, but it was not entirely unexpected. She was seven years his senior, a mercenary soldier and a Troian:

a delightful liaison for a season, adding the spice of the exotic and transgressive to the relatively dull life of a Parvan courtier-wizard. Even the fact that she was annemer, that she could neither feel nor understand magic, had been no deterrent, not to the person he had been then. Things were different now, and if he did not want her, then so be it. She would protect him with her life, and not for the sake of the money that his grandmother, Anna Paulina von Haarien, the head of the Banke Haarien in all but name, had promised her.

The road out of Karolinsberg was as deserted as Agido had ever seen it; the entire country of Norvena Parva was packed into the Plass Michivie to watch the coronation—those who were neither dead nor imprisoned in the wake of the autumn's war. She wished for a moment that they were among those crowds, she and Maur, sharing roasted chestnuts and laughing as he attempted to explain to her, for the fifteenth time, the government of his country.

Wishing was foolish and wasteful, and she shook the thought away, along with a scatter of snow-melt. She caught Maur's uneasy glance, but he said nothing.

In good weather, it was two weeks' ride from Karolinsberg to Igensbeck through the Pass of the Sisters. If winter came early, though, even with the excellent horses provided by the Banke Haarien and Anna Paulina's letter of authorization to the post-houses, they could easily be in the mountains until spring.

But waiting would drive Maur mad. Again.

They rode all day, not swiftly but steadily; the snow tapered off around noon. They slept that night in a post-house; Maur spoke neither to the couriers who shared their table nor to Agido, but she heard him cry out in nightmares through the thin partition between their sleeping chambers. In the morning, when she asked if he had slept well, he stared at her as if he could not remember what the words meant, then said, "Oh, yes. Quite. Like a babe in arms."

And that set the pattern for the next five days. They rode in silence, ate in silence; she pretended not to hear Maur's voice in the night because there was nothing she could do—nothing he would let her do. The glare in his blue eyes defied her, as if she were his enemy, as if she were one of the men who had hurt him, broken his hands and scarred his body, crippled his magic.

She missed the person he had been. If she let herself, she could remember her first sight of him, could remember the way he had stopped beside her table in the Kaffe Emilstrasse and said, "I beg your pardon—shockingly inquisitive of me—but you're Troian, aren't you?" And he had smiled at her, a smile that lit his pale face and made his sharp blue eyes dazzling. She had invited him to sit, and he had plied her with questions; she remembered now not the questions themselves, but the light in his eyes, his unabashed interest in her answers. She remembered, and grieved for, his fire, his all-consuming energy, his open delight in the world as it presented itself to him.

She had never been one for prayer, since the bleak and brutal ending of her childhood, but she found herself praying during the long cold nights, praying that the magisters of the Universitat could help Maur when his own teachers and colleagues could not.

And praying for patience.

But on the fifth day, as they started the climb up the southern Sister toward the pass, her prayers were answered with snow.

The clouds built up all morning; the first flakes, hard and bitter, began to fall around noon. The color of the sky presaged a real snowstorm, not the light, pretty, harmless snow that had attended their departure from Karolinsberg. Even city-bred Maur realized it; the third time Agido reined in, standing in her stirrups to look futilely for anything that might serve as shelter, he brought his horse up beside her and said, "We're in trouble, aren't we?"

"We may be," she said. There was no shelter, nothing but wind-scoured rocks and a few stunted, twisted trees; she had been warned that the Sisters did not welcome travelers, and, indeed, she felt prodigiously unwelcomed. "There's an inn just below the head of the pass, the last I knew. But we must push hard."

"And if it isn't there?"

"There will still be buildings, or at least a wall or a windbreak. Better than nothing," and she gestured around at the barren mountainside.

"The post-house—"

"Too far. The inn is closer, and they would have mentioned it at the post-house if it had been abandoned."

"If they knew," Maur said under his breath.

It was the sort of thing that happened in the high mountains. They had come across more than one deserted homestead—some destroyed by fire, others seeming entirely normal, except for the fact that they were empty. Silent tombs without even the dead to occupy them.

"If you prefer to be *certain* of your death, you can stay here," she said, glaring.

He hunched a little, his eyes flinching shut as if he thought she might strike him. She had been speaking out of frustration, not with any intent to wound; she hesitated a moment, but this was not the time for explanations and apologies. She said simply, "Keep up with me," and urged her horse forward again.

If she had needed further proof that those clouds meant trouble, she had it in the horses' behavior, their eyes rolling, the skittish dance of their hooves. The day degenerated into an endless misery of raw wind and the stinging lash of snow, riding alert as much to the footing as to the weather. By midafternoon, it was already dark as twilight, and a half-inch of snow covered the rough road they followed; Maur had fallen behind, and she had bitten her tongue and said nothing, because if he wanted to sulk, she could not prevent him. She almost didn't hear him call her name.

She turned in the saddle. His horse had stopped, the reins loose on its neck, and Maur was huddled around his crabbed, swollen-knuckled hands. Not sulking then, and she felt a scrape of bitterness, like the striking of a lucifer along her spine, that she had been so willing to think ill of him. She turned her horse hard and hurriedly, and went back.

"I can't," Maur said, his voice a bare thready whisper. "I'm sorry, I know you said . . . but I just can't." His face was ashen, and she could see blood on his lower lip where he'd bitten it. The black wool mittens hid the worst of the damage done to his hands, but she had seen them, broken, twisted, the first joint of two fingers on his right hand gone. And she could imagine what the cold was doing to the injured bones and tendons—and that made worse by the tension that had Maur as tightly strung as a violin.

"It's all right," she said, wishing she could offer better reassurance but not knowing what to say, and pulled the reins over his horse's head. "Just try not to fall off."

That got his head up, an indignant spark in his eyes. Maur, the child of wealth and privilege, had been taught to ride as soon as walk, had ridden with the Hoddferne Hunt since he was fourteen. She grinned at him, and for a moment thought he would respond with a blistering remark. And then his eyes dulled, and he looked away.

For the fiftieth time, her heart broke with grief and frustration, that she could not help him and that he could not seem to find a way to help himself. And, tugging hard on the reins of Maur's horse, she got them moving again. Her pity would do him no good if they were dead.

Hours later, the walls of the pass looming above them but doing nothing to shelter them from either snow or wind, they came to a wide place in the road, where a signpost, erected incongruously in the middle of the way, announced THE MARE'S NEST, with an arrow, pointing to the left, nailed beneath the sign. Although it was hard to tell in the gloom, she thought the paint looked fresh, and something that was not yet hope began to unfurl cautiously behind her ribs.

She reined in, jerked her collar higher on her neck, turned. And it was wise of them to have put up a sign, because otherwise she might have ridden right past the inn. The gate was set flush into the cliff wall and was barely wide enough for two horses to go abreast.

She said to Maur, over the noise of the wind, "Don't move yet," and dismounted, leading both horses to the gate. Which, closed and barred, seemed to deny that which the signpost promised.

She muttered a curse that was half a plea and thumped on the gate. Thumped again and was just wondering if either of these horses had been trained to kick at a door when she heard the blessed sound of a bar being lifted and the left-hand side of the gate swung open.

A youngish man, gangly and with an unfortunately misplaced belief in his ability to grow a beard, blinked at her. "Inn's full up," he said.

Her first instinct—to grab him by both bony shoulders and shake him until he rattled—she suppressed, and said pleasantly, "Then we will sleep in the stable."

He just goggled at her, and she wondered if it was because she was a woman, because she was Troian, or because he was feeble-minded. "Let us in, damn you," she said, "or we will die here in the pass and block your door with our stinking corpses."

He blinked, said, "Yes, maselle," and stepped aside.

Possibly he was not feeble-minded after all.

She led the horses in, through a narrow, low tunnel that neither of them liked—and, in fairness, she did not like it herself—and into a natural cavern, easily twice the size of the courtyard of the finest hotel in Karolinsberg, where a tall, fat man with alarming waxed mustaches came forward saying in a strong Ervenzian accent, "Ham! Idiot! Did I not tell you—"

"*She* said," the young man began, and then lowered his voice.

Agido ignored them, smiled thanks at the stableboy who came pattering up to hold the horses' heads. He nodded at her shyly, and then his attention was caught by something behind her, his eyes widening. She turned and saw Maur and did not blame the stableboy for staring.

Maur was still huddled as he had been every time she had looked back at him on the long cold dreariness of the climb up to the pass, his hands pressed against his stomach just below his sternum, shoulders hunched, head down. He was shivering, a fine all-over tremor, and his face was white as white.

"Maur," she said, and she could not help her voice gentling, could not help loving him, although it was painful and useless. "Let's go."

He shook his head, like a dog coming out of the water, looked down at her, frowning. Then he nodded curtly, swung his leg over and slid off the horse, neat and easy and she would have believed it, too, if it hadn't been for his knees buckling at the first step he took.

She caught him under one elbow, held him up, did not ask, *Are you all right?* for she knew the sneer that would answer her if she did. Instead she stood, waited as if there were nothing wrong, as if she were, perhaps, a tree or a pillar or some other inanimate object that had no opinion about the function it was asked to fulfill, and after a moment, he found himself again, caught his breath, straightened away from her.

But he did not jerk his arm free as if her touch was unpleasant, and that was more than she had expected.

He pushed damp strands of hair away from his face with his wrist and said, "So the inn is here, after all."

"Yes, although I am afraid we may be sleeping in the stable."

"Nonsense," said Maur. He stepped around her, strode up to the landlord as if he owned, not merely the inn, but also the pass and the Sisters themselves. He was a von Haarien; there was a good chance his grandmother did.

The conversation was intense, low-voiced, interrupted twice by the landlord sailing as majestically as a brigantine into the inn. Finally, after she had unbuckled their saddlebags and nodded to the boy to lead the horses away, Maur came back, scowling, and said abruptly, "We'll have to share a room."

"We've done that before."

He turned a slow, beautiful pink. "That isn't what . . . that is, Agido, I don't . . ."

"I was not propositioning you," she said stiffly. She shouldered the saddlebags and followed the gestures of the landlord into the public bar of The Mare's Nest.

Another cavern, not as large and possibly not quite as natural as the first. The bar was a long sinuous sweep of wood, glowing darkly in the light of oil-lamps and candles, and for a moment she stared, trying to imagine how they could have gotten it in here, let alone up the mountain in the first place.

"This way, messire, maselle, this way please." The landlord beckoned extravagantly. They followed him through the bar, up a staircase twisted as tightly as a corkscrew through the living rock, down a hall with such winding curves that it could only be a natural passageway. There were doors at irregular intervals, sometimes on one side, sometimes on the other, and at last, as she was wondering if they would find themselves in Norvena Magna before they reached their bed-chamber, the landlord stopped, unlocked one of the doors with a flourish, and held out the key.

He expected Maur to take it, but when Agido extended her hand, he gave it to her, along with one of the two lanterns he was carrying. "If you wish to bathe, messire, maselle, we have natural springs. Very hot."

Maur's face brightened perceptibly. Agido said, "Yes, please. How do we find them?"

"Continue to the end of this corridor. You will find a stair going down, like the stair we came up, yes? It will lead you to the baths."

And having ascertained that there was nothing more they needed, he bowed and smiled and waddled away.

The room was small, with a single window—barely more than an arrow slit—now shuttered tightly against the winter. The bed was a mattress with pillows and quilts and a goose-down duvet, all piled on a natural shelf in the rock. The odd nature of The Mare's Nest worked in their favor, Agido noted. That shelf was far wider than any bed she had ever had in a hotel or boarding house in any country she had visited.

She set the saddlebags down and turned to help Maur with his coat; they both knew he couldn't manage for himself, not tonight. He lifted his chin and stared determinedly over her shoulder while she undid the round horn buttons. She went behind him to hold the coat while he eased it off, both of them scarcely breathing until his hands were free of the sleeves, not caught or bumped by the folds of cloth. She hung the greatcoat on one of the hooks along the wall beside the door, then shrugged out of her own coat as well and sat down on the bed to take off her boots.

Maur sat down next to her; their silence was almost companionable. When she had finished with her boots, she knelt to take off his. It was maddening to be so close to his body and yet to treat him with the impersonal decorum of a valet. But he did not like to be touched now, and she was not going to force him to acknowledge an intimacy he no longer wanted. She put their boots beneath the coats and said, "You'd best let me take your mittens off, too."

He nodded once, tightly, manifestly unhappy, and held out his hands.

She did not make the mistake of trying to hurry. Maur was wrong to find this shameful. She eased first one mitten off, then the other, wincing in sympathy at his red and swollen knuckles, the clawed stiffness of his fingers.

"They are ugly, aren't they?" Maur said with studied lightness.

"No." She caught him very gently by the wrists, thereby effectively imprisoning him. Before he could ask what she thought she was doing, or demand that she let him go, she leaned forward and kissed his knuckles, first the left hand, then the right.

And then she released him, stood up, moved away, feeling her face burn and waiting for a withering remark about triteness and hypocrisy. But none came, and when she finally glanced at him, he was staring at her, his eyes wide, his hands still frozen exactly as she had held them.

She knew not to press her advantage. She smiled at him and said, "Shall we investigate the natural springs?"

And this time, for the first time in so long she could not even reckon the days, Maur smiled back.

THE NATURAL SPRINGS WERE, AS THE LANDLORD had promised, very hot. She unbraided her hair from its tight confinement against her skull, let it uncoil in slow ripples across the surface of the pool as she washed. The water darkened it from red to almost black, making the strands of gray show up vividly. It was no secret that she was nearly forty, growing old, growing tired. It was why she had come to Norvena Parva, searching for less strenuous work, not yet willing to face the pain and suffocation of returning to Troia, to her kin.

And she had found a war instead, a petty, stupid war, a vain and greedy man trying to take something that wasn't his. And if it had not been that he was trying to take it from a woman, there would have been no war at all. But there were factions in Norvena Parva that were willing to support Baron von Klemmerin against his cousin because they could not imagine a woman fit to rule them. Agido had no particular love for Anna Theresa von Klemmerin, but she had been, if not glad, then fiercely unapologetic to fight for the queen, to help her keep what was hers. And she had been, not glad, but deeply, wearily relieved, when Baron von Klemmerin was defeated, when the reactionaries, grumbling and resentful, bowed their heads and swore their oaths to their queen.

She and Maur were the only two people in the baths, and so she did not have to worry, as she usually did, about being propositioned by men who thought that if her sword was for hire, her body had to be as well. She arched her back, listening to the small, distinct noises of her vertebrae shifting, and Maur said, "You have scars. Why do I not remember you having scars?"

She turned to look at him, one eyebrow rising. He was standing in the waist-deep water, his hair dripping in ash-blond tendrils around his shoulders, hands submerged so that the heat could work on them. His own scars were plainly visible, flushed an ugly, hectic red across his chest and stomach, and it was that which kept her from saying something flippant and cruel.

Instead, she looked down at her body.

Scars on her hands and forearms, the sort that any sword-wielder acquired. Scars across her ribs from ugly close-quarter work fighting bandits in the Alinsons; those scars she mostly couldn't see because of the swell—and these days, the sag—of her breasts, though she knew their tracks, remembered the maddening itching as they healed. A thicker scar, older and uglier, across her left bicep and shoulder, where a fierce slash had gotten in over her guard. A vicious little war in southern Troia, and the last time she had let any Troian house have her loyalty, even temporarily, even for money. The man had been the size of a mountain, and she had paid dearly for assuming that he would not also be fast.

He had died, though, his face registering incredulous surprise as he fell.

The scar across her right thigh was hidden beneath the water; it was the newest of the lot, new enough that it was still shiny pink. The man who had caused it was dead, as well, although he had died by hanging, in front of Charsin Prison outside Karolinsberg, not at her hands.

She looked back at Maur and said, hearing the apology in her voice, "I do not often think of them."

"Of course," he said, looking away, "they are honorable scars."

"There is no particular honor in having been slower than a badly trained bandit."

She had said the wrong thing again. His eyes squeezed shut for a moment in a grimace of embarrassment; he said, "You must think me contemptible."

"No. I think you have been badly hurt." And then, because this ground was treacherous, she said, "I also think you need your hair washed, yes?"

He clearly wanted to disagree, but he could not deny he was as dirty and travel-weary as she was, nor that it fretted his fastidious nature. He let her wash his hair, and it was easy to move from that to massage, working on the iron stiffness of his neck and shoulders.

After a moment in which he seemed frozen with surprise, he allowed that, too. She heard his breath release with a sigh; she was beginning to hope that she had found a way to reach him, an expression

of concern which he would not instantly reject as pity, when she heard
voices in the outer chamber and felt him turn to stone beneath her
hands.

He moved away, ducking beneath the water to rinse off the last of
the soap, and when he reemerged, his eyes were cold and shuttered
again, and he said only, "Are you ready to go?"

The voices she had heard had been raised in argument; that much
was obvious from the strained silence that fell as soon as they realized
they had an audience. When she and Maur emerged, towel-wrapped,
into the anteroom with its discreetly curtained alcoves for changing,
there were two men standing awkwardly, the air chokingly thick with
the words they were not saying to each other.

Maur blanched and said, his voice perceptibly shaking, "Magister
von Plaadt. How . . . how pleasant to see you again." It could not
have been more patently a lie.

The elder of the two men frowned in an almost comically over-
done pantomime of searching his memory. "Von Haarien, isn't it?
How are you, dear boy?"

"Wet at the moment, and likely to catch a chill," Agido said, glaring Maur into the alcove where he had left his clothes. The fact that
he went meekly told her as much as she wanted to know about Magister von Plaadt.

Both the magister and his companion were staring at her now. She
smiled thinly, insincerely, and said, "He has been very ill. Now, if you
will excuse me—" She stepped into her own alcove and pulled the
curtain decisively shut.

The younger man said, "Magister, I—" and the older man
answered, "Not *now*, Eero, for the love of all the powers." Then, the
rattle of curtain rings, and she began drying her hair ferociously.

She dressed and went to help Maur; happily, Magister von Plaadt
and his companion had wasted no time in going into the baths
proper, and she and Maur were not afflicted with witnesses. Remembering how voices carried, though, she did not say anything, and neither did he. When they were both ready, she merely jerked her head at

him in a *come on* gesture and pushed the heavy curtain aside so that he could precede her out.

He went; she waited until they were climbing the stairs to ask, "And who, pray tell, is Magister von Plaadt?"

She drawled it, hard and mocking, and was rewarded by a nervous, almost spasmodic giggle. "He's the von Nalle Fellow at the Zauberhof," Maur said. "A . . . a specialist in thaumaturgical injury."

Oh, she carefully did not say, but waited to see if Maur would continue on his own. And after a moment, he did.

"They called him in. First, I mean. Because, powers, I think I must have seen every fellow the Zauberhof could throw at me before the end of it." He seemed about to say something more, but it wasn't until they were back in their room and she had closed and locked the door behind them that he got it out: "He said I was a hopeless case."

"Did he?" she said, keeping her voice level with an effort.

"It's all a matter of willpower, you see. If I truly *wished* to do magic, I could. Since I can't . . ." He shrugged.

"What a novel theory," she said. "Clearly the work of a man with the mental abilities of a sausage."

"You don't think . . . ?"

"Blessed Tetrarchs, Maur, I've never heard anything so ridiculous in my life." She realized from his shocked expression that he had expected her to agree with von Plaadt. *You must think me contemptible.*

Somewhere in the depths of the warren of tunnels that was The Mare's Nest, a bell rang. She shook off unprofitable thoughts about Magister von Plaadt's willpower versus six inches of steel in his guts, and said briskly, "Dinnertime. I'd better help you dress."

MEALS IN THE MARE'S NEST WERE SERVED COMMU-nally; the dining room was long and rather narrow, but it contained very neatly a massive table with ten chairs to each side. The food was hot and plentiful, and although not culinarily sophisticated, very good. The landlord, his buxom wife, and a rawboned maid stayed busy between kitchen and table, and the landlord, saying gloomily that if the snow kept up at its current rate it might be a week before the pass could be cleared enough for travel, was lavish with an unexpectedly excellent dark beer.

Aside from Maur and Agido, six travelers had been caught in The Mare's Nest by the snow. Magister von Plaadt, whom Agido liked no better on second meeting, and his companion Eero, who turned out to be a von Leistig who had finished his studies at the Zauberhof and was traveling to Igensbeck to take up a position as von Plaadt's research assistant. Von Plaadt told the table smugly, his glance lingering just perceptibly on Maur, that he had been offered an endowed chair. Von Plaadt dressed extremely well for an academic wizard; in his fine broadcloth coat and trousers and his midnight-blue brocade waistcoat, he looked more like one of Maur's banker-cousins than anything else. Von Leistig was tall, blond, rabbit-faced, and it was a little painful to see how completely von Plaadt had him under his thumb.

Two of the other travelers were men, each traveling alone. One, Skaarien by his accent, was a mercenary, his slight build and mild brown eyes alike deceptive; he was headed to Oskavia, seeking passage to the southern islands for reasons which he politely but unbudgingly refused to discuss. He gave his name as Nikk.

The other man, Sebastian Glas, was a lawyer's clerk, traveling with a strongbox of depositions. He folded his lips together primly and would not say more, but there was no need. A sufficient number of influential families had branches in both Norvenas, and the laws of inheritance were sufficiently complicated and contested, that even a foreigner could fill in the gaps.

There were two women traveling together: Corinna von Elstan and her governess, Anna Lucilla von Deiver. Maselle von Elstan, little more than a girl for all her ferocious scowl, had the Universitat stamped on her as clearly as the author's name on the spine of a book. Agido remembered hearing that they admitted women students only at Midwinter, for reasons which sounded plausible but which amounted to nothing more than the discouragement of students they had no particular desire to admit in the first place. Maselle von Elstan very sensibly kept her head lowered over her plate and avoided attracting Magister von Plaadt's attention. He was obviously the sort of man who had opinions about education for women and even more obviously would express them loudly and at great length. And Agido suspected that Maselle von Elstan had been getting enough of that already from her traveling companion.

Anna Lucilla von Deiver, who insisted on the *von* with the fervor one found only in those demanding privileges to which they had a tenuous claim at best, had been a governess for thirty years; her conversation was larded with references to illustrious pupils and veiled hints at the tragedy in her past that had forced her to the degrading expedient of working for a living. Her remarks about woman's proper role were not subtle. Agido watched the slow blush creeping up Maselle von Elstan's neck and face and wondered what pressures had been brought to bear on her, that she had agreed to travel with Maselle von Deiver. It was not the custom in the Norvenas for a woman to travel alone, but it was not unheard of, either—even for women who were respectable. Agido hoped, for Maselle von Elstan's sake, that she would be able to dispense with her duenna when she reached Igensbeck.

"And you, Messire von Haarien?" said Anna Lucilla von Deiver, leaning forward over the table. "Why are you—and your . . . *companion*—traveling to Norvena Magna at this unpleasant time of year?"

The other guests could tell there was something wrong with him, of course. The black gloves, fingertips carefully cut off where Maur still had fingertips to worry about, could mask the extent of the damage, but not that there had been damage done. Especially since holding a spoon was almost more than he could manage that evening. Agido was passionately grateful that the meal was a heavy stew, and he was thus spared the intricate agonies of knife and fork. But even if

Baron von Klemmerin's clever torturers hadn't chosen to cripple his hands, he was haggard, shadow-eyed. *He looks half-mad,* she thought and winced.

But he answered quite composedly, "I have been advised to consult a magister of the Universitat about my health."

Nicely noncommittal, giving away nothing that was not obvious, and he did not make the mistake of coming to Agido's defense. Let Maselle von Deiver think her a prostitute if it pleased her. But Maur's answer caught Magister von Plaadt's attention.

"About that same problem?" he boomed with hearty and entirely artificial goodwill. "Tell me, which of my new colleagues is it who thinks he can succeed where I have said there is nothing to be done?"

Maur said, looking darkly triumphant, "Magister Thornfeld," an attitude which Agido understood as she watched Magister von Plaadt swell with wrath.

"That common-bred mountebank?" he demanded with splendid contempt. "I told you, von Haarien, there's nothing wrong with you that a little determination and simple manly courage can't correct. And yet you go haring off to sit at the feet of Thornfeld, chasing rainbows like a child?"

Maur had gone white, and he put his spoon down to hide, not entirely successfully, the way his hands were beginning to shake. But he said with perfect waspishness, "Better to sit at the feet of a charlatan than an idiot."

It took a moment for von Plaadt to realize what he had actually said, and Agido gathered from the stricken and shocked look on von Leistig's face that people did not usually speak like that to the magister. Von Plaadt swelled still further, like a bullfrog, and she hoped for a moment a thunderclap coronary might deliver them all, but then he let his breath out and said in a slow, poisonous, lethally precise tone, "Is that any way to speak to the man who held you while you wept and screamed and begged for help? And who *gave* you that help, you ungrateful craven, though you whined and sniveled and said you could not do it? You can't be cured, von Haarien, because your illness is nothing but your own weakness, your own over-indulged imagination. And if you think Thornfeld can give you a miracle—"

"Magister von Plaadt," Agido said.

It brought him up short—mostly, she thought, because he was unprepared for a woman to interrupt him—and she continued before he could recoup: "Regardless of your theories on thaumaturgical injury, surely even you can have the common decency to *shut your mouth.*"

His mouth actually sagged open a little, but his silence was gratifying. She stood up, and her hand under his elbow ensured that Maur stood up with her.

"Messelles, messires," she said, bowing to the table generally, "you will forgive us, but I think it is in everyone's best interests if we bid you good night now. And, Magister, if you are not prepared to apologize the next time I see you—I suggest that you be sure I do not see you at all. Good night."

Maur moved with her when she went, and she was thankful for that.

They met no one in the halls on their way back to their room, and no one came after them. Agido locked the door behind them, and then sat down on the bed. Maur began pacing, short fierce strides up and back, his head down so that she could not read his face. He was swearing under his breath, a vicious mutter of ugliness and anger and despair.

She said, after a while, "Is what the magister says true?"

"Of course it's true!" He made an impassioned gesture, cut short as the incautious movement jarred his hand. "Mind you, I don't remember it all that clearly, between the morphia and the fact that I really was stark barking mad at the time." He stopped, eyeing her uncertainly. "Anna Paulina *did* tell you that part, didn't she? That I was completely insane for the first couple months I was in the Anna-maihopital?"

"I knew," she said, and did not say that she had not needed Anna Paulina to tell her.

"Good," he said, pacing again. "I mean, I wouldn't have liked to think that you—" He shook his head impatiently. "Anyway, I don't remember much, but I remember enough to know that . . ." Voice and pace slowed together. "That von Plaadt is telling the truth."

"I dislike that word *truth*," she said, forcing her voice to remain calm, almost disinterested. "In Norvenan it means too many different things."

She'd caught his attention, pulled him just a little away from his own pain. "Such as?"

"Well, there is the truth we receive from the world around us, as for example that snow is cold. There is the truth we receive from our teachers, which we agree to believe in order that all our time may not be spent in argument and war. And then there is the truth as each of us finds it for ourselves. And that truth is the most dangerous one."

"Are you talking about philosophy or ontology?"

"Either. Both. I am trying to say that I believe von Plaadt's *truth* is the third kind, not the first."

Maur considered that for a moment, then said, more thoughtfully, "I *do* remember some bits he didn't see fit to mention."

"Such as?"

"Well, hydrotherapy, for one."

"Hydro-what?"

"Hydrotherapy. That's where they hold you down in a tub of ice-cold water until you say what they want you to."

"And that's supposed to *help*? *How*?"

"Do you think I asked? And, anyway, it was better than the binding coat."

She said nothing, trying, horrified, to imagine something worse than what he had described, but Maur wasn't stopping, the words pouring out as if he had simply been waiting for someone to whom he could say them.

"It's canvas, smells of mildew and urine and vomit, straps and buckles everywhere. The arms are overlong, and they lace together like this." And he showed her, crossing his arms across his chest, wrenching his wrists as far around towards the small of his back as he could. "And they get you in it and cuff your feet to the bedframe, so you can't move, not at all, and then they *leave* you there. For hours, sometimes."

She could feel the gooseflesh marbling on her arms. Maur sat down beside her, heavily, all the febrile energy drained out of him. "It was for when I shouted at the magisters, or used unbecoming language, things like that. They said if I couldn't exercise decent self-control, they would have to impose it on me."

"They *punished* you? They punished you for *being hurt*?"

"I . . ." He stuck there, like a run-down clock, his mouth half-open, his eyes slightly blank. And then he said, "That doesn't make any sense, does it?"

"Of course it doesn't!" He winced, and she modulated her indignation. "I thought the magisters in the Annamaihopital were helping you."

"They cured me," he said, but he sounded uncertain.

"Did they?" she said, and he could not meet her eyes.

THEY BOTH SLEPT UNEASILY, MAUR LYING STIFFLY on his back to protect his hands, and Agido wishing desperately to have the freedom to touch him, to love him, to sleep with one arm thrown across his chest, and her legs entwined with his. Her dreams were not pleasant; Maur was restless, and he moaned once or twice, but he did not cry out.

Her time-sense, which was trustworthy, said it was about four in the morning when a small voice whispered, "Agido? Are you asleep?"

"No," she said.

"Nor am I," Maur said with a sound halfway between a chuckle and a sigh. "My hands are killing me."

He'd never said it so openly before, as if it was something he could trust her with; it took her a moment to find her voice. "Do you want to go back down to the baths?"

"It couldn't hurt," he said, which translated, she thought, into, *Please.*

"All right," she said and rolled thankfully out of bed. She lit the candle, found her shirt and trousers, looped her braids up out of the way, and turned back to help Maur with his clothes. He accepted her help, but stiffly, unwillingly. She didn't let her hands linger, didn't lean forward to press a kiss against the soft skin of his stomach.

He does not want you, Agido, she said to herself harshly.

She stood up again, collected lantern and keys, and they set forth into the sleeping darkness of The Mare's Nest. Neither spoke; somewhere, no doubt, the landlord and his wife were already preparing to face the day and the snow and the demands of their patrons, but the guest-quarters were still heavy with night.

Down and down in that tight spiral, past the strange short hallways that branched off at random intervals, the soft sound of Maur's bare feet against stone behind her. The bannister, carved like a trough into the wall, was smooth beneath her fingers, and she wondered how long The Mare's Nest had been here, and what it had been before it was an inn.

They undressed quickly, sharing an alcove. She told Maur to go ahead; she was almost dizzy with wanting him, with wanting what she could not have, and was glad to have a moment to herself, even if it was only folding their clothes neatly onto one of the roughly squared-out shelves at the back of the alcove.

And then Maur called her name, not loudly, but urgently.

She was through the doorway in a heartbeat and found him standing beside the pool, staring at an object in the water, a monstrous bloated starfish.

It was Magister von Plaadt, and he was dead.

"TOO DAMNABLY CONVENIENT," MAUR SAID, STALKing up the stairs ahead of her. "I hate the man, and lo and behold, he gets himself murdered. Enough to make me suspect I had something to do with it."

"I believe I would have noticed if you had," she said.

"Still, suspicious, don't you think?"

"Coincidence," she said, in the most uninterested voice she could manage. "Stranger things have happened."

"Yes, well, easy enough to *say*."

"Maur, you could not have killed him." The ghastly concavity in Magister von Plaadt's skull had been caused by something striking his head very hard, hard enough that there was a corresponding bruise on his forehead where he had been knocked into a wall or a table. With Maur's hands in their current state, he couldn't even have lifted an object heavy enough to have done that sort of damage, much less swung it at Magister von Plaadt's head. But it was Maur who had spotted the bruise, and had insisted on the closer examination that revealed other bruises indicating the magister had not fallen into the water on his own, but had been dragged to the baths from somewhere else.

The landlord was not grateful.

"No," Maur said over his shoulder, "but you could have."

"Why in the name of the blessed Tetrarchs would I kill Magister von Plaadt?"

"Well, you did more or less threaten to last night."

"That wasn't a threat." She opened the door to their room and all but shoved Maur inside, locking the door behind them with what she knew was an entirely delusional sense of relief. "It was fair warning."

Maur snorted. "Your hair-splitting technique is impressive, but not very helpful. Our host has already asked if I can vouch for your whereabouts."

"He gets no gratuity from me, then. What did you tell him?"

"That you couldn't have left the room last night without my hearing you. Which, of course, is exactly what I'd say if you'd killed von Plaadt on my behalf."

"Of course," she said.

"I did try to tell him that if you *had* killed Magister von Plaadt at my instigation and dumped him in the baths, we'd hardly have gone traipsing down there at four in the morning to fall over the body, but

I think the logic was a bit beyond him. Elgiv promises to bring up hot water, by the way. Can you bear to help me shave?"

"Yes, of course. Elgiv?"

"The maid. They don't quite know what to do about the pool, but considering the strength of the current, I said I thought the water Magister von Plaadt died in should have completely circulated out of the pool in twelve hours. Messire Bartolomeo found that logic much more congenial."

"I am sure he did," she said sourly.

"It worries me, though," Maur said.

"What does?"

"The first thing Bartolomeo will do, when the road is clear enough, is send someone for the Norvenwache."

"As he ought."

"And tell them that the murderer is most likely a Troian merce-nary. A woman whose half-mad crippled lover would lie for her at the drop of a pin."

"You aren't—"

"Please," Maur said, his voice tight with exasperation and self-loathing. "I *am* a half-mad cripple. There's no point trying to spare my feelings."

"You're not my lover, I was going to say."

They both flinched a little at the starkness of the words in the small room, and there was a difficult, silent awkwardness before Maur said, "Everyone here thinks I am. And the Norvenwache isn't going to believe either of us if we try to tell them otherwise."

"Yes, of course," she said, waspish with frustration. "I'm one of those immoral foreign mercenaries. I could hardly be expected to sleep in the same room with a desirable man and *not* ravish him."

Maur went scarlet, but managed to say, "It might be *my* morals they doubt, you know. Wizards have no better reputation than mer-cenaries."

No one with the full use of their senses would imagine Maur could ravish her. Though he was close to her own height, tall for a Norvenan, he was twenty pounds lighter—nearer forty these days—and even if he'd ever been taught to fight, those crippled hands would have made it impossible for him to use his knowledge. And he hadn't been taught to fight, beyond the polite sword work expected of gently-born Norvenan boys. And wizardry, of course, but that had been crippled, too.

She said none of that, although she could almost physically feel the words pushing at her throat when she swallowed them. Instead, carefully, she said, "So I'll be turned over to the Norvenwache."

"No," Maur said firmly. "I don't fancy the idea of watching them haul you off in chains."

"The strength of your regard warms my unworthy heart," she said—dryly, so that he would not guess that she spoke no more than the truth—and he laughed.

"Well, I do think—" he began, but cut himself off at the tap on the door that heralded the maid, and they lost the thread of the conversation for a while in the careful minutiae of getting him shaved and dressed. Agido did not nick him with the razor, and he managed to button his own waistcoat, so they both emerged more pleased with themselves than otherwise.

Maur said, "It seems to me that if we don't want you arrested for murder, we have to provide the Norvenwache with the real criminal. Who do you suppose would want Magister von Plaadt dead? Aside from me, that is, since I didn't kill him, and you didn't kill him for me."

"No one here *knows* him to want him dead—"

"Yes, fortunate I didn't ask that question in the Zauberhof."

"—except the man he was traveling with."

"Eero von Leistig," Maur said.

"Do you know him?"

"I recognized his name when he said it." Maur shrugged. "But I don't need to know him to know why he was traveling with Arnulf von Plaadt."

"Do you intend to enlighten me?" she said after a moment.

He shrugged again, mingled impatience and distaste. "Von Plaadt had a habit of preying on the more attractive of his male students."

"Preying how, exactly?"

"Oh, he pressured them into sleeping with him. He'd promise to help them get one of the Zauberhof's stipends or to introduce them to someone influential. He followed through on his promises if it suited him."

"And the Zauberhof knows?"

Maur wrinkled his nose. "Not . . . precisely. Everyone *at* the Zauberhof, with a few notable exceptions, but that's not the same thing."

"And did he . . . did you . . . ?"

"*Me*? Did you not hear me say quite distinctly his more *attractive* male students?"

"Hence my concern," she said, and he blushed.

"No, von Plaadt was never interested in me. Except as a patient, of course."

"Victim," she said, and Maur looked away. But he did not disagree.

"But Eero von Leistig," he said abruptly. "I find, bad-mannered of me though it is, that I am quite consumed with curiosity to discover what he and Magister von Plaadt were arguing about so fiercely yesterday. Do you want to tag along?"

"I suspect you will get more information out of Messire von Leistig without me. I must check on the horses. The stableboy seemed sensible enough, but Ham, I think, is not to be relied on."

"Ham? Oh, yes, the one who wasn't going to let us in. Well, do as you see fit. Anna Paulina trusts you; I can do no less."

Do you not trust me for your own sake? She said harshly, "I would have, if you had asked it of me."

"I'm sorry?"

"If you had wished it, I would have murdered Magister von Plaadt."

He stared at her, frowning a little. She could not tell what he was thinking. She turned away, impatient with her own folly. "Never mind. You did not ask, and I did not do it. Let us be about our business."

Maur said nothing, but he was still frowning when they went their separate ways.

THE STABLEBOY, SHORT AND SKINNY WITH AN UNTIDY thatch of mouse-brown hair overhanging his narrow, ferrety face, was indeed a sensible creature, and he had done well by the tired job-horses. "Don't worry about Ham, maselle," he said, having guessed accurately at the source of Agido's concern. "He don't come near the horses, now he's got me to do it."

She couldn't help her eyebrows going up. "Are you a recent development in Messire Ham's life?"

"Yes, maselle, if you mean by that I ain't been here long. Messire Bartolomeo only bought me last spring."

"*Bought* you? Do the Norvenans practice slavery? I had not known it."

"Bought out my indenture, I mean. I was just as glad. I like the horses, and Messire Bartolomeo don't hit me near as often as Messire Reyvik did."

"How long does your indenture last?"

"'Nother couple years. 'Til I turn eighteen."

He was older than she had thought him. "And you must put up with Ham until then?"

That made him laugh, his solemnity dissolving for a moment. "Ham ain't so bad. He's just lazy. But like I said, you don't need to worry about your horses. I'll look after 'em."

"I am certain you will," she said, and would have left him to his work except that he seemed to be hesitating. "Yes?"

"Beg pardon, maselle, if it's something I oughtn't to be asking, but the gentleman your companion, is he all right?"

All right? Oh, stableboy, you must learn to define your terms. "He has been very ill," she said, "but he is getting better."

"What happened to him, maselle?"

She could not help sighing, and on the instant, the boy said, "I beg pardon, maselle. I shouldn't have . . . I forgot myself, is all, and I'm sorry."

"You've done nothing wrong . . ." She raised her eyebrows, and he said, "Rose," adding defiantly, "named for the saint, not the flower."

"Rose. It's just that the story is not mine to tell." But she did not want him imagining that there was anything dishonorable in what had happened to Maur; she said carefully, "He was injured fighting for the queen."

"Oh." He considered that a moment and said, "Elgiv said there was an awful row at supper, with the gentleman that's been killed."

She looked at him closely and decided that he was not asking, obliquely or otherwise, if Maur was a murderer. "He was upset," she said, even more carefully, "but I think anyone would have been."

"If . . . if there's anything I can do to help." He was blushing fiercely, and she wondered which of them his sixteen-year-old passion had settled on, Maur or herself.

She was about to turn him aside, gently and with thanks, when it occurred to her that a sharp-eyed and intelligent ally in The Mare's Nest might not go at all amiss.

"Keep your eyes open," she said. "If you see anything unusual or suspicious, inform me. I did not murder Magister von Plaadt, and I should like to find out who did."

"Yes, maselle," he said, with such earnest grimness that she gathered he, too, had heard Bartolomeo's theories on the subject, and she left the stables feeling ridiculously comforted.

On entering the bar, she found Madame Bartolomea polishing every wooden surface in sight. Agido's Ervenzian was not particularly fluent, and under any other set of circumstances, she would have made no effort to engage the lady of The Mare's Nest in conversation. But she and Maur were trapped in this inn with a corpse, its murderer, and an innkeeper who apparently wished to assign the blame where it would be least inconvenient to himself.

It was not difficult to encourage Madame Bartolomea to talk. She was much younger than her husband, and she knew so little Norvenan that Agido gathered she had no one other than her husband to whom she could speak. By the same token, she couldn't offer very much information either about Magister von Plaadt's affairs on the last day of his life or about what her husband, with the advice of Messire Glas, was planning to do with the body. She did say that about an hour after supper, the magister had come into the bar alone and in a foul temper and had proceeded to drink two double whiskies in quick succession before storming out again. Madame Bartolomea had guessed that he was either drowning his sorrows after an argument or gathering his courage to start one.

"With Messire von Leistig?" Agido said.

"Him," Madame Bartolomea said with an expressive shrug. "They have been here two days, he and the magister, and if it wasn't one thing, it was another."

"They argued a great deal?"

"Not *argued* so much. But they were unhappy with each other. Elgiv says there was no pleasing Messire von Leistig."

"And Magister von Plaadt?"

Her smile was dimpled and twinkly. "The magister was the sort of man there was no pleasing regardless. Their first night here he made poor Elgiv cry. I imagine his wife could not keep housemaids. But surely, maselle, Messire von Haarien had more reason than anyone to be unhappy with the magister. Those dreadful things he said!"

Bartolomeo must have translated for his wife, Agido noted. Thoughtful of him. "He most certainly was not brawling with von Plaadt last night," she said, more tartly than she meant to.

"Ah, the poor dove," Madame Bartolomea said. "Was it the rebellion?"

"Yes," she said, and bit her tongue against the impulse to give the details, to prove just how unfair von Plaadt's attack had been. There was no reason to care what an innkeeper's not-very-bright wife thought of Maur; in any event, Madame Bartolomea did not seem inclined to take von Plaadt's side.

"A terrible thing," said Madame Bartolomea. "So wicked of Baron von Klemmerin, going to war against his cousin like that, and all because she wouldn't marry him."

"I would not have married him myself, cousin or no. She would have been dead within the year."

"Was he so cruel?"

"Ambitious. I am told he was much about King Paul Augustus in the last days of his life, angling to be named heir."

"And disown that blessed lamb?" Madame Bartolomea said disapprovingly. It was as much as Agido could do not to betray her opinion of the phrase *blessed lamb* used in conjunction with Queen Anna Theresa. But at least the queen and her generals had never resorted to torture. "Have you ever seen her? Do the pictures do her justice?"

More than justice, Agido thought, remembering that colorless face with its heavy eyebrows and protruding teeth. But she said only, "Yes." The queen had awarded Maur the Cross St. Clavere with her own hands; she deserved that much charity in return.

"I was hoping we'd get the coronation broadsheets this week," said Madame Bartolomea. "But the snow—"

"Sofia!" A bellow from somewhere in the depths of the inn. Madame Bartolomea jumped, flashed Agido a guilty, dimpled smile, and vanished like a rabbit down its hole.

Agido went in search of Maur and found him, scowling thoughtfully, in their room. "I don't think Eero killed him," he said when he saw her.

"No?"

"No."

"Is this a reasoned opinion or merely the promptings of intuition?"

"Wizards don't . . ." He made a frustrated, choppy gesture. "I don't say Eero *couldn't* have killed him, but I don't think he would have done it by hitting him over the head. Von Plaadt wouldn't have turned his back on him for one thing. We aren't Cabaline wizards with that handy built-in thaumaturgic armor. We watch each other carefully, especially when we are, ah, disagreeing strenuously."

"You think von Plaadt was killed by an annemer? Is that not even *less* likely than Messire von Leistig caving his skull in?"

"As a general rule, yes. But I just don't think . . ."

Wizards were notoriously difficult to kill. Even the safest and most academic spell-casting required fast reflexes, and although no school of wizardry save the Eusebians of Kekropia *condoned* using magic on annemer, few if any wizards were principled enough not to use every resource at their command to defend themselves. For an unaided annemer to kill a wizard, the wizard had to be taken by surprise, and had to be killed or incapacitated by the first blow.

Annemer had crippled Maur's hands, but wizards had crippled his magic first.

"The person who killed von Plaadt meant to do it," Maur said, "and Eero wouldn't have. Von Plaadt was his way into the Universitat, regardless of what Eero persisted in calling personal difficulties."

"So they were in fact having 'personal difficulties'?"

"Oh, powers, yes. Von Plaadt was throwing him over."

"Did he admit that?"

"Not in so many words. But von Plaadt had gotten what he wanted—Eero *could* have stayed at the Zauberhof as a fellow, you see."

"But you said Messire von Leistig wouldn't kill him because he was his entrée to the Universitat."

Maur looked at her blankly for a moment, not unlike a goldfish who had been asked to explain water. Then he said, "Staying at the Zauberhof would be safe, and within Norvena Parva, quite prestigious. But the Zauberhof is no more the Universitat than Karolinsberg is Igensbeck. And if Eero didn't get in on von Plaadt's coattails, it would be another twenty or thirty years before he might be a wizard of sufficient status and repute to be offered a chair. And he might never reach that point at all—he's not very powerful, and he doesn't strike me as a terribly original thinker."

"But being von Plaadt's research assistant . . . ?"

"The Universitat gives preference to its own magisters' students. If you don't start at the Universitat as a pupil—a child of fourteen or fifteen—getting yourself into their system is extraordinarily difficult. Most Parvan wizards don't even bother to try. So it would have been perfectly reasonable for Eero to say no to von Plaadt's offer, but once he said yes, he was committed. Now the poor fellow's going to have to explain to the Universitat Council just how he managed to lose their newest faculty member in such a dramatic and permanent fashion."

"Ah," she said. "*That*, I can understand."

His smile lit his face, there and gone like a flash of lightning. "I thought you might. But, you see, I can imagine Eero in a fit of rage trying to *throttle* von Plaadt or perhaps blacking his eye. Not smashing his skull in."

"Who *can* you imagine smashing his skull in?"

"That's the problem." He sighed. "All I seem to have managed this morning is to convince myself that the person with the most apparent reason to kill von Plaadt didn't do so."

"Well, von Plaadt's mood seems to have been ripe for murder last night," she offered, and told him what she'd learned from Madame Bartolomea.

"Gracious," said Maur. "I'm surprised he didn't come murder *me*."

"He would not have fared well had he made the attempt."

"And perhaps he knew it. From what Eero said, and from what he tried very hard *not* to say, I gathered that the magister had not exactly intended to break things off quite so precipitously. Or here, for that matter. So between that and the scene at dinner, he must have rather badly wanted someone to take his foul temper out on. Von Plaadt was always happier with a victim." His light, detached tone faltered, and it was a moment before he continued, "He must have made the mistake of choosing someone who was prepared to fight back. And who didn't believe in half-measures."

"But it makes no sense," she said. "We're only going to be immobilized here for a matter of days, and then most of us would never have seen von Plaadt again. If you say this was an intentional murder—"

"It wasn't a fight," Maur said. "That bruise on his forehead was the only injury on the front of his body. No one else is showing any signs of damage, and in any event, you don't get in a fistfight with a wizard and win by nonmagical means. Eero and I agree that that blow to the skull had nothing magical about it."

"Could the person responsible simply have misjudged the blow?"

"Why would you want to knock Magister von Plaadt unconscious if you didn't want to kill him? It's not as if you could buy time to escape. There's nowhere to escape to. Besides, Eero says he died by drowning."

"And how does Eero know that?"

"It's a perfectly straightforward spell—nothing necromantic about it. We all learned it in Magister Gruben's class on civil magic. But my point is, von Plaadt was still alive when he went into the water. Whoever killed him—well, either they believed he was already dead, or they knew he wasn't dead and decided to make sure. Either way, he didn't *drown* by accident, and that means that the person convicted of von Plaadt's murder will be beheaded." His eyes met hers with open concern.

"An irony I would prefer to avoid," she said, "to spend more than half my life riding to war and at last to be executed for the murder of a man like von Plaadt—even if I *had* killed him, it would be insupportable."

Maur smiled, appreciation lightening the worry in his eyes. But he said, "Once you are arrested—well, it is true that Norvenan justice rarely miscarries, but also true that it is very slow to let go of an idea once grasped. You might be imprisoned for more than a year, and . . ."

"You will not hurt my feelings by saying what we both know to be true. I am foreign and a woman and a soldier. I make your authorities nervous, no matter how useful they may sometimes find me. It would be a great deal easier for them if I were the murderer."

"I would go to the queen if I had to," Maur said. "I could, you know."

He could, and the von Haarien influence was enough that he would probably be listened to.

"Let us see if we can keep it from coming to that," she said, and he nodded almost gratefully.

"Then let's consider what we know. Do you think a woman could have killed him?"

"*I* could have."

"Let me be more specific. Do you think one of the other women here could have killed him?"

"It depends on how badly she wanted him dead."

He glared. She spread her hands helplessly and said, "As we don't know what he was hit with, or where—" She broke off as a thought struck her. "Maur, where are the magister's clothes?"

"His clothes?"

"He hadn't any when we found him."

"No," Maur said, and she could tell by his expression that he was remembering that bloated pink starfish, just as she was.

"And they weren't in the changing room. Or did someone find them?"

"I don't think anyone looked. Had we better?"

"Yes."

He followed her willingly; she thought he was glad to have someone else take the initiative. Even when he was not in bleak despair, his stamina was gone, the force of the self behind the blue eyes. It was that loss, Agido knew, that most worried his grandmother. Anna Paulina was annemer and understood wizards even less than Agido did, but she could see that something had been broken inside him, and it was something that she did not know how to fix. Neither did Agido. She was beginning to suspect that she did not even know what was truly wrong. She had thought it had been Baron von Klemmerin's torturers who had broken him, but what he had told her about binding coats and ice-water baths suggested a new and more terrible possibility. Baron von Klemmerin and his wizard cronies had broken

Maur's magic, but it might very well prove to be Magister von Plaadt who had driven him mad.

And if that was the case, then truly Maur's future would be decided in Igensbeck, and she prayed desperately that Magister Thornfeld would be able to help him, because it seemed to her that otherwise her fate would be to watch Maur wither and die like a tree denied rain.

There were no signs of Magister von Plaadt's clothes in the changing room, nor—when they went and looked—in the baths themselves.

Maur and Agido stared at each other.

"I refuse to believe that Magister von Plaadt walked down here starkers," Maur said finally. "But why in the world would anyone make off with his clothes?"

"Perhaps his clothes could have told us something about the murderer?"

"But *what*? I know, I know—if we knew that, we wouldn't need to worry about where his clothes had gone."

"Quite so," she said, and the bell of The Mare's Nest tolled through the warren, summoning them to lunch; they made faces of mutual exasperation at each other and went.

Lunch was an awkward experience. Half the table ate in silence, heads lowered over their plates to avoid making eye contact with anyone. The other half of the table indulged in gossip and speculation of the most indefensible type. Maur was prominent among the latter group, his eyes bright with mischief when he looked at Agido. And though she found his conduct deplorable, she could not help admiring his ability to extract scraps of actual fact from the conversation.

Anna Lucilla von Deiver and Corinna von Elstan were sharing a room; they had retired together. Although Agido suspected that Maselle von Deiver was a heavier sleeper than she wanted to admit, it nonetheless seemed unlikely that either lady could have left the room without alerting the other.

Eero von Leistig had volunteered to double up with the magister so that Maur and Agido would not have to sleep in the stables. He had had, of course, an ulterior motive for so doing, and it seemed as if it might have been that which had impelled the magister to his premature disavowal of affections. Certainly their quarrel explained why von Leistig had not been surprised at the magister's absence from their room the previous night.

He was white-faced, ill, clearly as much grieving as shocked. And although Agido supposed it might be possible for a man to murder his lover, coldly dispose of the still-breathing body, and nevertheless appear, or even genuinely be, grief-stricken the next day, she did not think von Leistig was up to that particular challenge. Little though she wanted to, she agreed with Maur: von Leistig was not the murderer. But she could see in several persons' eyes the awareness that he had had reason to be furious—even lethally furious—with von Plaadt, and had not even a problematic witness to attest that he had not acted on his anger. His position was, if anything, slightly worse than hers, although she did not think he had yet recognized that himself.

Neither Nikk nor Messire Glas had anyone who could say what they had been doing between dinner the previous night and the discovery of the body that morning, and although it was difficult to imagine either of them having any kind of a past with von Plaadt, much less one worthy of murder, they seemed the two most likely candidates from the simple perspective of opportunity. And then there was Madame Bartolomea's offhand remark about von Plaadt making Elgiv cry. If it was a simple case of a browbeaten chambermaid, that was one thing and sufficient motive for nothing more dire than spitting in the magister's coffee. But with the man murdered, the possibility could not be ignored that some more personal consideration had impelled Elgiv's tears.

Agido watched Elgiv thoughtfully as she came and went with bowls of soup and platters of bread and cheese and sliced smoked meat. She had been quick to report evil of von Plaadt to Rose in the stable—was it merely that the story was good gossip, or did she have some other reason to want word to spread of the magister's confrontation with Maur? Her eyes were watchful, and her broad-cheekboned face showed nothing of the mind behind it. She would have learned that early. There were women like her all across the two Norvenas: overworked, ill-educated. She might have been anywhere between eighteen and forty, an orphan or a widow or simply a working girl.

Toward the end of the meal, Bartolomeo came in and announced that it had stopped snowing, and that he and Ham and Rose would be clearing the pass that afternoon. Any guests who wished to join them were welcome, he added, his gaze blandly crossing Agido's. She smiled and said, equally blandly, that she would be delighted.

In the end, they were five—only Nikk among the other guests seemed to feel such manual labor not to be beneath him. He and Agido took south, toward Norvena Parva; Bartolomeo and Ham took north. Rose had the task of packing the snow into barrels to take back into The Mare's Nest to melt. Snow was an impediment, but water could always be useful.

Shoveling snow, while a job that created great camaraderie, did not lend itself to conversation. But afterward, when Bartolomeo said the springs were fit for use again, Nikk and Agido went down together to soak out the worst of their fatigue.

While they rested, propped against the edge of the pool, Nikk commented on her scars, as most men did, and that led easily to swapping stories about jobs they had had and campaigns they had fought in. Like Agido, he had spent a good deal of time in the patchwork of semicivilized baronies north of Norvena Magna, where there was always work for someone who could use a sword. Nikk told her the truth behind the marriage and subsequent swift demise of Baron Kruiver, and then, rather abruptly, as their laughter trailed off, said, "The fellow you're traveling with—you attached to him?"

"Yes," she said, although she was not, at least not in the specific sense Nikk meant.

"He doesn't look like he gives you much of a good time."

"Looks can be deceiving." She remembered lying in bed with

Maur—before Paul Augustus died and Baron von Klemmerin raised his banner against Anna Theresa—his clever tongue silent for once, but doing such sweet, wicked things.

"I don't know," Nikk said. "You seem to me like a woman who hasn't been getting what she wants for a while."

You have no idea, she thought, and grinned at him. The offer was tempting—from the light in his eyes, Nikk was the sort of man who knew how to give a woman what she wanted. It would be easy, meaning nothing but pleasure, satisfactory to both parties, and if they got lucky, remembered with fondness long after they could no longer recall each other's name. She was relatively sure Nikk was not the murderer; he had any annemer's healthy distrust of wizards, and his career had mostly been north and west of the Norvenas. She considered the possibility that someone had hired him to kill the magister, but although clever, there had been nothing professional about this job. And if Nikk had had anything to do with it, there would have been no telltale bruises to show the magister had been dragged into the baths from somewhere else. He knew as well as she did how to carry a dead or unconscious man.

But despite all that, she said, "No, thank you," and he shrugged philosophically and said, "Guess I'll try my luck with the chambermaid, then," and they separated.

And she wondered, all the way back up to the room to dress for dinner, what in the world had possessed her to turn him down. There was no point deluding herself that Maur would care; he couldn't even stand for her to touch him. He would probably have been relieved if she had spent the night in Nikk's room.

But when she opened the door, Maur looked up and gave her a blinding smile, and said, "*There* you are. I was just beginning to wonder if Messire Bartolomeo had left you in a snowdrift."

"I was in the baths," she said, and some perverse impulse made her add, "with Nikk."

His eyes went wide, and then his face became closed and cold. "I am relieved to hear that even mercenaries can be taught to appreciate the benefits of good hygiene." Said in his most affected, drawling voice, and if she had not seen that flash of hurt, he might have succeeded in provoking her. But she *had* seen—and perhaps she had been wrong to think Maur did not care. For that had looked and sounded a great deal like jealousy.

"He offered, but I declined," she said, answering that moment's unguarded pain.

He turned away from her and said wearily, "I can't imagine why."

"Can you not?"

"I know Anna Paulina hired you to babysit me to Igensbeck, but honestly I'd be fine on my own for a night."

"You think I'm here because Anna Paulina is paying me?"

"It's very kind of you to pretend otherwise, and I do appreciate it. I know I . . ." He couldn't seem to find a way to finish that sentence, saying abruptly, "You don't need to. I understand."

"Understand what, exactly?" she said. If he had been looking at her, he would have seen her hands clenching, seen the twitch of anger at the corner of her mouth. But he was looking down at his own hands where they rested, crabbed and twisted, in his lap.

"I'm not who I was. I know that. And I don't expect you to feel about me . . . You don't have any obligation to . . ."

"Maur, shut up." He had succeeded in provoking her after all, and he recoiled in startled dismay from the fury in her voice. She yanked her clean pullover on, said, "I'll see you at dinner," and walked out.

He didn't know, she reminded herself, stalking down to the bar. He didn't know that she'd gone every day to the Annamaihopital, asking for news of his progress, asking if she could see him; that she had sunk so low as to leave flowers before the statue of Anna Mai von Helfrin as if it were a shrine like those in the village where she had grown up. He did not know, because she had been desperately careful not to let him see, how much it had hurt her when he had pulled away from her touch, when his cold fingers had rested against hers barely long enough for politeness.

They had never discussed their past lovers, but she had not needed Maur to tell her that he had few to discuss. He had always been, she gathered, intent on his studies and never as attractive a catch as his annemer cousins. He had not come virgin to her bed, but it had also not been a secret between them that she was the teacher and he her student.

He had been both apt and eager; she had forgotten—had allowed herself to forget—how little he knew of desire, how ill-defended he was against the cruel voices of self-doubt and despair that von Plaadt had taught him to hear.

She had thought he did not want her, thought his coldness was embarrassed impatience with a discarded lover trailing after him like a stray dog. She was not ashamed of her varied sexual experiences, but she had wondered if he thought she should be. Her own pride had blinded her—her own pride and Maur's perfect cold façade—and all this time he had been assuming that she no longer desired him, no longer cared for him. And thus he had protected himself in the only way he could, by never giving her the chance to tell him what he believed to be the truth.

Nothing could have shown more eloquently how vulnerable he was, how fragile.

She stepped into the bar. Two bearded, scruffy-looking men were there, locals she judged, by the snowshoes propped against the hearth, and wondered what there was up here to be local to. The strong aroma of sheep that surrounded them gave her an answer.

Madame Bartolomea drew her a beer, and she sat at the bar to drink it. She remembered, for no good reason, a day in the spring. It had rained all night, dawning beautifully clear, and she had flung her windows open to the green, fresh-washed scent of the Park Corranin. The long white curtains had floated idly on the cross-breeze, and when Maur came in, he had brought her a great breathing armful of lilies.

She didn't even have to close her eyes to see him again as he had been that day, stretched out across her bed, his wrists bound with bright scarves, his eyes brilliant as diamonds. She remembered how both of them had reveled in her power over him, both of them, wizard and annemer, knowing that her power was part of a game with just enough undercurrent of truth to make it worthwhile. He could have ended the game anytime he wished: the truth was that he did not wish to.

She drank her beer and contemplated the new truth with which they were faced. Her power over him was no longer, even in part, a game. In that light, his rejection of her took on a new meaning; it was the only power he had. Once he admitted he wanted her, he had nothing left with which to negotiate, nothing he could do except wait to find out whether she would reject him or accept him, whether she would be cruel or kind. And she thought of Magister von Plaadt, who had claimed to help him and who had done nothing but hurt him, and she could not blame Maur for defending himself against a world that seemed poisoned with ambiguity and shifting truth.

She brooded over her beer, listening with half an ear to the shepherds' conversation. Local gossip, a long and involved discussion of winters past and the likely course of the winter ahead. The shepherds were polite to Madame Bartolomea and did not so much as make eye contact with Agido, but when Elgiv came in with a tray of clean glasses, they whistled and stomped and shouted things Agido was glad Madame Bartolomea did not have enough Norvenan to understand.

Elgiv met Agido's eyes and shrugged, a reaction which told her both that if Nikk did try his luck with the chambermaid, he was likely to find good fortune, and that if Elgiv had killed Magister von Plaadt, it had not been to protect herself. She answered the shepherds with something scurrilous and unrepeatable and clearly referring to old history, and left with her head high.

The bell rang for dinner as Agido finished her beer, and she made her way to the private dining room, frowning in thought. What she and Maur did or did not feel for each other would not matter if she was arrested by the Norvenwache, and all she was accomplishing, as Maur had said of himself earlier, was absolving possible murderers of blame. The only person left was the lawyer's clerk, Sebastian Glas, and he looked no more like a murderer than any of the others. She wondered if she should reconsider the case for her own guilt. Aside from the trifling fact that she had not done it, she recognized herself as the most plausible murderer of the lot.

Maur did not look at her when she entered the dining room, although his heightened color and the accelerated pace of his words showed that he was aware of her presence. He was talking to Corinna von Elstan about her proposed course of studies; on her other side, Messires von Leistig and Glas were engaged—or perhaps entangled— in conversation with Maselle von Deiver, who seemed convinced that they would be interested in hearing about her brothers, one of whom had been a fellow of the Zauberhof and the other a Statadvocat under Paul Augustus's father. "Before our Family Tragedy, of course," she said with a sigh worthy of a melodrama heroine.

Agido sat down next to Maur, smiled at Maselle von Elstan—who blushed, but smiled back—and applied herself to the food. It was the heavy bean soup, with garlic and cheese and toast on the side, that was a specialty of Norvena Parva and the southwestern part of Norvena Magna. And again there were platters of sliced cheese and sliced smoked meats and long loaves of bread: simple food, but plentiful, and almost all of it things that Maur could manage by himself. She did not think that was any part of the kitchen's plans, but she was grateful nonetheless. Silently, unobtrusively, she dealt with the toast and garlic for him, and then watched sidelong with what she hoped was well-concealed delight as he dipped the toast in the soup, wrapping long strings of melted cheese around it, and ate, all his attention focused on Maselle von Elstan and the questions she was asking him about thaumaturgical philosophy. His hands would never be normal—he would never be able to straighten his fingers fully, or spread them more than a few painful fractions of an inch—but he had some motion. They were not completely unusable, as the doctors of the Annamaihopital had feared they would be. And every shred of independence that could be returned to him was something to be treasured.

It was pointless to hate the dead, but Agido hated Baron von Klemmerin regardless. And hated Magister von Plaadt all the more.

Dessert was bread pudding in rum sauce, and over it conversation at the table became more general. The road down into Norvena Magna would probably be clear the day after tomorrow, said Glas, a veteran of the mountain passes between the Norvenas. "And then I have advised Messire Bartolomeo to send for the Norvenwache."

A ripple of unease ran around the table. The lawyer's clerk said patiently, "The murderer of Magister von Plaadt must be brought to justice."

"Of course," Maur said steadily. "But are you quite sure the Norvenwache is equipped to dispense justice in this case?"

"I have written a letter to the Zauberhof," von Leistig said. "We are justly famed for our judicial wizardry, you know."

"As a graduate of the Zauberhof, I do know that, Eero," Maur said with a smile of great and spurious sweetness, and von Leistig flushed up to the roots of his flaxen hair.

"But surely there's no difficulty," Maselle von Deiver began, with a pointed look down the table at Agido. "Isn't it clear that—"

"Anna Lucilla, hold your tongue!" Maselle von Elstan said sharply

"But Corinna, you know it—"

"Hold your tongue," Maselle von Elstan said again, blotchy with embarrassment but standing her ground.

"Far be it from me to cross my dear pupil," Maselle von Deiver said and tittered. Her laugh was high-pitched, grating.

Agido said abruptly, "Maur, I think we should call it a night."

Maur looked at her with unmistakable trepidation; she could see how much he didn't want to resume their interrupted conversation. But he nodded and rose and preceded her out of the room. Someone—she thought it was Nikk—muttered something about nursemaids. *Let them think what they want,* she said to herself grimly. *The truth belongs to no one but Maur and myself.*

They were silent in the hallways. When she closed and locked the bedroom door behind them, Maur tumbled into speech like falling down a flight of stairs: "Agido, I'm sorry, I didn't mean to imply that you were—that you would've—"

"Maur," she said, "my heart, how could you think that anyone would have to *pay* me to be with you?"

"But you . . . I didn't . . ." He had gone a florid crimson and, rather than sitting down, had backed into the corner. He was trembling, all his coldness dissolved into fear.

She sat down on the bed, said as gently as she could, "Are you afraid of me?"

He blanched, the hectic color draining out of his cheeks. But he shook his head. "N-not of you. But I . . . I . . . Agido, I *can't*."

"Can't what?"

"Can't . . ." He wrapped his arms around himself, as if for warmth or comfort, protecting his damaged hands. "I can't remember . . . can't remember who I was before. Can't remember how to be the person I was."

"Then you must learn how to be the person you are."

"Don't mock me. Please."

"I am not. I would not." She hesitated a long painful moment; she had never talked of her past to anyone, and it hurt like a gut wound to do so now, but she had to give him something, some anchor against the fear that was drowning him.

She said briskly, unemotionally, "When I was a child, the house to which my village owed fealty became involved in a feud with another house. I no longer remember the ins and outs of the quarrel, if ever I knew them, nor do I know how the matter was ultimately resolved, if it was resolved at all. Troian feuds sometimes are not. What I do know is that the feud is the reason my village no longer exists. The summer I was fourteen, the forces of the opposing house raided Iphigeneia. They burned every house to the ground, desecrated the temple, looted the public storehouses and granaries. And then they murdered, maimed, and raped their way through the population."

His eyes had gone wide. "You were . . ."

"Left for dead," she said flatly. "The Celebrants of Ianthos who found me accepted me into their order, taught me the sword, and did not try to hinder me when I left them. Thus, Maur, my heart, believe me when I say that I understand what you—"

"But . . . oh, this is ludicrous!" He started pacing, which she decided was preferable to having him huddled in the corner. "Agido, you can't trivialize what you suffered by comparing it to what happened to me."

"It's my experience. I can do what I like with it. Besides, I don't see how you can call it trivializing. You were driven mad."

He muttered something of which she caught only the word "weakness."

"Is that what von Plaadt told you?"

His badly controlled startle told her she was correct.

"I love you." She had not meant to say it, had not meant ever to say it to anyone. But the words were there, like embers burning her mouth and throat, forcing themselves past the barriers of teeth and lips, for the pain of speaking was less than the pain of keeping silent.

For a moment, he didn't seem to understand her. Then he was staring at her, jaw slack. His mouth worked once or twice, but no sound emerged.

"Nothing they did to you can change that," she said, determined now to get the truth, at least her part of it, out in plain sight. "Not von Klemmerin, not von Plaadt, not all the doctors of the Annamaihopital. Nothing von Plaadt told you about yourself can make me not love you, or make me not want you. I understand if you don't want me, but—"

"No," Maur said. "I do. I mean, I think I . . . I don't know how anymore, but I want . . . Agido, I . . . In the hospital . . ." His face was white, pinched, pain and honesty indistinguishable. "I tried to ask for help. It hurt, you know. My hands and my chest, and my . . . my . . . I don't know how to describe it."

He pressed both hands to his chest. "Something broken, and it didn't heal. And they said there was nothing wrong with me. That I was imagining things, that I was malingering, that I was mad. And von Plaadt said there was nothing wrong with me if I'd just pull myself together. And I couldn't . . . I couldn't . . . I asked for help. And they hurt me."

He swallowed hard and said the thing he hadn't said, all along, the thing he'd hinted at or circumvented or simply let her assume, but never *said*: "Help me."

She said promptly, simply: "What do you need?"

"Will you touch me? And not hurt me?"

She got up, feeling her heart thundering against her ribs. Took the few steps necessary to close the distance between them. Said in a voice she barely recognized as her own, "Maur, it is I. Open your eyes, my heart."

He obeyed, tilted his head to look up at her.

"If I hurt you, or frighten you, just tell me to stop, and I will. I promise you. Do you believe me?"

He hesitated a moment, which she found paradoxically reassuring. It meant that, whatever his answer, it wouldn't be a lie to placate her. And after that long moment, he nodded and then said, "Yes. I trust you."

"Good," she said, and didn't care if he could hear her voice waver. She raised her right hand, laid her fingertips very gently against his left cheekbone. His eyes never left hers. She pressed her palm against his jaw, felt him swallow, then felt him lean, infinitesimally, into the caress.

"It's you," he said, and he sounded surprised. "You touch me, and it's still you."

"Yes, my heart," she said.

"Will you . . ." He hesitated, and then met her eyes. "Will you kiss me?"

"*Yes*," she said, cupped his jaw in her hand to steady his head, and leaned in and kissed him.

His lips were soft against hers. After a moment, in which she could imagine him examining and cataloguing his own reactions, his mouth yielded to hers as it always had, allowing her to deepen the kiss, allowing her to taste him, a taste she had been deprived of for months. She kept the kiss gentle, encouraging him to respond, to taste her in return. And after some hesitation he did, with a sort of shy eagerness that hurt her as much as it delighted her.

Finally, she broke the kiss, moved back so that they both had room to breathe and so that she could see his face. "All right?" she said.

"Yes," he said. "Very much so." He raised one hand, then stopped, looking at its crabbed stiffness with frustration.

"Touch me," she said. "However you can."

He flushed red again, and did not meet her eyes, but he did reach out to press the back of his hand against her cheek. She could not have helped sighing with contentment if she had wanted to, and that brought his gaze up to her face. "You don't . . . you don't mind?"

"Why should I mind?"

"I . . . they're so ugly." But she heard what he meant, what he'd censored himself from saying: *I'm ugly.*

"Maur." She thought carefully about her words, even going so far as to say what she meant in Troian first, before translating into Norvenan. Language was such a fragile instrument, and what she needed to say was almost too heavy for it. "What happened to you is ugly. But it does not mean that *you* are ugly. Unless you let it."

"I've never heard you speak Troian before," he said, and she would have protested the non sequitur, except that there was something in his expression that looked like wonder.

She smiled at him, said, "I save it for the things that truly matter," and leaned in to kiss him again. This time, he did not hesitate to respond, seemed almost greedy for her touch, and his arms came up around her, wrists crossed at the back of her neck, hands carefully out of harm's way. She let her own hands slide down, slowly, ready to stop if he seemed in the least distressed. But he let her pull him closer, making a little pleased murmur as her fingers spread against the small of his back. And with their bodies pressed together, she could feel, through the layers of cloth, a promise of arousal.

He was fine-boned and still painfully thin. She swung round with him, and carefully they settled together on the wide bed. "We don't have to do any more than this, if you don't want it," she said, uncertain of where his boundaries were, of what would and would not be all right. She was excruciatingly aware of how easy it would be to pin him down, take what she wanted, ravish him as she had suggested earlier in bitter mockery.

She had always led, always dominated, and his own strength had been enough to ensure that aggression did not become coercion, that play did not become reality. But she could not trust in his strength unthinkingly anymore, because he had been taught he was not strong.

When he did not answer her immediately, she waited. She let him pull away from her, did not, although she wished to, reach to brush his hair out of his eyes. "You won't mind?" he said, biting his lip and watching her anxiously, as if he expected that she would mind, and would punish him for it.

"No," she said.

"I . . . I want to," he said. "At least, I think I want to. I don't know. I *want* to want to. Does that make any sense?"

"Yes," she said. And it did. She took a breath, cleared her own desire out of the way as much as she could, and said, "I will not do anything you do not want me to. But, Maur, my heart, that means you must tell me what you want."

"And if I don't know what I want?"

"Then we wait until you do. There's no hurry."

He looked at her even more doubtfully, as if he was not accustomed to having anyone be patient with him. And she supposed ruefully that he wouldn't be. There had never been any need for anyone to be patient with Maur von Haarien, his grandmother's darling, bright and talented, quick-witted, nimble-tongued . . . deft-fingered. She smiled back at him.

It took him two tries, but he said, "Will you help me with my buttons?"

They undressed together, slowly. She did the work of it, dealing with buttons and laces, pulling and pushing cloth about. Maur kissed her, her throat, her collarbones. When she took her shirt off, he stroked her arms and sides with the backs of his hands—small, halting caresses, but as sweet as the first taste of rain after a long drought. She kissed his scars, all of them, slowly, the painful need of her love turning into patience like an alchemy of the soul, and Maur blushed and bit his lip and let her. She eased his trousers and underclothes off, he lying there with his hands resting on the pillow above his head so that they would not be jarred, and then she took off her own remaining clothes and crawled up the bed to kiss his mouth, kiss away the anxiety she saw gathering in his eyes.

"I am not going to hurt you," she reminded him.

"Say it in Troian?"

"Why?"

"Please? Because . . ." He swallowed hard, but said doggedly, "Because it matters."

"It does matter," she agreed and said in Troian, "I swear, by the honor of my house and the witness of the Tetrarchs, I will not hurt you, and I will not do anything under the aegis of love that you do not wish."

"That got much longer, somehow," he said, a spark of humor starting to dance in his eyes.

"I embellished," she said and translated.

His face became very still for a moment, and she felt her entire self clench with the fear that she had said the wrong thing again, as she had been saying the wrong thing, it seemed, for weeks. Then he smiled, and it was the smile she remembered, lively with curiosity. He had understood, and when he spoke, she knew he had accepted what she was trying to offer.

"Why 'under the aegis of love'? What does that mean?"

"It means that I do not wish to lie to you, but I cannot promise *never* to do anything you do not wish me to."

"No?" he said, eyes brimming with mock sadness.

"No," she said firmly, repressing a smile. "But when we are like this, together, loving each other—"

"I understand. I had no idea Troians were such skilled logicians."

"We are an old and subtle people," she said gravely, and then they both started laughing.

But her oath, elaborate as it had been, seemed to comfort him; he kissed her with assurance now, and when her hand moved to caress his stomach, he did not object, and when it slipped lower, he arched, just a little, into her touch.

"What do you want, Maur?" she said against his ear.

His breath caught for a moment in something that was not quite a laugh. "I want Paul Gustaf von Klemmerin never to have gotten his bright idea. I want Soren von Kulp and Rikard von Estin not to have been such cruel and inventive beasts. I'm even starting to understand that I want Arnulf von Plaadt never to have come near me."

"Do I need to rephrase my question?" she asked dryly, and his laugh was startled, real.

"I want . . . I want to believe that you want this. That you want *me*."

"You should, my heart. Because it is true."

"But why?" he said, and although he tried to make it sound mock-plaintive, she heard the real pain beneath.

"I loved you in the spring," she said.

"You didn't let it show."

She shrugged a little, one-shouldered. "You did not need me to."

"You mean this is because I'm crippled?"

He started to struggle up, and she said hastily, "No, I'm sorry. I did not say it properly. It is difficult to explain."

He lay back, looking at her mistrustfully, wary again.

"I loved you," she said, "but what was I to you? A mercenary woman, a foreigner, an exotic liaison."

"I didn't—"

"Hush," she said and smiled at him. "I knew it, and I didn't mind. My love was of no use to you, do you see? You did not look for it."

He was frowning now, and said slowly, "And so you did not give it, because it would be a burden."

"Love should be like the gift of wings, or so I was taught as a child. And it is not the same as desire. I have never made any secret of desiring you." And she watched with delight as he blushed.

"But how did you know?" he said after a moment. "How did you know that I . . ." His voice was barely a whisper when he said, "That I have come to love you . . . since the spring."

"You . . ." Her voice cracked, and she had to start again: "You love me?"

They stared at each other, both wide-eyed now. "Yes," Maur said. "Hopelessly . . . I thought."

She kissed him, desperately, sweetly, and he clung to her with his mouth and with the awkward grip of his wrists against her shoulders. And the promise of arousal bloomed to truth, and when she asked, he said, "Yes," and "Yes," again as if the word itself were a joy and a wonder.

He lay on his back with his hands carefully above his head, and again she did the work, and again that was not what mattered. When she climaxed, it was with a shriek like that of a hunting cat, and she did not care if The Mare's Nest heard her or not. She hoped the Sisters rang with it.

She held Maur afterward, his hands cradled between their bodies like broken-winged birds. He looked at her, his eyes gentle without the weapons and walls he used to keep himself safe. "How do you say 'I love you' in Troian?"

She told him, and he repeated it back carefully. "Your accent is atrocious," she said, and he grinned at her sunnily, unrepentantly, and said it again. And very shortly thereafter was asleep.

She waited until she felt him sink into the deep bonelessness from which even he would not be easily roused, and then slid carefully out of bed. It was not worth making a foray down to the baths through the cold and dark, but the garderobe beside the stairhead was kept supplied with water. She pulled on shirt and trousers, found a clean handkerchief to serve as a washcloth, and quietly left the room, eschewing the candle because she did not want Maur to wake, if he should happen to, alone and in the dark.

Dark places were not uncomfortable to her, and the shielded lantern in the garderobe cast sufficient light for her purposes. She had not even particularly thought about the darkness she moved through, her mind dreaming gently of Maur, until, on the way back, a light emerged from a room two doors down from theirs, and a shaky voice said, "Wh-who's there?"

"Maselle von Elstan?"

"Oh, it's you." Corinna von Elstan shut the door behind her with a quite audible sigh of relief. "I beg pardon, Maselle Agido. I was afraid . . ."

Agido knew what she had feared and did not blame her. "I am sorry if I disturbed you," she said, although the girl would have needed ears like a rabbit's to have heard her.

"Oh, no," Maselle von Elstan said. "I didn't even know you were there. I was just . . ." Her candle wasn't strong enough to show if she blushed or not, but she looked away, flustered.

"Is Maselle von Deiver asleep then?" Agido said mildly.

Maselle von Elstan made a noise of profound contempt. "She's in the private parlor. 'Recruiting her strength.'" Her mimicry was savage, as was the pent-up fury with which she said, "I just wish she wouldn't treat me like a stupid *child*. Does she think I don't know what cherry brandy smells like? She reeks of it, you know. That's why she wears so much perfume."

"Ah," Agido said. "Does Maselle von Deiver often find it necessary to recruit her strength in this fashion?"

"Only every night," Maselle von Elstan said bitterly. "Usually she waits until she thinks I'm asleep, though. If you ask me, this inn is upsetting her."

"What do you mean?"

"Well, it *is* spooky, isn't it? Being under the mountains and with only these tiny windows, and we are trapped here in a way, aren't we?"

"Only for another day or two," Agido said, thinking that Maselle von Elstan was very probably ascribing her own nervousness to her companion—for there was no denying the girl was nervous.

"I know," she said, and managed a smile. "You won't tell anyone—about the cherry brandy, I mean? Anna Lucilla would be *livid*."

"I will not betray you," Agido said, and they parted; Agido returned to Maur, and Maselle von Elstan pursued whatever business it was that took her abroad in the night.

Sleepy as Agido was, and her mind mostly on other matters, it wasn't until she had snuffed the candle and was stretched out next to Maur that she realized the true import of Corinna von Elstan's complaint.

If Maselle von Deiver was in the habit of leaving their shared room after she believed Maselle von Elstan to be asleep, then there was nothing to exclude either one of them from being the murderer of Magister von Plaadt.

Agido turned that thought over in her mind. Neither woman seemed a particularly likely murderer—or murderess, since she suspected Maselle von Deiver would insist on the more genteel term. A girl barely out of the schoolroom or her drunken governess? Against a powerful middle-aged wizard?

But absurd as the idea was, it continued to nag at her all the way down into sleep.

Her dreams were uneasy, full of old battles, old grievances. She and Maur both woke early; she got up to light the candle, and when she turned back to the bed, he was hunched up again, sitting with his back against the wall, watching her with dream-darkened eyes.

"What's wrong?" she said.

He shook his head a little, impatient. "If I were what I should be, you wouldn't have to do that."

It was one of the benefits of being a wizard's lover; candles lit and extinguished themselves with a mere glance. "Perhaps Magister Thornfeld will be able to help." She crawled back under the blankets and noticed that he tensed at her proximity.

"It's a fool's hope, Agido. Magister von Plaadt was right."

"He was *not*." She reached out, laid one hand gently on his shoulder, felt it hunch. He did not flinch, quite, and he did not shrug her off, quite, but he was very close to both those things. "Maur, my heart, what is it?"

He scowled bleakly at the candle. "You shouldn't burden yourself with me."

"First of all, you're not a burden—"

"I most certainly am." His eyes were suddenly full of anger and light. "And it's no good saying maybe Magister Thornfeld can help, because he *can't*. Nothing can help. Nothing! I'm broken and useless, and, powers, I'm so *ashamed*—" His voice cracked and failed. He lowered his head, avoiding her eyes. "I'm such a coward."

"A *coward?*"

"You wouldn't have screamed the way I did. I wanted to tell them that, when they said I screamed like a girl. That *you* wouldn't have screamed, no matter what they did. But I couldn't even . . ."

"Maur—"

"No. Don't try to make me feel better with lies."

"I do not lie to you," she said, the words stark and hard as killing iron. "To scream does not make you a coward. It does not make you useless or any of these other things that you imagine you are."

He made a choked little noise that might have been either a laugh or a sob.

"I do not deny that you have been very badly hurt," she said and felt the tension in his shoulder ebb slightly. "But I will deny with my last breath that you are useless. You are not useless. Not to me."

He mumbled something, still not looking at her.

"What was that?"

"A gift of wings. That's what you said last night. Is it . . . is it still how you feel?" He couldn't quite bring himself to look at her, but she could see the trepidation and hope in his face.

Do you think me so fickle, my heart? But she understood that his asking had very little to do with her, and everything to do with the cold, barren brokenness that he now found within himself. "Yes," she said. "Always. I love you."

He looked up at her then, even though the tracks of tears were wet on his face. "I love you, too," he said, and they kissed as if to seal a bargain.

It was as she was helping him dress that she remembered her encounter with Maselle von Elstan the night before. She told him what the girl had said and was rewarded with a scowl that was thoughtful rather than bleak. "That's very interesting," he said. "Messire Glas has no one to vouch for his whereabouts, and he worked in the Zauberhof as a young man. So he must have known *of* von Plaadt, at least—although of course he said nothing disparaging about him to me."

They considered that a moment, and Agido offered, "I do not think, if Maselle von Elstan had murdered Magister von Plaadt, she would have been so quick to tell me about her companion's failures in chaperonage."

"No. It would have been very much in her interest to keep that quiet. And I cannot imagine that a girl of seventeen could have any reason to wish von Plaadt dead. A *boy* of seventeen, perhaps, but—"

"But that's the problem, isn't it? What reason has either Messire Glas or Maselle von Deiver to wish von Plaadt dead?"

"Well, that's what we don't know," Maur said and gave her a charming, crooked smile. "And I expect that's what I'll spend the morning finding out. You'll be shoveling again, won't you?"

"It seems the best way to keep Messire Bartolomeo from expounding on his belief that I am the murderer," she said, and Maur laughed.

"He sought me out yesterday and asked me, as a personal favor to him, not to think of leaving before the Norvenwache could get here. Of course, I asked him for snowshoe lessons immediately."

He caught her off-guard; she laughed, and his smile grew dazzling. "I told him we had no interest in hindering justice and would be delighted to stay as long as he wished. I believe I may also have said something about catching up on my correspondence with my cousins, so you may be confident that he will hold his tongue."

If the von Haariens did not run the government in Karolinsberg, it was only because none of them in the past two generations had had enough ambition to bother with consolidating their power. Maur's Cousin Orzibal was one of three or four hot contenders to succeed the current prime minister when that worthy stepped down in the spring.

"Clever," she said, and he grinned and said smugly, "Yes, I know."

They were both still snickering a little as they went down to breakfast, where Maselle von Deiver was clearly feeling the aftereffects of overindulgence in cherry brandy, but Nikk looked like he had indeed gotten lucky with Elgiv—and from the expression on her face when she came through the swinging doors with the first heavily laden tray, Elgiv had gotten lucky with Nikk.

Agido watched Messire Glas over breakfast, when she could do so without his observing—not difficult, as Maur had gotten him talking about the Karolinsberg Botanical Gardens. The lawyer's clerk became quite animated as he explained to Maur the differences between the three strains of Margrethe von Heber roses; Agido wondered if he had any other passions that roused him, and whether Magister von Plaadt might have run afoul of one of them. It seemed unlikely, but then so did the idea of Maselle von Deiver having the wherewithal to murder anyone.

After breakfast, she and Nikk joined the staff of The Mare's Nest in the pass. Typical for this early in the winter, the weather had warmed again, making their task easier but much soggier, as the melting snow clung wetly to everything it touched. Halfway through the morning, they were joined by men from the nearest village on the Magnan side, and by the time Madame Bartolomea called everyone in for lunch, the road was clear nearly the length of the pass.

Elgiv and Madame Bartolomea brought hot water out to the courtyard. As Agido and the men were cleaning off the worst of the mud, Rose came over to Agido, with a nervous glance at Bartolomeo, and said, "Maselle, may I speak to you about something?"

"Of course," she said. "Now?"

Another glance at Bartolomeo, who was frowning in their direction. "No, after lunch is fine. It may not be anything—"

"Rose!" The boy darted away from her like a cat splashed with water. Bartolomeo offered her a large fake smile. "Forgive him, maselle. He sometimes forgets his place."

She gave Bartolomeo a slow, flat, considering stare and said, "*He* forgets nothing, messire," then turned away and started toward the inn.

Elgiv, beside her, balancing a ewer on her shoulder as if it weighed no more than a puff of thistledown, said under her breath, "And if you aren't careful, he'll steal your young wizard away from you."

"Oh?" Agido said, and Elgiv grinned.

"Rare smitten is our Rose. Always pestering me for what Messire von Haarien said and did he look so ill as before." She shrugged tolerantly. "He's young yet, and suffering still seems like a storybook to him, you know?"

"Yes," she said, remembering other boys she had known, young and dreamy-eyed and brave. Remembering their deaths.

"He's a good boy, though. Good heart and a head on his shoulders, unlike some." And with that, she disappeared into the kitchens, and Agido made her way to the dining room.

The others had eaten earlier, and although she was a little disappointed that Maur did not come to bear her company, she was not surprised. He needed his dignity so badly, and even if no one mocked at him for being on her leading strings, he would hear the mockery in his own head.

She ate quickly, for she did not want to get Rose in trouble by making either him or herself late when their work-party reconvened for the afternoon. When she returned to the courtyard, Rose was standing in the entrance of the stable, eyes anxious, clearly waiting for her.

"What is it?" she asked as she reached him.

"Maselle, you said I should tell you. If there was anything strange. And I found something."

He led her into the stable, explaining over his shoulder as he went: "I was in the tack-room this morning, looking for a bit of leather to mend the oxen's harness with—Ham and Messire Bartolomeo are making the last run for winter supplies to Bronberg next week, and I thought I'd better make sure Steadfast and Stalwart were ready to go—Messire Bartolomeo's daughter named them, Elgiv says, but she died of the Winter Fever three years ago—and anyway I found *this*." He lifted a horse blanket off a row of snow-melt barrels.

Clothes. Crumpled and dirty, but Agido could recognize Magister von Plaadt's beautiful brocade waistcoat regardless.

"I moved them," Rose was saying anxiously, "because they didn't ought to be there, but they ain't mine, and they ain't Ham's, and I don't know—"

"They're the clothes Magister von Plaadt was wearing the night he was killed," Agido said. "You've done the right thing, Rose. Now be quiet a moment and let me think."

Obediently, he fell silent, and she examined von Plaadt's clothes. They stank of sweat, and of the ambergris he'd favored as a scent, and of . . .

She turned them over in her hands, searching carefully, and, yes, there, down shirt and waistcoat was a long spill of darkness, still slightly sticky to the touch and still smelling unmistakably, cloyingly, of cheap cherry brandy, the kind that wine merchants doctored with cherry syrup and sold to foolish ladies. Certainly nothing Bartolomeo would permit in his cellars.

She thought, clearly if rather inanely, *Now I know why the murderer had to hide von Plaadt's clothes.* And then she thought, *If Maur was talking to Messire Glas this morning . . .*

The pieces fell into place. The cherry brandy, the encounter with Maselle von Elstan, Maselle von Deiver's ugly eagerness to assert Agido was the murderer. Maur would find no guilt in Messire Glas's conversation; thus at lunch he would have turned his attention to Maselle von Deiver. And she, already raw-nerved with apprehension and anxiety, what would she do? She would not speak to him in a public place, that much was certain. And if she could murder a healthy wizard to protect whatever it was that she protected, then a man crippled both in his magic and in his hands would seem a pitifully easy target.

Agido's breath hissed in, hard; she dropped von Plaadt's clothes as if they'd burned her and bolted back to the inn, Rose bewildered but faithful at her heels.

"Maur," she barked at Messire Bartolomeo as he wallowed up from behind the bar. "Where is he?"

"You should not be so jealous of the poor young man, maselle," he said, smirking. "He is not—"

She jerked him forward across the bar by a double-handful of his shirt. "*Where is he?*"

"He, ah . . . I don't know, maselle. He was speaking to Maselle von Deiver at lunchtime, my wife tells me. Perhaps she—"

"You are a cloth-headed idiot," she said in Ervenzian, released him, and took the stairs three at a time. No one was in their room; in Maselle von Elstan and Maselle von Deiver's room, there was only Corinna von Elstan frowning over her books. Agido pressed the heels of her palms against her eyes, trying to think through a wash of mingled fury and fear. Maselle von Elstan had told her where Maselle von Deiver was last night, if she could just remember what the girl had said. Not in their bedroom, but—

"Where's your private parlor?" she demanded of Bartolomeo, who, like Rose, had followed her up the stairs.

"But, maselle, the private parlor has already been hired. The ladies wished—"

A place to drink in peace. And commit murder. "I don't want to hire it. Now, *where?*"

"This way, maselle," and for all his floundering bewilderment, he did at least lead her quickly. Down the stairs to the baths, a turn into one of the odd little hallways that jutted off from it like spikes, a door marked in a literate Ervenzian hand, PRIVATE PARLOR. And locked.

She pounded on the door, and heard a rustle, a noise like a gasp. "Open this damned door!" she shouted, and when there was no response, she leaned back and kicked the door hard, just under the latch. Bartolomeo made an agonized squawk of protest, the door flew open, and Maur said weakly, "Oh, *there* you are."

He was sitting on the hearthstone, chalk-white, hunched up around his hands like a hedgehog. "She keeps saying she doesn't want to kill me, but the more often she says it the less I believe her."

Anna Lucilla von Deiver, in a swirl of skirts, snatched the poker from the hearth and backed away, baring her teeth in a startling and unladylike snarl. "So possessive of your lover, harlot?"

"To the extent that I will not allow you to kill him, yes."

She laughed shrilly. "You don't mean you *believed* him? You must know he's mad, no matter how besotted you are."

Agido saw Maur's flinch from the corner of her eye, but kept her voice reasonable when she said, "You're the one holding the poker."

"You broke down the door. And we all know there's a murderer in this inn."

"And we all know that the murderer is you." Agido began to circle right, drawing Maselle von Deiver's attention away from Maur. "I found von Plaadt's clothes."

An innocent woman would have been confused. A woman with the nerve and intelligence for the game Maselle von Deiver was trying to play would have bluffed. Anna Lucilla von Deiver went ashen, made an inarticulate noise of fear and fury mixed, and rushed at Agido, the poker upraised.

It was both futile and foolish, and would have been even had she succeeded. As it was, Agido shifted sideways and caught Maselle von Deiver's wrist as she began to bring the poker down. A hard, simple twist, and the poker clattered harmlessly to the floor.

Maselle von Deiver clutched her broken wrist and screamed.

Agido turned away from her, knelt in front of Maur. "My heart, are you all right?"

He nodded tightly, said past her, "She murdered von Plaadt, Bartolomeo. Do you have a storeroom or a cellar you can lock her in?"

Rose and Bartolomeo began to deal with the murderess, who was rapidly working herself into a hysterical fit; Maur looked at Agido and said, "I'm fine. I should have known better than to try to get the key away from her." He gave her a lopsided smile. "I'm not really meant to be a hero."

"That depends on the definition you choose." She closed her hands gently around his forearms, glorying in the heat of him, in his pulse beneath her fingertips, in the way he relaxed just slightly as she touched him, leaned just a little toward her.

Bartolomeo was bawling like a cow in the hallway, his calls for his wife mingling cacophonously with Maselle von Deiver's shrieks. But Agido thought she could categorize that situation as being under control. Maur was a von Haarien; Bartolomeo would do as he was told.

The world was in Maur's eyes as he reached up and very gently brushed her cheek with the back of his hand.

The norvenwache arrived the next morning, prompt and courteous and flatteringly attentive to everything Maur had to say. He received them in the private parlor like an emperor out of a Tibernian novel, and Agido stood behind his chair like an imperial bodyguard.

They were pleased by the evidence of the clothes, and the flask still a quarter-full of cherry brandy which Elgiv found among Maselle von Deiver's belongings, and the rather awed testimony of Corinna von Elstan. "But," said the wachekapitan, middle-aged, blond going gray, the sort of man you could trust with any job he turned his hand to, "why? What cause had she to hate Magister von Plaadt?"

"Oh, she didn't hate him," Maur said, "although she must have been in a rare fury when she cracked his skull with that poker. She was afraid of him."

"But that makes no more sense than the other."

"No, she had good reason to be afraid of him. And he was the sort of man who couldn't resist using that. She told me a little—in between assurances that she didn't *want* to kill me—and I actually remember being told about the scandal when I was at the Zauberhof. I just never learned the poor man's name."

The wachekapitan waited, eyebrows politely raised.

"About thirty years ago, a fellow of the Zauberhof—whose name, I now know, was Mathias von Deiver—was accused and convicted of embezzling funds out of the von Zef Trust. It came out in the course of the trial that he'd used the money to settle his gambling debts, and from his sister's rather incoherent remarks, I gather he was generally living above his means, trying to keep up with the fashionable set he wanted to belong to. A set which included Arnulf von Plaadt."

"So the social climbing was a family trait," Agido murmured, not loud enough for anyone but Maur to hear her.

He tilted his head to flash her a smile, and continued: "Von Deiver's ambition got the better of him. He always insisted he meant to pay the money back, and after the trial he hanged himself. His younger brother and sister, both annemer, were suspected of complicity, but nothing was ever proven against them. I don't know what became of the brother, although I daresay you'll be able to get Maselle von Deiver to tell you. She receded into obscurity, taking governess positions in what she describes as the 'hinterlands,' by which she seems to mean Skaar and Mira and northern Kekropia. And gradually she worked her way back into Norvena Parva. She was counting on the respectable and wealthy Parvan annemer not to remember a scandal among wizards, and she was quite right. It was simply her bad luck to run into a respectable and wealthy *wizard*, and one moreover who had been an associate of her brother's. I do not use the word 'friend,' for I don't imagine it would accurately reflect the feelings of either party."

"And he recognized her?" said the wachekapitan.

"Or remembered her name," Maur said. "She, of course, had no idea who he was—until he came upon her that evening, after he had had a most unsatisfactory scene with me and a quarrel with a lover he had come to find tiresome. And he discovered her getting drunk on cherry brandy while her charge slept."

Agido could imagine Magister von Plaadt's satisfaction, and although she neither liked nor sympathized with Maselle von Deiver, she could not help a shiver of empathy.

"She did not wish to discuss their encounter, although she admits that during the course of it, she threw a snifter of cherry brandy in his face. Whereupon he said he felt he had no choice except to write and inform Messire von Elstan what sort of person he had entrusted his daughter to. And turned to leave."

"And died," Agido said.

"Somewhat later, yes. Whether or not she meant to hit him—she says she didn't, says she doesn't know what came over her—I'm afraid she did quite cold-bloodedly decide to kill him. You don't, in the fine fierce rapture of your maenadic frenzy, take a man larger than yourself, strip him, and dump him in a pool to drown slowly. And she knew he was alive when he went in the water. She said as much."

The wachekapitan cleared his throat uncomfortably and said, "Thank you, Messire von Haarien. I think we need not trouble you further."

"Oh good," Maur said leaning back to look at Agido. "Because I think I've had quite enough trouble for one year."

Puzzled, the wachekapitan made his bow and departed with his men. Agido came and knelt by Maur's chair and kissed him, and said, "What now?"

"Well, actually," he said, "I was hoping for just a bit more trouble."

"Oh?"

"Yes. I was hoping I could trouble you to come back to bed with me."

"That, my heart," Agido said, "is no trouble at all."

Epilogue

✳

AGIDO MET MAUR IN THE KAFFE PALATIO-
Heber, across the Plass Ingevar from the great gloomy
towers of the Universitat. Igensbeck was beautiful in the
winter, the sky a crisp astonishing blue above its gray
slate roofs, the snow heaping cornices and ledges like
sugar sifted down by some giant confectioner.

She caught a glimpse of Maur as he came out of the
gates, still looking like a molting crow in the black
greatcoat he would not part with, his braided hair hanging over one shoulder, the crimson ribbon like a banner
of defiance. The five-year-old daughter of their landlady
had given it to him, for inscrutable five-year-old reasons, and Maur had worn it ever since.

Agido had learned through the long cold months to
judge whether his day had been good or bad by the
way he moved through the crowds between the Universitat and the kaffe. On bad days, he seemed almost to
disappear, shoulders hunched, dodging the other pedes-
trians as if they were hostile. On good days, he kept his

chin up and walked like someone who had a right to take up space in the world.

Today, he was *striding*, head high, and when he ducked around people, he did it neatly, almost delightedly, as if it were a step in some beautiful, intricate minuet that he was dancing with the entire world. She came to her feet involuntarily, and his smile when he saw her was bright enough to melt the snow.

He made straight for her, his eyes brilliant, seeming as if he might at any moment break into a run like a child. He did not take his hands out of his pockets—even with half-gloves and mittens, the cold still hurt them cruelly—but he marched up to her and said, "I lit a candle. By myself."

She let out a war-whoop she had learned from the spear-maidens of the Osfahan Archipelago. Heads turned toward them from all corners of the Plass Ingevar, but at that moment, neither she nor Maur cared.

She caught his face between her hands, said, "The gift of wings, my heart," and kissed him.

And Maur kissed her back.